DEAL With the
Devil

and 13 Short Stories

Photo by Cristiana Pecheanu. Hair and makeup by Mario Ortega.

DEAL With the the Devil

and 13 Short Stories

by Elaine Viets

Crippen & Landru Publishers
Cincinnati, Ohio
2018

For information contact:

Crippen & Landru, Publishers

P. O. Box 532057

Cincinnati, OH 45253 USA

Web: www.crippenlandru.com

E-mail: Info@crippenlandru.com

ISBN (signed numbered cloth edition) 978-1-936363-27-8

ISBN (trade softcover) 978-1-936363-28-5

First Edition: April 2018

10 9 8 7 6 5 4 3 2 1

Table of Contents

Introduction

Weird things happen to me. A cigar chomper in a red Mercedes convertible really did try to buy my car – and my house – and maybe me – when I was in a bank drive-in line in Fort Lauderdale, Florida. I should have told him to buzz off. But then I wouldn't have written "A Deal With the Devil."

That incident bedeviled my brain for more than two years, before I finally turned it into a story. That's how many of my stories start – something offbeat sticks in my mind until it turns into a story.

My grandmother, Frances Vierling, believed she had second sight, and people she loved stopped by to see her before they left on their final journey. Grandma hid this strange secret, because she feared her unwelcome ability would get her "locked up in Arsenal Street." That's where the home for the mentally ill was in Saint Louis. Grandma told me she had second sight shortly before she died. Her unwanted gift triggered "The Bedroom Door."

I wrote "Red Meat" after my husband got a stunning blonde trainer. Don was the envy of every man on the beach when he jogged by with his golden goddess. Then he discovered one man's dream is another's nightmare.

"Vampire Hours" was inspired by the condo across the way. Our condo is on the Intracoastal Waterway, and there's a little canal that runs along the side of the building. I can see right into the condos across the canal – it's like looking into a dollhouse. One condo had elegant midnight parties: handsome men in black tie and beautiful women in long black gowns swirled through candlelit rooms. Then, one night, they were all gone.

Does our condo have a condo commando? Of course not. "Death of a Condo Commando" is pure fiction, and as of this writing the annoying snoop is alive and well.

If you read my mystery series, you'll recognize some of my characters. "Gotta Go" introduces Death Investigator Angela Richman, who works in mythical Chouteau County, which is a lot like the richer parts of Saint Louis County. Angela debuted in *Alfred Hitchcock's Mystery Magazine*. Thank you, editor Linda Landrigan.

Helen Hawthorne makes two appearances outside the Dead-End Job series. "Sex and Bingo" was written right after *Shop Till You Drop,* the first mystery in that series. Helen is still on the run from Rob, her unfaithful ex, and she takes a job on a cruise ship, where she gets an advanced education in cheating.

"Good and Dead" was written after my last Dead-End Job mystery, *The Art of Murder.* Helen has changed after fifteen mysteries: Now she's married Phil Sagemont. They've opened their private eye agency, Coronado Investigations, on the second floor of Coronado Tropic Apartments, where they live. In "Good and Dead," Helen and Margery Flax, her seventy-six-year-old landlady, take a case in New Orleans. This story was inspired by a scruffy French Quarter convention hotel where my friend Doris Ann Norris and I shared a room. Doris Ann, like Margery, is a serious smoker, and she encountered a young drug dealer using the outside smokers to camouflage his business.

"His Funkalicous Majesty," featuring newspaper reporter Francesca Vierling from my first mystery series, is also based on a nugget of truth. I was a Saint Louis newspaper columnist, and early in my career I had to cover a black gala, a sly protest against a local institution for the one-percent, the Veiled Prophet Ball. The details of the VP Ball are real. So was the protest party, under a different name.

"Wedding Knife" was my first short story. Every woman has had to wear an ugly bridesmaid dress in the name of friendship. I actually wore the pink monstrosity in the story. I didn't kill the bride. But I wanted to.

I hope you'll enjoy reading these short stories as much as I did writing them.

Elaine Viets
December 13, 2017

A Deal With the Devil

Do you believe in the devil? Who else would drive a convertible on a sweltering July afternoon in South Florida? The real question is, can you outwit him?

I met the devil in the bank drive-in lane. I'm not talking about Satan himself – I don't flatter myself I'm so important the big guy Down There would be interested. But I'm pretty sure I met one of his minions. A devil, not the devil. There are lots of them, sort of like infernal interns. This one was wearing a pink polo and driving a 1986 Mercedes two-seater convertible.

Wednesday was payday at Fort Lauderdale College. Blackie and I stopped at the bank on the way home. The middle lane had no cars. My paycheck was sucked through the vacuum tube to the clerk behind the bulletproof glass.

"Nice car," said the man in the drive-in lane on my left.

Nice? Blackie, my '86 Jaguar, is flat-out gorgeous. Sleekly curved, Black Beauty's ebony body is so well polished I can see my face in it. A fiery pinstripe streaks down his slim body, the same color as his leather seats.

"Thank you." My tone was cold and unfriendly. I was used to gushing compliments about Blackie. This man had denigrated my car – and by extension – me.

"How much?" he asked.

"What?" Now I turned to look at the man. He was a beef-faced fifty with a cigar stuck in his mouth at an angry angle. His face was flame red, nearly the same color as his Mercedes convertible. His round bald head gushed sweat. Why would anyone drive with the July sun beating down on him? How could he stand that hellish heat? I had my window down for my bank dealings, but even with Blackie's air-conditioner blasting icy air, I was sweltering.

"I said, how much?" His tone was aggressive, demanding, a little frightening. I couldn't quite place his accent.

"He's not for sale." Sell Blackie! I'd sooner sell my right hand.

"You live around here?" The Mercedes man's voice was thrusting, intrusive, rough. I should have driven away right then, but I wanted my bank receipt.

"Yes." Why was I answering him? He was a stranger, yet I felt compelled to talk to him. What was wrong with me?

"You have a house? How much you want for it?"

"It's not for sale, either."

His teeth were white and cruel. Who did this overfed businessman think he was, asking to buy my car and my house?

"You're nice, too." His smile around the cigar was obscenely suggestive.

Me? Did he want to buy me, too? I am a forty-year-old instructor at a third-tier college, good-looking enough that sophomore boys sometimes crushed on me. You'd never guess to look at me, but I have stage four metastatic liver cancer. No, Mercedes man wouldn't be interested in me. Men like him wanted brainless blonde babes. And I definitely wasn't interested in him. He was no match for Jess, my husband of twenty years.

Whooosh. Thump! I jumped at the sound of the vacuum tube. My deposit slip had arrived. My fingers shook when I retrieved it from the canister. I wanted out of there, but for some odd reason I didn't want to offend Mercedes man.

"I like your car," I said, eyeing his vintage red beauty. Why did I compliment this man? I should leave. Now.

I had to force myself to put the car in gear. It took extra effort to shift from park to drive, as if some force was holding back my hand. Please don't let there be a problem with Blackie's transmission, I thought. Finally, I did it. Before I could escape, Mercedes man stuck a business card in my face.

"Here, take this." He'd handed me his card without seeming to leave his car. "If you're interested in a deal, meet me for lunch at the Flames at twelve noon tomorrow."

The card was expensively engraved in an antique font on thick cream stock. HL Acheron, it said. The last name was vaguely familiar. Was he a real estate agent?

Blackie and I raced out of the bank lane like a bat out of hell, nearly sideswiping an innocent white Soul. Once I was away from the bank, I felt like some sort of spell was broken. I was a fool, an idiot . . . I was intrigued.

I couldn't wait to tell Jess about my strange encounter with Acheron the real estate agent. As I drove past the multimillion-dollar homes in my neighborhood, I kept thinking about what he'd said: "You have a house? How much you want for it?"

Jess and I have a seventh-floor condo in Sky House, where the glass apartments float in the sky above the Intracoastal Waterway. If Acheron was in real estate, he'd be interested in Sky House. Our condos were underpriced and rarely on the market. We were one of the few condo buildings that allowed pets.

I parked Blackie in the Sky House garage and waited impatiently for the elevator, then hurried along the hallway and unlocked our door. Our copper-eyed Chartreux, Mystery, met me by the door. I picked her up and stroked her soft smoky-gray fur, reassured by her familiar purr.

And stopped a second to admire the stunning view. We can see the ocean from our living room. The water was a restless, molten silver this afternoon. Straight down, in the wide swath of the Intracoastal, a millionaire's yacht plowed haughtily toward the drawbridge over Commercial Boulevard.

Our condo was deliciously scented with coffee, so I knew my husband was working.

"Jess?" I called, setting our cat back on the floor.

"In the kitchen. I'm testing Ethiopians." Jess ran his fingers through his shaggy dirty-blond hair when he was working, and it stuck up all over. His kind blue eyes were shrewdly studying the color of the coffee samples in little glass cups. His arm muscles bulged and his stomach was flat. Regular workouts in the condo gym helped prevent writer's paunch.

Overindulging was a danger with Jess' current book contract. He was writing his "Jess's Best" series: the best vodka, the best mail-order steak, the best sixty-inch TV. He was currently working on the best coffee book. He saw me and smiled.

"Come taste this. I think it has the richest flavor, and no hint of bitterness." He handed me a small, clear cup of a dark steaming brew.

I inhaled it, then took a sip. "It is rich. And strong. Too bad coffee doesn't taste as good as it smells."

"Spoken like a true tea drinker," he said. "How are you feeling?"

"I'm fine." I saw the worry shadow his eyes. "Really. No symptoms at all."

I wanted to change the subject – fast. "I had a strange encounter in the bank line." I told him about Acheron. I left out that the man scared me – that was my imagination.

"He gave me his card. He wants to meet at the Flames tomorrow at noon," I said.

"You aren't going, are you?"

"I might," I said. "I don't have class on Thursday. Acheron's name is familiar. I think he's in real estate."

"What do you think this Acheron can do for you? Do you want to sell Blackie?"

"Of course not. But what if Acheron made us a good deal for this condo?"

"How good?"

"If we got double what it's worth, we could pay off my medical bills, so you wouldn't be stuck with a huge debt when we run out of chemo options." And I run out of chances.

He took me in his arms and kissed me. "That's not going to happen."

I loved his warmth and reassurance. But I had to make him see the grim reality.

"I'm stage four, Jess. I see Dr. Sullivan next week. If the latest blood tests aren't good, he's going to switch to the next option, that awful IV stuff, and I might have some bad reactions. I could lose my hair. I've managed to keep it so far."

He held me again and ran his fingers through my thick blonde hair. There was nothing to say. Dr. Sullivan had said there were at least forty different kinds of chemo he could try to keep me going, but this next option signaled serious changes. I was desperate. We both knew it.

"This Acheron could prove to be a blessing, Jess."

"Maybe. I don't like you going alone, Selena. You don't know this man."

"The Flames is a steakhouse. At noon, it's packed with business people."

Jess kissed me and went back to his coffee research. I went into my home office and Googled Acheron's name. No mention of a real estate company, or any indication that he was a Realtor. The local Realtors and real estate associations had never heard of him. I wondered if he had one of those small, exclusive companies that only dealt with the richest of the rich. I hoped not. If he was in that league, he wouldn't be interested in our condo. That deal would be too small for a major player.

I must be doing something wrong, I decided. I widened my search and found one more mention: Acheron was one of the rivers of Hades – the River of Woe.

That night, I slept restlessly, and finally got up about three in the morning to avoid waking Jess. I watched the silvered moon on the restless ocean, and the go-fast boats skimming down the Intracoastal with their running lights off. What was their illegal cargo: smuggled people, drugs, weapons? Dawn was breaking when I finally fell asleep. I felt safe once I saw the morning light on the horizon, promising a new day. I woke at ten-thirty to the smell of fresh coffee: Arabica, Jess told me. His research continued.

I had a cup of Dragonwell green tea in the kitchen, watching my husband fuss over his coffee samples, all the while wondering: Who was Acheron? What was he? What did he want? And why did he choose me? As I scrambled eggs for my breakfast, I asked Jess, "What if Acheron made a good offer for the condo?"

"How good?" He was wary.

"A million dollars."

"Whew!" He blew out his lips. "That's twice what it's worth. If we took his offer, where would we live? I don't want to leave Sky House."

"At the last barbecue night, Ellie and Martin in 9173 said they were thinking about selling their two bedroom. We could afford their smaller unit and still pay my medical bills."

"It would sure solve a lot of problems," Jess said, as he held a clear cup of Arabica up to the light.

Then he turned to look at me. "But I'm still worried about this meeting, Selena. Call me when you get there, and call me when you leave. Promise? If you're not home by four o'clock, I'm going over there."

"I'll be home long before that," I said. "Lunch is over by three and we live ten minutes away."

I dressed conservatively in a crisp white blouse, tailored black pants, black heels and the pearl earrings Jess gave me for our wedding, then patted the cat and promised Jess I'd call as soon as I got to the restaurant. He followed me to the door and kissed me on the lips. He was a world-class kisser, and I wanted to forget all about lunch with Acheron. But I was afraid to lose this opportunity. I reluctantly said goodbye, then got in Blackie and drove to the Flames.

The Flames was dark as a cave, with a roaring fire in the center of the restaurant, and booths extending from the fire pit like spokes in a wheel. Acheron was in the black lobby. He wasn't waiting, or looking at his watch. He expected me to show up at noon and I did.

He wore a shining dark suit that I suspected was a Brioni – I'd seen one like it when Jess was researching the best men's fashion – and a black shirt that fitted like a second skin. His red tie was a slash of designer silk. For all the expense, the effect was oddly cheap and slightly clownish. Suits, especially dark suits with black shirts, are rare in a South Florida summer.

"Good to see you, Selena," he said. "I have a booth near the fire." All around us businessmen – and a few women – in light summerweight suits were talking on cell phones, taking notes on iPads, talking to each other, opening briefcases, shaking hands. The Flame was where deals got done.

We settled into the comfortable black leather booth. I was close enough to touch the fire, but the air conditioning was so frosty I was glad I wore a high-necked blouse with long sleeves. Sweat was streaming off Acheron's naked head and the front of his black shirt was soaked.

When the server arrived – a pale young man in black with spiked hair – we knew what we wanted. Acheron ordered a twenty-four-ounce steak blood rare.

Really? I thought. That much meat for lunch?

"Tear it off the cow and walk it through the kitchen," he said. "I hate overdone meat." He glared at the server, who seemed to go even paler. I asked for a shrimp salad. We ignored the Flame's extensive wine list. Acheron ordered a Coke and I wanted a club soda.

The server quickly brought our food: a luscious green salad with fat shrimp for me, and a steak so bloody it really did look like it had been ripped off a live cow. Acheron reached for his steak knife, a serrated dagger. His red eyes gleamed and he smacked his lips. I couldn't bear to watch him devour it, and concentrated on my salad.

Except for slurps, cracks, and crunches, neither of us said a word until the server took our plates. Acheron ordered coffee for both of us, without asking if I drank it, and patted his greasy lips with a white napkin nearly as big as a tablecloth.

I was nervous now. I knew business was conducted after meals. I waited for him to speak first.

The uneasy silence stretched on, broken only by the server asking, "May I bring you cream or sugar? How about dessert or an aperitif?" Acheron's "No!" was so fierce the server shriveled and blew away.

"So," Acheron said, "I understand you have a Chartreux, a pedigreed show cat with copper eyes. She bit a judge at her first show and was banned from the ring for life. My kind of cat."

He smiled. I felt so cold I edged closer to the fire. How did he know this? I'd only told a few friends. That information had never been published, not even on Facebook.

Cats are the devil's familiar. Acheron, the River of Woe, was the devil. Now I had no doubt. I felt the shrimp rise in my throat and fought to not throw up. Mystery was a member of our family. I couldn't give her up – especially not to this devil.

"Mystery's not for sale, either." I hoped my voice was steady.

"I wouldn't take your family cat, dear lady. I'm not that barbaric."

"We could make a deal for our condo," I said. "We'd be willing to sell it for a million dollars."

"HAW, HAW, HAW!" His rude laugh was so loud and harsh people at the nearby tables turned to stare.

He finally quit laughing and lowered his voice. "I'm sure you would like to sell it for a million. But it's only worth half that – and you haven't updated your kitchen and bathrooms, so it's worth even less."

How did he know that? I was truly frightened. He was definitely the devil.

"My dear lady, I'm interested in serious deals." Acheron looked satanic in the flickering firelight. He leaned forward, his bulk blocking the fire's glow. I pushed against the back of the booth, as far away as I could get from him without bolting.

"You can't have my soul." I wanted to sound defiant, but I was a Chihuahua yapping at a mastiff.

"YOUR SOUL!" His laugh was even louder. The few diners left in the restaurant stared at us. "WHAT WOULD I DO WITH A SOUL? HANG IT IN A CLOSET?"

This meeting was a waste of time. He wasn't going to buy our condo. He couldn't help me. I wasn't going to sit here and be mocked. I reached into my purse, threw twenty dollars on the table and started to slide out of the booth.

He stopped laughing, grabbed my hand and pressed my twenty into it. His plump hands were smooth and carefully manicured, but the skin felt warm and curiously pawlike. "Selena. Let me explain. I have no use for a soul. I came here to make a deal. I know you've got stage four cancer and it's spreading."

"How do you know that?"

"It's my business to know. I make deals and I need information. I know Doc Sullivan is running out of easy options. If you fail your blood tests next week, all that's left are the treatments that will make you really sick, until you get to the choices that will keep you alive but you'll wish they didn't."

That was the harsh truth. The truth I couldn't make Jess see.

"I can help you, Selena."

"How?"

"I need you to do me a simple favor. It won't cost you anything. I'm also a drug company representative."

Figures, I thought. Everyone knew Big Pharma was in league with the devil.

"I can give Doc Sullivan one sample of a new drug that would help you. That is, if you're willing to help me."

"What do I have to do?" My heart was pounding so loud I was sure he could hear it rattling against my ribs. What would he want me to do? Kill someone? Dance naked in the moonlight? Betray my husband?

"Come, come, Selena, let's not be melodramatic."

I jumped and wondered if he could read my mind. "You have a student in your Advanced English Literature class named Amy, Amy Beauchamp?"

Amy, my least favorite student. I could picture her now, a senior dressed like a woman of thirty in a demure blouse, knee-length skirt, and expensive flats. Her long, shimmering bleached blonde hair was so straight it looked ironed, even in the brutal Florida humidity. Her smile was wide, white and insincere. She was a straight-A student and dumber than a sack of potatoes. I had no idea how she'd gotten in my advanced English class, much less in the gifted track. When she bothered to show up in class, Amy spent her time texting.

Yet teacher after teacher gave her the highest grades. Not me. I was going to flunk her.

"You're wondering how she got all those As, aren't you?" Acheron asked.

I nodded.

"I want you to flunk her." The flames danced in the fire pit, making his shining bald head glow.

"Is that all?" I shouldn't have blurted that. I had a lot to learn about dealing with the devil.

"That's all. I'm very displeased with little Amy." He examined his manicure while he talked. "We had a deal and she broke it. I want to give her a little warning."

"I can do that," I said.

"So we have a deal?" He presented his paw. I screwed up my courage and shook his plump hand, fighting to hide the shudder when I felt that pawlike palm.

"Well, if that's all, I should be going." I gathered my purse. He snapped his fingers to summon the pale waiter, who said, "Lunch is on the house, sir."

"Good, good," Acheron said, turned to me and bragged, "I'm friends with the owner." He left a dollar tip and I escaped, relieved to go home.

Back at our condo, Jess was brewing Colombian coffee. "So you got off easy this time," he said. "You were going to flunk the girl anyway. What's he going to ask for next time?" He sipped from a small clear glass cup of Colombian, shook his head, and made a note on a pad.

"I'm not sure there will be a next time," I said. "We didn't exchange phone numbers."

"He'll find you," Jess said. "And when he does and has another request, get a contract, get it in writing. And give yourself an escape clause."

"What's that mean?"

"When he contacts you again, get it in writing that if you fulfill his next assignment, you are free and clear and have no further obligation."

"Good idea," I said. "How do you know so much about dealing with the devil?"

"Twenty years of dealing with editors," Jess said. "Before you go all woo-woo on me, this bird could be just a clever con man."

"Isn't the devil a con man?" I asked.

Jess sighed. "I'm trying to say that Acheron didn't perform any amazing feats. You drive a distinctive car. Everyone in the neighborhood knows about Blackie. You live a regular life. All Acheron had to do was follow you for a few days and he'd know where you live, where you work, where you go for chemo, and where you bank. He could easily find out when payday is for the college. He could bribe someone at Doc Sullivan's office for information about your case."

"And what about Mystery?"

"If he saw you at the supermarket, he knows you have a cat. You always buy Fancy Feast, or litter liners and cat litter. You never put that story about Mystery on Facebook, but you have posted her picture and said she was a Chartreux. There are only three or four Chartreux breeders in the US. He could have found Mystery's breeder online, just like we did."

"And Amy? Why would he want her flunked?"

"Old boyfriend? Ex-lover? Someone with a grudge? It's not magic," Jess said. "There is no devil. But you look damn sexy. Come to bed."

And so I did.

A nasty surprise was waiting for me at the English Department the next morning: Eric, the department chair, and Acheron, wearing an evil grin and another shiny black suit with an orange and yellow tie, like a dancing flame.

"What are you doing here?" I blurted.

"Selena!" Eric looked mortified. "That's no way to treat Mr. Acheron. He's an honored guest, and he's thinking of making a substantial donation to the department's student liberal arts theater program."

That was Eric's pet project, and I suspected it gave our department head an excuse to interview aspiring young actresses.

"I like to encourage young talent," Acheron said. His smile was so smug I had to clench my hands to keep from slapping his sweaty face.

Eric patted him on the back. "Mr. Acheron is interested in the workings of our department and would like to shadow you for the day. You have a class in . . ."

"Half an hour, in room C12, and there's barely room for the five of us," I said. "Mr. Acheron would be very uncomfortable in that closet-sized room."

And he'd scare the hell out of my students, I thought.

"I have office hours from eleven to two today," I said. "Student conferences are confidential."

"Perhaps I might talk to Ms. Steadman in her office after her class, from ten to eleven," Acheron said. "I'd be honored. I know this is an unexpected intrusion."

It sure as hell is. I hated how he oozed false humility.

"I'm hoping she'll tell me what else your department needs," Acheron said. "It's good to have a woman's viewpoint. Meanwhile I'll sit here, check my phone and drink coffee."

Eric's smile lit the dingy room. "Mr. Acheron gifted the department with a new Keurig machine and a year's supply of K-cups." The new coffee machine was enshrined on a small utility table, and the fax machine had been moved to the department secretary's desk. Trish was off today, but she'd be spitting mad when she saw the fax machine taking up most of her desk – and the boxes of K-cups looming over it. Eric had long coveted a Keurig, but the department's budget barely covered paperclips and pens. No wonder he was fawning over Acheron.

"Lovely," I said. "Now if you gentlemen will excuse me, I'll go to my class. See you in an hour, Mr. Acheron."

"Looking forward to it," he said.

I sure wasn't, but I was looking forward to my advanced English class. Four of my five students were delights: bright, funny, insightful. I was glad those times when Amy didn't show up and it was just my four favorites. Today's discussion and the essays about whether Shakespeare wrote those plays would count for sixty percent of their grade.

They were all there today, including Amy, a picture of pink perfection from her twin set to her flats with little bows on the toes, and her matching cell phone. She was texting, her shell-pink thumbs flying over the phone. A large Starbucks cup sat at her place. The other students were nervously checking their papers. Yes, I was old school and preferred paper essays.

"Good to see you all," I said. "We'll start with the oral part of the test. You may consult your paper while you talk. You first, Amy." I knew she wasn't prepared and I didn't want her to pick up any ideas from the other students. "Did Shakespeare write those plays?"

Amy reluctantly put down her phone and picked up her paper, a scrawny two pages instead of the required twenty. "No, he couldn't have," she said. "He never went to college or got any education to write plays. They were written by someone else. A guy called Baxton . . . Baxster. I can't remember the name, but it started with a B and he was lots more educated and stuff."

She stopped. Amy had just earned an F, but I wanted to make it ironclad. "And what are your sources to support your conclusion?"

"Uh, sources . . . You wanted sources?"

"At least five," I said.

"Uh, nobody told me that. But here's my paper." She sat down, clueless that this time the charm wouldn't work. She'd flunked.

"I disagree with Amy's conclusion," Brooke said. "Lots of

learned people have said Shakespeare didn't write those plays, even Mark Twain and Orson Welles. But other people say he did, and I agree with them."

"Are you ready with your presentation?" I asked.

"Yes, I am. My paper's longer than twenty pages. More like thirty. I hope you don't mind. I got excited about the subject and got carried away."

That sounded like Brooke, a freckled redhead with a sweet smile and endless enthusiasm. But today, something was slightly off: Her long hair needed a wash and she had dark shadows under her startling violet eyes. Were they red from crying? I hoped everything was okay.

Brooke's presentation was impressively researched, well thought out and detailed, and the citations were excellent, but the spark was missing. Still, she'd done her work and done it well. If her paper was as good as her oral presentation – and I expected it would be – Brooke would get an A. Karissa's presentation was almost as good as Brooke's, though she didn't cite as many sources. A B-plus. If her paper was well written, she might bring her grade up to an A-minus. Karissa was pro-Shakespeare, too. So was Cole, and he ended his presentation: "So in conclusion, Shakespeare's plays were either written by him or someone with the same name."

Everyone laughed but Amy, who was texting.

"Good work, class," I said. "I've enjoyed the discussion. Your grades will be posted on the board outside the English Department next week."

Unfortunately, class was over, and I had to meet with Acheron. Someone, probably Eric, the department chair, had let that creature into my office. A violation of protocol, but I knew there was no way I could complain – not about a potential donor.

Acheron seemed to fill my tiny office and block the light from the arrow-slit window. Worse, he stank of sweat masked by expensive cologne. I hadn't noticed that yesterday in the well-ventilated restaurant. I flipped on the overhead light and left the door partly open.

"Do you have to turn that light on?" he complained. I flicked it off, then turned on my desk lamp and bumped the shade slightly so the light hit him right in the eyes.

"What do you want?"

"To make another deal," he said. "You've flunked Amy."

"I haven't read her paper yet."

"You may not have read Amy's paper, but you've seen it. It's two pages when it should be twenty."

How did he know that? I wondered. He wasn't in my classroom.

"If I know Amy, she didn't even bother reading Wikipedia, much less do any research," Acheron said. "For her presentation, she recited a mishmash of some things she overheard or half-remembered from class. You're all set to give her an F. In fact, you're itching to do it."

I kept silent, but my thoughts were racing like a runaway car. I couldn't stop them. Again and again I asked myself: is he a devil or a con man? How does he know this? He could have seen Amy's paper before class. Maybe she wrote it at Starbucks and he saw it there.

"I didn't ask you to do anything you don't want to do, my dear." His voice was silky. "It will give you real pleasure to flunk Amy. You'll enjoy it. Maybe not as much pleasure as you enjoyed with your husband yesterday, but it will still be good."

I could feel the heat rising in my neck and traveling to my face. We did make love yesterday. Was he guessing, or did he know?

"Because you've been so good . . ." Acheron's smirk was vile ". . . when you go to the oncologist at three-thirty today, you'll receive a very pleasant surprise."

I felt hope blooming in me. I'd been so worried about my blood tests. Would the news be good? Would I be spared the torment of that new IV chemo: the vomiting, the rashes, the hair loss? I ran my fingers through my thick wavy hair. I'd hate to lose it. I'd had long hair since I was in high school.

"Now I have another little favor," he said. "I want the department head to catch Roger Maltby en flagrante with a student, Brooke della Femina."

"Roger?" My voice was a peep when it should have been a roar. "Why Roger?"

"BECAUSE I SAID SO!" Acheron howled. My office seemed to shrink as his anger swelled. "We all know he has an eye for the ladies." Acheron's reddish eyes were bloody pools of malice. His smile revealed his sharp canines. His voice was soft and sympathetic. "Lately, he's been interested in a young redhead in his Contemporary English Literature class – Brooke della Femina. She's the one I want to teach a lesson. Brooke needed money to get through college and I gave it to her. All she had to do was a simple seduction. At the last minute, she turned goody-goody on me and said she couldn't screw the man because he was married. But she'd taken my money and couldn't pay it back. I want her humiliated."

"But why Roger?" I asked.

"Because you know him and I can humiliate her through you. Roger is simply collateral damage. It's hard – if you'll pardon the tacky pun – for a bachelor like Roger to be around all this young stuff, especially when your school has that ridiculous policy that faculty can't date students. The new professor of Contemporary English Lit is only twenty-nine."

"But –"

"I know, I know, Roger is your best friend. He's the only one who knows how sick you really are. He covers for you when you can't teach class. He never tells Eric anything."

"I can't −"

"You'll be doing him a favor. You know he can't stand the Florida humidity. He spends all his free time in the southwest. He could get a job at a college in Arizona or New Mexico."

He'd like that, I thought. But not if he got caught with this student. Who'd hire him then?

"Roger's not ambitious," Acheron said. "He's never going to land a post at Harvard. He doesn't even want to be chair of this piddly department. Roger really wants to move out west, but he needs a little push. Otherwise, he'll work comfortably here for five, ten, twenty, thirty years, and then − poof! − it's too late and he's in his sixties and stuck for good.

"But you could give him that little shove he needs, and send him on his way."

"Why would I do that?" My voice was a guilty croak.

"Because when you go to your oncologist today, Doc Sullivan will give you the good news: Your blood tests are excellent. Even better, he has this new drug. But the bad news is it's in short supply, and he doesn't know if he can get enough or if your insurance will cover it. He won't know for at least a week.

"If you help me out, I'll help you out. Then Doc Sullivan will get good news, and so will you, week after week. You'll get an unlimited supply of this new drug, and your insurance will cover all of it. No co-pay. This new drug can work wonders. It can even cure, if you take it long enough. It all depends on you.

"Do this little thing for me and I'll do something for your husband, too."

My anger flared up. "You keep him out of this!"

"Are you sure? I know a lot of editors. New York publishers are fickle. How long do you think that Jess's Best series can last?"

My husband. Jess had told me that Acheron would be back − and he was. Jess also told me to get a contract.

"Last time, we had a handshake deal," I said. "This time I want a contract."

"A contract?" he said. "With me? Don't you trust me?"

"No. That's why I'll write the contract."

He looked amused, like a mean little kid who's thinking of torturing a puppy. "You think you're smart enough to deal with the likes of me? Was that contract your idea or your husband's?"

My face gave me away. "Hah! It's your husband's idea. He thinks dealing with New York editors means he knows how to handle me. Be careful, my dear. Next thing you know, Jess could be writing about the best unemployment agencies. HAW, HAW, HAW!"

I'd had enough. "Begone!"

He stood up suddenly. Now his voice trembled with red rage. "I'll be back in one week, and I expect results – or else. Just do this one little favor for me, and for Roger, and your chemo will be easier. You'll go into remission. Otherwise, think how you'll look bald."

I touched my soft brown curls. I couldn't help it.

He pointed his finger at me. Spit flew from his thin lips as he said with a snarl, "That's right. Think about it. You're on a campus with hundreds of young beauties with thick, shiny hair. Of course some women do just fine when they lose their hair. They look cute in baseball caps. They get wigs, although those are hot in Florida. Some gutsy ones go bald like me." He gleefully rubbed his sweating bowling ball of a head. "So many choices. Make yours by next week."

There was a puff of smoke and a bad smell. Damn! My desk lamp was smoking. I quickly yanked the plug out of the wall. The cord had melted. The lamp was ruined and the department wouldn't buy me another. Acheron was gone. He didn't even stop to help me.

I barely had time to wrap the burned desk lamp in a plastic bag, bury it in the trash can down the hall, and spray the room with Febreze before my first student showed up. It was Brooke, the redhead I'd thought had been crying. She really was crying now.

"Brooke, what's wrong?" I handed her a tissue.

"It's Mr. Maltby." Sniffle, snerch. She blew her nose, but the tears gushed again. I handed her another tissue.

"What did he do?" Brooke was luscious. Her creamy skin looked almost edible and the sprinkling of freckles were like cinnamon. She smelled of strawberries. Her red hair rippled like spun silk. I could see where Roger Maltby would be tempted by her.

"Nothing!" Another wave of tears from those lovely violet eyes. "I love him. I've loved him since the moment I saw him in class. He's the smartest, funniest man I've ever known. And I know he loves me. I can tell by how he looks at me. He's never made a move, but we communicate with our eyes. I know the class is supposed to be for everyone, but it feels like I'm the only one in the room."

Roger was that kind of teacher. He could make every student feel that way. But what if it's true? some imp whispered in my ear. What if he really is in love with this girl? He can't say anything, not with your school's stupid no-dating policy. You could help them.

"We're reading Maya Angelou," Brooke said. "The black lady poet. Mr. Maltby played us a recording of her reading 'I Still Rise.' Knowing about her life, what he told us about her, that poem is just beautiful. It's so profound. I'm sorry she's dead, but her words will live forever. That's what Mr. Maltby said. He told us writing is immortality."

"He's right," I said. "What's the problem?"

"I want to be a writer and Mr. Maltby mentioned that the free paper, the *Lauderdale Gazette*, is looking for a theater reviewer. He knows the editor. I want that job. I want to write for a newspaper and this would be my big break. I want to talk to Mr. Maltby about it."

"There's nothing wrong with asking Mr. Maltby for advice," I said. "He is your teacher. You can stop by during his office hours." You're doing it, the imp whispered. Way to go. Remind her he has office hours today. I swatted at my left ear as if a fly was crawling on it, but the little voice continued, She'll walk in with that flaming hair and light his fire.

"But I love him," Brooke said. "If he dates me, he'll get fired."

"How old are you, Brooke?"

She looked startled. "Twenty-one. I graduate at the end of this semester. Why?"

Just checking to make sure you're not jail bait, I thought. She's ripe and ready, the imp whispered. And just as green as her outfit. Maltby won't be able to resist that innocent act. He'll jump her bones in no time.

"You're a grown woman, Brooke. You can handle yourself. I have confidence in you. Just ask Mr. Maltby about the reviewing job. I'm sure he'll help. There's nothing wrong in doing that."

Brooke brightened. Now her pretty violet eyes shone. She had a muddy eyeliner smudge down her tear trail. "You really think so?"

"Yes, I do, Brooke. And I think you're good enough to write for the Gazette. If you want to be a writer, you need to build up a portfolio."

"Thanks!"

So far everything I'd said was exactly what an honorable advisor would do. But then I stepped over the line. "By the way," I said, "you may want to fix your eye make-up. Mr. Maltby is having office hours right now." Yes, you've done it! The imp was shrieking now. The trap is set.

The trap was set, and I felt guilty. I tried to grade my students' papers during my office hours, but I couldn't concentrate. I wrote down the points I would put in a contract with Acheron. I checked e-mail and found a memo from Eric: We had a mandatory department meeting next week. Only one other student stopped by, Mark Tadden, a freshman in my Intro to English Lit class at 7:40 in the morning.

Mark was a big, lumpy black kid with unruly dark hair and a shy smile, who looked like he needed about twenty hours of sleep. A good student, he always sat in the front of class and asked sharp questions. I was surprised when he didn't show up for the test last week. I was certain he knew the material.

Mark gave me that shy smile and slouched into the visitor's chair. "I missed the test."

"I noticed."

"I'm sorry I wasn't there, but my grandmother died." His brown eyes shifted. He wouldn't look at me.

"That's your third dead grandmother this semester, Mark. My limit is two. What's really going on? You can tell me." I leaned forward on my desk and gave him what I hoped was a friendly smile. I was trying to atone for what I'd done to Brooke.

He looked at the ceiling, where the fluorescent light was buzzing, then said, "I was delivering pizzas the night before and worked until midnight. I overslept the next morning."

He hung his head.

"Are you working your way through school?"

"Yes, I work most nights and study while I wait for a pizza run. But that night, we were nonstop busy. I was so tired I slept until ten the next morning. Please don't flunk me."

"I won't if you'll write me a paper about the theme of sacrifice in *A Tale of Two Cities*. Five pages."

"No prob." His smile widened. "When do you want it?"

"Next class." I tried to look stern.

He stood up, grinning happily and nearly knocked over his chair. "Thanks, Mrs. Steadman. I really appreciate it."

He left. And I left for my appointment with Doc Sullivan, where the news was incredibly good: my blood tests were spectacular and he had one sample of this new chemo drug he wanted me to try.

The drug was as good as Doc Sullivan hoped. I didn't get any side effects, not even nausea. But what was happening at the college made me slightly sick. Trish, our department secretary and gossip central, told me when I showed up Monday morning – after she finished grousing about the new coffee machine. "I can't believe Eric let that donor guy dump this fax machine on my desk." She glared at the shiny black machine, then tucked her short brown hair behind one ear. "Look at that useless thing. Now there's barely room for my computer. I had to put my IN box on it."

Trish sat back, crossed her arms, and scowled at the silent machine. We depended on this efficient woman of forty to run the office smoothly on a tiny budget, and she did. But now she was riled.

"I can't see out my window because of the coffee boxes. My plant's dying from lack of sunlight and so am I." The green plant on her desk did look wilted. No, it looked indignant, its yellowing leaves stiff with outrage.

"That fax machine takes up half my desk. I told Eric, 'Now that I got half a desk, I should do half as much work.' I don't think he heard. He was too busy fixing himself another French roast.

"And speaking of busy," she lowered her voice. "You won't believe what Maltby's been up to." My heart dropped like an elevator with cut cables, but I managed to say, "What?"

"He spends all day in his office with that cute little redhead, what's her name – she's in your class . . .?"

"Brooke?" The word stuck in my throat, but I finally got it out.

"That's her. She went in last Friday to ask him about a reviewing job at that free paper, and he's been reviewing her ever since."

"Maybe he's helping her with her article," I said.

"Ha! He's helping himself to Miss Peaches and Cream. They're in there for hours, with the door shut! You know professors aren't supposed to shut the door when they have students in their offices. He only leaves when he has a class. First she comes out, her hair a mess, her make-up smudged, looking guilty as hell. Five minutes later, he comes out, whistling and buttoning his shirt. His shirt! I say, get a motel if you're going to do that."

"Uh, maybe his shirt button popped open. Roger's not the snazziest dresser. He looks like he shops at Goodwill."

Trish snorted like a water buffalo. "He was here all weekend 'helping' her." Trish made air quotes with her red-tipped fingernails. "Helping her out of her clothes is more like it. He put the department keys back on the wrong hook. If Eric finds out, there will be hell to pay. He has zero tolerance."

I went through my Monday classes on autopilot. Mark handed in his *Tale of Two Cities* essay and thanked me. Brooke showed up in my class with a glow that could be seen from outer space. Her red hair tumbled down her back, a scorching fire. Her creamy skin was lit from within. She waited until after class to talk to me.

"Thank you, thank you, Mrs. Steadman. I got the reviewing job. Roger – I mean Mr. Maltby and I – went to the theater Friday night."

Oh, no! They were dating. If anyone from the college saw them together, Roger would be fired. But Roger could say he was helping a student. Would the faculty ethics council buy that?

"Roger – Mr. Maltby – and I spent the rest of the weekend brainstorming ideas."

Brainstorming. Right. I hoped he was focused on her fine mind. "I turned in a list of twenty ideas Sunday," Brooke said, "and the editor e-mailed me first thing this morning – he bought five of them. I start my first assignment today. I'm going to be a real journalist!"

"I'm really happy for you, Brooke. But please be careful."

"Why?"

"There are rules that forbid faculty from dating students."

"But we're not dating. He's helping me. Isn't that the point of a school like this – to prepare students to get jobs?"

"Well, yes, but be careful. Please?"

I could tell she didn't hear a word I'd said. My useless warning didn't salve my aching conscience, either. The gossip swirled around our department and spread through the other departments like a nasty virus. All week I heard salacious remarks, saw the winks and nods. I tried to defend my friend, but it didn't work. The whole college knew, as a psychology prof gleefully said, that "Roger was rogering a redhead." So far, Eric was so enamored with his coffee machine, he didn't notice the rumors. But I knew the day was coming.

That day was Friday, my deadline. Acheron showed up after my seven-forty class with a new plant for Trish – a malevolent orchid with a flower like a skull. She adored it. Acheron also had two workers in white overalls carry in shelving from an office supply store.

"I hope you don't mind," he told Eric, who was fixing himself a cup of hazelnut coffee. "I took the liberty of buying shelves for your fax machine and your coffee supply. We can't have the lovely Trish unhappy, can we? She puts up with enough."

Trish blushed like a bride, and adjusted the collar of her blue lace blouse.

"The shelves should fit nicely over there, by the door," Acheron said.

Eric simply nodded at this takeover of his department.

"And while these gentlemen are working on the shelves – I hope you'll excuse the noise, it's just a temporary inconvenience – I'd like to consult with Mrs. Steadman. Just briefly, if she can spare me the time. I know there's a mandatory department meeting at nine-thirty."

"Of course she has time," Eric said, without consulting me.

I glanced at Roger's door with dread. It was closed, but he was here – I'd talked to him this morning.

"Come along," Acheron said, and I felt like a prisoner as he marched me to my own office. When he sat in the chair in front of my desk, it was like the sun had gone behind a cloud. His suit was the darkest shade of black I'd ever seen. It absorbed light. His tie was slick black leather.

I left my door open, and refused to turn on the overhead light.

"Now, my dear, your week is up and it's time for our agreement." He tried to sound avuncular, but he looked sly and malicious. "You must take the next step and tell Eric what's going on in that room with Professor Maltby and Ms. Brooke."

"I –"

"I'll give you an easy out. Rather than tattle on the good professor, you can simply ask where he is just before the department meeting starts. Eric will be forced to knock on Maltby's door and – voila!
It's all over. He makes his discovery, and it's done. No muss, no fuss.
You'll get an endless supply of chemo until you're completely recovered. Roger's your friend. You know he'd do anything for you. He'd
want this for you. What do you say?"

What did I say? Roger would do anything for me, but he should
have a choice. He should know what he's getting into. But maybe
Eric would open Roger's door and find my friend and Brooke working on her next article. People had such dirty minds when a pretty
young woman was with a man. They automatically assumed the couple was having sex. Roger HAD gotten Brooke that reviewing job,
and she WAS a campus correspondent for the paper. I had no doubt
that was true. I recalled what my husband had said. This bird could
keep coming back and bugging me. I had to get rid of Acheron, and
it looked like he was going to be a permanent fixture in the department.

"I want that contract we talked about," I said.

Acheron's round face was the color of raw liver. Was that steam
coming out of his ears? Surely not. "I warned you about dealing with
me, but you still want a contract. Why?"

"So once we're done, you'll go away. I'll type it up now."

So I did. I brought out the points I'd jotted down, and made
sure they covered everything: I would have an unlimited supply of
the new chemo until I was cured. My insurance would cover all the
medical expenses. Jess's Best contracts would be renewed as long as
he lived – and each book would stay on the *New York Times* bestseller
list at least ten weeks. In return, Roger Maltby would be discovered
en flagrante with Brooke della Femina. After that, Acheron would
never speak to me or have any further contact with me, and neither
would his agents and assigns. Forever and ever.

I printed out a copy for Acheron. He put on a pair of drugstore
reading glasses and studied it. "Wait! What's this part about your
husband on the *Times* list?"

"You can do it," I said. Jess deserved something extra. This contract was his idea.

"Uh, look, there's a problem," Acheron said. "The contract says I
can't have any contact with you forever and ever. But you realize this
contract is only good up here."

"What do you mean?"

"Well, if you should wind up Down There, we might run into
each other."

"I'll worry about that when it happens," I said.

"I want to remind you: there's a special place there for people who betray their friends."

"Roger will understand. Are you going to sign?" He nodded.

"Do you want to sign it in blood?" I asked.

He looked amused. "Why? Don't you have a pen? I don't want to risk ruining my suit." That black suit had a peculiar texture that shimmered like a holograph.

I printed out another copy, then reached for my silver pen, a gift from Jess. No, I wouldn't let Acheron's paws sully it. Instead, I found a plastic pen I'd swiped from a hotel. Acheron signed both copies with a flourish. I started to sign mine, but I felt sick.

I paused, my pen hovering over the contract. Could I really betray Roger, the man who'd held my hair out of my face when I'd knelt over the toilet and barfed my guts out in the faculty bathroom after a bad round of chemo? My friend who'd told Eric I'd had the flu when another round of chemo had laid me low and I couldn't teach for a week?

"Do you really want to lose your hair?" Acheron said. "It's quite beautiful, you know. You're twenty years older than the girls here, but there's something about a woman in her prime. Oh, well, never mind. I certainly know bald is beautiful. I suppose you could live without your hair – lots of women do, and they wait for it to grow back. But without the new chemo, your hair may not grow back. You're stage four. Once this cancer continues to spread, your weight will drop to nothing, and you'll be a hairless bag of bones, stinking, puking, tubes and wires all over your body . . .

"Make up your mind. The department meeting is in thirteen minutes."

I thought of Acheron hanging around my office forever. I hoped Roger really was helping Brooke. No, I knew he was. I signed the contract and gave Acheron a copy.

"Nice doing business with you." He folded the contract in thirds and stuffed it in his shirt pocket. "Shall we go? I'd like to have a cup of coffee and check on my shelves."

The shiny black shelves were on the wall, and the whole department – all six instructors – was singing their praises. All except Roger. His door was still closed. It seemed to throb like a boil. He's in there, I thought. Brooke is writing an article and Roger is helping edit it for her. He's crossing out words and suggesting better ones and that's the only suggestive thing he's doing.

But I remembered Brooke's glorious hair, her wide pansy-colored eyes, and lips like ripe strawberries. She loved him with all the force of young love. Roger would need superhuman strength to resist that. But my friend could do that. I knew it. I knew him.

"Mr. Acheron, these shelves are superb," Eric said. "There's room for all the coffee you gave us."

"And the fax machine is at just the right level," Trish said. I'd never seen her smile like that, not even after two drinks at the faculty holiday party. I noticed her poor, struggling plant had been tossed in her waste can, and the skull-like orchid reigned on her desk.

"I'm delighted you like my little addition." Acheron rubbed his paws together. "Eric, isn't the department meeting now?"

"Oh, my, yes, I nearly forgot. Is everyone here?"

"Go ahead," Acheron whispered to me. "Ask about Maltby. Remember your contract. Maybe he really is editing Brooke's article instead of dipping his pen in the red ink."

I wanted to slap that smirk off his face. But I knew only the truth would remove it. So I said, "Where's Roger? Isn't he coming?"

I heard a nasty snicker. Acheron turned everything into a dirty joke. But I had faith in my friend.

"Roger?" Eric looked befuddled. "I know he's here. He said hello when he came in this morning. But his door is closed."

"You can knock on it," Acheron said. "You're the chair. You have every right. Assert yourself." He was stroking his black leather tie. Was that snake skin?

Eric looked doubtful. It was a breach of professorial protocol to open that door. But he looked at Acheron and got an approving nod. Eric walked over, squared his narrow shoulders, and knocked on the door so forcefully it swung open.

Brooke was lying on Roger's sofa, her glorious hair fanned out, her back arched, her creamy breasts with their pink aureoles exposed. Roger was . . . well, Roger was in a state of excitement, as the Victorians said.

"The beast with two backs," Acheron whispered in my ear. "My favorite animal."

Roger quickly threw a coverlet over Brooke, then pulled up his pants and zipped them. The department staff crowded around the door to gawk.

Eric was speechless, but not for long. "Professor Maltby!" His voice started as a shout, then turned high and reedy. "You are banned from campus. You will appear before the faculty ethics committee in two weeks. Until then, pack up your things and leave."

Roger was too stunned to move. Brooke cowered under the coverlet. I could hear her weeping with shame. But no one was more ashamed than I was. I'd done this. I'd deluded myself that Roger could withstand Brooke's overpowering love. I'd betrayed my best friend.

The embarrassed faculty filed out and disappeared. Roger helped the weeping Brooke get dressed, threw some things in a box, and they slipped out together.

Only Acheron and I were left. His triumphant smile was uglier than his orchid. "Nice work," he said with a sneer, then did an embarrassingly good job of imitating my earlier attempt at defiance: "'You can't have my soul.'" He laughed and patted the pocket with my contract. "I've already got it, right here. Remember what I said. There's a special place for people like you."

"Get out of here," I hissed. "You got what you wanted. I don't have to talk to you any more. It's in the contract."

He hesitated.

"Begone!" I said.

"See you later," he said. There was a puff of smoke, and the Keurig machine burst into flames. By the time I'd shouted for help and grabbed the fire extinguisher, Acheron was gone. When the firefighters arrived, the flames had consumed the coffee maker, the new shelves, and the fax machine. The year's supply of coffee was soaked. Trish's orchid was knocked off her desk and trampled.

Because of the smoke and fire damage, classes were canceled for a week. I spent the first few days in bed, but not because of the chemo side effects. I was sickened by what I'd done to Roger and Brooke. I keep seeing my friend's office door swing open, and his startled face. I felt scalded by Brooke's humiliation, and heard her wounded weeping under that coverlet. I couldn't eat. I couldn't sleep. Jess was so worried about me he couldn't work on his book, and I was too ashamed to tell him what I'd done.

On the following Friday, a shamefaced Roger Maltby showed up at my condo. "Do you want to see me after what I've done?" He couldn't look at me.

"Of course I do." I gave him a kiss, and hoped my false lips wouldn't sear his scratchy cheek. He looked so worn and haggard I wanted to cry. I'd done this to him. I'd ruined my best friend.

"I brought you these." He produced an enormous bouquet of pink stargazer lilies. I breathed in their heavenly scent. "My favorite. Thank you, Roger. Come have some coffee. Lord knows we had enough of it. Jess is testing coffee for his next book. So far, he have the Ethiopian best. Come into the kitchen and I'll brew you some."

He followed me into the kitchen and sat at the table while I made coffee for him and tea for me. While the coffee perked, I clipped the stems on the lilies, and filled a vase with water, then put them on the table. These homely tasks helped me forget the awful thing I'd done to him and the woman he loved – just for a few minutes. When his coffee was ready, I filled a mug, fixed him a ham sandwich and cut him a big slice of apple crumb cake.

"You've lost weight," I said.

"I haven't been able to eat." His face was ravaged and his brown eyes were bagged. But he devoured the sandwich so quickly, I fixed him another and gave him a bag of chips and a bowl of fresh fruit.

After he ate all that, and the apple cake, I refilled his mug. He was finally ready to talk.

"I've done a terrible thing," he said. "And everyone knows. Everyone saw me. Worse, everyone saw Brooke." His eyes filled with tears. "I can't bear to know that she's been hurt so badly."

"How is she?" I asked. I imagined I felt a little of her pain, but I knew it was only my throbbing conscience.

"Devastated. Humiliated. I have a hearing in front of the faculty ethics committee next week. It's six of the starchiest faculty members. How are they going to understand love at first sight? I fell for Brooke the moment I saw her. During my class, I tried to talk to my other students, but she was the only one in that room. Yes, she's stunning. I've never seen anyone so beautiful. But she's also brilliant. She wants to be a writer and she's a good one. You know that – she's in your class. I got her that reviewing job at the paper, but she deserved it. And she came up with so many good feature ideas the editor made her a campus correspondent. She got that on her own. Our first date was when we went to the theater together, and I proposed to her that night. She accepted, even though I said, 'Do you really want an instructor at a nowhere college?' and she said, 'I want you and I love you.'"

"Wait a minute. You're engaged?"

"We're getting married at the end of the semester, when she graduates." For just a second, I saw a flash of quiet pride and contentment.

"Then you were in your office with your fiancée?"

"Yes."

Hallelujah! This was my salvation. I tried to hide my relief and excitement. "Does Brooke have enough credits to audit your class and still graduate?"

"Yes, I think so, but why would she do that?"

"So she isn't boinking her professor, silly. It isn't fair to the other students if she's taking a class taught by her fiancé. You can't grade her. That's an ethics breach. But if she audits your class and doesn't get a grade. . . ."

"Then she's not technically my student," Roger said.

"And there's no ethics breach. You simply got carried away with your fiancée in your office behind closed doors and Eric walked in on you."

Roger suddenly looked ten years younger. I poured him more coffee and cut him another slice of cake. He ate every crumb of cake, drained his coffee, then shyly pulled a blue velvet box out of his pocket. "Here's Brooke's engagement ring." It was a delicate red-gold with two diamonds and a ruby.

"It's lovely," I said.

"I found it in an antique shop. It's unique, like her. We're getting married in September. Will you be my – I don't know the right word – best woman, best person? Will you stand up for me at our wedding?"

"I'd be honored," I said.

"We're moving out west after the wedding," he said. "I hate the Florida heat and humidity. In the summer, this place is the gateway to hell."

"You're telling me," I said.

"I'm lucky Brooke agrees. She can't stand the hurricanes and what the locals call 'palmetto bugs.' She says that's a fancy name for giant roaches."

"She's right," I said. "Where will you be going?"

"Phoenix. Her favorite aunt lives there, and she's a dean at a small private college. She says there's an opening in the English department. Brooke is going to pursue her writing out there. After what happened last Friday, we both want to leave the school."

"Sounds like a perfect plan." I hugged him goodbye. "Make sure Brooke sees the school registrar first thing Monday. That's the last day to change her status to auditing your class. I'm so happy for you both."

And for me. I didn't deserve it, but I beat the devil. Okay, a devil.

The faculty ethics committee did not sanction Roger for having sex with his fiancée in his office. It helped that Roger and Brooke had set a date for their wedding and were leaving the college – and the state – at the end of the semester.

My blood tests stayed good. I took the new chemo for eight months, and then my cancer went into remission. Doc Sullivan was surprised but said it happened sometimes. I'm cured now.

My contract with Acheron had one little error. In it, I said that Jess would "write the Jess's Best series as long as he lived." The series is a huge success, but Jess is sick of it, and thanks to me, he can't get away from it. When his agent sent Jess a new contract for Jess's Best Divorce Lawyers, I knew my little mistake had hurt our marriage. He's fallen in love with a doctor. I'm single now, but Jess's Best Single Life Choices is a great comfort.

I never saw Acheron again. I don't know if I'll wind up Down There. I hope not. But I'm a full-time Floridian. We're not afraid of heat.

The Seven

I grew up in a split-level in a Saint Louis suburb. My mother's friends stopped by for coffee and conversation. Thanks to a well-placed heating duct in my bedroom, I heard them talk about how trapped they felt. These stay-at-home moms had had careers before marriage, but their husbands decreed "no wife of mine will ever work," and the conventions backed them up. My mother's friends said, "I'd do anything to go back to work." Would they go as far as The Seven?

Betty checked herself once more in the bedroom mirror. Her short black hair was stylishly curled, and defiantly unwilted in the sweltering St. Louis heat. She thought her Besame Red lipstick was bold, but it went well with her pale skin. Betty's red-and-white polka-dot dress was cinched with a wide white patent leather belt that matched her white heels. It was June 1950, so it was safe to wear white shoes. Betty wouldn't dare wear white before Memorial Day. The starched, frilly apron over her full skirt was a sweet domestic touch.

Portrait of the Perfect Atomic Age Housewife, Betty thought.

Bill's always liked this outfit. I've made his favorite dinner tonight, too. That will put him in a good mood. This has to work. I don't want to kill him, but if Bill doesn't change his mind tonight, either he dies – or I do.

She heard his Chevy pull into the driveway, and hurried to meet her man, heels clicking across the waxed kitchen linoleum. She greeted her husband of five years with a kiss and his favorite drink, a light scotch. With his chiseled chin and Princeton cut, Bill looked like the perfect young insurance executive. He also looked beat by the heat. He'd rolled up his white shirt sleeves and loosened his tie. His seersucker suit jacket hung over one arm, covering his monogrammed briefcase.

"Daddy's home," four-year-old Pattie squealed, and wrapped her short, plump arms around Bill's pants leg.

"Careful there, sweetie," Bill said, his voice sharp. "Don't spill Daddy's drink."

Pattie's lower lip trembled, but she knew better than to cry. Daddy didn't like crying children after a long, hot day at the office.

Betty fought to hide her panic. She couldn't have her plan unravel because of Pattie. Not tonight. It was Number Seven.

"Why don't you wash up, honey," Betty said. "Pattie and I will finish getting dinner ready."

"I can't wait to get out of this suit," Bill said. "It's ninety-two degrees."

While Bill changed in the bedroom, Betty turned up the kitchen window fan, and under the cover of its soothing whirr said, "You look so cute in your ruffled pink playsuit, darling. You know Daddy doesn't mean to snap at you. He's just tired."

Pattie nodded, her soft dark curls bobbing in the fan's breeze.

"Sit at the table," Betty said, helping her into her booster seat, "and I'll fix you your own cocktail."

Betty poured 7-Up and ice into a plastic glass, added maraschino cherry juice and two fat cherries, then a candy-striped straw. "Cheers!"

Pattie managed a smile.

Betty prepared the summer salad: cool lime Jell-O with chopped celery and radishes on iceberg lettuce leaves. She poured tall glasses of iced tea for Bill and herself.

She heard the shower shut off. Time to take the casserole out of the warming oven. Perfect. It wasn't dried out at all. She heaped Bill's plate with tuna noodle casserole topped with her secret ingredient for extra crunch – cornflakes – then dished out smaller portions for herself and Pattie.

Bill strolled into the kitchen, looking cool and refreshed in a short-sleeved plaid shirt and khakis. "Well, what have we here? Tuna noodle casserole!" He smiled at Betty.

"It's not too hot for a casserole, is it?" she asked, her voice anxious. Everything depended on pleasing him tonight.

"Never! Nobody makes tuna and noodles like you do, sweetie. It's even better than my mother's."

Betty knew that. That's why she'd made it.

Number Seven was Bill's last chance. And hers. Tonight was Wednesday. The Sevens meeting was tomorrow night at seven. If she couldn't get him to say yes, then Friday it was curtains for one of them, and she sure wasn't going to get killed.

Betty was too tense to eat more than a few bites, but Bill didn't notice. She asked about his work day. "Miserable," he said. "The ceiling fans moved the hot air around, and my desk fan was broken. By noon, I was sweating like a stevedore. The stupid secretary couldn't find my paperweight and the ceiling fan nearly blew my paperwork out the window. I had to use my coffee cup to keep it on the desk."

Betty made sympathetic noises while she cleared his plate, then served homemade brownies and vanilla ice cream. He wolfed down his dessert while she talked about her day. "I washed and ironed two loads of laundry in the basement, where it's reasonably cool. After lunch, I read Pattie a story at nap time. She's starting to read, Bill. Our Pattie is so smart." Pattie smiled at her mother.

"Too bad those brains are wasted on a girl," Bill said. Pattie stared at her dessert plate, her smile gone.

Betty wanted to say it was important for women to be smart too, but she bit back her comment. She couldn't afford an argument. Not on Number Seven. "While Pattie napped, I waxed the kitchen floor," she said, "then . . ."

Bill wasn't interested, and Betty couldn't blame him. She knew her day was boring. He interrupted her. "Another good dinner, sweetie. Your brownies are the best."

"Thank you, honey," Betty said, carrying his dessert plate to the sink.

"Can I have more brownies?" Pattie asked, her voice small and crushed down.

"May I have more brownies, please?" Betty corrected. "Yes, you may have one more. You can watch television while I talk to Daddy."

She carried a brownie on a paper plate into the den and turned on the Philco TV. Once her little girl was settled, Betty took a deep breath, then rushed into the bedroom to fluff her hair and put on fresh lipstick. This was it. Number Seven had to work or she'd have to kill him. She had no choice.

She freshened Bill's tea. Here goes, she thought, and plunged ahead.

"Bill, dear, remember Mike Roberts? I worked at his law office before the war. He wants me to come back as his executive secretary."

"What?" Bill set down his glass so hard the tea slopped onto the tablecloth. "Betty, we've had this conversation before. Five times."

Six, Betty thought, but rushed on with her rehearsed reasons.

"Yes, I know, but he's offering more money – five cents an hour more. I want to go back to work." Deep breaths, she reminded herself. Don't sound hysterical. Be reasonable.

"With all the men out of work, Mike should be able to find a good executive secretary. I've told you before: No wife of mine is working."

Bill's face was bright red with fury, his thin lips were pulled into a snarl, and his voice was steadily rising. Betty turned up the window fan to the highest speed. Mrs. Raines next door was pretty deaf, but she couldn't risk a neighbor hearing them argue.

"What will people say?" Bill said. "They'll think I can't support you."

Betty twisted her starched apron under the table, where he couldn't see how nervous she was. Don't offend him, she thought.

Convince him. "Bill, please. I'm trapped in this house all day. I need to get out. I need a job."

"You have a job!" he said. "Your job is taking care of our house, cooking and cleaning, darning my socks, ironing my shirts and rearing my daughter. That's your job – your only job. If you went to work, who'd watch Pattie?"

"My mother," Betty said. Her heart was beating faster now. She had to make him understand. For her sake – and his. "Pattie goes to kiddie summer camp for a half-day now, and starts kindergarten in September. Mother said she'd enjoy watching her grandchild after school."

"And what about my dinner?" Bill said. It was a demand.

"You'll still have your dinner," she said. She hated the way she had to wheedle and soothe him, as if he were a spoiled child. She no longer loved him, but she had to save him. "I'll get home an hour before you. Plenty of time to cook a nourishing meal. You love casseroles. I'll prepare them the night before and pop them in the oven. I'll make all your favorites: my green bean bake, Hawaiian ham casserole, chicken casserole . . ."

Bill cut her off. "And the housework?"

"I can do it in my spare time. On weekends." She was sounding desperate. He wasn't listening, and his stubbornness was going to kill him.

Bill talked to her as if she were a disobedient child. "Betty, I've given you everything a woman could want. You have a new brick home in Clayton, one of the best suburbs in St. Louis. You have a patio with sliding glass doors and huge walk-in closets to hold all the clothes I buy you. I gave you a new stove, a washing machine, a refrigerator, and you have the first television on the block. I put this food on the table. What more could you want?"

"I want to do something meaningful, Bill, like I did in the war. I was a third officer in the Women's Army Corps."

"And I was a second lieutenant. Now I'm a paper pusher at an insurance agency."

"You're not, Bill," she said. "You're a rising young executive."

"Who can provide for his family," Bill said. "You'll hurt my prospects if you get a job. Our daughter will grow up to be a juvenile delinquent. Motherhood is a woman's highest calling."

Betty chose her next words carefully. The wrong ones would send one of them to their death. "I agree, Bill. I love being Pattie's mother, watching her discover the world. But a woman can have other callings besides motherhood. I was an officer, just like you during the war. A third officer in the WACs was the same rank as a second lieutenant."

Bill's laugh was cruel. "You can't compare your war work with mine, Betty. I was part of the Normandy invasion. You were one of our crack troops."

Betty flinched at the insult. "Bill! Don't you dare use that vulgar term for a WAC," she said. "I took a job in the military to free up a man for the front."

"Where he could get killed! Everyone knows WACs were hookers in uniform, Victory Girls eager to give relief to the troops."

"You of all people, know that's not true," Betty said. "I was a virgin on our wedding night."

"Of course you were, or I wouldn't have married you," he said. "The war's over. I've had to join the rat race. And I don't understand why any woman would want an office job when you could stay home in a nice house."

Please listen to me, she thought. I don't want to kill you. "Bill, every day I vacuum, dust, make the beds and mop the floors. I cook your meals. But it's the same thing over and over."

"That's life, Betty. You have plenty of diversions. How many clubs have you joined?"

"Three. The book club, the church's ladies' auxiliary, and the Seven."

"That should be enough," he said. "The Seven was hard to get into. It took you more than a year to be a full member."

"It's very exclusive, Bill. I was lucky to be accepted. I met Claire at the book club, and we went for coffee afterward."

That's where our friendship started, Betty thought. Claire has a sixth sense for finding women like me. Restless women who want more. Week after week, we drank coffee while she carefully sounded me out: What did I do during the war? Did I want to be a housewife? Was I happy in a new subdivision house with all the modern conveniences? Was it enough?

Little by little, I told Claire how I really felt. How I'd enjoyed my wartime freedom, and missed it when it was taken away. Claire understood. She'd been there. She'd been a radio operator in the WACs, just like me. Only the brightest women were chosen for that job.

After fourteen months of coffee, Claire invited me to the first meeting of the Seven: Seven smart, educated, accomplished women, all widows, except for Muriel, the newest member. Betty wanted to join this dazzling, sophisticated group.

"All the other Seven work, Bill," Betty said. "They have important jobs. Alice is an office manager. Louise is director of nursing at a hospital. Mitzi's an accountant. Ann is head of the notions department at Famous-Barr. Claire teaches deaf students. Edith is a college professor."

"At a girls' school," Bill said. She hated his sneer, as if teaching young women wasn't as important as teaching men. "Are these women putting this crazy idea about getting a job in your head?"

"No," Betty said. "This is my own idea. I only see them once a week on Thursday night."

"Maybe you should see them less," Bill said.

"You need them too, Bill. They're very influential. Mitzi's husband, Tom, hired you."

"I liked Tom," Bill said. "He died too young. A heart attack at thirty-five. See, that's what I meant about the rat race."

"But your new supervisor, Bryson, likes you, too. Maybe more than Tom," Betty said. "You're on the fast track to promotion. Please, Bill, don't say no. Please let me go back to work."

"If you want something to do, give me a son."

"But we have Pattie." One child was more than enough. They'd agreed on that before they were married. When Bill started climbing the corporate ladder, he changed his mind. He wanted two children, a boy and a girl, like the other top executives. Betty's opinion no longer mattered.

"She's cute, but a man needs a son. Someone I can take to the ball game and play catch with in the yard."

"You can do those things with Pattie. She loves the Browns."

"I won't have a tomboy. She's going to be a girl, a real girl who plays with dolls. No more of those playsuits, Betty. My daughter should know that men wear the pants. America went off the rails during the war, but it's been over for five years."

He slapped five dollars on the table. "Here. Buy yourself something. Whatever you want. Don't ever say I don't give you enough money."

Betty didn't want money. She wanted a job with money she earned. Fear gripped her heart. She made one last effort to save her husband. "Bill, what if I put my salary in an account for Pattie, so she can go to college?"

"Girls don't need college. She's going to get married."

"All right then, I'll use the money for her wedding."

"No!" Bill pounded the table. "No! No! You are a mother and a housewife, Betty, and that's enough for any woman. This is my final word on the subject. Understand? MY FINAL WORD."

"As you wish," Betty said.

"I'm going to read my newspaper," he said.

Betty was relieved when he stomped out of the kitchen. As she washed the dishes, she told herself, You tried. It's not your fault. If you don't kill him, you'll die. And then what will happen to your daughter? Bill won't send your smart little girl to college. She'll be trapped just like her mother.

Betty's tears dripped into the dishpan as she scrubbed at the baked-on noodles in the casserole dish. She rinsed it clean, took out a fresh dishtowel and began drying. Bill didn't like dishes in the drainer overnight.

When did my husband turn into a tyrant? she wondered. She'd thought he was her soul mate when she met him in 1944. Unlike many soldiers, he was respectful and a little shy. They'd talked about everything, especially the war, and he'd listened – really listened.

She knew then that Bill was the man for her. They were discharged about the same time, and he'd proposed. They were married in December 1945. Betty wore a wedding dress made of parachute silk and her mother's veil. She carried gardenias. And Bill had looked so handsome. She got pregnant on their honeymoon. She was delighted to be a mother. Bill seemed happy when Pattie was born, but as their little girl started growing, he often mentioned how he wanted a boy – as if Pattie was nothing.

That night, Betty waited until Bill was asleep before she climbed into bed. The heat gave her a good excuse to hug her side of the bed. Only one more night of sharing a bed with him.

Thursday flew by. Bill let her serve Swanson TV dinners to him and Pattie on the Seven meeting nights, and Betty baked two pineapple upside-down cakes, one for dinner and another for the Seven meeting. She made sure Bill and Pattie were eating at their TV trays in front of the Philco. Pattie had been bathed and dressed in her pjs, so Bill could put her in bed. Betty thanked her husband for babysitting, then carried her cake to Claire's house, two blocks away, where the Seven would deliver the inevitable verdict.

Claire's ranch house was tastefully furnished. Five of the Seven were chatting on the matching Danish modern living room suite, nibbling Trix Mix and garlic olives. The dining room table held a buffet: pineapple fingers wrapped in bacon, deviled eggs, pinwheel sandwiches, and cream puffs filled with hot chicken salad served in a silver chafing dish. She saw a rainbow pudding made with Del Monte fruit cocktail. Betty's cake and a bouquet of red garden roses were the centerpiece. They drank Lipton tea planter's punch, made with tea and frozen lemonade. Betty was glad the Seven did not drink at meetings. They had to make sober decisions. Besides, if she came home with alcohol on her breath, Bill would never let her go to another meeting.

"Help yourselves to the buffet, ladies," Claire said, "then we'll start the meeting."

Betty put a cream puff stuffed with chicken salad and a pineapple finger on her plate to be polite, but she wasn't hungry. She already knew the verdict. She also knew what would happen if she lost her nerve. No one understood how Muriel Johnson had fallen in front of the Clayton-Skinker bus. No one except the Seven. Muriel had lost her nerve to kill Roger at the last minute, and lost her life.

Louise had been with Muriel that fatal afternoon. They'd gone to lunch and then shopping. Louise told the police that Muriel had had a manhattan at lunch and was a little unsteady. She must have tripped running for the bus. Muriel's untimely death opened up a spot for Betty as one of the Seven, but now it was her turn to prove herself.

Claire took a club chair. Once the rest of the Seven were seated, Claire called the meeting to order.

"Today we begin with a celebration. Edith is engaged! She's marrying Dr. Jack Gatesworth, a professor of mathematics. They're moving to San Francisco, where they both have professorships at local colleges."

"Ooh," the other women said, gathering to admire Edith's engagement ring. Betty praised the sparkling square-cut diamond, but she was too nervous to join in the excited chatter.

"Edith will be a member of the Seven in San Francisco," Claire said. "We're a nationwide organization, Betty dear, but we keep a low profile."

"Publicity would be unladylike," Mitzi giggled.

"Thanks to you, I can marry my dream man," Edith said, blushing prettily.

"You've caught a good one," Mitzi said.

"There are lots of good men," Edith said. "We're not man haters. We give even the most difficult men seven chances to see reason before we declare them incorrigible."

And put them down like dogs, Betty thought. Like I'm going to do.

"I have a new recruit," Claire said. "We'll meet her next meeting when we'll have an opening. Or maybe two."

Everyone applauded, except Betty. She'd just received a death threat.

Betty was trembling when Claire said, "Betty, let's hear your report."

She told them about last night. Everything. They gasped at Bill's insults about WACs and looked sad when Betty said her husband had reprimanded Pattie for hugging him and nearly spilling his drink.

"I'm so sorry that he makes your little girl feel unwanted," Mitzi said.

"Children are resilient," Edith said, with professorial authority. "And you'll do your best to give her confidence, once this is over."

"Is that all?" Claire asked. "Ladies, shall we put this to a vote?"

The verdict was swift and unanimous. While Bill was pronounced "incorrigible, without hope of redemption," Betty folded her hands in her lap to keep them from shaking.

"Before we proceed, let me ask a few questions," Claire said. "You and Bill haven't had a fight recently?"

"No, I've been very careful. We had that disagreement last night, that's all."

"But nothing the neighbors could hear?" Claire asked.

"No. I was careful to turn up the window fan to the highest speed beforehand, and my neighbor on the kitchen window side, Mrs. Raines, is seventy and deaf."

"Good," Claire said. "And Bill's life insurance is paid up."

"Oh, yes," Betty said. "We also have mortgage insurance, so if anything happens to him, I'll own the house free and clear. We made our wills when I was carrying Pattie. Our affairs are in order."

"Good," Claire said. "Now, for the details of your mission. It's my turn to help you." She handed Betty a Welch's jelly jar filled with about thirty shiny light brown beans with dark brown spots. They were about the size of pinto beans, and Betty thought they were pretty.

"These are castor beans," Claire said. "From the ornamental plants in my backyard."

"The tall ones that grow along the edge of your patio?" Edith asked. "I've always admired those plants with their big purplish, red-veined leaves."

"They're a super privacy barrier," Claire said. "I can't see the neighbors on the other side."

"Who would guess such a cute plant is poisonous?" Ann said. She wore a cool yellow sundress. Ann was the best dressed of the Seven, since she got her clothes at a discount at the department store.

"Castor beans are one of the deadliest poisons on earth," Claire said.

Betty looked alarmed. "But I give my little girl castor oil," she said.

"Every mother does," Claire said. "Castor oil is perfectly safe. I think the heat during the treatment destroys the poison. I do know that castor beans are poison if the outer shell is broken or chewed. It's the pulp that's fatal. Three beans are enough to kill a grown man, but you should use all of them, just to be safe."

"How do you know this?" Betty asked, forcing her voice not to tremble.

"My husband was a chemist," she said.

"Late husband, thanks to me," Mitzi said. She giggled again and sipped her punch. Mitzi came straight from the office and still wore her summer-weight beige business suit. Her untidy blonde hair was frizzy.

Claire said, "You will serve your husband castor beans tomorrow night with his dinner. Will your mother watch Pattie?"

"Of course."

"Tell her you want a second honeymoon with Bill. Pattie shouldn't be around when the police are at your house or when he's in the hospital. That's too difficult for a child. When you go home tonight, tell Bill we talked you into having that son, and you want to have the whole weekend with him. He'll spend Friday at work in a good mood. That will give you the perfect alibi."

"Bill is too much of a gentleman to mention our private life," Betty said.

"Maybe," Claire said. "But his co-workers will notice he's happy and whistling in this dreadful heat. He may even drop a few hints. "What's Bill's favorite appetizer?"

"Sour cream-and-chive dip with lots of garlic. Real garlic, not garlic powder. I chop my own."

"Perfect," Betty said.

"Add extra garlic this time, and chop up the castor beans with the garlic. The garlic and chives should mask any unusual taste, if there is one. Give Bill a double scotch tomorrow night and have him eat as much dip as possible. Does Bill like steak?"

"What man doesn't?" Betty said.

"Then broil him a big juicy T-bone."

"But it's fifty-nine cents a pound," Betty said. "That will blow my household budget for the month."

"He gave you that five dollars," Claire said. "You can afford it."

"And he told you to buy something you wanted," Louise said. The other women laughed.

"Exactly," Claire said. "Serve him baked potatoes heaped with butter and sour cream. I gather he likes chives in his sour cream?"

"Loves it," Betty said. "And garlic, too."

"A double dose," Claire said. "The more the better."

"I can put garlic in his mashed potatoes, too," Betty said.

"You can, but don't bother putting castor beans in the mashed potatoes. The heat may make the poison ineffective. Don't forget to bake his favorite cake for dessert. Do you wear rubber gloves when you clean?" Claire glanced at Betty's smooth white hands and perfect manicure. Betty nodded.

"Wear them when you peel and mash the beans. Throw out anything you use to prepare the castor beans. Break the bowl and toss it in the trash. Hide the rubber gloves, paring knife, the seed peelings, this jelly jar and anything else you use to chop and prepare the castor beans, until you can safely dispose of them."

"Where will I hide them if the police search the house?" Betty's voice was shaking.

Claire lowered her voice. "In a Kotex box. You keep one in the bathroom, right?"

"Yes, in the linen closet, behind the hamper. Bill doesn't even like to see the box. He says it's disgusting."

"Most men feel that way," Claire said. "Including the police. Put a few pads on top and they'll never check. After the funeral, when the fuss has died down, you can throw that box away. But not in your trash can."

Claire patted Betty's hand. "Don't worry, darling. No one will ever suspect you. And the symptoms of castor bean poisoning are similar to so many other things. Depending on how many beans he eats, the symptoms will show up in about three or four hours."

The other women toasted Betty with their punch.

As she left, Claire told her, "Remember, Betty. You owe this to your daughter. To all our daughters."

"And our sons," said Alice, who had a six-year-old boy. "We can't have them growing up to be men who don't respect women."

The Seven wished her luck, and Betty left.

She was surprised how well the plan worked. Bill was ecstatic that she wanted to be alone with him for the weekend. It was a muggy eighty-seven degrees when he went to work Friday morning, but he was whistling cheerfully. Pattie was excited to spend the whole weekend with Grandma. And Betty spent the day slaving in the hot kitchen, baking a sensational banana chocolate layer cake, and chopping heaps of garlic and all thirty castor beans.

By the time Bill came home, the kitchen was cleaned, the potatoes were baked and the steaks were ready for broiling. Betty wore her slinky black dress. The table was set with flowers and candles. She greeted Bill with a double scotch and a kiss, and tonight, Bill's kiss lingered. After he showered, she brought his favorite dip into the den and sat on his lap, feeding him chunks of rye bread dunked in the dip. He never noticed that she didn't eat any. An hour later, only a few spoonfuls remained when she said, "Why don't you finish the dip, honey, and I'll put the steaks on?"

"Can't wait," he said. "I'm still hungry as a bear."

Bill looked a little shamefaced when she called him into dinner. "I'm glad you weren't watching me," he said. "I used the rest of the rye bread to mop up the last of that dip."

He ate every bite of his T-bone and heaped all the sour cream on his baked potato. "None for me, thanks," Betty said. "I'll never fit into this dress if I eat sour cream."

Betty cut him a thick slice of cake. Bill watched TV patiently while she did the dishes. Betty washed the dip bowl and the sour cream bowl separately after the other dishes, and stacked them on the counter. She'd throw them out later.

"Oh, Betty," Bill called from the den. "Are you ready yet?"

"Almost," Betty said. She blew out the candles and hurried into the den. Bill led her into the bedroom and unzipped her dress with trembling fingers, then doubled over in pain.

"Honey, what's wrong?" she asked.

"Some kind of flu bug," he said, running for the bathroom.

Bill's flu worsened. He was sweating and running a temperature, mumbling things that didn't make sense. His heart was racing and his skin was waxy-gray. Betty called an ambulance and went with Bill to the hospital. While she waited through the long night, she called her mother, who promised to take care of Pattie.

When the doctor asked what Bill had eaten, she told them about her special meal. "The sour cream must have gone off in the heat," the doctor said.

Bill died Saturday afternoon. Food poisoning was the most likely suspect. An exhausted Betty accompanied the kindly police detective back to her home. He took the empty sour cream container and denuded T-bones in the trash under the sink, along with the rest of the cake. Bill's neighbors and co-workers said he had a perfect marriage. The tests found nothing wrong with the food. The doctors concluded Bill died of a mysterious virus.

Bill's wake and funeral overflowed with friends and co-workers. Every one of the Seven sent flowers to the funeral home or to the house. The most dramatic arrangement was from clever Claire. It included gladioli and the huge, starfish-shaped leaves of the castor bean plant. "We will never forget," the card said.

Betty got the message. She would be the next one to set another woman free.

She waited for a week after the funeral before she called Mike Roberts and said she'd take the job.

"No, next week's not too soon to go back to work, Mr. Roberts," Betty said. "It will take my mind off Bill."

His Funkalicious Majesty

Newspaper columnist Francesca Vierling is the star of my first series. "His Funkalicious Majesty" took place early in her career, when she was a lowly fashion writer fighting to be taken seriously. Francesca and I both had to cover society balls, wearing twelve-button gloves and evening gowns. Saint Louis still has a Veiled Prophet Ball for its one percent. In the 1970s, black protestors held their own soiree to parody the Veiled Prophet Ball. Yes, that's real. So are pig ear sandwiches, a delicious artery-clogging delicacy. I've eaten them.

"Hey, you'll never guess what I saw at today's slice and dice," Cutup Katie said.

"Do I want to know this over dinner?" I asked, pushing reheated Chinese around on my plate. I'm Francesca Vierling, future Pulitzer Prize winning reporter. For now, I'm stuck with the lowest, girliest job at the *Saint Louis City Gazette*. I'm a fashion writer, but I won't be for long.

My roommate is the newly hatched Doctor Katherine Kelly Stern, a.k.a. Cutup Katie. She earned her nickname as a pathology resident. She's in the last year of her residency now. Katie is small, brown-haired and practical. She says she has no interest in fashion, and doesn't believe me that her comfortable sweaters, T-shirts, and jeans are the latest seventies style.

We share a rundown redbrick flat on Saint Louis's south side, the old German neighborhood near the brewery. Our place is big, cheap, and drafty.

Katie has a cast-iron stomach and likes to bring up interesting things she sees at the morgue – which makes me want to bring up my dinner.

"Last night, before I could stop you," I said, "you told me about the gobs of yellow fat you found around a dead guy's heart. I couldn't finish my food."

"I was saving your life," Katie said. "Burgers and fries killed him – and that's what you were eating." She was munching on a monster salad festooned with tomatoes and sliced California avocado. She'd saved the seed again. Katie keeps trying to grow avocado plants. So far, none have sprouted.

"Newspaper reporters aren't known for their healthy lifestyles," I said.

"At least you don't drink much," Katie said. "For a reporter." She took a big bite of lettuce.

"Not since you told me you could smell the booze when you opened the stomach of that dead DWI," I said.

"Doesn't stop me from enjoying a stiff one," Katie said.

"Are you talking about booze or dead bodies?" I said.

"Do you want to bitch or learn something that will land you a real reporting job?" Katie pointed at me with a forkful of greens.

"Go ahead," I said, but I was wary.

Everyone said how lucky I was to get hired right out of journalism school at the *Saint Louis City Gazette* two years ago. Like every other reporter, I have raging Watergate fever, and I offered the paper a real deal: They could have Woodward AND Bernstein for the price of one reporter. Instead they made me a fashion writer.

My qualifications? I was a woman and I wore clothes.

"Don't you want out of your girlie job?" Katie said.

"You bet. The editors are all men and they don't know a damn thing about fashion, or they would have noticed I was wearing a McCall's pattern dress made by my grandmother."

"A very short dress," Katie said. "That's probably why you got hired."

"Hey, I'm a good reporter."

"Who shows lots of leg," Katie said. "Those old guys in the newsroom must have coronaries over their Smith-Coronas when you walk by."

"Let 'em. Fashion will be my ticket to serious reporting."

"Then let me tell you what I saw today. There's no blood. I promise."

My dinner was congealing on my plate. I thought I saw a bean sprout move in my reheated egg foo young. After three days in the fridge, it wasn't quite so young any more. I nodded and Katie started her story.

"We had this dead man on the slab in the lab," Katie said. "Thirty two, WWM." That's Katie's shorthand for well-nourished white male, a standard autopsy phrase.

"Hard hat type, lotta muscles, wide shoulders. Weighed two-twenty. Looked perfectly healthy, except he was dead.

"Before Dr. Evans sawed him open, he told us to examine the body and find out what killed the construction worker. He gave us a hint: The dead guy had been stabbed by his wife, who weighed maybe ninety pounds.

"We didn't see any blood. The dead hard hat was hairy as a bear, but we didn't find any stab wounds on his chest, in his gut, or his groin. We flipped the guy over on his stomach – it took four of us. Talk about dead weight. Still didn't see anything.

"Finally, Doc Evans had to point it out: A little cut on the back of the man's neck, hidden by his dark hair.

"According to the police report, the guy had yelled at his old lady for making hash again for dinner. She was peeling potatoes, and he ticked her off. When he turned his back and bent down to get a beer out of the fridge, she stabbed him in the neck with her paring knife. He dropped like a stone. She'd severed his spinal cord with one cut."

"He was dead?"

"Just like that." Katie snapped her fingers. "Little nothing cut this big." She held out her fingertips the width of a paring knife blade. "One cut and he couldn't walk, talk, or complain about hash any more. Just a lucky stab."

"Not for him," I said.

"See, not too bloody. Just news you can use." Katie was rooting through the pile of lettuce for cucumber and radish slices.

"Not in my job," I said, and scraped the egg foo young down the disposal. I'd lost my appetite, but it wasn't Katie's fault. "No chance there will be any stabbings at my next assignments."

"No stiletto heels?" Katie asked.

"Out of style," I said. "And I'm not covering fashion for the next two weeks. No more stories on the Big Look. I've already reported that platform heels are so high you can commit suicide jumping off them. And readers have finally recovered from the thrilling news that New York designers Geoffrey Beene and Halston were elected to the Coty Hall of Fame."

Katie speared a wayward slice of avocado in her big wooden salad bowl. "What are you writing instead of fashion?"

"I'm covering society stories for the rest of the month. The Winter Wonderland Ball is next Saturday night. I have to wear a long dress and twelve-button gloves."

"Ritzy," Katie said.

"Boring," I said. "How can I make a story out of thirty people saying, 'We're having a wonderful time'? The women's make-up cracks if they smile."

"Doesn't the paper know it's 1974?" Katie asked.

"Maybe. My editor Charlie said I don't have to cover the Veiled Prophet Parade or the VP Ball this year."

"That's the big society do for rich people?"

"You got it. Since you're not from here, you probably don't know that the peons are supposed to wave to the muckety-mucks on their parade floats. When I was a kid, we got to watch their daughters make their society debuts on TV. I had to cover the parade and the ball last December."

"I remember the nonstop whining," Katie said. She searched the lettuce for more goodies, then gave up.

"At least I caught a break this Saturday night," I said. "The Gazette's letting me cover the Funkadelic Afro-Unlimited Court of Love and Social Justice People's Party."

"I'm impressed you could say the whole name," Katie said. "What's the catch? Your editor Charlie has never done you any favors. Why would the little toad suddenly give you a good assignment?"

"Maybe Charlie had a change of heart," I said.

Katie snorted and began singing that fairytales could come true, "it could happen to you..."

"All right, all right."

"There has to be a trap somewhere," Katie said. "Where is this Funkadelic People's Party?"

"In North Saint Louis," I said. "At the Moonlight Ballroom on Delmar."

"In an all-black neighborhood. Isn't that an iffy section of town?"

"It's getting better," I said.

"Really? You're driving there alone? And coming home late at night?"

"I can take care of myself," I said. "I'm not some suburban scaredy cat."

"Don't get so defensive," Katie said. "I'm just asking. Is this the black version of the Veiled Prophet Ball, run by that ACTION guy?"

"You mean Percy Green? Nope. Different party all together." White Saint Louis considers Percy a rabble rouser, but all he wants is jobs for black men. Percy and his protestors are peaceful. They handcuff themselves to the Veiled Prophet Parade floats and get arrested. Then the police have to haul them away to jail and that slows down the snowflake celebration.

"The Funkadelic People's Party is run by someone different, Alistair Huntington. The local rich white folks think he's more radical than Percy Green."

"Do you?" Katie asked.

"Not really. Alistair's not throwing bombs or burning buildings. He's another peaceful protestor."

"What's Alistair want?" Katie asked.

"He says black men should make the same money as white men and run the city's businesses."

"What about black women?" Katie asked.

"Alistair's not that radical," I said. "Alistair says his name means 'defender of the people.' Here. Check out the party invitation."

I rummaged through a pile of paper on the kitchen counter

until I found the glossy invite. An orange, black and green African warrior's shield was on one side. The other side read,

His Funkalicious Majesty invites you to the People's Court of Love and Social Justice to meet His Brown Satin Queen of Love and her Ladies. Boogie down at the Moonlight Ballroom. By order of FM.

"Who's FM?" Katie asked.

"His Funkalicious Majesty," I said. "The title is a parody of the Veiled Prophet Ball invitation, which says 'by order of the GO.' That's the Veiled Prophet, also known as the Grand Oracle to insiders."

"Well, I'm definitely not one," Katie said. "Since I'm a Missouri farm girl, you'd better enlighten me."

"The Veiled Prophet goes back almost a hundred years," I said. "In 1878, the city bigwigs started a parade and a ball for the richest of the rich. The Veiled Prophet is from the Kingdom of Khorasan."

"Where's that?" Katie asked.

"Persia or some place in the so-called mysterious east. For those birds, the farthest east they've been is New York City.

"The Veiled Prophet is a rich white guy chosen by other white guys. The VP dresses like a Klansman in drag with a crown, a veil, and a robe."

"You're joking." Katie was wide-eyed with disbelief.

"I am not making this up. He has a court with a Queen of Love and Beauty and everyone's whiter than Wonder Bread. The debs wear dresses that cost more than I make in a year. And they bow down to some old guy with a veil over his face – a faceless male member. Hasn't anyone read their Freud?"

"Why hasn't anyone laughed this guy off the stage?" Katie asked.

"Rich people take themselves and their money seriously," I said. "You know what's sad? The VP Ball could be a real story, if the paper would turn me loose. I want to really talk to those people."

"What makes you think they'd talk to an outsider like you?" Katie said.

"Some of them would. Two years ago, Percy Green persuaded a VP Maid of Honor to rip the veil off His Majesty and everyone saw who the super-secret leader was. The *Gazette* editors nearly turned themselves inside out arguing if they should reveal the name the whole city now knew.

"I'm a good reporter. I'd keep trying until I found someone who'd talk. I'd ask the debutantes how they feel being part of this charade. I want to know how they like dancing to music that's older than they are. The VP Ball's idea of a new hit tune is 'Baby Elephant Walk.'"

"No Disco Tex and the Sex-O-Lettes singing 'Get Dancin'?" Katie asked.

"Not even the Average White Band," I said, and grinned. "The debs and their partners dance to their grandparents' music. The debs have to hate that.

"They've been away at college, so I'd ask them if they care that the only black people at the VP Ball are waiting tables and parking their cars. Somebody must."

"So why don't you write the story?" Katie asked. She washed her salad bowl in the sink and dried it.

"Because the *Gazette's* publisher is one of the powers behind the VP throne. For all I know, he's this year's Veiled Prophet. The paper has to take this shindig seriously – or else."

"Will you take the Funkadelic People's Party seriously?"

"Of course. I'm even dressing up in my long gown, like it's any other important formal occasion."

"And you think they'll take you seriously?" Katie asked. "You're a South Side white girl with no connection to their world."

"We'll find out tomorrow night," I said.

Despite my tough talk, I was shivering when I drove down Delmar to the Moonlight Ballroom, and not just because it was fifteen degrees. The neighborhood looked scary. I had one comfort – even a wino wouldn't hijack the Blue Bomber, my ten-year-old rattletrap.

Seventy years ago, when this section of Delmar was a mansion-lined boulevard, a white woman dressed like me would have felt at home wearing a floor-sweeping evening gown and twelve-button gloves on a cold winter night. A gentleman in white tie would have escorted me to a flower-filled ballroom, bright with crystal chandeliers and Tiffany art glass windows. I would have danced all night in my silver shoes.

Now the art glass windows were shattered or stolen, the mansions' limestone carvings were salvaged and sold in antique shops, and the streetlights were shot out.

Tonight, the dark street looked like a war zone. Boarded up, abandoned brick buildings huddled next to empty, rubble-filled lots. Ragged men tried to warm themselves around oil drum fires, drinking booze from pint bottles. Broken glass glittered like diamonds amid patches of dirty ice. A lean, mangy hound trotted along the cracked concrete sidewalk past a payphone with its guts hanging out. I had yet to see a phone that wasn't vandalized. If my Blue Bomber died, I couldn't even call anyone for help.

You wanted to be in the big time, I told myself. Act like it. If you were a war correspondent in Egypt or Syria, it would be just as scary. Then I saw the glowing blue neon sign for the Moonlight Ballroom, a converted redbrick mansion with white classical columns. A black canopy sheltered the couples hurrying up the massive stone stairs to the brightly lit ballroom.

Limousines and shiny luxury cars were lined up along the street. I joined the line creeping forward. My Blue Bomber was older and more battered than any other vehicle. Despite my fancy dress, I felt like trash.

A Mercedes stopped in front of the ballroom. The uniformed chauffeur, a pudgy white man, opened the door and out stepped a regal woman in a magnificent kente-cloth gown with a red, yellow, green and black geometric design. The woman's long neck and fine-boned face made her look like the Egyptian queen, Nefertiti. Her escort, a slender light-skinned black man with a fashionable mustache and thick sideburns, wore an elegant dinner jacket nipped in at the waist. A wing collar finished his outfit with a flourish. I'd seen that tux and shirt somewhere: Esquire? GQ?

I wasn't sure, but I knew this was more style than I'd ever seen at the white society parties I covered, where the men's tuxes were shiny with age and the older women hauled out the same tatty couture gowns year after year. The showy money was spent on their marriageable daughters.

The handsome couple swept up the Moonlight's red carpet and into the ballroom as a limo disgorged its passengers. This woman's outfit made Cher look like a Sunday school teacher. Her lean, shapely brown body was set off to perfection in a sheer white bra top. Her toned midriff was bare and her transparent skirt slit up to there. Her dashiki-clad escort looked dazzled, as did every other man.

I carried a clipboard to take notes for my stories. I dug a pen out of my silver purse and jotted notes about the couples' outfits. The *Gazette* photo desk had promised to send a photographer, but he was covering a sports event and wouldn't show up until later. I'd have to rely on word pictures unless he showed. This story wasn't a *Gazette* priority.

Now that I was closer to the ballroom, I could see an orange neon sign promising public parking. I swung past the shiny cars still dropping off their glamorous passengers and steered the Bomber to the potholed parking lot next door. I gave the attendant five bucks and my tires crunched over glass and debris. I hoped I wouldn't get a nail in my retreads.

I grabbed my clipboard and silver purse, and carefully walked across the uneven pavement. I could hear Sly and the Family Stone's "Dance to the Music."

Above the catchy music, I heard rude whistles, catcalls and yells. I froze. Were those jeers coming from the Moonlight Ballroom?

No, from the other side of the parking lot. Three men were hanging out on the sagging wooden porch of the rundown house next door. I could just make them out by the porch's bare light bulb. Two men were hoisting Schlitz cans and one was hidden in a cloud of reefer smoke. The scent of burning leaves drifted my way.

The tallest man on the porch had an Afro the size of a shrub. I liked his orange disco suit and brown satin shirt with the flared collar.

Next to him was a Shaft lookalike, only much shorter than Richard Roundtree, wearing a red turtleneck and fawn hip huggers. The third man in the reefer cloud was perched on the porch railing. He had greasy dreads and a baggy T-shirt that said "Marijuana – Nature's Way of Saying Hi." The reefer didn't mellow him out. He seemed to be arguing with his companions in between hassling me.

All three men stayed on the porch. I ignored them and headed toward the sidewalk, where I saw a familiar Saturday night sight in African-American neighborhoods – the pig ear sandwich man selling his crispy delicacies. That was the name painted on his cart, parked on the street side of the lot.

Pig ear sandwiches are just what they sound like –a pig's ear on a bun. This particular pig ear sandwich man deep-fried the pig ears, then slathered them in Saint Louis's sweet tomato barbecue sauce and topped the ears with mayonnaise potato salad. Deep-fried pig ears taste like pork rinds. I'd had them before, but they are a sandwich best eaten alone with a bale of paper napkins. The pillowy white bun tends to collapse under the sloppy red sauce and yellow potato salad.

"Pig ear sandwich, honey?" the sandwich man asked. He was about sixty years old, a dark-skinned man with a gentle face and close-cropped gray hair.

"Not while I'm wearing this dress," I said, and smiled. "I'm Francesca Vierling, a reporter for the *Gazette*. I'm covering the Funkadelic People's Party."

"The white folks' paper actually sent someone?" he said, and looked surprised.

"Me," I said. "I can't eat while I work, but your sandwiches sure smell good."

"I'm James Brown, but I'm no singer. I make the best pig ear sandwiches in town," he said. "Good snoots, too." Those were pig noses. I couldn't work up the same enthusiasm for them. I could barely hear the man over the hoots and hollers of the rowdy bunch on the peeling front porch. Afro Man hurled a Schlitz beer can at me. I ducked and it sailed over my head and bounced harmlessly against a tree. The three on the porch howled with laughter and cranked up their stereo. The funky sounds of their music – the "Bertha Butt Boogie" – drowned out the softer "Soul Train" at the Moonlight Ballroom.

I rather liked the Bertha boogie, though the angry, drunken men made me nervous.

Mr. Brown seemed embarrassed by the music and the men. "Pay that trash no mind," the pig ear sandwich man said, raising his baritone voice so I could hear him. "They've been drinking and smoking all day. They're nothing but drug dealers, and they're trying to cause trouble for Mr. Alistair. They want the police here so folks can say the People's Party is a bunch of troublemakers. If you wait just a minute, I'll find someone to safely escort you inside. I'll get Kenny at the parking lot entrance to watch my cart."

He whistled and waved at Kenny, and the khaki-uniformed attendant hurried over. He was about my age, somewhere in his early twenties, and those broad shoulders weren't gym muscles. Kenny was respectful to the older man. "What can I do for you, Mr. Brown?" he asked.

"Watch my cart while I find someone to escort this young lady to the party."

"I can do that," Kenny said, and his smile was dazzling.

"No, I need someone young and strong to watch things here." Mr. Brown nodded toward the porch. "Those three have been looking for trouble all day."

Then he looked toward the ballroom and smiled. "Ah, looks like help is on the way. Here comes Mr. Alistair himself."

I tried to keep from staring. No disco funk here. Alistair Huntington was slim and elegant. Think an African-American Fred Astaire, right down to the impeccable double-breasted black evening suit with wide lapels and a silver tie. The suit wasn't custom-tailored — Alistair Huntington was born to wear it. He was carrying something silver-tipped in his hand. A scepter?

No, a cane. A smart silver cane completed his outfit.

"Mr. James Brown," Alistair said politely. "You seem distressed."

I was enchanted by his beautiful voice. He spoke British English, and I wondered if he – or his family – was from a Caribbean island.

The catcalls increased, and I heard cries of "Hey, Tom!"

Alistair ignored them and asked, "Who is this lovely lady?"

I extended my hand. "I'm Francesca Vierling, reporter for the *Saint Louis City Gazette*. I was assigned to cover the People's Party."

He shook my hand and quirked a thin eyebrow in surprise. "You were, huh? Someone must have really hated you, girl."

I thought of Charlie, my fat, mean boss, squatting behind his paper-piled desk, but said nothing. Charlie did hate me, but there was no point in mentioning that to Alistair.

"I plan to do a good, fair job reporting your party," I said.

"I'm sure you do," he said, "but it's not safe for you to wander around here alone. My lieutenant, Mr. Carleton, should be here shortly. He can escort you while you do your story. He's one of my Imperial Guards."

The cries of "Tom! Yo, Tom," were louder.

Tom? I wondered. Who's Tom?

But then I heard, "Hey, Uncle? Why you looking like the Man?"

They were calling Alistair an Uncle Tom, a deadly insult in that community, but Alistair appeared not to hear them.

"Ah, here's Mr. Carleton," he said.

Imperial was the right word. I tried to keep my mouth from dropping open. This Imperial Guard lived up to his name. The man was a slab of solid mahogany, at least six feet three, not including his Afro and orange-and-red platforms. His yellow-and-orange dashiki didn't hide his rippling muscles. A gold medallion the size of a saucer looked small on his broad chest.

I'd expected Carleton to look ridiculous standing next to the dapper Alistair, or for Alistair to look effete. But they didn't. Both men were completely, confidently themselves.

"Is there a problem, Mr. Brown?" Carleton asked, his big voice rumbling.

"No, Mr. Carleton," the pig ear sandwich man said. "But this here is Miss Francesca Vierling. She's been sent by the *Gazette* newspaper to cover the People's Party, and those rowdies on the porch are threatening her. They already tossed a beer can at her."

"Will you escort Ms. Vierling to the party?" Alistair asked.

"My pleasure," Carleton said, but he wasn't flirting. He was simply being polite.

Before we could leave for the Moonlight Ballroom, our way was blocked by the three men from the porch. They'd slithered through the parked cars and confronted us on the sidewalk, arms crossed defiantly.

Afro Man in the orange disco suit stood in front of Alistair, with short Shaft in the red turtleneck at his side. Reefer Man stood a little off to the side, his rat red eyes fearful, mumbling to himself. I was getting a contact high standing two feet away.

Carleton put himself between me and the angry men, and Mr. Brown grabbed my hand and dragged me behind the pig ear sandwich cart. "Get down," he whispered. He looked worried. "I don't want you hurt. This kinda trouble isn't good for Mr. Alistair."

I put my clipboard and purse on the sidewalk and hunkered down, then peeked around the edge of the metal sandwich cart. I saw Carleton standing at Alistair's side and Kenny next to him. Two lines of three furious men were glaring at one another, like the start of a Wild West shootout.

"You been ignoring us, Oreo," Afro Man said to Alistair, his voice soft and sneery. "Hell, you even dress like one. Black on the outside, but creamy white inside." He smiled, showing yellow teeth.

"Yah!" the Shaft shadow said, his brown eyes small, mean and hard.

"Why you disrespecting us?" Reefer Man said, his voice shrill. He was braver now that he'd joined the group.

"You gentlemen are not worthy of my respect or my notice," Alistair said mildly.

Reefer Man did a prissy imitation of Alistair's speech, holding a pinkie crooked, as if he were taking tea.

"Why you talk like the Man?" the Shaft shadow said.

"I speak like an educated man, Terrence," Alistair said. "Why do you talk like ghetto trash? You three are a disgrace to your people, bringing them down, ruining them with drugs. We don't need white people to destroy us when we have traitors like you living among us."

"Hey, if we didn't sell shit, someone else would," Reefer Man said. "At least we keep the money in the neighborhood."

"You could have finished school and made something of yourselves," Alistair said. "Randolph!" He glared at Afro Man. "Your poor mother worked herself to death scrubbing white people's floors, trying to give you a good start in life. You've dishonored her work and disgraced her name."

Afro Man's face was dark with fury, and a long thin knife materialized in his hand. A switchblade? I'd never seen one except in an old movie, but I was pretty sure that's what Randolph had in his hand. The knife looked narrow, long and lethal.

Little Reefer Man tugged on Randolph's orange disco suit jacket and said, "C'mon, man, you don't want to do this."

"Shut your mouth, Lonnie," Randolph said. "I'm tired of your shit. Get outta here. You ain't gonna get your money nowhere, no how."

"And you, Lonnie," Alistair turned to face Reefer Man. "A grown man, living off his grandmother's Social Security check. For shame."

"What you mean? I bring home money." Lonnie stared at Alistair, and His Funkalicious Majesty stared back, not bothering to hide his contempt.

Lonnie's eyes wavered first and he said, "I do give her money. When they pay me what I'm owed. And they owe me five hundred dollars."

Now the street was silent. I couldn't even hear the cars arriving. The potholed parking lot was a moonscape, washed in cold, white light.

At the Moonlight Ballroom, The Trammps were singing "Stop and Think" but it didn't look like there was going to be any stopping this impending disaster. Carleton was standing steady at Alistair's side, with Kenny next to him. Mr. James Brown gripped my gloved hand so tightly it hurt, and I thought the sandwich man might be praying.

Randolph gave such a contemptuous snort, his towering Afro wobbled. "Shit," he said, dragging the word out to four syllables and laughing at Lonnie. "We don't owe you shit."

"You do owe me," Lonnie insisted, and his own flick knife appeared. Several inches bigger than Randolph's, this knife's thick, gold-plated blade gleamed in the winter light.

For a brief, hopeful moment, I thought the two drug thugs were going to turn on each other.

Instead, skinny little Lonnie lunged at Alistair, who knocked the flick knife out of his hand with the silver-headed cane. Lonnie reached to retrieve his knife and Alistair whacked him on the side of the head, hard.

I could see Randolph telegraphing his attack, but Alistair's cane hit Randolph's knife hand so hard I heard bone crack.

Shadow Shaft was no action hero. Terrence stood there, unmoving, while Alistair effortlessly disarmed both his friends. Lonnie had collapsed on the sidewalk.

"Go on," Alistair said. "Get out of here. Both of you. And take Lonnie with you. Now!"

Carleton and Kenny took two threatening steps forward, but that's all they had to do. Randolph scrambled for his thin switchblade, while short Shaft grabbed Lonnie's knife. Then they each took one of Lonnie's arms and dragged him along the broken sidewalk. Lonnie's bony legs bumped along the broken concrete. The two weren't careful about protecting Lonnie's head when they dragged him over the weed-choked lawn to the porch.

But the rough treatment must have been reviving. By the time the drug dealers got Lonnie to the sagging porch stairs, he was able to sit down on the bottom step. He groaned loudly but his companions didn't bother to check how he was feeling. They left him alone and went inside.

I watched the scrawny pothead drag himself up the porch stairs by the wobbly railing, and wondered if it could hold even his light weight. Lonnie made it to the top step and plunked himself down.

By that time, I heard the disco beat of "Uptown Saturday Night." Bill Harris was singing, "Then I'm gonna be all right…" and I thought things really were going to be all right. I could hear Randolph and Terrence arguing with Lonnie, who insisted "you owe me five hundred dollars."

The more Lonnie demanded his money, the more the other two taunted him.

"Whacha gonna do?" Terrence said to him. "Call the police?"

"No, call the Crime Tip Hotline," Lonnie said. "Get my five hundred one way or t'other."

I lost track of the argument when Mr. James Brown helped me up off the sidewalk. Alistair retrieved my clipboard and purse and presented them to me. "Are you unharmed, Francesca?" he asked.

"I'm fine," I said, though I was shaking. I hoped he didn't notice.

Alistair was cooler than an Arctic winter. His outfit was as perfect as his diction. "I apologize on behalf of my misbegotten brothers."

"Not your fault," I said, dusting the dirt off my dress. "I'm not responsible for every white person, and you don't have to account for every black one." I had a few smudges on my twelve-button gloves, but they didn't look too bad.

"You're sure you're okay?" Kenny the parking lot guy asked. "You look a little pale."

"I am pale," I said. "There's nothing wrong. I'm a bit shaken, that's all. I'm ready to go to work, if Carleton will take me to the Moonlight Ballroom."

"My pleasure," Carleton said, same as before.

I thought the evening was going to pick up from when he'd said that same line earlier.

I could hear Barry White's mellow "Can't Get Enough of Your Love, Babe" drifting from the ballroom, and I wondered if the couples were slow-dancing under the shimmering disco ball. I hoped the Gazette photographer would be along soon. I wanted some interviews and I was out of there.

A screech cut through Barry's smooth sounds. A man yelled, "He's dead! Gawd damn, he's dead. You killed Lonnie, Alistair."

Randolph was shouting from the porch, his eyes big and wild, his huge hair flailing like a storm-tossed bush.

"Terrence," he screamed at the Shaft shadow, "call the police. Alistair's Oreo ass is going to jail."

"Wait!" I said, and Terrence froze on the porch step. "How do you know Alistair killed Lonnie?"

"He's got a big lump on his head from where Alistair brained him," Randolph said. "Little bitty Lonnie died of a concussion. Happens all the time."

I had to act fast. The police would love to throw Alistair in jail, no questions asked.

"Let me see," I said, and marched boldly across the weedy yard, trailed by Alistair, Carleton, Kenny and the pig ear sandwich man. Terrence stayed put on the porch. Lonnie was slumped forward on the top step, his frail upper body flopped toward his lap. He definitely looked dead.

Randolph regarded me with bemusement. "What do you gots to say for yourself, Snowflake?" he asked.

"I want to see Lonnie's fatal injury," I said.

"Right there," Randolph said and pointed out a sizeable goose egg on Lonnie's right temple.

I could see the dark bruising, but no broken skin. What did Cutup Katie call this injury? A hema-something. Hematoma.

"Hematomas aren't necessarily fatal," I said.

"The hell they aren't," Randolph said. "His Funkalicious Majesty" – he gilded Alistair's title with mockery – "hit Lonnie hard. He killed him."

"Lonnie was alive and arguing with you on the porch a few minutes ago," I said.

"So?"

"How do I know you didn't kill Lonnie?" I said. "He wanted his money."

"He followed us inside and got his money," Terrence said. The Shaft shadow pulled a wad of bills out of Lonnie's back pocket. I wasn't going to stand there and count it, but I knew something wasn't right.

"How long was Lonnie inside with you?" I said.

"Long enough to get his money. Then he said he didn't feel good and he wanted us to sit outside."

"After he had his money, instead of leaving, he wanted to sit on the porch in the cold?" I said. "It's twenty degrees."

"We been out here all day. We're used to it. One minute he was laughing and talking. Next thing he was dead. Just like that."

Dead. Just like that...Katie.

Why was I thinking about my roommate, Katie? I saw her at dinner in our kitchen the night before, talking about that morning's autopsy and the man whose angry wife had "severed his spinal cord with one cut ... dead ...Just like that." Katie snapped her fingers. "Little nothing cut this big." She held out her fingertips the width of a paring knife blade. "One cut and he couldn't walk, talk, or complain about hash any more. Just a lucky stab."

I looked at Lonnie's exposed neck. Under the dim light I could barely see a cut the size of a paring knife at the base of his neck. No, not a paring knife...

"Where's your switchblade?" I asked Randolph.

"My what?" he said.

But Alistair and Carleton heard something in my voice. They grabbed Randolph and held him still while Kenny and Mr. James Brown searched him. The switchblade was in the pocket of his orange disco suit.

The police found traces of blood and spinal fluid on the tip, but it was enough to convict Randolph for the murder of Lonnie Larkin Estep.

Sex and Bingo

One of Helen Hawthorne's early dead-end jobs was on a cruise ship, where she learned about high stakes gambling and cheating. Sex and Bingo *was written right after* Shop Till You Drop, *my first Dead-End Job mystery, and Helen was still on the run from her ex-husband.*

This cruise ship adventure was nominated for an Agatha Award for Best Short Story.

It was a summer of sex and bingo.

Where Helen Hawthorne came from, bingo had nothing to do with sex. In her hometown of Saint Louis, bingo was a game for women gamblers. They were serious and gray-haired. Stick cigars in their mouths, and they'd look like the men who played high-stakes poker.

But on a cruise ship, everything was different. Even bingo.

Serious bingo was silent as a church, except for the intoning of the numbers and the hallelujah cry of "Bingo!" Here bingo players chattered like flocks of parrots.

Real bingo players would sneer at these frivolous women who played one card. Serious players could handle ten or fifteen cards.

Only one thing was serious about cruise ship bingo: The money.

Twenty thousand dollars was the grand prize on this cruise. That was more money than Helen made in a year. And Helen couldn't win a dime. She worked on the Caribbean Wave, and cruise ship employees were not eligible for bingo prizes.

But Helen was sure there was a scam. She knew an employee had walked away with a ten-thousand-dollar bingo prize on the last cruise. This time, he was going to double his money and go for twenty grand.

She knew it, and she couldn't prove it. She was totally at sea, in all senses of the word.

Helen knew who to blame for that: her landlady at the Coronado Tropic Apartments. Good old Margery Flax.

Seven weeks ago, Helen had been exhausted by the discouraging job of looking for a job in Fort Lauderdale. One night, as Helen trudged back to her apartment, hot, sweaty, dejected and rejected, she was met by her landlady. Margery was wearing purple, as usual. Her purple shorts were spattered with red starbursts. Her red toenails were spattered with purple stars. Her purple sandals ended in bows at the ankles. The Florida sun had turned Margery's face as wrinkled and brown as an old lunch sack, but she had good legs and liked to show them off.

"How'd you like to get paid to go on a Caribbean cruise?" Margery had said. Her landlady had on her best sweet old lady face. Helen was instantly suspicious. There was nothing sweet or old about Margery, even if she was seventy-six.

"I'd love it. I'd also like a million bucks, but there's no chance of that, either."

"But I can get you the cruise. My friend, Jane Gilbert, manages the fancy clothing boutique on the Caribbean Wave cruise ship. It's part of the Royal Wave cruise line, the best in the world. The service is superb. And the food ... what are you living on these days? Peanut butter?"

"Scrambled eggs. Ninety-nine cents a dozen," Helen said. "I get six meals out of a carton."

"And a cholesterol count in the stratosphere," Margery said. She was puffing on a Marlboro.

"Listen, take the cruise and help out my friend. Jane broke her leg and won't be back in action for two months. Jobs on a cruise ship are hard to come by. Jane needs someone to take her job who won't take her job, if you know what I mean. I said you'd be perfect. You'll get room and board and make four hundred dollars a month. Cash." At the word "cash," Margery expelled a huge cloud of smoke. Helen waved it away.

Helen always worked for cash. It made her harder to trace.

"But Margery –" Helen said.

"Plus commission," Margery cut her off. "You'll get a commission, too. There are some high rollers on those cruise ships. When they win in the casino, they buy big." More smoke.

"But Margery, what will I do about my apartment here?"

"You won't have to pay any rent. My sister Cora's latest marriage just broke up. She wants to stay with me for a few months while she gets another facelift. I can put her up at your place."

Margery was still blowing smoke, but suddenly, it was all clear. Margery needed a place to put the much-divorced Cora, who she usually called "my obnoxious sister Cora." In fact, Helen thought Cora's first name was Obnoxious. Helen wouldn't have been surprised if Margery had tripped Jane and broken her leg, just so Helen would go to sea and leave her apartment for Cora.

Helen took the job. She had no choice. She needed the money.

She'd only been on board the Caribbean Wave two days when she realized she wasn't being paid to take a cruise. She was being paid to stand ten hours on a hard tile floor. After a day in the shop, her feet hurt, no matter how sensible her shoes. Helen could feel the spider veins breaking out on her legs. When the sea was rough, the merchandise swayed and danced on the hangers and Helen's stomach shifted and lurched. The walls seemed to close in on her. It was worse in her room. Her inside cabin was the size of a coffin, but not as plush.

But Helen loved the sea. She could stare at the ocean for hours. Some days it was the green of old Chinese jade. Other times, it was a brilliant turquoise with dark purple patches. On rainy days it looked like wrinkled gray silk, and when it stormed the water swelled and roiled like it was on to boil.

Today was a turquoise day. It was also her day off. Helen sat in a deck chair with a fat paperback, alternately staring at the ocean and reading about a woman who murdered her unfaithful husband. Helen hoped she got away with it.

She still remembered how murderous she'd felt the day she'd come home from work early and found her husband Rob with their neighbor, Sandy. Rob had always claimed he didn't like Sandy, but he could have fooled Helen with that lip-lock. In fact, he had fooled her. That's why Helen picked up the crowbar and . . . well, never mind. The crowbar made such a satisfying crunching sound. It was one reason why Helen had to leave Saint Louis abruptly and change her name. She could no longer make six figures as an employee benefits director in a big corporation. She'd be too easy to find. Instead, Helen took a series of dead-end jobs that paid cash and kept her out of the computers. She rarely made more than six-seventy an hour. But if she had to do it all over again, she'd still do it all over again.

On a cruise ship, nobody cared that she was on the run. Everyone was running from something: old debts, old lovers, old lives. Nobody cared what she did, period. Seventies' hedonism wasn't dead. It had sailed away on the cruise ships. There were old drugs, new drugs, everything from pot to heroin and beyond. There was every combination of sex Helen could imagine and some she couldn't.

Helen enjoyed the free atmosphere, but she didn't indulge. Drugs made her muzzy-headed. Love made her stupid. She was still recovering from a romance gone wrong. She'd made yet another bad choice in men, and she didn't trust her judgement. For this cruise, she was a noncombatant in the war of the sexes.

Helen just wanted to read her book and stare at the ocean. Now a huge shadow blocked her view.

"What's a pretty little thing like you doing reading that great big book?" a good old boy voice said. Actually, it sounded like, "Wad's uh purdy lil thang lack yew . . ."

Helen gave the guy her patented Saint Louis glare, which could singe the hide off a rhino. It had no effect on him. He sat down next to her. He was cute, if you liked men who liked dumb women. He looked like Tom Sawyer all grown up. His face was lean, tanned and freckled. His hair was silky blond. One curl hung down over his eye. Nice muscular body. Friendly smile that stopped at his mean slitty eyes.

"Name's Jimmy," he said, extending a thick tanned hand highlighted with little golden hairs. "You're new. You work at the boutique. I'm the bar manager and bingo caller."

"I'm Helen," she said, leaving the hand dangling, untouched. "Even though I'm a woman, I can read and write."

"Aww, now don't take offense. It's just that anybody with those long legs shouldn't be wasting her time cuddling up to a book."

"I like smart things," Helen said, sticking her nose back in her book. Even Jimmy should get that hint.

He did. "You know, pretty boxes kept on the shelf too long get so's nobody wants them any more." His country boy smile brimmed with malice.

"Beat it," Helen said. "Before I report you for sexual harassment."

"Plenty of ladies are happy to be harassed by me."

"Can any of them read?"

"Don't need to. What I teach them makes 'em forget all about books." Jimmy grinned, but it stopped before it reached his eyes. Then he walked off.

The creep was gone. But Helen's ocean view was still blocked. This obstruction was much better. It was Derreck, the musclebound cabin steward. Derreck looked like a god. Unfortunately for the women, he was a Greek god. Derreck was gay.

"I see you met the ship's legendary ladies' man," he said.

"That's him? He's disgusting."

"The small-town ladies from Michigan and Minnesota love him."

"I'd rather be marooned on a desert isle."

"I guess I better warn you about the Italian waiters, too. They're very macho and great womanizers. Don't tick them off. The waiters control access to the passenger food. If you're ever hungry for a steak, the waiters can provide it, but you may have to provide something back."

"I lived on eggs for two months before I got this job," Helen said. "I can do without steak."

"I'm just trying to explain how a cruise ship works. Jimmy, as the bar manager, is an important person. His cabin has recessed speakers and other luxuries, all provided by thirsty staffers."

"Power I can understand. But I don't see how that slob scores with the women. Do you find him attractive?" Helen said.

"He's not my type," Derreck said and shrugged.

"Is it true he has a new romance with a passenger every cruise and most are married?"

Derreck sighed. "Helen, Helen. You can take the girl out of the Midwest, but you can't take the Midwest out of the girl. Jimmy provides a public service. Our female passengers want a fling on their cruise. They also want it to be over when the cruise is over. They'll never see Jimmy again and he'll never see them. He gives them a nice guilt-free romance. You know, ships that pass in the night."

"One of those ships is going to hit an iceberg," she said.

"I doubt it. Jimmy excels at three shipboard activities: bartending, bingo-calling, and banging passengers. He's never made a mistake in ten years."

"There's always a first time."

"What time is the midnight buffet?" asked a chunky gentleman in a red shirt splashed with parrots and palm leaves. He was about sixty, and looked like he was wearing a tropical disease.

"Twelve p.m.," Helen answered with a straight face.

The guy was buying the boutique's gaudiest cruise wear, so she was very respectful. Not only did she get a commission, she got the ugliest stock out of the shop. Mr. Shirt had won big at the blackjack tables and now he was showering his girlfriend with gifts.

"She's my little gold good luck charm," he said, patting her round gold bottom. "I call her Lucky, and I plan to get Lucky all the time."

Lucky giggled.

The pint-sized blonde was definitely attracted to gold. Everything she chose shimmered and glittered, from the Gucci evening gown to the Armani jogging suit. Lucky was one of those women who looked like a knockout at first glance. She had a fabulous figure and blonde hair to her waist. On second glance, she wasn't quite so stunning. Despite the clever make-up, her eyes were small and squinty, as if she used a jeweler's loupe to estimate the value of everything. Her lips were thin and her long blonde hair was brassy and bristling with split ends. But she was built, no doubt about it.

Mr. Shirt kept patting her, as if to reassure himself she wouldn't disappear. Helen figured Lucky would stick with him as long as he had money.

"These platforms are cute," Lucky said. "Do you have them in gold?" The shoe soles were the size of paving stones, but they looked sexy on her tiny feet. Helen noticed her toenails were painted gold.

"Let me check in the back." A quick glance told Helen there were no platforms in the small stockroom.

"I'll go look in the big storage room down the hall," Helen said.

"No problem. There are lots of clothes to try on here." Lucky held a black-and-gold beaded crop top to her jutting chest. Mr. Shirt beamed as if she'd done something clever.

Helen unlocked the storage room and nearly dropped the keys in surprise. She hadn't seen Jimmy since their encounter on deck at the beginning of the cruise. Now she saw more of him than she wanted. Jimmy was wrapped around a slender brunette passenger. She was moaning and writhing under him. He was lowering her to a table bolted to the floor.

The woman's white linen skirt was hiked up and her long dark hair had tumbled loose from its seashell clip. She had a wide gold wedding band on her left hand. Jimmy's large red hands were working their way across the woman's bare back, like two crabs on a beach. They had nearly reached the string on her green halter top. The woman's face was turned away from the door, but Jimmy saw Helen and gave that flat-eyed grin. The woman didn't notice her.

Helen found the gold shoes and tiptoed out. She returned to the boutique a little rattled, and talked too much to cover her confusion.

"So," she said to Lucky, "do you ever use that luck for yourself? Do you gamble?"

"Nah, she plays bingo," Mr. Shirt said, answering for her.

"That's gambling," Lucky pouted.

"Bingo is an old lady's game," Mr. Shirt said.

"It is not! The last game of the cruise is at three this afternoon. It's a ten-thousand-dollar jackpot. So there. That's real money. You'll see just how Lucky I am."

She asked Helen, "Are you going to be there?"

"You're wasting your time," Mr. Shirt said. "Blackjack is real gambling. Nobody with brains plays bingo."

If he hadn't said that, Helen might have skipped bingo. Now she felt it was a matter of sisterly solidarity.

"I can't play, but I'll watch," Helen said, thinking that described her life these days.

Helen missed lunch so she could take an hour for bingo. At two-fifty-five, she put out the "On Break" sign and went to the Sea Star lounge. It was packed with bingo players.

Helen sat in the back, sipped coffee and talked with Trevor the Bahamian bartender. Helen loved to listen to Trevor. He had the most beautiful accent.

Then Lucky flounced in, dressed in a tight gold-braided Escada pantsuit. She bought a bingo card and sat next to Helen. Jimmy got up on stage and told corny jokes like a third-rate comic: "You know why mice have such small balls?" Long pause. A wink and a grin. "Because they don't dance."

The women lapped it up like cats with a saucer of cream. Finally he said, "You all ready to win?"

At last, he was calling the numbers. "I-18. B-4."

Lucky squealed. "That's two. See. I am lucky."

She had a long way to go. The grand prize was for a coverall, all twenty-four numbers on the card.

Helen watched, comparing this game to bingo back home. She'd learned the game at the old city bingo halls in Saint Louis. Her Aunt Gertrude babysat her on Sunday afternoon. Gert was supposed to take Helen some place educational, like the zoo or the planetarium, but Gert and Helen were bored with them. Instead, Helen got an education in the bingo halls.

She learned to keep her mouth shut. If she said a word about their Sunday bingo games, she and Gert would really have to go to the zoo.

She learned to lie. Helen would come home babbling about the baby penguins or the star show until her parents tuned her out.

She learned that sometimes you had to take a risk. Gert lived mainly on her Social Security money. When she lost at bingo, she ate chicken necks until the next check. When her aunt won the five-hundred-dollar jackpot, she would have new slipcovers for the couch and filet mignon at Tony's, the best restaurant in St. Louis. She'd never get those on Social Security.

Helen learned that sin was more fun than virtue. Her mother made her eat sugar-free cereal and vegetables and drink her milk. Her well-padded aunt let her have hot dogs, greasy fries, a chunk of chocolate cake the size of Gert's purse, and all the Coke she wanted.

Helen would sit and sip and watch. When she was seven, Gert got Helen her own bingo card. Helen attributed her number-crunching abilities to the reverent way the bingo callers said the numbers. B-6. G-54. N-43. You knew these numbers were important. They could change lives. They meant the difference between chicken necks and steak.

This cruise ship game didn't seem like bingo to Helen. Bingo gamblers did not wear size-two Escada. Aunt Gert wore a JC Penney dress the size of a pup tent and smelled of Evening in Paris. She'd never touch the cute candy-colored bingo chips that Lucky used to cover her numbers. Serious players like Aunt Gert used daubers, which were sort of like highlighter pens. Daubers were quicker than picking up little chips. Gert could handle fifteen or twenty cards per game.

Serious bingo players didn't say they were lucky. They brought their own luck. Gert had an orange-haired troll, a Saint Christopher medal and a plastic poodle lined up by her cards. She kept them in a purple velvet Royal Crown bag.

Serious players would never tolerate Jimmy, the jokey country boy caller. Aunt Gert would have stomped out by now – or stomped Jimmy.

There were so many differences between cruise ship bingo and real bingo, Helen couldn't keep track of them all. Her list was interrupted by Lucky's joyful shriek.

"0-66!" Jimmy called.

"Two more and I have bingo," Lucky said. "I hope someone else doesn't get it first."

"I doubt it," Helen said. "Jimmy's only called forty numbers."

Lucky looked at her curiously. "How do you know?" she said.

"I'm good with numbers and I played bingo every Sunday with my aunt. A coverall for a small crowd like this will take at least fifty-five to fifty-nine numbers."

"Bingo!" a woman shouted.

"Yeah, you really know bingo," Lucky said sarcastically.

But Helen did know bingo. It was technically possible, but highly improbable, to have a coverall winner when only forty numbers were called. That bingo was either a scam or a mistake.

She'd seen a scam once. It had caused a huge scandal at Saint Philomena Catholic Church. An investigation showed the crooked bingo caller was splitting the pot with her best friend. The pastor was so disgusted, he banned bingo for a full year. Aunt Gert never went back. "Gambling is a matter of trust," she said. "When that's broken, it can't be fixed. Something is wrong there."

Something was wrong here, too.

A staffer who'd been holding up the back wall rushed to the winner's wildly waving hand. He began calling back the numbers. "And the last one is O-66," he said.

"That's it!" Jimmy said. "Congratulations, darling, you're the big winner. Step up here to get your jackpot prize of ten thousand dollars."

"Who won the money?" Lucky asked.

Helen could see a woman pushing her way through the crowd to the stage. The winner had dark hair caught up in a seashell clip, a white linen skirt, a green halter top, and a gold wedding ring.

It was the woman who'd been in the storeroom with Jimmy.

"It's a scam," Helen said to Derreck that night. "Sure as I'm sitting here."

They were drinking in the crew bar above the rope deck, which was really the poop deck. Royal Wave ships did not use the word poop. Crew bar prices were cheap and the ship's staff sailed on an ocean of booze, except for the ones in dry dock at the onboard AA meetings.

Derreck was drinking with Helen to avoid a different temptation. The hunky cabin steward was in a committed relationship with Jon, a graphic artist in Miami, and didn't want to flirt with the crew.

"Are you sure, Helen?" Derreck said. "You don't like Jimmy. And it is possible to win after forty numbers." His jutting jaw was cleft, like George of the Jungle's. The man was ridiculously, heart-stoppingly handsome.

"What's the possibility that his current squeeze would win?" Helen said.

Derreck widened his already big blue eyes. "Really? The little redhead on the Panorama Deck won ten thousand bucks?"

"What redhead?" Helen said. "This was a brunette."

"Then you got it wrong," Derreck said. "He picked up a redhead this cruise. A school teacher from Akron. Divorced, cute and a little naive, just the way Jimmy likes them."

"Oh, yeah? I caught him doing the wild thing in the stockroom with a married brunette, about an hour before the bingo game."

"Interesting," Derreck said, and took a thoughtful sip of his beer.

"I thought the crew couldn't fraternize with the passengers," Helen said. "I sure got a lecture on that subject."

"Well, they can and they can't," Derreck said. "Technically, the staff is forbidden. In reality, affairs by officers and uniformed staff like Jimmy are tolerated, but deckhands and below-stairs help would be instantly dismissed. It's sort of an upstairs-downstairs thing. You know, a Victorian lady could have a fling with her handsome footman, but heaven help her if she was caught with the bootblack.

"There is one unbreakable rule: No one on staff can take a passenger to his or her room. The cruise line put up cameras all over the crew sleeping areas to watch us. Cut the rape complaints way back."

"So where do the crew and passengers meet, besides my stockroom?" Helen said.

"Well, there are the lifeboats. We're always finding used condoms and wine bottles in the lifeboats. The top decks are another trysting place."

"I thought the security guards did rounds up there," Helen said.

"They do. Every thirty-five or forty minutes. They're easy to time. You just wait till the guard passes. Then you have at least half an hour."

"Are you speaking from personal experience?" Helen said.

"Not lately," Derreck said, and virtuously finished his beer.

"How do you keep those flat abs when you drink beer?" Helen said.

"Beer has food value. It's made of all natural ingredients, malt, grain, and hops. Now, if I can continue my sex lecture, the crew has one more choice. In most ports there are flea bag hotels that rent rooms on an hourly basis. Want another wine?"

"No, thanks."

Derreck went for another beer. Helen stared out into the ocean's infinite emptiness. There was nothing, not even the lights of another ship. It did not make her feel lonely. She felt secure. No one could find her in this blackness.

Derreck returned with his beer and Helen returned to the subject of sex and bingo. "Why isn't the cruise director calling bingo? I thought that was his job."

"Because Jimmy's popular with the passengers and the cruise director is more interested in pleasing them than playing power games. Listen, even if Jimmy is guilty, how can you prove it?"

"I can't," Helen said. "Not this time. The cruise is nearly over. It was only seven days. We'll be back in Fort Lauderdale tomorrow. I'm going to watch him this next cruise."

"If he's crooked, that one is the big bait. It's twenty-one days, with twelve days at sea. Lots of sea days means more bingo games for the bored passengers, and a big jackpot prize. Twenty thousand dollars."

Helen whistled. Aunt Gert would have thought she'd died and gone to heaven if she played bingo on a cruise ship with a prize that big. Gert had been dead for years, and Helen hoped she was playing bingo in some celestial hall with angel callers and golden daubers.

"Is there that much money in cruise ship bingo?" she said.

"Gambling is big business on cruises," he said. "Along with bingo, there's Caribbean stud poker and the progressive slots. There's money in those, too, and cruise ships get a break the casinos don't. Casino jackpots have to keep going up each time the slots are played. Ships can roll the progressive slots back down after each voyage. Less of a payout. Casinos can't get away with that."

Derreck's second beer was almost gone, but he still had questions. "Here's what I don't get: How do you cheat at bingo? It's basically a lottery. Is he fixing the numbers or what?"

"I'm not sure," Helen said. "I think he's getting his ladies to work with him somehow. I have a theory he has two girlfriends, one for show and one on the QT. That's the one he's cheating with. But this is a different game of bingo than I'm used to. These players are not all that sophisticated. It would be easy to get things past them. It's not right. Will you help me nail him?"

"Might as well," Derreck said. "Now that I'm faithful to Jon, I have lots of time for a cheater."

How was Jimmy doing it? That was the question. How did that bingo scam work at St. Philomena's all those years ago? Helen couldn't ask her long-dead aunt. Helen couldn't call anyone in her family. Only her sister Kathy knew where Helen was, and Kathy couldn't tell a bingo dauber from a mud dauber. Aunt Gert's illicit bingo excursions took place before Kathy was born, but she would have never participated. Kathy was a straight arrow.

The twenty-one-day Ultimate Caribbean Adventure embarked from Fort Lauderdale and sailed the eastern and western Caribbean. Lucky and Mr. Shirt were replaced by other couples, some married, some not. There were the usual collection of single and divorced women, hoping for a shipboard romance, as well as older people enjoying the good meals and sea air.

The ship had barely reached Nassau in the Bahamas before Jimmy was flirting with a giggly little CPA who had a face like a china doll and thick, muscular dancer's legs. The CPA, whose name was Emma, must have been very good with money. She was staying in an eight-thousand-dollar Royal Wave suite with two ocean-view windows, a king-size bed, and a Jacuzzi. Jimmy courted her with free drinks and bottles of wine at dinner. She giggled at his corny jokes.

Derreck pointed her out to Helen. "That's Emma, Jimmy's pick this cruise."

"That's his show girl," Helen said. "If he's running the same scam as last time, then he'll have someone else stashed in the background."

"That's going to be the tough part," Derreck said. "Keeping the second one secret. A cruise ship is worse than a small town. We all know each other's business. Speaking of which, Lourdes, the Vista Deck maid, told me that guy nobody wants to sit next to at meals because of his awful BO doesn't shower. He hasn't touched a bath towel since the cruise started and his shower is dry as a bone."

"Sometimes," Helen said, "you can have too much information."

Working in the boutique, Helen met most of the women onboard. She listened while they talked about their husbands, boyfriends and exes. The Royal Wave operated on a cashless card system, and that seemed to encourage spending. Helen was fascinated. Before she'd picked up that crowbar, she spent as carelessly as they did. But now that she was on the run, she'd grown used to living on minimum wage money. She'd learned to watch her pennies.

Nobody bought anything because they needed it. Men bought clothes for women to show off their own power. Neglected wives bought expensive outfits to punish their husbands. Women bought to celebrate a special occasion, get even with their man, or because they were on vacation and had to buy something. Emma the CPA spent lavishly, treating herself to delicate designs and light colors that flattered her china doll face.

Occasionally, someone would lose too much in the casino, and then the trophy buys would have to be returned. Helen dreaded those times. The loud silences, unshed tears, the pulsating, palpable embarrassment nearly crowded her out of the room.

She listened carefully for the women to mention Jimmy, but they never did, not even Emma. He was a servant, part of the ship's fittings. Helen watched the storeroom like a cat watched a mouse hole, but Jimmy never went near it.

He's too smart for that, Helen thought. He knows I know. He's found another hiding place. That would be easy. Cruise ships had more hiding places than the mountains of Afghanistan.

She followed him when he went ashore at San Juan, Saint Thomas (which the crew called Saint Toilet), and Georgetown on Grand Cayman Island. He did all the things the other crew members did. He ate in little local restaurants away from the crowds. He stopped at American fast-food places because travel made you crave Big Macs and KFC, even if you rarely ate them at home. He drank in the bars and went for walks. Sometimes he took the giggly CPA with him, and sometimes he didn't.

"He's sticking with Emma. I've never caught him with another woman passenger," Helen complained to Derreck.

"Jimmy has become your great white whale," Derreck said. "You're following him like Captain Ahab." Derreck laughed when he said that, but Helen saw the concern in his eyes. Following Jimmy had become an obsession.

"Helen, why are you doing this? You know the cruise line won't reward you if you discover Jimmy's fraud," he said. "They don't appreciate having their eyes opened to unpleasant things."

She knew that. But she couldn't stop.

"I'm tracking him for women like Lucky, who didn't know they were being cheated," she said righteously. Derreck gave her the fish eye, but said nothing else.

Helen knew in her secret heart that she hated Jimmy and she hated cheaters. Jimmy was one of the destroyers, the men who preyed on unhappy women and shaky marriages. She thought again of her husband Rob, who'd made such a fool of her with their neighbor Sandy. That's why she wanted Jimmy, and that's why she was going to get him.

At first Helen was afraid that Jimmy might realize she was following him. But soon she saw when the cruise ships docked in these Caribbean ports, they flooded the little towns with tourists. Crew members met one another coming and going. If she ran into Jimmy on a side street, well, she was trying to escape the crowds just like he was. She nodded coldly and kept walking.

Helen met Derreck in the crew bar the night before they docked in Cozumel, Mexico. She'd made no progress. "I'm getting desperate. We only have two more ports."

"Something is going to happen," Derreck said. "Emma the CPA was giggling even more than usual."

Helen wanted to ask Derreck to go with her on the next shore trip, but he seemed distracted. He was suspiciously silent on the subject of Jon.

This time, Helen followed Emma off the ship instead of Jimmy. Some of the passengers went on the shore excursions. Others headed for the duty-free shops. Helen wondered how much Lalique, Royal Doulton, and Waterford people could look at.

Emma stayed by herself. The CPA wandered through T-shirt shops and souvenir stands, getting farther and farther from the cruise ship crowd. Helen lost track of Emma in a shop that sold onyx bookends and coconut carvings. Half a block later, she spotted Emma again, but she was no longer alone. She was hanging onto Jimmy like he was the last lifeboat on the Titanic.

The couple went to a dingy little hotel, blocks away from the bright new tourist hotels that lined the shore. It was painted turquoise, hence its name, La Turquesa. Helen was afraid they would see her. She was surrounded by swarms of grubby children selling her souvenirs, begging for money, offering to show her the sights. Their older brothers tried to sell her drugs and themselves. But Jimmy and Emma were too wrapped up in each other to notice. Helen pushed her way through the begging crowds and went back to the ship. She didn't say anything about the tryst, but by the first dinner seating, the whole crew knew where Jimmy had spent the afternoon. It was amazing how gossip spread on the ship.

"I've read this all wrong," Helen told Derreck in the crew bar that night. "He's not carrying on with anyone but the CPA. The cruise is almost over. Tomorrow there's a stop in Progreso."

Derreck grunted a response. He was in no mood to talk, but he did listen.

"You could say I've been gambling, too. Progreso is my last chance. The day after is our last sea day and the jackpot bingo."

Progreso was anything but, in Helen's opinion. It was a dirty little port city. Emma, like most passengers, took the shore excursion to the Mayan ruins at Chichen Itza. Jimmy rode in the tender with the crew and walked around Progreso. Helen followed, thinking how strange land felt. She'd grown so used to the ship's movement she felt oddly flatfooted.

Jimmy stopped at a restaurant that had more flies and dogs than customers. Helen wasn't about to eat there. Instead, she went down the street to a pickup truck, where a man was lopping the tops off coconuts with a machete. She drank the sweet, warm coconut milk, then picked at the meat.

Finally, Jimmy came out of the restaurant talking to a tall, horse-faced blonde with elaborately curled hair. Helen recognized her from the cruise ship. She was Jackie, a beautician from Springfield, Missouri. She was married with two kids, she'd told Helen. Jackie must have scraped together every penny to take this trip with her girlfriend, Lila. They shared an inside stateroom on the lowest deck, a shoebox-sized room.

Jackie spent hours in Helen's boutique, looking at clothes she knew and Helen knew she could never afford. Eventually, she did buy a seashell hairclip. Jackie wore it today with what was obviously her best outfit, a peach dress with ruffles. She also wore a wedding ring.

Jimmy kissed Jackie. They walked up a steep rutted road, Jackie's high-heeled sandals slipping on the rocks and potholes, to a hotel that looked like a noir movie set: a single bare bulb, a whirring fan on a sagging registration desk. The lobby was painted a vile yellow. Helen hoped the beautician thought it was romantic.

Jimmy signed the register and paid the clerk up front. Bingo! Helen thought. She was right.

She couldn't wait to tell Derreck what she'd seen, but she waited anyway. He wasn't himself that night when they met in the crew bar.

He hadn't heard from Jon in six days. His lover wasn't answering his letters, phone calls, or e-mails. "Maybe he's out of town," Helen said. "Maybe his e-mail server is down."

Each excuse sounded lamer than the last and seemed to make Derreck drink more. Finally she gave up trying to make Derreck feel better before he was too trashed to help her at all. Besides, being sad only made him better-looking. He wouldn't be lonely for long. Helen was sure of that.

"You won't believe what I saw today," she said. Helen told him about the flyspecked restaurant and the flea bag hotel.

"There seems to be an insect theme here," Derreck said.

"There was only one reason you'd go to that hotel," she said.

"To collect cockroaches?"

"I've got Jimmy," she said. "The beautician is his accomplice."

"But what have you got?" Derreck said.

That was what she didn't know.

Helen was determined to be at the jackpot bingo game early, to watch every move. Derreck was there, too, and rather grumpy.

There was still no word from Jon.

Helen scanned the audience. Emma, Jimmy's show girl, was sitting up front, flirting outrageously with him. She'd bought her bingo card when she walked in the door, waiting in a long line. The only reason Emma had a seat up front was Jimmy had saved it for her.

Jackie the beautician was a little savvier. She'd bought her card when they went on sale that morning and avoided the rush. She sat in the back. Helen wondered if Jimmy wanted her there. Helen liked the seating arrangement. She could see the beautician's bingo card.

"Remember, it's a coverall," Helen told Derreck. "The winner has to have all twenty-four numbers on the card. There shouldn't be a jackpot until fifty-five or sixty numbers are called. If the coverall number drops below forty-seven, it's a scam."

"If he's cooking the numbers, why doesn't he just wait until fifty-five?" Derreck said.

"Because someone else could win, too, and they'd have to share the prize."

Jimmy had told his jokes, and the audience had oohed and ahhed over the grand prize of twenty thousand dollars. Finally, Jimmy started calling the numbers. The women were laughing and talking so loud, Helen could hardly hear the numbers.

"O-70. I-26. G-56."

She watched Jackie the beautician. She had covered all three of those numbers.

"I-30. B-1. O-69." Jackie had one of those numbers. Out of six called so far, she had four numbers.

Helen nudged Derreck. "Something's going on," she said. "Look how many she has already."

"How's she doing it?" Derreck said.

Helen didn't know. She stared at Jackie, but saw nothing out of the ordinary, except that she was covering her card at an amazing rate.

Helen looked at the stage and saw all the standard equipment: the bingo blower was shooting out the numbers. The display board lighted up when Jimmy placed a ball in the master board slot for that number.

"N-34," he called. The number went up on the display board, and Jackie covered yet another space.

"How many numbers have been called?" Derreck said. "Have you been keeping track?"

"Yes. Thirty-eight. It's going to happen soon. Jackie only needs two more."

"Three," Derreck corrected. "The center space on her card is empty."

"That's the free space," Helen said. "You're hopeless."

But she was, too. She stared at the stage. Jimmy was laughing, flirting and flapping around like a wounded crow. But something was off. Something was missing. She couldn't remember what it was. It nagged at her. She thought back to her bingo games with Aunt Gert. What was missing?

"O-63. N-36."

"Bingo!" Jackie screamed.

"Balls!" Derreck said.

"That's it," Helen cried, and sprinted for the stage. Suddenly, everything had fallen into place, and she knew what was wrong. She knocked Mrs. Edmond McGregor, sixty-one, off her motorized scooter, but Helen kept going, running as fast as she could.

Jimmy saw her charging through the audience, and tried to pick up the balls he'd called, but Helen threw her body over the master board. Jimmy grabbed her and tried to pull her away. But Helen hung onto the master board and kicked him hard in the crotch. He fell to the floor.

"Arrrgh. My balls," Jimmy screamed. Helen wasn't sure if he was yelling about the bingo balls, or something more personal and tender.

"My hip," howled Mrs. McGregor, the woman Helen had knocked off the motorized scooter.

"My money," Jackie the beautician screamed. "Where's my three thousand dollars?"

Three? The jackpot was twenty thousand dollars. Now the last piece of the puzzle was complete.

"You cheated on your husband. And you cheated on bingo," Helen said. The stage microphone picked up her voice and it rang forth from the speakers, the voice of an angry goddess. People were screaming in panic now, and running from the room, knocking over chairs and tables, spilling drinks and bingo cards.

Jackie fell to the floor, weeping. "I just wanted a little fun," she said.

"Bingo is serious," Helen said, and her voice thundered through the room. Six security guards and the chief purser stormed through the doors. Bingo was serious indeed.

"So what happened after the purser and security showed up?" Derreck said.

They were in Helen's cabin. Her door was open to let the crew know everything was on the up-and-up, but the staff avoided her like a rabid lionfish. Only Derreck came to see her while she packed. She would be off the ship first thing tomorrow.

"I couldn't see anything," he complained. "The room was closed and locked and the rest of us were thrown out. Except for Mrs. Mc-Gregor, who went to the ship's hospital."

Helen winced, and stuffed a pile of T-shirts into her suitcase. "I'm so sorry I flipped over her cart. How is that poor woman?"

"Alive and well and calling for her lawyer."

"Ouch," Helen said. Three pairs of shorts followed the T-shirts. "What made you try a flying tackle on Jimmy?"

"I had to," she said. "If he got those bingo balls, I couldn't prove how he was cheating. I'd been staring at that stage. I knew something was missing. When you yelled, 'Balls!' I realized what it was. Nobody was on stage verifying the numbers Jimmy called.

"That's the fastest way to have fraud. It's so easy on a cruise ship. The players don't know the game. In a shoreside bingo hall the other players would scream foul if someone wasn't called up from the audience to verify the bingo numbers as they're called. Even then, you can get collusion. It happened in a church bingo game when I was a kid. That's why many serious bingo halls have video surveillance with monitors the players can see. They wouldn't tolerate this lax security."

"But I still don't know how Jimmy did it," Derreck said.

Helen threw her tennis shoes on top the shorts. She wondered if the dirty soles would leave marks on her clean clothes, but she didn't care enough to rearrange her suitcase.

"First, he found an accomplice. He knew how to pick them. The women liked to cheat and some of them, like Jackie, didn't have much money. Three thousand dollars was a lot to them.

"Jimmy would find his mark, romance her, and then say, 'How would you like to win three thousand dollars?'"

"Three? The jackpot was twenty thousand," Derreck interrupted.

A pair of sandals followed the tennis shoes into Helen's suitcase. "Jimmy couldn't help cheating any way he could. He couldn't even split the winnings with that poor woman, Jackie. He told her – and probably all the others – that he also had to split the take with a greedy housekeeper. Jackie believed him. The cruise line says there was no crooked housekeeper. Jimmy was taking that share, too."

"At the risk of repeating myself, let me ask again: how did he do it?" Derreck said.

"Cruise ship bingo cards are sold ahead of time on the day of the cruise. He asked his accomplice – Jackie – to buy a card when they first went on sale that morning. Then Jimmy had her call him and read all her card numbers to him. He wasn't in his cabin, but Jackie left the message on his answering machine. He didn't even bother erasing the tape. The cruise line has him cold."

"He got lazy," Derreck said. "Jimmy's been working here for ten years. I wonder how long he's been scamming the cruise line?"

"He didn't say. In fact, he wasn't talking at all. But Jackie sure babbled. She was scared to death. I don't know which she was more afraid of – divorce or prosecution."

Helen found a pair of socks on the floor and crammed them into the suitcase.

"When Jackie called with her card numbers, Jimmy was in the lounge to verify the setup of the game. The stage staff, the grunt labor, did the actual physical installation of the bingo blower and display board. Jimmy stood around and supervised. He simply excused himself for a moment, went to a phone, and retrieved the message with the bingo numbers Jackie had left for him."

"I still don't get it. How did he get the blower to put out the right numbers?" Derreck asked.

"He didn't," Helen said. "The ball would be B-5, but he'd call Jackie's number, B-12. Then he'd drop it in the B-12 slot on the master board and it would flash on the display board, because the system doesn't know the real number of the ball that's dropped in the slot. It just knows if a ball is there. Only the most sophisticated machines actually verify the ball is put in the correct slot, and cruise ships rarely have those.

"A bingo hall would have someone from the audience come up on stage and verify that the number was being accurately repeated, but most cruise ships don't. Jimmy conveniently forgot that step. And I couldn't remember it. My Aunt Gert would have never let him get away with it."

Helen found more socks in the drawer and stuffed them inside her tennis shoes. "Jimmy would call out forty numbers or so before making his girlfriend the winner. Once the girlfriend called Bingo! a second cruise staff person would go to her seat and call her numbers back.

"This person was not in on the scam. Jimmy, the caller onstage, confirmed the numbers and announced, 'That's a winner!'

"The winner was handed a bundle of cash – most of which she later handed back to Jimmy. But Jimmy knew how to pick his women. His partner was happy with her earnings. She knew it was more money than she would have made in an honest bingo game."

Helen made a final search of the tiny cabin. Her clothes for tomorrow were laid out on the single chair. She was ready to go.

"Jimmy was fired," she said. "He's confined to quarters until the cruise is over and banned from any Royal Wave ship for life. Do you think he will go to jail?"

"Not a chance," Derreck said. "The Royal Wave line does not want any bad publicity. I suspect Jimmy will retire in comfort with his ill-gotten gains."

"At least he won't be ruining any more shipboard bingo games,"

Helen said.

Derreck told her good night. Helen wished him good luck with Jon, but they both knew that romance was over. Helen suspected Derreck was relieved. Celibacy did not suit him.

Helen got a rather chilly thank you from the cruise line, and a not-so-gentle hint that she was no longer welcome as a boutique employee, even if it was a subcontracted position. But Jane Gilbert was tired of sitting around the house. Her broken leg had healed and she was happy to return early to her job on the cruise. She gave Helen a nice thousand-dollar bonus in commissions.

Helen's landlady, Margery Flax, was happy to have an excuse to put her obnoxious sister Cora on the plane home a week early.

Helen's little apartment seemed big as a mansion after so many weeks in that cramped cabin. She enjoyed sleeping in her own bed. She dreamed of Aunt Gert and a piece of chocolate cake as big as a purse.

Jackie the beautician was allowed to catch the next plane back to Missouri. She was barred from Royal Wave cruises forever, but the cruise line did not prosecute her, nor did they tell her husband. She was happy, too.

No one got the twenty-thousand-dollar jackpot money. But someone did win the jackpot.

Mrs. Edmond McGregor, whose motorized scooter tipped over in the bingo debacle, settled out of court with the Royal Wave line for an undisclosed amount. It was rumored to be two hundred thousand dollars.

Despite her unfortunate experience, she did take another cruise – on the QE II.

The Bride Wore Blood

"Weddings made everyone crazy, and on-board ship, the weirdness escalated," said the chief purser on the Royal Wave cruise ship. But this bride had blood in her eye – and on her hands.

The groom was bashing the hell out of his cabin door with a champagne bottle. Four thousand bucks worth of polished mahogany, and he was beating it to pieces.

Blood ran down his high, handsome forehead and onto his tux. His white shirtfront was almost red.

"Sir, may I help you?" We were trained to be polite on the Royal Wave Cruise Lines, no matter how trying the circumstances.

"She's locked me out," the groom said. More blood dripped down the shirtfront of Symington Noonan the Fifth, known as Quint. "She can't do that. It's our honeymoon."

"Why don't you put the bottle down, Mr. Noonan, sir, and I'll talk to her."

My job title is chief purser. I handle the financial side of the cruise ship, but since I rank right under the captain, I often get called when the crew doesn't know what to do. Like now, when a blood-soaked groom was assaulting and battering a stateroom door.

Our security staff was first-rate for locating lost watches and misplaced walkers, but they didn't know what to do with the gory groom. The three security officers stood there like tree stumps. They didn't even try to wrestle the champagne bottle away from Quint.

Fortunately, Quint dropped the bottle. Now that the groom had stopped hammering on the door, I could hear another expensive sound: glass shattering in the stateroom. Lots of glass. Mirrors, I thought. The bride's breaking mirrors.

"Mrs. Noonan?" I called through the door.

"Don't use that son of a bitch's name," the bride screamed.

The mothers arrived now. The bride's mother, Loretta Aldean, was on my left, a stout woman draped in pink lace. The groom's mother, Regina Danvers Noonan, was on my right, a tall woman in sleek dark blue. Both women looked upset.

"Tiffany?" I could hear sniffling. I tried again. "Tiffany, we're worried about you. Would you open the door?"

She would not. But now I could hear Tiffany crying softly. At least she'd stopped breaking things.

"Tiffany, please open the door," I said.

"Honey," the groom said.

"Shut up, you pervert. I never want to speak to you again."

Oops. I turned to the groom. "Mr. Noonan, your wife seems a little upset. Perhaps you would like to go with your mother."

"I told you she wasn't good enough for you," the groom's mother said. The bride's mother bristled, but security finally woke up and hustled the Noonans away before more trouble developed.

"He's gone now, Tiffany. Please come out," I said.

"Tiffany, sweetheart, it's your mother," Loretta Aldean said.

That did it. There was another sniff, then the sound of a lock clicking. The bride opened the door. Her mother gasped in horror.

Tiffany looked like the bride of Frankenstein. Her Alencon lace and silk-illusion gown was shredded and smeared with blood. Her blonde hair was matted with blood, hair spray, and wilting flowers.

The six-thousand-dollar Royal Wave suite looked like it had been used to slaughter sheep. Blood was smeared on the wall-to-wall carpet. There were bloody handprints on the upholstered chairs and the bedsheets were sliced.

Broken mirrors were everywhere. Tiffany had racked up ninety-six years of bad luck, if you believed a broken mirror brought seven years of misery.

"Are you okay, Tiffany?" I asked.

She sniffled again and nodded yes. Tiffany had a cut on her forehead, which didn't look serious, but it bled a lot, giving her that unforgettable horror movie look. The cut on her arm was no more than a scratch. Most of the damage had been deflected by her lace sleeves. Her hands were speckled with small bloody nicks, probably from when she broke the mirrors.

Most of the blood was probably the groom's. Tiffany must have knocked him silly when she whacked him with a champagne bottle. I'd seen her serve on the ship's tennis courts and that woman packed power. Quint was lucky to get out alive. Heaven knows why he wanted back in.

"Baby, what did he do to you?" her mother asked.

"He screwed someone else. On our wedding night," she said. Fury flared in her blue eyes and for a moment I almost felt sorry for the groom.

Loretta went white with shock. "Who?" she said. "Who?" She looked and sounded like a small owl.

"A dancer," the bride said, and started weeping again.

Figures, I thought. Dancers were nothing but trouble on shipboard. They only worked three shows a week and spent the rest of the time causing mischief. But this was the limit. I wondered which one it was: Tanya? Geneen? Hazel?

"I'll kill the bitch," Mom said, gathering her sobbing daughter into her arms. As her maternal instincts kicked in, she looked more like an eagle than an owl.

"It's a guy," the bride said. "His name is Rico."

Oh, no. No wonder she'd trashed the suite. It was bad enough to be thrown over for another woman. But when her groom cheated on Tiffany with another man, she must have felt like her insides were ripped out.

Poor Tiffany. Poor us. Weddings made everyone crazy, and on-board ship, the weirdness escalated.

"Where did you find them?" Loretta asked. "In here?"

Not possible, I thought. Staff members weren't allowed in passengers' rooms, except on duty. It was a firing offense. Even Rico wouldn't be that stupid.

"I went for a walk on deck," the bride said, between hiccoughing sobs. "The reception was winding down and most of the guests had left. I heard noises coming from a lifeboat."

Ah, that explained it. The lifeboats were favorite onboard hookup spots. Thanks to the lifeboat drill, everyone knew where to find them. Once a week the crew had to "clean the lifeboats," a euphemism for removing half-empty liquor bottles, beer bottles, used condoms, and other love-worn detritus.

We had cameras recording almost every inch of this ship, but if I checked them, I'd bet my next paycheck someone in a hoodie had spray-painted the lens near the love boat – and that someone was Rico.

"This man was moaning and I thought he was hurt," the bride said. "So I ran to the boat and I saw . . . I saw . . ."

A fresh wave of tears overwhelmed her. "Quint," she managed. "With that man from the show Friday night."

"That beast," her mother hissed, as Tiffany sobbed on her shoulder.

"I ran back to our cabin, but Quint followed me," the bride said. "I can't run fast in these heels. He followed me inside our suite and I saw the bottle of champagne our cabin steward had opened for us and I picked it up and hit him as hard as I could. He grabbed the bottle . . ."

"He didn't hit you, darling, did he?" her mother asked.

"No, I shoved him outside the suite door. Then I lost it. This was supposed to be the happiest day of my life."

Tiffany cried on her mother's shoulder. "Daddy mustn't know," she said. "He didn't want me to marry Quint."

"Sh! We'll work it out," her mother soothed, and rocked her bloodstained baby.

"I had no idea Quint was like that," the bride said.

Quint was in the closet in this day and age? One look at the groom's frosty, forbidding mother and I knew poor Quint would never come out. He'd married at thirty-five. I wondered how Regina had prodded him down the aisle.

"But I know he's not gay," she said. "I'm pregnant. And he was so happy."

"Of course, dear," her mother said.

About half our brides were pregnant, and they always blamed their queasy stomachs on seasickness. The raging pregnancy hormones only added to the wedding fun.

"What better reason to live with your parents," her mother said. "That big old Noonan house is in the boonies, and needs so many repairs. We live on Main Street, where you'll be close to the care you need."

"But Quint is a doctor," the bride said.

"Who graduated at the bottom of his class," her mother said. "I wouldn't take a sick dog to him. Your father and I will make sure you see the best doctors near Noonanville. If necessary, we'll take you to Kirksville, or Columbia, even Saint Louis. We can afford it."

Daddy owned the John Deere franchise in Noonanville, a wealthy farming community of about twenty thousand in northern Missouri. He also had the McDonald's on Highway 63. The Aldeans were small-town rich.

The Noonans were small-town aristocracy, and Regina Danvers Noonan made Queen Elizabeth seem like a backslapping good-time gal.

I was extremely good at collecting tidbits of information and putting two and two together, vital skills for one in my position. Mrs. Noonan made sure I knew that Quint's ancestor, Dr. Symington Noonan the First, founded Noonanville in 1879, and the town had had a Doc Noonan ever since. I figured out that the money had disappeared about forty years ago, but the Noonans were still local king makers.

Tiffany and Quint had started the sixth member of the medical dynasty. A hasty marriage had been arranged along with a lavish reception aboard the Royal Wave. Mr. Aldean paid for caviar and surf-and-turf dinners for two hundred guests, airfare and week-long Caribbean cruises for the wedding party and the widowed Mrs. Noonan, as well as his future son-in-law.

I cleared my throat and said, "If I may make a suggestion, I'd like to move you to another room. We don't have another stateroom like this, but I can make you comfortable. I'll have our staff move you to the junior suite next to your parents' and then I'll send the ship's doctor to check you out. I'm concerned about that glass."

"Good idea," Mom said approvingly. "And send the bill to her father."

"Yes, madam," I said. I'd planned to do that anyway.

"Now, I'll leave you to change into something comfortable before I send our staff to assist with the move." I slipped out and walked down the empty corridor to Mrs. Noonan's suite at the other end of the hall. I was immensely relieved that the new couple's fight hadn't attracted any curious passengers.

Mrs. Noonan had the Do Not Disturb sign on her door. I have sharp ears and there's a sweet spot near the doorknob where I can hear voices even as soft as Mrs. Noonan's.

"You idiot!" she hissed. "If you want to inherit your father's hunting lodge, our family home, and the house at the lake, you'll patch things up with that pregnant trailer trash. You won't get a thing until you have an heir and you know it."

The poor bride. She didn't deserve this calculating pair.

"But Mumsy," he whined.

"Don't Mumsy me," she said, her voice softly dangerous. "You couldn't wait a week until you were back home? Instead you have a fling with a dancer. A foreigner! Who knows what diseases he has!"

Another whine.

"The disgrace! What if she divorces you? Ah! I feel faint. My nerves! Get me my medication now."

"Which one?" Quint asked.

"The Xanax, you idiot! My nerves are wrecked!"

I heard the click of pills and the glug of water poured into a glass. "Thank you," she said, her voice feeble.

Now seemed like a good time to knock. "Mrs. Noonan? Mr. Noonan?" I asked.

"Please come in," Regina Noonan said, as if granting me an audience.

"I'm checking to see how you're feeling," I said. "Mr. Noonan, I'm sending the ship's doctor to examine you. That cut on your head may require stitches. I've moved Tiffany" – I was afraid that calling her Mrs. Noonan would provoke another outburst – "to the stateroom next to her parents' cabin. Your suite will need to be cleaned. May I relocate you to a stateroom at this end of the hall?"

"No, Quint prefers to stay with me," Regina said.

He glared at his mother, but said nothing. The son was under house arrest.

"Very good," I said. "The staff will pack up your belongings and convey them here."

"And if the wedding guests ask why the bride and groom are not staying in their suite?" Mrs. Noonan asked.

"A pipe burst," I said. "Most unfortunate, but the couple has been relocated to another stateroom. No one expects to see the bride and groom for the first two or three days after the wedding, madam. After that, we'll be in our first port and the guests will be busy with shore excursions."

"Yes, of course," Regina said, as if that was what had happened. "Poor Quint tripped on the stairs when the seas were rough and cut his head."

The woman had an amazing ability to rewrite history.

"Is there anything else I can do to assist you?" I asked.

"No. You may leave."

Dismissed, without even a thank you.

Back in my office, I rang for Rico. It was now four in the morning, and the hungover Rico was so pale, he could have been marble. The dancer was so finely made, he managed not to look ridiculous in Italian tailoring.

"You!" I said. "What were you thinking, sleeping with a guest?"

"We were not sleeping," he said. Rico's English is a bit literal.

"I know what you were doing in that lifeboat and it's a firing offense."

"Please, don't fire me," he said. "I need to send money to mia mamma. She is sick."

"Then she'd better get well fast," I said. "This is your last cruise."

"It is not my fault," he said. "He ask me. I no ask him. I do no harm. His mamma is a dragon. He is handsome, but a country pumpkin."

"Bumpkin," I corrected. "The Noonans may be not be city sophisticates, but they're far from bumpkins."

He shrugged, which could mean anything. "It is over," he said.

"Damn right, it is. So is your job with Royal Wave."

He left, head bowed, shoulders slumped under his exquisite tailoring. Dancers!

By noon, the bride and groom were settled in their new separate quarters, both barricaded behind Do Not Disturb signs. The ship's doctor put six stitches in the groom's head while his mother paced, oblivious to his yelps of pain.

The bride stayed in her stateroom, her mother at her side. The room service waiter reported that Loretta ordered ginger ale and soda crackers for her daughter, but nothing for herself.

The next day, I listened carefully, but the rest of the wedding guests seemed unaware of the domestic drama. They made sniggery jokes about the couple staying in their suite. Everyone seemed to assume they were lost in bridal bliss.

The bride didn't venture out until Wednesday, when most of the passengers were at a picnic and snorkeling trip at a private island owned by the cruise line.

Tiffany walked along the nearly deserted deck. She must have had her hair done at the salon. It was sprayed so stiffly the ocean breezes didn't move it. Heck, an F5 tornado couldn't ruffle those golden curls. Tiffany was delicately painted and candy box pretty.

The groom joined her when she was halfway around the deck. Quint's Cardinals ball cap hid his stitches and the ugly bruise on his forehead. Tiffany folded her arms defensively, looking like walking origami. The couple didn't touch, but they didn't argue, either. After a few words, she went back to her cabin and he disappeared into his mother's stateroom.

The next morning, most of the passengers were on an all-day tour of a sugar plantation. I saw Tiffany stretched out in a deck chair, reading a paperback, both her hair and her back stiff. Her pink linen pants didn't dare wrinkle.

Quint sat in the chair next to hers. She ignored him at first, but soon they were talking softly. Some sort of negotiation seemed to be going on. I moved downwind and began straightening deck chairs. That wasn't my job, but I could hear everything.

"If I forgive you and take you back," Tiffany said, "you'll escort me to the Christmas DAR ball?"

"I promise, sugar."

"And the Friday night dances at the club?"

"Of course."

"And you'll attend the Episcopal services every Sunday?"

"Except for my once-a-month weekend at the lake," he said.

"And you agree that if you can have special friends, I can, too?" she asked.

Sauce for the goose, I thought.

"As long as our son is named Symington Noonan the Sixth," he said. "I can't wait to take Sixtus to his first ball game."

"And if our baby is a girl, we'll call her Loretta for my mother," the bride said.

"Agreed." Quint attempted a relieved smile. I got the feeling there was only going to be one child in this marriage.

They sealed the deal with a passionless kiss, like two clerks rubber-stamping a document.

"Good!" Quint said. "Let's go tell Mumsey."

An hour later, I was summoned to Regina's stateroom. She received me in the living room, using the lavender club chair as her throne. She held out her hand as if she expected me to kiss it. I gave it a gentle squeeze. She gave me a cold smile.

On a table next to her was a vase of tropical flowers and a cup of tea. Behind her on the credenza was a phalanx of medicine bottles. Big ones, the kind that held ninety-day supplies. I couldn't read the labels, but I recognized the distinctive pink-orange Zocor tablets in one. Another was brimful of white aspirin-like tablets. I squinted at the label. Xanax.

Quint hovered by his mother, but I saw no trace of Tiffany.

Regina handed me a thick cream envelope. "I would like you to give this to that dancer, Rocco. It's a good-bye present of a thousand dollars."

"Rico?" I said. "That's not necessary. I assure you, he'll never communicate with you or your family again."

"I didn't say it was necessary," Regina said. "I've always found it better to end things on a positive note. I hope you will oblige an old woman."

She gave me a shark's smile. I fought to suppress a shudder. "Certainly, madam," I said, and took the envelope. It felt fat. I told myself this would make Rico's departure easier. Money always burned a hole in Rico's pocket. He'd be eager to blow this in the port bars.

Back in my office, I called Rico and gave him the envelope. "The pumpkin feels guilty," he said with a sardonic smile.

"Bumpkin," I corrected him again. "Listen, city boy, the Noonans are small town, but they aren't stupid. Regina Noonan doesn't know the meaning of the word guilt. Take this and be grateful. You won't get any severance from us."

"I will be fine," he said, his smile revealing white, even teeth. His perfectly cut black hair had a slight curl, and he filled out his black Egyptian cotton shirt perfectly. Rico seemed unencumbered by a conscience.

I was glad to see him go. On Saturday, Rico would be off the ship permanently and someone else's problem.

The rest of the afternoon passed pleasantly until a little after six when Christopher, the shipboard entertainment director, rushed into my office.

"We can't find Rico," he said, "and the show starts at seven."

Christopher, whip-thin and artistic in black, was skilled at herding the wayward hoofers. He managed to find ones who could keep dancing in rough weather when the stage shifted under them.

"Did you check the —" I began.

"Lifeboats? Yes. And all his other usual haunts," Christopher said. "No one's seen him since he went back to his cabin a little after three with a bottle of wine. The door is locked or jammed from the inside and his roommate can't open it. I want to break down the door, in case he's sick."

Or drunk. Or high. Anything was possible with Rico. But Christopher knew the right euphemisms.

"I'll come with you," I said, and summoned the ship's doctor, just in case. It took ten minutes to get the door open, and the moment I stepped into his cabin, I knew there was no need for the doctor. Rico stared sightlessly at the ceiling.

"He's dead," Christopher said, his voice shaky. He looked barely alive himself.

"Go rearrange the show," I said. "I'll handle this."

Rico did not look romantically beautiful in death. He was an ugly gray. Next to him was a nearly empty wine bottle. Mrs. Noonan's cream-colored envelope had been hastily ripped open, and near it was a pile of fifty dollar bills and a plastic baggy containing a tiny bit of white powder.

One bill had been rolled into a tube and had a powdery residue on it. Cocaine? There was still a light dusting on the scratched mirror on the nightstand by Rico's bunk.

Drugs were a problem onboard, and more than one staffer tried to make a fortune smuggling coke, especially when we cruised the Caribbean. I'd seen enough cocaine to know what it looked like.

This wasn't the pearly white of pure coke. It was off-white, like coke that had been cut with anything from baby powder to baking soda. But something was wrong about the color and texture.

Fortunately, we sailed under the Panamanian flag of convenience, so we wouldn't have to worry about a US investigation into Rico's death. A few well-placed words backed with a gift or two, and Rico's body would be flown home to Rome and he'd be quickly forgotten.

I told a shaken staffer, "Get me a large zip-lock bag and a canvas carryall."

While the staffer was gone, I made sure Rico's body, the wine bottle, the envelope, the money, and the drug paraphernalia were photographed.

When the staffer returned, I gathered up the vestiges of Rico's last party. I planned to test the suspicious white powder with a police field kit I kept in my office, and check the plastic baggy for prints. I had one last chore.

I summoned Regina's cabin steward, William. "Has Mrs. Noonan been taking her meals in her cabin?" I asked.

"Yes," William said. "Has she complained about the service?"

"Certainly not. Bring me one of her water glasses."

"She's just rung and asked room service to pick up her tea tray," William said. "There's usually a water glass on it."

"Good. Bring it to my office."

By eight p.m. I'd finished my investigation and the field test. It was not too late to call upon Regina Noonan.

When I knocked on her door, she said "Yes?"

"Are you alone?" I asked.

"I am," she said. "My son and his wife have reached a rapprochement. They're sharing her stateroom."

She wore a soft yellow robe and slippers, but her hair was iron and her back was stick straight. She settled into the lavender chair, but didn't invite me to sit.

"I'd like to discuss your gift to Rico," I said.

She frowned. "A thousand dollars wasn't generous enough? Do you want something, too?"

"Yes, madam. What was that white powder you included in the packet of money?"

"I'm sure I don't know what you're talking about," she said.

"I'm sure you do. Your fingerprints were all over the plastic baggy. Let me guess. It was Xanax. You take it for anxiety. Your ninety-day supply is nearly gone, but the last time I was in your stateroom, the bottle was almost full.

"When combined with alcohol, Xanax has a synergistic effect on the central nervous system. It can lead to dizziness, coma and death. That's what happened to Rico. Your son must have told you the dancer liked to party with wine and coke. Xanax and red wine were a fatal combination for him."

"You're accusing me of his death?" Regina didn't bother sounding indignant. Nor did she ask if Rico was dead.

"I'm simply mentioning the remarkable coincidence," I said.

She shrugged. "The man was trash. No telling what someone like that would do. The world is better off without him."

"I'll be sure and tell his mother. Good evening, madam."

I shut her stateroom door with more force than usual. I'd be glad to see the last of the Noonans.

Friday morning, most of the guests had disembarked at nine o'clock for a shopping expedition in port, buying designer purses, watches, and duty-free rum.

About an hour later, a frantic William knocked on my office door, his face as white as his uniform.

"We have a problem," the cabin steward said. "You need to come to Mrs. Noonan's suite."

"What happened?"

"Mrs. Noonan, sir. She's dead. Orlando, the room service waiter, found her."

"Heart attack?"

"I don't think so. There was a note on her nightstand and a nearly empty bottle of sleeping tablets near it. Orlando is quite shaken. He delivered her tea at ten, as she'd requested. She'd left her stateroom door unlocked."

"Have you informed her son?" I asked.

"Not yet. I thought you'd want to read her note first."

Regina Noonan had thoughtfully left her note unsealed. I opened the creamy stationery and read:

My Son,

I've done everything to ensure your future and your success. The man who tempted you is gone. Now it is my turn to lay down my burdens. I am tired, my son, but I know you and your bride will live according to the Noonan legacy and pass it on to the next generation. It gives me great satisfaction to know that you are married and expecting a son.

Mother

It was a chilling letter. Regina never mentioned the bride's name. There was no "love." I suspected there never was. The woman had gotten away with murder and blackmailed her son into marriage and a family.

Quint and Tiffany were enjoying a late breakfast on their balcony when I informed them that Regina was dead. They didn't ask to see the body, but they read the letter. Quint showed no emotion. Tiffany asked, "Will anyone know that my mother-in-law killed herself?"

"She was quite elderly," I said. "It's possible that she miscounted the number of sleeping tablets she needed. There's no need for an inquest."

The bride and groom looked relieved. Neither one pretended to be saddened by Mrs. Noonan's death, but they said the right things and assumed mournful faces. They dined in their suite that night and everyone understood.

On Saturday, I was gratified by the generous tips the Noonans gave everyone, including me.

They did not disembark with the other passengers, but waited until everyone had left the ship and the funeral director arrived with a discreet black van and a chauffeured black Lincoln Town Car.

Tiffany and Quint Noonan left the ship walking shoulder to shoulder, though they did not touch.

Their black car slowly followed the van bearing Regina's body, as if her dead hand was pulling it into the future.

Gotta Go

Death investigators are the paralegals of forensic world – they're not pathologists but they're trained to investigate deaths at the scene. I'm fascinated by this profession created in the 1970s. I passed the Medicolegal Death Investigators training course at Saint Louis University. The result was Death Investigator Angela Richman, who found Chouteau County's one percent a rich subject for murder.

If you want to be a good-looking corpse, carbon monoxide is the way to go. Your skin is a lovely shade of pink. Cookie Cabanne, a society beauty, died in style inside her black Bentley, wrapped in a thousand-dollar cashmere sweater with an empty bottle of Grey Goose at her feet.

She was the most beautiful dead woman I've ever seen – and I've seen a few.

I'm Angela Richman, death investigator for Chouteau County, Missouri. I live on the Du Pres estate in Chouteau Forest, the main town in this ten-square-mile pocket of white privilege. I don't own the estate. My Mom and Dad worked for the Du Pres family, and catered to their daily needs until cancer took them both. Now I serve the Forest by caring for its dead.

I investigate all unexpected and unexplained deaths in the county that don't happen under a doctor's care: accidents, murders, suicides. I work for the Chouteau County medical examiner. I'm responsible for the dead person. The police handle the scene – everything but the body.

The newly dead aren't silent. They're shouting for our attention. But it can be hard to hear them when your first reaction is "Oh, my God." Don't believe what you see on TV. Death isn't pretty. It's dirty, smelly, and ugly. Some days, it's hard to see past the blood, brain matter, and skin slippage to listen to the dead person.

Cookie, with her swoop of styled blonde hair and her unnaturally pink skin, was one of the lucky ones. Except she was dead, of course. I almost didn't hear what she had to say because Detective Ray Greiman wouldn't shut up.

Death investigators and homicide detectives are colleagues, and we work well together. Unless I get Detective Ray Greiman, the most careless detective on the Forest force.

Cookie Cabanne lived in a twelve-thousand-square-foot French chateau, built by her family at the turn of the century. Chouteau County is thirty miles west of St. Louis, and Cookie was the star of the society columns. I'd seen photos of her in a black velvet Valentino gown on her winding marble staircase. Cookie's husband, the smoldering dark-haired Randolph D. Cabanne, was photographed wearing a smoking jacket in the billiard room – the same room where Forest gossip said Cookie caught randy Randolph with the upstairs maid.

But I saw none of this splendor when I came to the Cabanne estate as a death investigator that cold Monday afternoon in January. Cookie had died in the garage. I drove my black Dodge Charger through the wrought iron service gates to the fourteen-vehicle garage, and parked near the yellow crime scene tape. From the Cabanne house, the garage was a short walk across a stone courtyard with a topiary menagerie. For some reason, rich people like torturing shrubs into cats, owls and other animals.

Now the flashing emergency lights parked in front of the garage gave the fanciful creatures a blood bath. I saw a twenty-something blonde weeping inside an ambulance. I pulled my death investigator kit out of the trunk. My kit includes everything I need for my investigations.

Information check lists, forms for property evidence, and releases are loaded on my iPad. My camera for scene documentation, my digital recorder, a digital meat thermometer for taking the body temperature, syringes for blood draws, tweezers, a flashlight, clean white sheets in sealed plastic bags, and latex gloves are also stuffed inside. This was a relatively fresh body, so I wouldn't need a protective mask, goggles, or jumpsuit.

I said hi to Warren, the uniform on duty. Detective Ray Foster Greiman met me at the yellow crime scene tape. In his gray cashmere topcoat, the Forest detective looked like he was at a fashion shoot. As far as I was concerned, Greiman used his detective skills to hunt expensive clothes.

"The stiff's in the garage," he said. "She was a no hoper."

He said that to rile me. He knows I don't call dead people "floaters," "crispy critters," or other disrespectful names.

"The hydrant humpers are checking for carbon monoxide. They should give the all-clear shortly." I could see two firefighters in full turnout gear with SCBAs – Self Contained Breathing Apparatus – walking inside the garage with their meters.

"Who found the body?" I asked. The last person to see the victim alive and the first person to find the body have valuable information.

"The blonde in the ambulance," Greiman said. "She's the vic's younger sister." He checked his notes. "Her name is Arabella 'Bella' Duvall, age twenty-four, single, lives in the Forest with her parents. She opened the garage door, saw her sister and ran to the car. She tried to pull her out, but was nearly overcome by the exhaust fumes. She dialed 911, stumbled out of the garage and passed out on the lawn. The ambulance crew had to revive her. Bella's refusing treatment.

"It's suicide," Greiman said. "The car ran out of gas by the time the sister found her. Cookie got drunk, shut the garage door, turned on the car and offed herself."

"Why would Cookie kill herself?" I asked. "She was blonde, beautiful, and had ten million dollars in very old money."

"Her old man left her," Greiman said.

"I heard she kicked him out," I said.

The local gossip was that Cookie's husband, Randolph D. Cabanne, was a hound, and an indiscreet one at that. She walked into the billiard room and saw Randolph with the twenty-year-old maid. The pretty brunette was on her knees, and she wasn't shining his shoes. Cookie fired the woman and had her lawyer draw up a separation agreement. She was through with the handsome leech. Randolph's latest cheap fling had cost him his rich marriage.

"You can talk to the sister now." Greiman checked his Patek Phillippe watch. Where did a homicide detective get a thirty-five-thousand-dollar watch?

"Then do your DI inspection and wrap this up," he said. "Fast. I gotta go in an hour. My shift is up at four."

Oh, no, I thought. I don't take orders from cops. Especially not this "errorist." That's cop slang for somebody who makes lots of mistakes.

"The ERT didn't do too much damage to the scene," Greiman said. "They tried to revive the stiff, but it's definitely suicide."

Some days, I needed a translator to talk to Ray. ERT is the Evidence Eradication Team. Like many cops, he hates when firefighters and paramedics trample a scene trying to save lives.

"I'll check with the paramedics first and then interview Cookie's sister in the house," I said.

"Okay, but hurry. The city's cut back on OT. This is a slam dunk."

I didn't bother answering. I fired up my iPad and opened the Death Scene Investigation form. I saw Mike the paramedic help a shivering Bella Duvall out of the back of the ambulance. Despite her chic red fake fur coat and matching beanie, Bella's lips were blue with cold.

"I still advise you to see a doctor, Miss Duvall," Mike told her. "But if you absolutely refuse hospital treatment, please sign this paper."

The curly-haired hunk gave Bella a heart-melting smile. She shook her head no and signed the paperwork.

"Miss Duvall," I said. "I'm Angela Richman. I'm sorry for your loss. I'm the death investigator for your sister's case. I'd like to talk to you as soon as I speak to the paramedics. Please meet me inside, where you can warm up."

"I'd rather stay here, thank you," Bella said, but she moved out of earshot.

"Hey, gorgeous, good to see you," Mike said. "When can we go out?"

"You're wasting your time flirting with a happily married woman, Mike," I said.

"I can dream, can't I? I love leggy, long-haired brunettes."

I flipped on my digital recorder and Mike turned all business. After I recited the date and time, Mike's title, and spelled his name, he said, "I entered the garage about two p.m. with Dan Watts, another paramedic. We both wore SCBAs. We found the victim in full rigor. I'm guessing she was dead maybe twelve-fifteen hours, depending on how warm the car was. The victim was too stiff for us to remove, so we left her behind the wheel."

"Was the car running?" I asked.

"No. It looked like the car had run out of gas, but I didn't get a good look at the key's position."

"The medical examiner told me cars don't run out of gas in CO_2 deaths," I said. "As the garage is deprived of oxygen, the engine chokes before the car runs out of gas."

"If you say so." Mike shrugged. "I saw a vodka bottle near the gas pedal, but I don't know how much was in it. I didn't see any suicide note, purse or anything else, but I didn't examine the car."

"Were the garage lights on?" I asked.

"They go on automatically when the garage door is open, so yes."

"Did you touch the car door handle?" I asked.

"Yes, with gloves on."

"Any hoses connected to the tailpipe?"

"I didn't see anything," Mike said. "That's really all I can tell you."

Dan, another hunk who looked like he bench-pressed Bentleys, basically repeated Mike's account. As soon as Dan finished, the paramedics roared off on another call.

The firefighters still hadn't cleared the garage. Detective Greiman looked pointedly at his watch as Bella and I hurried to the house. My fingers were numb with cold, even with my thick wool gloves.

"Cookie's house has two kitchens," Bella said, as our shoes clip-clopped across the flagstone courtyard and my death investigator suitcase bumped behind me. "Fran does the real cooking back here. It's a good place to talk."

"Do you know who was the last person to see your sister alive?"

"Probably Fran," Bella said. "I know she was supposed to fix the reconciliation dinner last night, serve it and then go home."

Cookie's sister looked ghost pale in her bright coat. Even her blonde French braid seemed to have lost color. Bella fought back her tears until Fran met us at the back door.

"Oh, Miss Bella," the short, grandmotherly cook said. "I can't believe it's true. Our Cookie's really gone."

Bella gathered Fran into her arms, and the two women wept. Fran was round and work-worn with permed gray hair and faded blue eyes. Her tidy kitchen smelled of coffee and cinnamon. I smiled when I saw a fat ceramic frog squatting beside the sink, a scouring pad in its mouth. My grandmother had had one of those.

Bella gave Fran a final hug, then said to me, "I heard what that detective said, Angela. My sister would never kill herself."

"Not over that worthless excuse for a man," Fran said.

"Was your sister upset that she and Mr. Cabanne had separated?" I asked.

"Hell, no," Bella said. "She threw the bastard out. She only agreed to the dinner last night because Mother asked her to see Randolph again. Mother is a devout Catholic and doesn't believe in divorce."

Bella and I sat at the pine kitchen table and Fran brought us coffee in thin flowered china cups. We thanked her, but she stayed by the table, wringing her hands. Fran wanted to say something.

"Were you the last person to see Ms. Cabanne, Fran?" I asked.

"I believe so," Fran said. "Except for her killer. And that's her cold-blooded husband."

"Will you sit down and talk to me for my report?"

Fran sat, but she wasn't comfortable doing it. I took her basic information, then asked the questions for a suspected suicide, "Was Ms. Cabanne depressed?"

"Of course not," Fran said. "Miss Cookie would never bring such grief on her family. She was making plans for the future. She always wanted to be an interior designer, but she quit before graduation to marry that man.

"Once he was out of the way, she enrolled at Maryville College in Saint Louis to finish her degree. She's just started the new semester a week ago and she's loving it. She wants to open her own business after she graduates, and why shouldn't she? She has the talent and the money to do what she wants. Better yet, Miss Cookie has ambition, which is more than I could say for him."

Fran couldn't seem to bring herself to say Randolph's name. She still spoke about Cookie Cabanne in the present tense. She hadn't accepted her death yet. "How long was she separated from Mr. Cabanne?" I asked.

"About two months," Fran said. "When that man moved out, Miss Cookie said it was like a weight was lifted from her shoulders. She would have never gone back with him. Never. But she was a good daughter and wanted to please her mother."

Fran's lip trembled and she fought back her tears. Bella patted her hand until Fran was able to continue. "Miss Cookie asked me to fix a nice little dinner for two. Everything he liked – steak and lobster tails, my creamed spinach, and twice-baked potatoes. He came here about seven o'clock with a big bouquet of red roses. That's them on the kitchen counter."

She nodded at the showy, velvety hot house flowers.

"Married ten years they were," Fran said, "And he still didn't know she hates cut flowers. She doesn't like to watch them die. I served dinner at the table in the den at eight.

"I could tell the reconciliation wasn't going well. Miss Cookie was drinking too much – nearly half the bottle of Grey Goose was gone – and she'd barely touched her food. I took away her plate. She'd only taken a bite or two."

"Does Mr. Cabanne drink vodka?" I asked.

"Scotch," Fran said. "He only had one, and he didn't finish it. He asked me to remove his glass. But he ate like an over-the-road trucker while Miss Cookie picked at her food.

"She didn't even touch her dessert, and it was her favorite, bitter chocolate mousse. I was bringing in their coffee when I heard her say, 'It's over, Randolph. I'm not going back with you and you're not getting any more money. You promised last time you'd never be unfaithful again, but . . .'

"Miss Cookie shut up when I walked in with the coffee carafe. She told me to leave it and said I could go home. It was about eight-thirty. That's the last time I saw her alive. I should have never left her alone with him."

"Was anyone else here?" I asked.

"Just the live-in housekeeper, Mrs. Bevans, but her rooms are on the other side. She watches her shows at night. I doubt she saw anything. Security was on duty at the main gatehouse. They'd know if anyone else came here and what time he left. But as far as I can tell, I was the last one to see Miss Cookie."

"Did she change her routine yesterday?" I asked.

"No, she left for her early morning class at Maryville and stayed until two o'clock, like she always does. Then she had her hair done at Killer Cuts." That was the fashionable Forest salon.

"She was home by four. Miss Cookie had a project due for her class next week and she spent the rest of the afternoon working in her studio on the third floor. About five o'clock, I brought her tea. About seven, she showered and got dressed for dinner with him. She wore her favorite cashmere sweater, poor lamb. I think it comforted her. I know she didn't get any comfort from him." She gave an angry sniff.

"Where is Mr. Cabanne today?" I asked.

"He's in New York," Fran said, wiping her eyes with her apron. "He left early this morning. He's flying home now. Can I get you more coffee? What about a cinnamon roll?"

"Yes, please," Bella said for both of us.

"What about those nice firefighters and the policemen?" Fran asked me.

"I'm sure they'd be grateful for hot coffee and cinnamon rolls," I said. I also thought the work might distract Fran from her grief.

While the cook busied herself with the coffee and pulled a huge pan of cinnamon rolls out of the oven, I went back to Cookie's sister, Bella.

"You said you believe your sister didn't kill herself," I said.

"I know it," Bella said. "My father and I tried to talk her out of marrying Randolph, but she was madly in love. He charmed Mother, but Daddy and I saw through his act. Daddy made him sign a pre-nup and insisted on a penalty clause if Randolph was unfaithful. If Cookie . . ."

Bella stopped, then seemed to gather her strength and said the word: " . . . died, he'd inherit everything. About ten million, plus this house.

"Daddy thought he was protecting my sister with that pre-nup, but now it looks like he wrote her death warrant. Randolph doesn't have a nickel to his name, but the Cabannes are a very good, very old family."

Forest dwellers are ancestor worshippers. Bella rushed on, and I let her talk. Now was the best time to interview her. Suicide victims' families often closed ranks once they had time to think. Then they'd change their stories to fit the facts they wished had happened.

"We all knew Randolph was running around on her," Bella said. "He started soon after the honeymoon. It was the talk of the Forest. Even Cookie couldn't keep her eyes shut forever. She knew he'd had at least three other women. I knew he'd had more. Each time, he'd promise it would never happen again and she believed him. Then she caught him with the maid. You heard that story?"

I nodded.

"That was the last straw. Cookie walked in on them. It's one thing to hear your husband is unfaithful and quite another to see it. Cookie drove straight to her lawyer. She had his things packed that afternoon and sent to his lawyer's office. He was gone by dinner."

Fran brought our warm cinnamon rolls. I took a small bite.

"And she didn't miss him," Bella said. "He tried to get back with her, but she wanted nothing to do with him. She wouldn't take his calls. She sent back his flowers. Then he went sneaking behind her back, crying his crocodile tears and telling Mother he wanted to reconcile with the love of his life. Mother urged Cookie to give her marriage another try. Cookie went through the motions for Mother. And now this!"

Bella's tears turned into harsh, heartbroken sobs. Fran hurried over with a box of tissues, and patted her back. I waited until Cookie's sister stopped crying, then asked, "Why did you come here this afternoon?"

Bella wiped her eyes. "We were supposed to meet for lunch at Solange's, the new French restaurant in the Forest," she said. "At one o'clock."

Another sniffle, then she stopped crying. I abandoned my cinnamon roll. I couldn't eat when she was in so much pain.

"Cookie's always on time. When she didn't show up at the restaurant by one fifteen, I called her cell. She didn't answer. Then I called Fran, and she said she hadn't seen Cookie yet, but my sister had left instructions that she wanted to sleep late. Fran said her bedroom door was closed. She checked Cookie's bed and it hadn't been slept in. That's when I came straight here.

"I had a bad feeling, and I was right. Cookie kept her car in the garage bay closest to the house. I opened it to see if her car was there, but I prayed it wasn't. My sister liked to drive around and think when she was upset. I'd hoped she'd gone for a drive and then stayed at the Ritz in Saint Louis.

"But I smelled the car exhaust as soon as I opened the garage door, and I saw Cookie's blonde hair against the driver's headrest. Her car wasn't running. I was choking on the exhaust fumes. I had to fight my way to the car, I was so dizzy.

"As soon as I opened the door, I knew she was dead, even if she looked like she was asleep. I grabbed her and she was stiff! It was horrible. I wanted to get her out of there, but I felt so sick. I called 911 and then somehow I made it outside and blacked out. When I woke up, I was in the ambulance."

"How do you feel now?" I asked.

"My sister's dead," Bella said. "How do you think I feel?" She shrugged out of her heavy coat and let it fall back on the chair.

I tried to soften my voice. "I know your sister's death –"

"Murder," Bella interrupted.

"– is difficult for you. But you blacked out from carbon monoxide."

"Don't you start," Bella said. "I'm not going to the hospital. Period. Anything else you want to ask me about my sister?"

I went back to the questions for a carbon monoxide suicide. "Does your sister's garage door have a manual or an electric opener?"

"Electric," Bella said. "Cookie has twenty-four hour security, so all one has to do is press a button by the garage door to open it. She has an opener in her car, of course."

"Was the car radio or CD player on?"

"No."

"Were the windows up?"

"Yes. It was winter," she said.

"Was the heater on?"

"I don't know. I saw a bottle of Grey Goose by her feet, but I didn't notice anything else."

"Did your sister smoke cigarettes?"

"No."

Now came the tricky questions. I tried to be tactful. "Does she have a problem with alcohol?"

"You mean is she an alcoholic? No. Fran said she was drinking last night, but that was rare. Cookie opened a bottle of champagne when she threw him out, but that was a celebration, not a binge drunk."

"What about medications?"

"We can check her bedroom. I believe she takes birth control pills and sleeping pills. Otherwise, she is perfectly healthy."

"Any history of other drugs? Street drugs?"

Bella hesitated and I knew the answer. "Look, I'm not the police," I said. "Nobody's going to get in trouble. I need to know for my investigation."

"She smokes a little weed," Bella said. "I think she gets it at school."

"Has she ever mentioned any suicidal thoughts?"

"No! I told you. My sister didn't kill herself. She isn't depressed. She isn't seeing a psychiatrist, and she doesn't abuse drugs or alcohol." Bella folded her arms in front of her. Fran wasn't the only one unable to grasp Cookie's death.

"Will you show me her room, please?" I asked.

I followed Bella up the plain service stairs to the second floor, then gloved up in the hall so I wouldn't leave prints.

Cookie's bedroom faced the front of the house, with French doors overlooking the front gardens. The room looked like it had been airlifted from Versailles. The last time I saw that much gold and mirrors was when I did a death investigation at the home of a Forest convenience store clerk. She'd died of a heart attack, but that woman liked gold furniture.

I'm always amazed that the super-rich and very poor have similar taste. I was sure the gold and crystal chandeliers in Cookie's room were real, and tried not to gape like a hick at the luxury.

There were no night stands next to her ornate bed. "That's my sister's jewel case on the left," Bella said, pointing to a fancy gold-inlaid chest the size of a sideboard.

I crossed the room to open the jewel case. "Don't –" Bella said. But I'd already opened the door and spotted the antique ormo-lu jewel casket filled with what Detective Greiman would call a "green leafy substance."

I caught the oily, slightly skunky herbal odor of pot, but found no pills, coke, or other drugs in her stash box. I checked the jewel case and the satin-draped bed for a suicide note. Nothing.

"Cookie keeps her medications in her bath." Bella opened the gold-paneled door to a bathroom that would have made Marie Antoinette gape. The medicine cabinet was behind a mirror. Gold framed, of course.

Bella knew her sister well. There was a compact of birth control pills and a mild sleeping pill prescribed by a Forest doctor. I checked the prescription date, then counted the pills. She'd taken two in the past three weeks. Cookie was not a heavy prescription drug user. The rest of the medications were mundane over-the-counter items – aspirin, Midol, Pepto-Bismol. I bagged everything. They would go with the body to the medical examiner.

I checked the bathroom wastebasket and found an empty package for "100% pure organzine silk socks." Cookie had paid sixty dollars for one pair of off-white silk socks.

Her studio was up one floor in a vast room with the north light that artists love. The jewel-toned Persian rug probably cost more than my annual salary. The studio was a professional setup, with a desk and a tilted drawing table. No gold up here.

I saw half-finished sketches of a living room and bedroom, with swatches of material clipped to the drawing board. In a small alcove were a comfortable couch, two overstuffed chairs and a table piled with interior design books, including *Perspective for Interior Designers* and *Color in Interior Design*.

Yellow Post-it Notes stuck out of both books. Cookie was serious about her chosen profession.

I turned on her computer, but saw no suicide note. She did not accumulate paper, so the room was easy to search. Bella seemed relieved when I couldn't find a suicide note.

"No note," she said. "That's proof my sister didn't kill herself."

"Not necessarily," I said. "Only about a third of suicides leave notes."

But most give clues that they're going to kill themselves, I thought. I remembered the death investigation of an executive who'd been fired. After twenty-five years of service, he was cruelly stripped of his job and title when he came into work one morning, and marched out of the building by two security guards. His office was locked and he was told his belongings would be shipped to his house.

The fired executive went home and told his wife he had to run an errand. "Give me one last kiss," he said.

She was in a hurry to go to a meeting, and didn't notice the odd phrasing. The executive left a note on their bed that said, "At sixty-two, I won't get another job, sugar. You'll be better off without me."

Then he grabbed the gun he kept in their bedroom, parked his Lincoln outside the CEO's house, and blew off his head. The CEO's daughter found his body when she came home from high school.

But Cookie, according to her sister and her cook, had none of the classic signs of suicide.

It was time for me to do the body actualization in the garage. Bella put on her coat and tried to follow me. "No," I said. "You can't go to the scene. I need you to stay inside the house."

Her pale face flushed an angry red and her mouth was set in a stubborn line.

"For your sister's sake," I said. I could feel her angry stare as I hurried across the wind-whipped courtyard. The temperature was dropping.

Detective Greiman met me by a topiary squirrel. "You girls have a good gab fest?" he said.

"I've finished my interviews," I said, ignoring his sarcasm.

"Photographs have been taken and the car's been printed," he said. "It's three-ten. If you hurry, we can be out by four. The meat wagon is on the way."

I wasn't hurrying. This was too important. I opened up the Death Scene Investigation form on my iPad. Bella had already given me the basic information, including Cookie's date of birth and Social Security number. I noted the weather – overcast – and the temperature: twenty-three degrees outside, thirty-two degrees inside the garage.

I photographed a wide shot of the garage and the Bentley, then a midrange photo of the car, and finally a close-up of the body behind the padded steering wheel. The driver's door was open and gray fingerprint powder covered the door, the dash, and other surfaces. The key was in the "on" position and the gas tank was almost empty. I photographed it all.

I noted that Cookie's car was parked in the first garage bay, facing east, and she was sitting upright in the driver's seat, with her feet on the floor and her hands at her side. Cookie's body was still stiff from rigor, and she'd settled back into the seat. Her blonde head was framed by the Bentley "wings" embroidered on the headrest.

According to her sister, Cookie was thirty-two. The dead woman's lips were slightly parted and her eyes were closed. I photographed her, starting with her head. Her hair was perfect. She was wearing a pale pink cashmere sweater, winter white wool pants, those sixty-dollar off-white silk socks, and no shoes.

I noted on the form that she was dressed appropriately for someone who'd had a casual dinner at home.

"It's getting late," Greiman reminded me, looking at his watch. "You can see it's a suicide. I gotta go. You done?"

"Not yet," I said. "But if you want to speed this up, help me move the body."

The garage was big enough that I could spread out a clean white sheet for the body actualization, the inspection.

I kept clean white sheets in my DI kit. I opened one on the garage floor and put on four pairs of latex gloves. I'd strip them off as I examined the body, and avoid contaminating it.

Greiman helped me pull the body out of the car. Cookie only weighed about a hundred pounds, but it was a struggle. She was still stiff. I photographed the driver's seat. It was stained from where her bowels and bladder had relaxed.

Then I opened the Body Inspection (Actualization) form on my iPad, while Greiman paced impatiently and muttered, "Come on."

I lifted that thousand-dollar sweater, and made a small slit in her skin, just under her rib cage, then took her temperature with a digital meat thermometer. I circled and initialed the slit with a black Sharpie so the ME would know I'd made that cut – "defect" – in her skin. The meat thermometer is more accurate than the professional thermometers, and a reminder that we are a hundred-plus pounds of meat.

I checked that the zipper and buttons on her sweater and pants were properly closed. Her front-closure bra was hooked and the straps weren't twisted. She'd dressed herself. I saw no visible tattoos.

I'd worked a murder scene where the husband had claimed his wife came home from work, tripped and "accidentally" hit her head on the sharp-edged table by the front door. He said he'd found her on the hall floor.

If so, she must have walked in naked through the front door. Her sweater was on backward and the side zipper on her skirt was in back. Homicide discovered someone had tried to clean the blood on the bedroom carpet with bleach.

The husband confessed that the couple had fought while she was undressing in their bedroom after work, and he'd slugged her with a bedside lamp. He tried – and failed – to make her death look accidental.

Now Greiman's face was as black as his hair. The badge bunnies thought he looked "cute." I ignored him and continued the body actualization.

Cookie's temperature was ninety degrees. Thanks to the cold weather, the temperature in the car and in the garage, the ME would have a tough time calculating the time of death.

I studied the body, starting at the head. There were no insects on the body. I saw no contusions, cuts, broken fingernails or blood. Her clean, undamaged hands were especially important. I saw no defensive wounds or cuts. Cookie had not fought for her life.

I recognized her Tiffany twist gold earrings, but I couldn't say that. Death investigators don't appraise jewelry. Instead, I said she wore yellow metal earrings in the shape of a bow. She wore no other jewelry, including rings.

I saw a short, dark brown hair on her right sleeve at the biceps area. I showed it to Greiman, then photographed it, removed it with my tweezers, and bagged it.

"Yeah, yeah," he said. "A dark hair. Big deal. She still offed herself. Will you hurry up? I gotta go."

But I continued my methodical examination, working my way down the front of her body. There was a black smear on the right knee of her pants.

"Look at this," I said, as I photographed, then measured the two-inch smear. "Looks like she got oil or something on her white pants."

"Probably from the door when she got in the car," he said.

"A woman who wore white pants would be more careful," I said.

"For chrissakes!" Greiman said. "She got in the car to kill herself. Why would she care if she got a smudge on her pants?"

His impatient remark triggered something in my mind. She got in the car . . . I looked at her feet. In white socks. Clean white silk socks. With no dirt on the soles. No runs or damage to the thin material. So how did Cookie get to the car? She'd have to walk across a flagstone courtyard.

Unless . . .

"Are you ready now?" Greiman looked at his watch again. "Any idiot can see it's a suicide."

"You're right, Ray," I said. "Any idiot can see that. An idiot wouldn't notice her socks."

"They're white," he said. "So?"

"They're clean, Ray. How did she get from the house to the garage across that stone courtyard? Fly?

"Her killer carried her," I said. "And I'll bet my next paycheck that's her estranged husband, who inherits ten million bucks if she dies.

"But murder investigations are your job, Ray. Looks like you'll be staying late."

The Bedroom Door

Francine knew her business partner would be dead in three days, and she couldn't save Abby. Worse, Abby would die naked in bed, and her death would be a crime. Francine suspected her husband was the reason Abby ripped off her clothes. Was this a crime of passion?

"I saw your partner Abby in my bedroom door," Grandma said.

"Abby, my interior design partner?" I asked. "That Abby?"

"The skinny one with the red hair," Grandma said.

"Damn. She's a good partner," I said. "I'll hate to lose her. She's going to be dead in three days."

A shrill scream split the air, and I jumped. Then I realized it was the teakettle boiling on Grandma's Magic Chef stove. She dropped two tea bags in a blue pot, poured in boiling water, and cut me a slab of homemade apple pie.

That gave me time to recover. I'd blurted something horribly selfish. Abby was going to die, and my first thought was how it would inconvenience me.

"I wanted to warn you in case something happened," Grandma said.

Something bad.

My grandmother had second sight, but it wasn't a gift anyone would want. She couldn't say, "Sell your stock this afternoon. The market's going to tank." Grandma saw only misery with her second sight.

The doorway to Grandma's bedroom was a portal to the other side. For ten years, people appeared in Grandma's bedroom doorway three days before they died. Some were friends, some were family, but all had a connection to Grandma.

The soon-to-be dead showed themselves at night bathed in warm light, while Grandma shook and shivered under her chenille spread. They never appeared when she took an afternoon nap or had a sick headache. They never said anything. They were just there, and then they weren't.

I asked the crucial question. "What was Abby wearing?"

The dead in the doorway always wore whatever they had on

when they passed to the other side.

"Not a stitch," Grandma said, disapproval in her voice. "And let me tell you, she's not a natural redhead."

"She's not a natural anything, Grandma. Abby puts on heels and a suit to take out the trash. This is good pie."

"Thanks," Grandma said. "I put up the apples last fall."

"If you saw Abby naked, maybe she had a heart attack in the shower," I said.

"I don't think so," Grandma said. "I saw your Aunt Tillie when she had her stroke in the bathtub. Her hair was wet and she clutched a bar of Palmolive soap. Tillie was my own sister, but that woman had serious cellulite. Abby was perfectly dry and looked like she'd just gotten out of bed. Her hair was mussed and her lipstick was smeared."

"Maybe I should say something to her," I said, taking another bite of pie.

"No!" Grandma said. "You can't! Remember Bill."

Her favorite brother had shown up in Grandma's doorway wearing a green hospital gown. Grandma was so upset, she called Bill at two in the morning about her deadly vision and scared the stuffing out of the man. When Bill had chest pains three days later, he refused to go to the hospital. By the time he collapsed and was taken to Saint Mary's by ambulance, it was too late. Bill died in the ER wearing a hospital gown.

Grandma swore she'd never say anything to anyone again. She kept silent when my father showed up in her doorway minus his head and his wedding ring. Grandma never liked Dad. She knew he cheated on her daughter. Heck, the whole neighborhood knew. Mom always forgave my father and took him back. Grandma thought her daughter would be better off without him. Three days later, when Dad was supposed to be at work, an irate husband blew away my father's head with a shotgun as he slipped out of a hot sheet motel. The errant wife locked herself in the bathroom and survived.

Somehow, Mom found out that Grandma knew about Dad's death in advance. She never forgave Grandma – or spoke to her again. Two years later, Mom appeared in Grandma's bedroom doorway in a hospital gown. She was dying of cancer. Grandma rushed to Saint John's Mercy and begged her daughter to forgive her. Mom went to her grave in stone-hard silence.

My Cousin Jimmy wore jungle fatigues in Grandma's doorway. Grandma wept when she saw her favorite grandson with a seeping chest wound. Then she called the Red Cross and said she needed to get in touch with Jimmy – it was an emergency.

"Does this concern a death in the family?" the Red Cross contact said.

"Not yet," Grandma said.

The Red Cross dismissed her as a harmless nutcase. Three days later Cousin Jimmy was shot in Vietnam, but we didn't know about his death for two weeks.

Grandma mourned Jimmy and blamed herself. "I should have lied," she said. "I should have said his mother had died and then they would have let my grandbaby come home." But she was unable to lie about what she saw. It was part of her unwanted gift.

Here's the weird thing about my grandmother: She looked like a picture-book grandma. She had a comfortable flour-sack figure and permed gray hair. She put up grape jelly, made apple butter in a big kettle, baked pies with flaky crusts, canned her own tomatoes – and saw dead people in her bedroom doorway.

My grandfather did not stop by Grandma's door before his heart attack. Grandma believed that was her punishment for her silence when my father was murdered. She found her husband of fifty years dead at the kitchen table, a deck of cards spread out on the Formica top. He'd been cheating at solitaire.

Why did Grandma see the dead three days before they passed over – when they were still alive? Grandma said time didn't run in a straight line, the way we saw it in school books. "Time is all around us," she said. "It's happening all at once." That was a pretty fair explanation of quantum physics from a woman who'd never finished grade school.

Much of what Grandma saw didn't make sense until after it happened. Aunt Leila appeared in the doorway wearing a raincoat and fluffy pink bedroom slippers. Grandma thought that outfit was so ridiculous, she blamed the pickled herring she'd had for dinner.

After three Tums, she decided to warn Leila. Grandma's younger sister lived in a snooty suburb of Saint Louis called Ladue. Leila thought Grandma's town, Mehlville, was low-rent.

"I was wearing a raincoat and slippers? What have you been drinking, Emma?" Leila asked. "I wouldn't be caught dead in that getup."

But she was. Three days later, Leila overslept and her daughter Annie missed the school bus. Annie could lose her perfect attendance award. Aunt Leila threw her raincoat over her night gown, grabbed her purse and drove Annie to school. Aunt Leila was killed driving home when a woman ran a stop sign on McKnight Road. Leila was wearing fluffy pink slippers and a raincoat.

"I should have tried harder," Grandma wept. "She wouldn't believe me. Now I'm warning you."

"What was I wearing in your doorway?" I asked. I couldn't keep the fear out of my voice. I had a fifteen-year-old daughter. I wanted to see my Sarah go to her senior prom. I wanted to be there when she graduated from college, and at her wedding. I wanted to hold my grandchild in my arms.

"Oh, I didn't see you," Grandma said. "I just had a feeling."

I took a deep breath and relaxed. Grandma's "feelings" were right maybe half the time. I had a fifty percent chance of escape.

In 2006, Grandma "had a feeling" the Saint Louis Cardinals would win the World Series, and talked me into getting season tickets with her. She was triumphant when they won. Of course, she also thought the Cards would win in 2007. They had a miserable season. The Philadelphia Phillies won the World Series against the Tampa Bay Rays.

I took Grandma to the race track twice because she "had a feeling." The first time, she won twenty-seven dollars. The second time, she lost fifty bucks on broken-down nags in what I called the Dog Food Trifecta – all three of her horses came in last.

Still, Grandma might be right this time. I fortified myself with more pie and asked, "Well, if I didn't stop in your doorway, what's going to happen?"

"I'm not sure," Grandma said. "But it involves you and Abby and a crime."

"Abby in a crime? No one is more honest than Abby. She keeps our books and insists on an independent audit every year. Besides, our design business doesn't make enough money for her to steal."

"I didn't say she was stealing," Grandma said. "Your Jack is working late a lot lately, isn't he?"

"Jack's architectural firm won the renovation project for the old NorCo shoe company building. They're turning it into loft apartments. His proposal is due in two weeks."

Why the sudden shift from my business partner to my husband? Oh, no. Jack wouldn't. She wouldn't. Abby was no angel, but she wouldn't have an affair with my husband. Would she?

I put down my pie fork. "Grandma, Jack is working late. And he doesn't like Abby. She's not interested in him, either."

"That's what your father used to say, until—" Grandma said.

"He was shot," I interrupted. "Jack is nothing like my father. That's why I married him."

"But what about Abby? She's a good-looking woman."

"Much better looking than me," I said.

"Francine! I would never say that," Grandma said.

"No, but you think it, like everyone else. Abby has a boyfriend. Actually, he's a friend with benefits."

"What's that?" Grandma asked.

"It means she likes him and she sleeps with him sometimes when she feels like it."

"In my day, we called that a husband," Grandma said.

"I'd better go," I said. "It's getting late, and I need to get home before Sarah."

"You worry too much," Grandma said. "She's not a little girl any more."

"She's a teenager, which is even more dangerous."

"Sarah's not using drugs, is she?" Grandma asked.

"No, she's just surly. I can't do anything right."

"She'll grow out of it," Grandma said. "Take her some apple pie. Do you think it's boy trouble?"

"She says boys are gross," I said. "I'm happy she believes that for now."

"So many young girls get in trouble," Grandma said, as she put half a pie in a Tupperware container. "I'm thankful Sarah's still a child." Grandma handed the pie to me.

I kissed her forehead. "I guess I'm overprotective," I said. "But Sarah is a young fifteen."

"She doesn't dress like a young girl," Grandma said. "At Thanksgiving, she was wearing an outfit that made her look like—"

"A slut," I finished.

Grandma's lips tightened into a thin, angry line. "I would never say that about my great-grandbaby. But that short skirt and belly-baring top did make her look older than her years."

"That's how girls dress now, Grandma," I said. "It looks slutty by our standards, but I didn't want her to be what I was in high school."

"What? An A-student?" Grandma said.

"A nerd," I said. "A misfit. Thanks for the pie. I'm sure she'll love it."

Grandma followed me to her front door. "Francine, if you need money for anything, you can always come to me. I only have a couple hundred in the bank, but I own this house. It's not worth much, but the land is valuable. Some developer wants to build another subdivision on this road. He's made an offer for that lot across the street and my five acres."

"Thanks, Grandma, but where would you live? You keep your house and your independence."

"Okay, but the money is yours when you need it. Lawyers are expensive."

"I don't need a lawyer," I said. "Where did that come from?"

"Just a feeling," Grandma said.

Grandma had bought the green three-room rambler when Mehlville was still the middle of nowhere. New highways around

Saint Louis had made the suburb more accessible, and the land more valuable.

I worried all the way to my next stop, my Maplewood design office. I tried to remember what I knew about Abby's "friend with benefits." His name was Allan, he was a CPA, and Abby had redecorated his office in what we privately called "clubby classic." Allan wanted leather wing chairs, forest green walls and hunting prints. Not terribly innovative, but most people didn't want an innovative accountant. I gathered Allan wasn't much more exciting outside the office. Abby had said he was a presentable escort and "okay in the sack, but he won't set the world on fire. Besides, I like them young, you know what I mean? Allan's my age. He's too old for me." She'd laughed.

Lately, Abby had been uncommonly cheerful. Her pale complexion had the glow of a well-loved woman. Maybe she did have a new boyfriend. Good for her.

I knew Abby didn't have time for an affair with my husband. She was too busy mentoring Megan, the new intern from the university's design school. Thanks to Abby, we got the school's best young talent working for us. Interns were good at tracking down online resources and running out for paint samples, material swatches, and coffee. They were low-paid errand girls, but they got terrific recommendation letters and experience. Our firm, Smart Women, was a good name to put on their resumes.

I didn't like dealing with the college students. The girls showed up late, hungover, or not at all. They needed constant attention. They whined that their parents didn't give them enough money. I'd worked my way through college and thought most were spoiled brats. Abby said working with young talent was invigorating. She could have them.

Even my own daughter, who wanted to be an interior designer, would rather work with Abby. Sarah said all I did was criticize her. I only suggested a few small improvements. I was happy my daughter wanted to follow in my footsteps. Sarah's rejection hurt, but maybe we needed a buffer for now. We'd just had a fight over the October cell phone bill. Sarah had texted another two hundred dollars onto it.

Sarah must have cried on Abby's shoulder. Abby told me many parents had monster texting bills from their kids. She emailed me some family phone plans with unlimited text messaging. "Sarah needs to stay in touch with her friends," Abby said. "It's harmless. All the kids do it."

Exactly what Sarah had said. I didn't want to reward my daughter for running up bills, but maybe I should look into those plans. When I was in high school, I'd spent hours talking on the phone to my best friend, Sue. I couldn't remember a word we'd said, but those calls were vital to me at Sarah's age. My daughter was a good kid. Heaven knows what I'd put my mother through when I was fifteen.

Smart Women, our interior design office, was close to my home. Ten years ago, Abby and I had bought an old two-story brick building on Manchester Road for a good price. We'd created an amazing office with lots of natural light, open space and hardwood floors. Smart Women was close to three major highways and the rich areas that used our services. Maplewood, an older Saint Louis suburb, had become trendy and our property value skyrocketed.

It was dark when I parked my Lexus in back of the building and slipped quietly through the side door. I could see my daughter and my design partner standing over a drawing board. I knew they were working on the McDaniel's vacation condo at the Lake of the Ozarks. The overhead lights turned Abby's red hair into fire. My daughter's long blonde hair was spun gold. Sarah seemed older in the dim light, and I could see the young woman she would soon become. Both women were dressed in black sweaters and pants

I watched the scene without making a sound.

"We could use a beachy theme in the great room, which has the best view of the lake," Abby said. "What about a conversation group of wicker chairs and a white couch facing those big windows? We could use the blue accent pillows."

Ordinary, I thought. The McDaniels would want something more stylish. That's why they hired Smart Women.

"What happens when one of the McDaniel's boys visits?" my daughter said. "The condo only has one bedroom. That couch won't stay white if the boys crash on it. I go to school with the youngest, Judson. He's a slob. I've seen him eat spaghetti out of the can. Maybe we should think about a pullout sofa to give the room flexibility."

"Good idea," Abby said. "What do you think of coral for the sofa?"

"It's spaghetti-colored," my daughter said, then paused. "I meant that as a joke, Abby. I love the color, and we can keep your blue accent pillows, too. You've made the room vibrant."

I was so proud of my daughter. Sarah was smart, talented—and tactful. I could see my daughter's name on our letterhead in a few years.

In the meantime, I was hungry. I tiptoed out and carefully shut the door so I wouldn't disturb them. Then I called my husband. It was only five-thirty, and Jack was still at work. I asked him if he'd like to meet me for dinner at Acero, his favorite Maplewood restaurant.

"I was just finishing up," Jack said. "I should have this project done before the deadline. Probably tomorrow night."

"Good," I said. "Maybe you'll get a bonus."

"Only if the clients like it. Are you serious about Acero?"

"My treat," I said.

"Could I order the mushroom ravioli with black truffles?"

"You can have whatever your heart desires," I said. "Including me."

"You're dessert," he said. "Black truffles first. I'll be there in ten minutes."

Acero wasn't a spaghetti-and-meatball Italian restaurant. I ordered the grilled skate wing in browned butter. The meat looked like a large, plump wing. It was hard to believe it came from such a prehistoric-looking creature as the raylike skate.

"This is heavenly," I told Jack.

"Maybe it's an angel wing," he teased.

We finished dinner and drove by Smart Women on the way home. The lights were still on. "Our daughter is working with Abby tonight," I said. "That means we have the house to ourselves."

"Are you propositioning me?" Jack asked.

"Absolutely. I'm a smart woman, remember?" We hurried home.

Sarah walked in the door at eight o'clock. Jack and I were watching a movie in the media room, holding hands. We'd had an hour to make love.

"Hi, honey, how was your day?" Jack joked.

Sarah smiled at her father and said, "Good. I worked with Abby on the McDaniel's beach house and we came up with this cool idea for the great room."

Our daughter talked a mile a minute, the way she did when she was happy. Then she kissed her father goodnight, ignored me, and went upstairs.

She's going to be upset when Abby dies, I thought, meanly. But maybe I'll get my daughter back. Sarah will have to work with me.

I slept badly that night. In my dreams, a ghostly Abby pleaded with me not to let her die. I woke up drenched with sweat and went to the kitchen to fix a calming cup of tea. I couldn't save Abby, and she wouldn't believe me if I told her she'd soon be dead.

I was trapped and she was doomed. I wished Grandma had never told me about Abby. I knew her supernatural knowledge was a dark burden, but I didn't want it, either. I didn't sleep the rest of that night.

The next day, I was tired and preoccupied. At work I botched an order for upholstery fabric, gave the wrong number for my trade discount to a wholesale house, and spilled a mug of coffee all over my desk.

"What's wrong?" Abby asked. "You look pale."

So did Abby. Maybe it was her new light pink lipstick. It was a shade I hadn't seen since the 1960s. It must be back in style, or Abby wouldn't wear it.

"I'm probably coming down with the flu," I said.

"Why don't you go home?" Abby said. "I can finish up here."

I was glad to leave. I couldn't meet her eyes, knowing she had one more day to live. Trouble was coming and all I could do was avoid it. But I was worried about my daughter. What if Sarah was with Abby when my partner died? What if Sarah was hurt, too? Or caught up somehow in Grandma's mysterious crime? I had to keep my daughter safe tomorrow.

When school was out, I called Sarah on her cell phone. "Hi," she said, her voice flat and sullen.

"Sarah, your father should be finishing his big project tomorrow. I thought we could take him out to dinner to celebrate."

"Can't, Mom," she said. "I'm rehearsing for the school musical, remember?"

"Right," I said. "I forgot."

What musical? When did she tell me that? "You never talk about your part," I said.

"I'm in the chorus and a crowd scene. Big whoop."

There it was again, that surly teenage voice. I tamped down my anger. If Sarah was at school, she wouldn't be around Abby on a dangerous day.

I called my husband at work to invite him to dinner tomorrow night.

"I just hope I get everything finished, after I bragged to you how well it was going," he said. "I've hit a snag. I'll be working late tonight and maybe tomorrow. Don't wait for dinner, promise?"

"Sure."

Sarah came home about six and went straight to her room without greeting me.

"Do you want dinner, honey?" I asked.

"Not hungry," she said. The two words were dropped on me like flat stones. I spent the night brooding on the couch, aimlessly channel surfing. When would Sarah return to her cheerful self? Why was her father working late? Jack wouldn't lie to me, would he? Not after the way he'd loved me last night. Of course, my father had lied to my mother. Easily.

Jack came home after midnight and woke me up. I'd fallen asleep on the couch. "Come on, sweetheart," he whispered. "You'll be more comfortable in our bed. I want to hold you."

I followed him upstairs, trying to drown out the voices that said he was betraying me. Jack took off his tie and rumpled suit jacket. "I have a lipstick stain on my collar," he said. "Do we have any stain remover?"

"How did you get lipstick on your collar?" I asked, trying to sound light and unconcerned.

"Sandy, the office manager, is moving to Seattle with her new husband. You remember her. The pretty one with the brown eyes and dark hair. We had a party at the office and she gave me a good-bye kiss."

That sounded like the kind of excuse my father used, I thought. My father the cheater.

"Just drop it in the laundry basket," I said. "I'll treat the stain in the morning."

The lipstick on the collar nagged at me. I spent another restless night, then got up to kiss Jack good-bye and see my daughter off to school. She was wearing a tiny skirt and a scoop-necked top.

"Sarah, is that outfit appropriate for school?" I asked.

"Mom," she said. "Everybody dresses like this. Anyway, I'm going to be late for the bus."

"At least put a jacket over it." I handed her the cropped jacket we'd bought as part of her back-to-school wardrobe.

"Gotta run," she said, and was out the door before I could tell if she'd put on the jacket or stuffed it in her backpack. I sighed. At least she hadn't dropped the jacket on a chair.

I examined the lipstick stain on my husband's shirt. The lipstick was a pale pink. Would a brunette wear that color? Didn't Sandy wear darker colors? But Abby was wearing something similar. It must be back in style.

Abby. What if that wasn't Sandy's lipstick on my husband's shirt collar? What if it was Abby's?

"Your Jack is working late a lot lately, isn't he?" my grandmother had asked. I'd defended him. He didn't get in until midnight last night. He was working late tonight, too. On his project – or on Abby?

I had to know. I wasn't going to be a fool like my mother. I drove over to Jack's office in downtown Kirkwood. His car was parked in the company lot in his reserved space. I parked across the street and waited. At twelve-fifteen, he left the building and went to Spencer's Grill. I got out, pulled my winter hat low and walked past the old-fashioned diner. Jack was sitting at the counter, reading a magazine and munching a grilled cheese sandwich.

I watched him walk back to his office while I stood in a store across the street. Jack had a corner office, and I could see him at his desk. The lights were on in the gray winter afternoon and the building was too busy for a dalliance. I went home until five-thirty and called him.

"Still have to work late, honey?" I asked.

"Afraid so," he said. "I'm sorry to leave you home alone again, but you can spend the time thinking what you can do with the extra money. Maybe we can take a February vacation to some place warm."

"I'd love to go to the Caribbean. What about Saint Bart's? Or Saint Lucia?"

"Any saint you want," he said.

He hung up and I started brooding again. My husband had sounded suspiciously cheery—the way my father did when he was cheating on my mother. Mom took it, year after year. Well, I wasn't going to be Jack's doormat. If he was cheating, I wanted to know. Then I'd get the best divorce lawyer.

I waited until seven o'clock, when I knew Jack would be getting hungry, and drove to a Maplewood brew pub, the Schlafly Bottleworks. I ordered a bison burger. I'd surprise him with his favorite sandwich if he was at the office working. If not, well, he'd get a different surprise.

I saw Jack's light was on and his blinds were drawn. I barged right into his office.

"Surprise!" I yelled.

Jack was surprised. He was sitting at his drawing board, with paper spread everywhere.

I felt foolish, standing there with a bison burger. "I brought you a present." I handed him the bag.

Jack's face lit up when he unwrapped his burger. "You didn't have to," he said. "But you've saved me from eating pretzels from the snack machine."

"That's free-range bison," I said. "I wonder where in the US the buffalo roam."

"Like me, not far from home," he said, kissing me on the nose. "Now I really do have to get back to work."

"I have to get home," I said. "Sarah's rehearsing for the school musical. She should be back any moment."

It was so cold my car didn't warm up on the short drive home. I passed Smart Women and saw the lights were off. I hoped Abby was enjoying her last night on earth. She only had four hours left, if Grandma was right. Of course, Grandma had been wrong about my husband, Jack. Maybe she was wrong about Abby, too. Maybe she was turning as strange as her brother, Oswald, who lived in the state mental institution and talked to imaginary people.

Our house was dark when I parked in front of it. I killed the lights and went in the front door. Sarah wasn't home yet, unless she'd fallen asleep.

I heard a noise upstairs. "Hello?" I called.

No answer.

I armed myself with the fireplace poker. I took out my cell phone and pressed 911, but didn't hit the call button. I slipped it in my pocket and tiptoed upstairs.

More noise, thumping and moaning. The sounds were coming from our bedroom. A burglar was hurting Sarah. I raced down the hall, flipped on the bedroom light, and saw Abby in my bed. Naked.

With my daughter.

Their clothes were scattered all over the floor.

"You slut," I shrieked. "That's my innocent daughter!"

I struck out with the poker and hit Abby on the head. I heard Sarah scream, "No, Mom, you don't understand!" She tried to grab my arm, but I shook her away.

I kept hitting Abby until I realized that brilliant red was not her hair, but her blood. By then Abby was dead and my sobbing daughter had called the police.

When my husband got home at midnight, I was being led away in handcuffs.

M y daughter still won't speak to me. Sarah told the police and the reporters that she loved Abby and they were planning to marry. Sarah said she didn't tell me about their romance because she was afraid I'd overreact, and Abby's murder proved she was right. I didn't want my daughter to be known as a nerd, and she isn't. The tabloids call her the Lesbian Lolita.

Will I be convicted of murder?

My lawyer says it depends on the jury. The law is tricky in Missouri. Seventeen is the age of consent, but if Abby believed Sarah was older and my daughter had given her consent, then Abby would not have been guilty of sex with a minor.

But Abby knew Sarah was only fifteen. She went to our daughter's birthday dinner with us. My husband can't find the photos to prove that. I wonder if my daughter destroyed them. She's testifying for the prosecution. They're saying my little Sarah was sexually emancipated. A TV talk show shrink said when Sarah brought her lover into her parents' bedroom she was declaring herself a sexual being. He didn't mention that bed was a lot bigger than hers.

Jack sold our house to help pay for the best criminal lawyer in the city. He and Sarah rent a small apartment near his office. Grandma sleeps on a pullout sofa in the living room. She's moved in with them. She sold her house to pay for my legal bills. My grandmother wants to testify on my behalf. My lawyer says she'll help prove a family history of mental illness.

The last time Grandma visited me in jail, I asked if she saw my future. Grandma said she saw nothing. The dead no longer visit her in the new apartment. She's glad her so-called gift is gone.

Her tiny house has been leveled and an upscale subdivision is being built on the site. These grand houses will have two baths, marble fireplaces, three bedrooms and walk-in closets.

I wonder if one will have a walk-in bedroom doorway.

Vampire Hours

On the eve of her birthday, Katherine had only one choice – death. But which kind: her real death, the living death of middle age, or death-in-life?

"It's three o'clock in the morning, Katherine. Go to sleep."
My husband, the surgeon. Eric barked orders even in the middle of the night.

"I can't sleep," I said.

"I have to be at the hospital in three hours. Turn off the light. And go see a doctor, will you? You're a pain in the ass."

Eric rolled away from me and pulled the pillow over his face.

I turned off the light. I felt like a disobedient child in my own home, as I listened to my husband of twenty-five years snore into his pillow. Eric could fall asleep anywhere, any time. Especially when he was in bed with me.

If I pushed his face into the pillow, could I smother him?

Probably not. Years of late-night emergency calls had given Eric an instant, unnatural alertness.

I lay alone on my side of the vast bed, stiff as a corpse in a coffin. My white negligee seemed more like a shroud than sexy sleepwear. My marriage to Eric was dead, and I knew it. I wanted him to love me, and hated myself for wanting a man so cold.

He wasn't like that when we were first married. Then, he'd ripped off so many of my nightgowns, he'd bought me a thousand-dollar gift certificate at Victoria's Secret. I'd model the latest addition and he'd rip it off again. Back then, he didn't care if he had early surgery. We'd had wild, all-night sex.

A tear slipped down my cheek, and I cursed it. Tears came too easily these days, ever since menopause. "The change," my mother had called it. Once, before I knew what those changes were, I'd looked forward to menopause. I wanted the monthly flow of blood to stop. I was tired of the bloat, the cramps, and the pain.

But the change was infinitely worse. Oh, the blood stopped, as promised. But nobody told me what would start: the weight gain, no matter how hard I dieted. How could I get fat on rice cakes and lettuce?

The change brought other changes. My skin started to sag along the jaw. The lines from my nose to my lips deepened into trenches. My neck looked like it belonged on a stewing hen.

And my husband, the old rooster, was chasing young chicks. I knew it, but I didn't dare confront him. I'd seen what happened to my friends when they'd faced down their rich, powerful husbands. Elizabeth, courageous, I-won't-stand-for-this Elizabeth, had been destroyed. She'd caught Zack, her husband of thirty years, groping some not-so-sweet young thing in the dim lights of the local bar. Elizabeth had fearlessly confronted Zack on the spot. She'd embarrassed him in front of his backslapping cronies.

Good old Zack hired a pinstriped shark – one of his bar buddies. Now the elegant Elizabeth lived in a cramped hotbox of an apartment, with a cat and a rattling air conditioner. She worked as a checker at the supermarket and barely made the rent. Elizabeth was on her feet all day and had the varicose veins to prove it.

I'd taken her out to a dreary lunch last month. I'd wanted to do something nice. We went to the club, where we'd always lunched in the old days, when she was still a member. Some of our friends didn't recognize her. Poor Elizabeth, with her home-permed hair and unwaxed eyebrows, looked older than her mother. She was so exhausted, she could hardly keep up a conversation.

That same fate awaited me. I had to stall as long as I could, until I could figure out what to do with my life. If Eric dumped me now, I'd be at the supermarket asking my former friends, "Would you like paper or plastic?"

I'd be one more useless, used-up, middle-aged woman.

I was already. In seven days, I'll be fifty-five years old. My future had never looked bleaker. I had no money and no job skills. My husband didn't love me any more. Happy birthday, Katherine.

"Lie still," Eric snarled. "Quit twitching."

I didn't think I'd moved. Maybe Eric felt my inner restlessness. Maybe we were still connected enough for that.

But I couldn't lie there another moment. Not even to save myself. I slid out of bed.

"Now what? Where are you going at this hour?" Eric demanded.

"I thought I'd get some fresh air. I'm going for a walk."

Eric sat straight up, his gray hair wild, his long surgeon's hands clutching the sheet to his hairy chest. "Are you crazy? You want to go outside in the middle of the night? After that woman was murdered two streets away?"

"People get murdered all the time in Fort Lauderdale," I said.

"Not like that. Some freak drained her blood. They didn't put that little detail in the papers. The city commission wants to avoid scaring the tourists. Dave at the medical examiner's office told me.

That woman hardly had a drop of blood left in her. She went for a walk at three in the morning and turned up drained dry. For Chrissakes, use your head."

"All right," I said. "I'll sit on the balcony. I didn't want to wake you."

I put on my peignoir and padded into the living room. I never tired of the view from our condo. To the east was the dark, endless expanse of the Atlantic Ocean, lit by ancient stars. Straight down were the black waters of the Intracoastal. Across the little canal that ran alongside our building were the Dark Harbor condos. Those places started at three million dollars. But it wasn't the money that fascinated me. Florida had lots of expensive condos. There was something about Dark Harbor. Something mysterious. Exciting. Exotic. Even at three in the morning.

I slid open the glass doors, careful not to make a sound. The warm night air caressed my cheek. I loved the night. Always had. Moon glow was kinder than the harsh Florida sun. I could hear the water softly lapping at the pilings on the dock, seven stories below.

Laughter drifted across the water, and the faint sounds of a chanteuse singing something in French. It was an old Edith Piaf song of love and loss.

There was a party in the Dark Harbor penthouse. Such a glamorous party. The men wore black tie. The women wore sleek black. They looked like me, only better, smoother, thinner. These people were in charge of their futures. They didn't have my half-life as the soon-to-be-shed wife. They were more alive than I would ever be.

I sighed and turned away from my beautiful neighbors. I drifted back into our bedroom like a lost soul, crawled in next to my unloving husband, and fell into a fitful sleep.

Eric woke me up at five-thirty when he left for the hospital.

"Good-bye," I said.

His only answer was a slammed door.

That night, while getting ready for bed, I looked in my dressing room mirror and panicked. I'd always had a cute figure, but now it had thickened. I had love handles. Where did those come from? I swear I didn't have them two days ago. I burst into tears. I couldn't help it.

I ran into the bathroom to stifle the sobs I knew would irritate Eric. But it was too late. "Now what?" he snarled. "I can't take these mood swings. Get hormone replacement therapy or something."

He was definitely getting something. I'd found the Viagra bottle in his drawer when I put away his socks. It was half empty. He wasn't popping those pills for me. We hadn't made love in months.

No pill would cure my problem. Not unless I took a whole bunch at once and drifted into the long sleep. That prospect was looking more attractive every day. Didn't someone say, "The idea is to die young as late as possible"? Time was running out for me.

I spent another restless night, haunting the balcony like a ghost, watching another party across the way at Dark Harbor. Once again, I drifted off to sleep as Eric was getting ready for work.

Tuesday was a brilliant, sunlit day. Even I couldn't feel gloomy. I was living in paradise. I put on my new Escada outfit – tight black jeans and a white jacket so soft, it was pettable. I smiled into the mirror. I looked good, thanks to topnotch tailoring and a body shaper that nearly strangled my middle.

I didn't care. It nipped in my waist, lifted my behind and thrust out my boobs. I sashayed out to the condo garage like a model on a catwalk. A sexy, young model.

I had a charity lunch at the Aldritch Hotel. I was eating – or rather, not eating – lunch to support the Drexal School. I didn't have any children, but everyone in our circle supported the Drex. As a Drexal Angel, I paid one hundred dollars for a limp chicken Caesar salad and stale rolls.

My silver Jaguar roared up under the hotel portico. A hunky valet raced out to take my keys. The muscular valet ogled my long legs and sensational spike heels, and I felt that little frisson a woman gets when a handsome man thinks she's hot.

Then his eyes reached my face and I saw his disappointment. The valet didn't bother to hide it. I was old.

I handed him my keys. The valet tore off my ticket without another glance at me. I felt like he'd ripped my heart in half. I used to be a beauty. Heads would turn when I strutted into a room. Now if anyone stared at me, it was because I had a soup stain on my suit or toilet paper stuck on my shoe. I was becoming invisible.

I caught a glimpse of myself in the hotel's automatic doors. Who was I kidding in my overpriced, overdressed outfit? I was losing my looks – and my husband.

I stopped in the ladies room to check my make-up. My lipstick had a nasty habit of creeping into the cracks at the lip line. I used my liner pencil, then stopped in a stall, grateful it had a floor-to-ceiling louvered door. I needed extra privacy to wriggle out of the body shaper.

I heard the restroom door open. Two women were talking. One sounded like my best friend, Margaret. The other was my neighbor, Patricia. I'd known them for years. I nearly called out, but they were deep in conversation and I didn't want to interrupt.

". . . such a cliché," Margaret said, in her rich-girl drawl.

"I can't believe it," Patricia said. Her voice was a New York honk. "Eric is boinking his secretary?"

Eric. My husband, Eric? Panic squeezed me tighter than any

body shaper. There were lots of Erics.

"Office manager," Margaret said. "But it's the same thing. She's twenty-five, blonde, and desperate to catch a doctor. It looks like Eric will let himself get caught."

"Can you blame him?" Patricia honked. "Katherine's let herself go."

Katherine. No, there weren't many Erics with Katherines. I felt sick. I sat down on the toilet seat and listened.

"She won't even get an eye job," Patricia said. "And her own husband is a plastic surgeon. How rejecting is that? Eric did my eyes. Then he did the rest of me." Her words filled the room. I couldn't escape them.

"You slept with him?" Margaret sounded mildly shocked.

"Everyone does," Patricia said.

I could almost hear her shrug. I wanted to rush out and strangle her. I wanted to blacken her stretched eyelids. But I was half-dressed, and my jiggly middle would prove she was right.

"It's part of the package," Patricia said. "My skin never looked better than when I was getting Dr. Eric's special injections."

"You're awful," Margaret said. Then my best friend laughed.

"It's part of my charm," Patricia said. "But someone better clue in Katherine, so she can line up a good divorce lawyer before it's too late."

"It's already too late," Margaret said. "Eric's already seen the best lawyer in Lauderdale, Jack Kellern."

"And you didn't tell Katherine that Eric hired Jack the Ripper?"

"How could I? He's my husband."

And you, Margaret, are my best friend. Or rather, you were. Margaret had also had her eyes done by Jack. Did she get the full package, too?

I waited until my faithless friends shut the restroom door. I rocked back and forth on the toilet in stunned misery. It was one thing to suspect your husband was playing around. It was another to learn of his betrayal – and your best friend's. I was a joke, a laughing-stock. I had even less time than I thought.

I pulled my clothes together, pasted on a smile, and found my table. A waitress set my salad in front of me. I studied the woman. She was about my age, with a weary face, limp brown hair, and thick, sensible shoes. This time next year, would I be serving salads to the ladies who lunched?

Only if I were lucky. I didn't even have the skills to be a waitress. I picked at my salad, but couldn't eat a bite. No one noticed. Well-bred women didn't have appetites.

A polite clink of silverware on glasses signaled that the head-master was at the podium. He was a lean man with a good suit and a sycophantic smile.

"You've heard that Drexal has one of the finest academic re-
cords . . ." he began. My thoughts soon drifted away.

Menopause had killed my marriage, but it had been dying for a
long time. I knew exactly when it had received the fatal wound: the
day my husband asked to cut on me.

I was thirty-five, but looked ten years younger. Eric was itching
to get out his scalpel and work on my face.

"Just let me do your eyes," he said, "and take a few tucks. If you
start early, you'll look younger longer."

"I look fine," I said.

"You don't trust me," he said.

"Of course I do," I said. "You're the most successful plastic surgeon in Broward County."

But not the most skilled. Eric was right. I didn't trust him.
He'd never killed anyone, unlike some Florida face sculptors. But I
saw his work everywhere. I could recognize his patients: Caucasian
women of a certain age with the telltale slanted eyes and stretched
skin.

Eric gave them facelifts when no other doctor would. He'd give
them as many as seven or eight, until their skin was so tight they
could bikini wax their upper lip.

I pleaded fear of anesthesia. I invented an aunt who died from
minor surgery when I was a child. But Eric knew the truth: I was
afraid to let him touch me. I was his in every way, except one. I
would not surrender to his knife.

For ten years, he never stopped trying. He nagged me for a full
facelift at forty. At forty-five, I knew I could probably use one, but
still I wouldn't submit.

"Nothing can make me twenty-five again," I said. "I'll take my
chances with wrinkles."

It was the worst rejection a plastic surgeon could have. I made
him look bad. Everyone could see my lines and wrinkles. These
normal signs of aging became an accusation. They said every woman but his wife believed Eric was a fine surgeon.

When I turned fifty, Eric quit asking. That's when our hot
nights together cooled. I suspected there were other women, but
knew the affairs weren't serious. Now, things had changed. Eric
was going to marry a twenty-five-year-old blonde. In another five
years, she'd submit to his knife.

Suddenly, I was back in the hotel ballroom. The headmaster's
speech had reached its crescendo. "We have almost everything we
need to make the Drexal School the finest educational institution
in Broward County," he said. "Only one thing is missing. After
today, we'll have it all. I'm pleased to announce the creation of the

Drexal Panthers – our own football team. Your donations have made it possible."

The lunching mothers cheered wildly.

I looked down at my plate and realized I'd eaten an entire slice of chocolate cheesecake with raspberry sauce.

Worse, I hadn't tasted one bite.

No wonder I was fat.

On the way home, I picked up some college catalogues. I made myself a stiff drink and settled into my favorite chair in the great room to study the glossy catalogues. I looked at careers for legal aides, dental assistants, and licensed practical nurses. One choice seemed more depressing than the other.

What had I wanted to be before I met Eric?

An English teacher. Back then, I saw myself teaching poetry to eager young minds, watching them open like flowers with the beauty of the written word. Now, I knew I couldn't cope with the young ruffians at the public schools. Would the Drexal School hire an Angel down on her luck? Would the headmaster remember how often I'd lunched to make his dream team possible?

If I went back to college, how many years would I need to complete my degree? Would my life experience count for anything? What had I done in fifty-five years?

I fell asleep on the pile of catalogues. I woke up at midnight when I heard Eric unlock the door. I hid the catalogues with my arms, but he never noticed them. Or me. He went straight to bed without even saying good night.

I woke up at three. I couldn't sleep through the night any more. I kept vampire hours now. I drifted into the living room and watched the condo across the way. There was another party tonight. This time, the music seemed livelier, the guests more keyed up, more dramatically dressed, as if they were at some special ceremony.

Our condo walls seemed to close in on me. I slipped on my jeans and a cotton shirt. I was going for a walk along the water, even if it killed me. I'd rather risk death than suffocate inside.

The night air was delicious, cool but not cold. I was drawn to the lights of the Dark Harbor party, and picked my way along the docks until I was almost underneath its windows. I couldn't see anything, but I could feel the contained excitement inside. The walls seemed to pulse with life.

"Wish you were here?"

I jumped at the voice – very rich, very male.

The man who came out of the shadows wore evening dress. His skin looked luminous in the moonlight. His hair was black with a slight curl. There was strength in his face, and a hint of cruelty. I couldn't tell his age. He seemed beyond such ordinary measures.

"I'm sorry. I didn't mean to trespass," I said.

"You aren't trespassing, Katherine," he said. "You spend a lot of time watching us, don't you?"

"Am I that obvious?" I said.

"No," he said. "But I feel your yearning. It makes you very beautiful – and very vulnerable."

Inside the condo, there was a shriek of triumph, followed by polite tennis-match applause.

"Excuse me," he said. "I must return to my guests. My name is Michael, by the way."

"Will I see you again?" I said.

"If you want to," he said.

He was gone. Only then did I wonder how he knew my name.

I floated back to my condo wrapped in soft, warm clouds of fantasy. How long had it been since any man had called me beautiful?

I was beautiful. Michael made me feel that way. I crawled into bed beside my husband, and dreamed of another man.

In the morning, I woke up smiling and refreshed. For the first time in months, I didn't check my mirror for more ravages. I didn't need to. I was beautiful. Michael had said so. I was dreamy as a lovesick teenager, until the phone shattered the sweet silence at eleven a.m.

"Katherine, it's Patricia." Of course it was. She'd slept with my husband, and confessed it in a public restroom. I'd know her honking voice anywhere. Except today it had a different note. She sounded subdued, even frightened. "Have you heard about Jack?"

"Jack who?" I said.

"Margaret's Jack. They found his body in the parking lot of his law offices early this morning."

"What happened?" I said. "Was he mugged?"

"They don't think so," Patricia said. "The police say the murder didn't take place there. They think he was abducted."

"Kidnapped and murdered? But why?" Which wife killed him, I wondered. How many deserted women wished him dead?

"No one knows. But it gets worse. Jack's body was drained of blood. Completely dry."

"That's awful," I said. "I'll go see Margaret immediately."

I hung up the phone quickly, hoping to hide my elation. Jack the Ripper was dead – horribly dead. My husband no longer had a divorce lawyer. I felt a brief stab of shame for my selfish thoughts, but Jack's death was poetic justice. Someone had sucked the blood out of the city's biggest bloodsucker. Someone had given me more time.

I put on a navy pantsuit and a long face, and stopped by a smart specialty shop for a cheese tray and a bottle of wine. My long-dead mother would be proud. She'd taught me to bring food to a house of mourning.

There were other cars in Margaret's driveway, including what looked like unmarked police cars and three silver Lexuses. Lawyers' cars.

Margaret was a wreck. Her eyes were deeply bagged and swollen. Her jawline sagged nearly as badly as mine. All my husband's fine work was undone. I felt petty for noticing. She's a new widow, I told myself. Show some pity.

"Katherine!" Margaret ran weeping into my arms, smearing my jacket with makeup.

"I'm sorry," I said, patting her nearly fleshless back. I could feel her thin bones. It wasn't a lie. I was sorry for so many things, including the death of our friendship. Women need the sympathy of our own kind. Margaret had destroyed even that small comfort for me.

"Come into the garden where we can talk," she said. "The police are searching Jack's home office. Three lawyers from his firm and a court-appointed guardian are arguing over what papers they can take."

We sat at an umbrella table near a bubbling fountain. Palms rustled overhead. Impatiens bloomed at our feet. It looked like every other garden in Florida. A Hispanic maid brought iced tea, lemon slices, and two kinds of artificial sweetener.

"May I have sugar, please?" I asked.

"Sugar?" the maid said, as if she'd never heard the word.

"You use sugar?" Margaret might be dazed with grief, but she was still surprised by my request. In our crowd, sleeping with a friend's husband was a faux pas. Taking sugar in your tea was a serious sin.

"Doctor's orders," I said. "Sweeteners are out. Cancer in the family."

Actually, I liked real sugar. And it was only eighteen calories a spoonful.

"How are you?" I asked.

"I don't know," Margaret said. Two more tears escaped her swollen eyelids. "I thought Jack was seeing someone, and that's why he worked late so often these last few weeks. I was furious, but I couldn't say anything. I was too afraid."

"I understand," I said.

She flushed with guilt.

"My husband went to see Jack," I said. "So I know how you feel."

Margaret had the grace to say nothing. I appreciated that.

"Do you think Jack's lover killed him?" I asked.

"I don't know. I don't even know now if he had a lover. One of the firm's associates found Jack in the parking lot when she came to work at six this morning. Maybe he really had been working late. I had to identify him. Jack didn't look dead so much as . . . empty.

Someone took all his blood. It wasn't some slashing attack. Just two holes in the side of his neck. There were bruises, too. Terrible bruises on his wrists, legs and shoulders."

"Was he beaten?"

"No. They think someone – or maybe more than one person – held him down while he was – while they –" Margaret couldn't go on.

"Do the police think it was a serial killer?" I asked.

"They won't say. But the way they're acting, I know it's strange. There were other attacks like this in Lauderdale. Jack wasn't the only person to die like this."

"No," I said. "Eric told me that the woman found off of Bayview had been drained dry, too. He heard that from the medical examiner's office. The police kept it out of the papers."

"It's like some nightmare," Margaret said, "except I can't wake up. Mindy is flying home this afternoon from college. This will be so hard for our daughter. Mindy idolized her father." Margaret started weeping again.

I wasn't sure what to do. If we'd still been friends, I would have folded Margaret in my arms. But she had betrayed me. I knew it, and she knew it.

I was saved by a homicide detective and a lawyer.

"Margaret," the lawyer said, "I'm sorry to disturb you, but we have some more questions about your husband."

"I'd better go," I said. "I'll let myself out." I air-kissed her cheek. It took all my self-control to keep from running for my car.

Once, I would have called my husband and told him the awful news. Now I didn't. What could I say? You know that lawyer you hired to strip me of my last dime? The son of a bitch was murdered. Couldn't happen to a nicer guy.

I suspected Eric already knew about Jack's death. He was probably looking for a new blood sucker.

I spent the afternoon taking calls from Margaret's shocked friends, pretending to be sad and concerned and hating myself because I couldn't feel any of it. Instead, I felt oddly excited. I broiled a skinless chicken breast, steamed some broccoli, and waited for my husband to come home.

At eleven o'clock, there was still no sign of Eric. He didn't bother to phone me. I didn't humiliate myself by calling around asking for him.

What if he turned up dead, like Jack? I wondered. Then my troubles would be over. I felt guilty even thinking that. But it was true.

At three in the morning, I woke up alone and drenched in sweat. Night sweats, another menopausal delight. I punched my soggy pillow and tried to settle back to sleep. At three-thirty, I gave up. I reached for my jeans, then abandoned that idea. Instead, I pulled out a long, nearly sheer hostess gown that looked glamorous in the soft moonlight.

I wasn't going for a walk. I was going hunting. For Michael.

There was no party tonight. His condo was dark except for flickering candles in the living room and the opalescent light of a television. Michael was alone, like me. He couldn't sleep, either.

He was waiting for me down by the Dark Harbor docks. At first, I heard nothing but the gentle slap of the water and the clinking of the halyards as the boats rocked back and forth. It was a peaceful sound. A light breeze ruffled my hair and pressed my gown against my body.

"You dressed for me, didn't you?" he said.

Michael seemed to appear from nowhere. His white shirt, open at the throat and rolled at the sleeves, glowed in the moonlight. His hair was black as onyx, but so soft. I longed to run my fingers through it

"Yes," I said.

His hand touched my hair and traced the line of my neck. I stepped back. It wouldn't do to seem too eager too soon.

Michael smiled, as if he could read my mind. "You don't have to play games," he said.

"I'm not playing games," I said. "I'm being cautious. I don't know anything about you. Are you married?"

"My wife has been dead for many years. I live alone."

"You have such lovely parties." I couldn't keep the wistful note out of my voice.

"I have many friends. We enjoy the night."

"I do, too," I said. "I'm tired of the Florida sun. It burns the life out of everything."

"You may be one of us," Michael said. "I'd like to see more of you, before I go."

"Go?" The word clutched at my heart. "Where are you going?"

"I'm selling the condo. Nobody stays long in Florida. You know that. Will you be here tomorrow night? May I see you again?"

"Three o'clock," I said. "Same time, same place."

There. I'd done it. I'd made a date with another man. My marriage was over, except for the legalities. It was time to face the future. Maybe, if I was lucky, I'd have Michael in my life. If not, I'd find someone else. He'd shown me that I was still attractive. I was grateful for that. I'd let Eric destroy my confidence.

I turned around for one last look, but Michael was gone. Only then did I realize he hadn't asked if I was married. I wondered if he knew. Or cared.

Eric was waiting for me when I returned, tapping his foot like an impatient parent.

"Where were you?"

"I could ask you the same question," I said.

"I was with a patient," he said.

"Administering more special injections?" I said. "Patricia says they're wonderful for the complexion. I wouldn't know. It's been so long I've forgotten."

"You're certifiable." Eric turned the attack back on me. He was good at that. "Jack is dead. Murdered! Some freak drank his blood. And you're roaming the streets at night like an Alzheimer's patient. I should hire a keeper."

I should hire a hit man, I thought. But I held in my harsh words. I didn't need Eric now. I had Michael.

"Good night," I said. "I'm sleeping in the guest room."

"You can't –"

I didn't stop to hear what I couldn't do. I locked the guestroom door and put fresh sheets on the bed. What am I doing? I wondered. I have a three a.m. rendezvous with a man I don't know. There's a murderer running loose in my neighborhood. Yet I'd never felt safer or more at peace. I slept blissfully until ten in the morning. I woke up with just enough time to get ready for my literacy board meeting.

As I walked into the dark paneled board room, I caught snatches of conversation: "he was drained dry . . . don't know when they'll have a funeral . . . Margaret is devastated."

All anyone could talk about was Jack's murder, at least until the board meeting started. Then we had to listen to Nancy blather on about bylaws changes. She'd kept the board tied up with this pointless minutia for the last eight months.

Once, I saw myself as a philanthropist, dispensing our money to improve the lives of the disadvantaged. But I'd sat on too many charity boards. Now I knew how little was possible. Here I was in another endless meeting, listening to a debate about whether the organization's president should remain a figurehead or have a vote on the board.

How did this debate help one poor child learn to read? I wondered.

"Katherine?"

I looked up. The entire board was staring at me.

"How do you vote on the motion: yes or no?" Nancy asked.

"Yes." I wasn't saying yes to the motion, whatever it was. I was saying yes to a new life.

Mercifully, the board meeting was over at noon. I dodged any offers of lunch and went straight home. I spent three hours on the Internet, looking at my career options. Work couldn't be any worse than board meetings. Then I'd get ready for my date with Michael.

By four that afternoon, I'd decided to become a librarian. It would only take another three years of college. The pay was decent. The benefits were not bad. The job prospects were good. I'd be a useful member of society, which was more than I could say for myself now.

I pushed away the memory of Elizabeth's dreary apartment and made an appointment with a feminist lawyer. Tomorrow, we would discuss my divorce. Today, I wanted to think about my date with Michael.

I washed my hair, so it would have a soft curl. I applied a mango-honey face mask and swiped Eric's razor to de-fuzz my legs. Eric hated when I did that. I hoped the dull razor would rip his face off tomorrow morning. I sprayed his shaving cream on my long legs. I was now covered with goo from head to toe. Naturally, the doorbell rang.

Who was that?

I looked out the peephole. A young woman with a cheap blonde dye job was on my doorstep. Her skirt was some bright, shiny material, and her tight halter top barely covered her massive breasts. I'd seen her before, at Eric's office.

"Just a minute," I called, and quickly wiped off the shaving cream and the mango mask.

When I opened the door, I was hit by a gust of perfume.

"Yes?" I said. "You're from Eric's office. Is there a problem?"

"There is." She boldly walked into my home and sat down on my couch. "My name is Dawn. I'm Eric's office manager."

And his lover. The recognition was a punch in the face. Eric was leaving me for this big-titted cliché. I stood there in silence, hoping to make this husband-stealing tramp squirm. She'd have to do the talking.

Dawn came right out with her request. "We want to get married," she said.

"We?"

"Eric and I."

"He's married to me," I said.

"That's the problem, isn't it?" Dawn smiled. She had small, feral teeth and smooth skin. Eric would revel in that flawless skin. How my husband would love to put a knife into it. He had the gall to try to improve perfection.

"If you make it easy for me, I'll make it easy for you," Dawn said. "I'll make sure you get a nice allowance. You drag us through the courts, and I'll fight you every step of the way."

"You're threatening me in my own living room?" I said.

"It won't be yours for long," Dawn said. She looked around at my carefully decorated room. "No wonder Eric doesn't like to hang here.

It's like a funeral parlor. White couches in Florida. Hello? Can you say corny? This place needs some life.

"Oh, dear, you've got some gunk on your forehead. Those do-it-yourself beauty treatments don't work. Should have gone to your husband for help. You might still have him. But maybe not. He can only do so much."

I sat there, speechless, while the little slut sauntered past me. I picked up the first thing I could find, a delicate gold-trimmed Limoges dish – a wedding present – and threw it at her. Too late. She'd already shut the door.

The dish shattered with a satisfying sound. Plates, glasses, candy dishes, even a soup tureen followed, until the hall's marble floor was crunchy with smashed crockery and broken glass. It took me an hour to sweep it up and drop it down the trash chute. I knew Eric wouldn't miss any of it. He wouldn't even notice anything was gone. These were the things I loved. I wondered if the slut would be dining off my best china and drinking from my remaining wedding crystal. Over my dead body. Better yet, over hers.

I cleaned off the remnants of the mango-honey mask and shaved my legs with a shaky hand. I had a date with a man at three o'clock in the morning. What kind of time was that? I nicked my leg and watched a small drop of blood well up. Blood.

Three a.m. was a good time for a vampire.

That's what Michael was, wasn't he? Who else had drained Jack dry but a vampire? What else could Michael and his sleek, night-loving friends be?

I expected to feel shocked and horrified, but I didn't. Michael and his friends did me a favor by killing Jack. If they'd killed Eric, I would have been the center of a murder investigation. Instead, they gave me a little more time to arrange my life before it self-destructed.

Was Michael a danger to me? I didn't think so. If he'd wanted to kill me, he'd had many opportunities. No, Michael wanted more than a quick kill. But what, exactly? His conversation was full of innuendoes, invitations, and explanations.

"I feel your yearning. It makes you very beautiful – and very vulnerable."

"My wife has been dead for many years. I live alone."

"I have many friends. We enjoy the night."

"You may be one of us."

Michael had told me what he was, if I listened carefully. Did I want to be one of his beautiful friends? Could I kill other people?

Depends, I thought. I could kill lawyers like Jack, doctors like my husband, and that little bitch who waltzed into my house and claimed my husband like a piece of lost luggage.

I wondered about the other woman who'd been drained dry. Who was she? Did she deserve to die? I didn't have her name, but I knew the date she'd died and the street where she was found – Forty-seventh, off of Bayview.

A quick Internet search found the story in the Sun-Sentinel. The dead woman was forty-five, divorced, an IRS auditor. Another deserving victim. Another bloodsucker. Eric and I'd been audited one long, hot summer. The IRS found one small error, but the accountant and lawyer bills to defend ourselves were tremendous. We would have had more rights if we'd been accused of murder, instead of cheating on our income tax.

Yes, I could kill an IRS auditor. I could hand out justice to the unjust. In my new life, I would punish the wicked. I would be superwoman – invisible by day, fearless by night. That beat being a divorced librarian living in a garden apartment.

I hardly tasted my dinner, I was so excited by my new life. Not that my dinner had much flavor: four ounces of boneless, skinless, joyless chicken and romaine with fat-free dressing.

For dessert, I treated myself to two ounces of dark chocolate and a delicious daydream of Michael. It had been a long time since any man had wanted me. And this man had so much to give me.

I watched the full moon rise, and paced my condo. Eric didn't come home that night. I didn't expect him to. I was glad. I was in no mood to confront him.

I dug out my favorite black Armani dress. It was specially designed to cover my flaws. The high neck hid the crepe under my chin. The sleeves disguised the unsightly wings under my arms that no workouts could eliminate. The short hem showed my legs at their best. I put on sexy high-heeled sandals. They were dangerous on the docks, but I was living dangerously these days.

Michael was waiting for me outside my condo. He'd come to me this time. His hair was black as a midnight ocean. His luminous skin was like moonlight on snow. He kissed me, and his lips were soft and surprisingly warm.

"You know who we are, don't you?" he said.

"Yes," I said. "I want to be like you."

"You must be sure. You must have no illusions before you adopt our way of life. You must ask me any questions tonight."

"Are you immortal?"

"Almost," he said. "We can be killed by fire, by sunlight, and by wooden stakes through the heart. All natural elements."

"What about crosses and holy water?"

He laughed. "There were vampires long before there were Christians."

"What will happen to me? How will I become one of you?"

"I will make you a vampire by giving you my blood. I will take yours. Don't be frightened. It's not painful. You'll find it quite exhilarating. Once the transference is complete, you must make your first kill."

"Will I change? Will I look different?"

"You'll look like yourself, only more beautiful. Any wrinkles will vanish. Any physical flaws will disappear. You'll quickly attain your ideal weight. Our people are never fat."

Vampirism – the ultimate low-fat diet. I wanted to smile. But suddenly, I couldn't joke. The changes were profound, and frightening. "I'll never be able to eat food again." I felt a sudden desperate pain at what I would have to give up.

"Do you eat now?" Michael asked.

The question seemed ridiculous. "Of course."

"But do you like what you eat? Do you actually hunger for carrot sticks? Do you long for steamed broccoli and romaine with diet dressing?" He put his warm lips next to my ear and whispered, "When was the last time you had food you really wanted?"

I thought of the meals of my youth, when I could eat anything: fried chicken and cheeseburgers, crispy french fries lightly sprinkled with salt, hot fudge sundaes with warm whipped cream, crusty bread and butter.

"You haven't had any of those in years, have you?" Michael said.

He could read my mind. I knew that now.

"You'll never experience the pain of dieting again," he said. "You will have no need for ordinary food. You will drink the food of the gods. Blood is offered to them as a sacrifice. You will take it for your own pleasure. It is a thrill you cannot imagine. You will still hunger, but now you will be satisfied. You are hungry, aren't you? Even now, after your supper of skinless chicken."

"Yes." The pale, pathetic hunk of bird nearly turned my stomach. "I can do good, too," I said. "I can feed on those who deserve to die."

His eyes were suddenly darker, and I realized he was angry. "No! You must embrace the dark side like a lover. Any good you do will be accidental."

"But Jack –" I began.

"When Rosette killed that bloodsucking lawyer, she made a lot of scorned wives happy. But Jack will be mourned by his daughter. Randall killed the IRS agent because she'd been auditing his books. She nearly drove him crazy, and he was innocent. But she was the sole support of her elderly mother. And, irritating though she was, the agent was an honest woman.

"You cannot fool yourself into believing that you will only feed on serial killers or child molesters. That is romantic nonsense.

"You are evil and you must choose it. Your killing will not make the world a better place. We kill for revenge, for sport, for reasons that are impossibly petty. Marissa once killed a dress shop clerk on Las Olas because she wouldn't wait on her."

"So you've killed more people in Fort Lauderdale than Jack and the IRS agent?" I asked.

"Many more," Michael said. "The details about the other bodies being exsanguinated did not make the papers. The police try to hide that information. When it becomes public, then it's time for us to leave. That's why we're going tomorrow night."

"What happened to the other bodies?"

Michael said nothing. He didn't have to. I realized we were looking at the wide black ocean.

"Where will you go when you leave?" I said.

"The south of France," he said. "I have a cottage by the sea. The air smells of lavender and the sound of the waves is wonderfully soothing."

A small sigh escaped me. He was offering me such a beautiful life.

"Why me?" I asked. "There are millions of women like me, a little past our prime, abandoned by our husbands."

"Do you define yourself only by your husband?" he asked. "I don't think so. Americans have such boring ideas about age. Older cultures celebrate all aspects of a woman's life. Americans only want youth, which can be the dullest time. I prefer a woman who has lived.

"And you are not like the others. You are strong. You have resisted the lemming-like urge for plastic surgery. It's become a national obsession, but you fought it, even though it cost you your marriage and your comfortable life. You knew it wasn't the right choice for you. That takes courage. You know who you are. Do you know what you are?"

For the first time, I knew I was someone special.

He took my hand. "I'd like you to join us," he said. "I want you. Now that you know, you have only two choices: join us or die."

"May I have twenty-four hours? I have some loose ends to tie up."

"Yes. But remember, no one will believe you if you go to the police. And we will be gone before they can get a search warrant."

"I would never betray you," I said. "You've already helped me. Did you encourage Rosette to kill Jack? For my sake?"

"I wish I could take credit," Michael said. "But Jack was her idea. Still, I'm glad it helped you."

Then he kissed my hand. "You have much to think about," he said. "I hope you make the right decision."

I left him feeling oddly lighthearted for a woman whose only choice was death: my real death, the living death of middle age, or the death-in-life of a vampire.

I slept well that night, or what was left of it. Then, at five-thirty, I was awakened by Eric slamming doors and opening drawers. He had four white shirts in plastic bags. I'd picked up those shirts for him from the best laundry in Lauderdale, prepared precisely the way he liked: hangers, no starch.

I sat up groggily in bed. "From now on," I said, "have your slut pick up your laundry. That's the last errand I'm running for you."

"Don't you dare call Dawn that," Eric said.

"Dawn! Has it dawned on you how trite you are?" My bitterness burst like a lanced boil, and I was screaming like a fishwife. My husband yelled right back.

Our argument was interrupted by pounding on our front door. Marvin, our condo security guard, was standing on the doorstep. He looked embarrassed. "I'm sorry," he said. "But there have been complaints about the noise."

We both apologized to the guard. Now my humiliation was complete. Eric walked out a few minutes later, clutching his fresh shirts by the hangers. "You'll hear from my lawyer," he said.

That was it. That was how he ended our quarter-century marriage, the day before my birthday.

He'd forgotten that, of course. He couldn't even say, "I'm sorry, I've found someone else." Eric wasn't sorry, was he? But he would be.

I watched the sun rise on the last morning of my life. The new morning turned the air a pearlescent pink, and a shimmering fog drifted across the water. White birds skimmed along the Intracoastal Waterway.

I will never see this beauty again, I thought. But I didn't have time to wallow in regret. I had things to do. I stopped at a diner for a last, lavish breakfast. The young, busty waitress was too busy flirting with a table full of businessmen to pay any attention to me. I could hear the cook ringing the bell in the kitchen. When the waitress finally brought my breakfast, the eggs had congealed to rubber, and the home fries were coated with grease.

"This food is cold," I said to the waitress.

"Huh?" she said, as if she'd just noticed me for the first time. Once again, I was the incredible, invisible middle-aged woman.

"I'll get the cook to warm it up," she said.

"Never mind," I said. "I'm not hungry after all."

I threw some money on the table and left. I'd lost my taste for food.

At ten o'clock, I was weeping in my lawyer's office. The tears came easily, and they weren't entirely false. Only the accusations were made up.

"Please help me," I sobbed. "My husband is divorcing me. He has a new girlfriend and he hates me. They're fighting about how soon they can get married. I'm in the way. I'm afraid Eric will harm me."

"Harm you how?" the lawyer asked.

She would look perfect on the witness stand during Eric's murder trial, I thought. She was serious enough for the women to believe her, but sexy enough to get the men's attention. There was something about her tailored black suit, tightly pulled back hair, and horn-rimmed glasses that made men wonder what she'd look like without them.

"K-kill me," I said. "Eric doesn't let anyone stand in his way."

"Have there been any threats?" the lawyer said.

"Nothing in front of witnesses," I said. "But we had a terrible fight this morning, and he said he'd kill me if I didn't give him a divorce and . . . I'm so embarrassed. Condo security had to knock on our door."

"That's good," the lawyer said. "I mean, it's not good, but it will help."

She made plans to get a restraining order and told me to change the locks. Of course, I would tragically disappear before I could carry out her instructions.

It was after noon when I left the lawyer's office, my least favorite time of day in Florida. The parking lot was baking in the harsh sun. It showed all the cracks in the buildings and the sidewalks – and in my lips and skin. I won't miss this, I thought. Not one bit.

I wanted to treat myself to a special dress for this evening, my coming out. I strolled along Las Olas Boulevard, where all the smart shops were. The windows glowed with dresses in dramatic black and fabulous colors.

Black, I thought. Black was the right choice when you're going to the dark side.

I entered the cool shop. A young saleswoman, who looked like a thinner version of Dawn, was talking to another clerk. They didn't look up when I came in. They didn't notice me.

"Excuse me," I said. "May I have some help?"

The two young women smirked and rolled their eyes, and I understood why Marissa had killed her salesclerk. If I had more time in Lauderdale, I'd come back for this one.

But I didn't. I bought the first dress I tried on. It didn't fit quite right. I could see my drooping back in the mirror, the little rolls of fat at my waist. But they would be gone soon. In my new life, this dress would be spectacular.

As I left, I knew I'd made the right decision. Not about the dress. About my life. I would be invisible, but it would be my choice.

I would be powerful.

I would be beautiful forever.

I would get the blood back. It would flow again. It would flow into me, and I would feel the ecstasy. I would not be young, but I didn't want to be young. The young were vulnerable, trusting, hurting. I never wanted to feel that way again.

I sat in my condo and thought about the rest of the night and the beginning of my new life.

When the sky began to bleed red, I walked once more through my condo, saying good-bye to all my things. It would be easy to give them up. I sat on the balcony until the sun set and the sky turned dark velvet. Then I dressed for my final night.

At midnight, I met Michael down by the docks. He was frighteningly beautiful.

"Have you made your choice?" he asked.

"I choose you," I said.

He kissed me. "I'm so glad," he whispered. "Everyone is waiting for you. Who will be your first kill?"

"Dawn, Eric's office manager. The police will find her bloodless body outside his clinic."

"What about your husband?"

"I'll let him live. It will be fun to see how he explains his drained and dead girlfriend and his missing wife. I'll be gone, but I won't take anything with me – no money from our bank account, no stocks, not even my jewelry. I'll follow the trial on the Internet from the south of France."

Michael smiled. "I'm sure we'll all be entertained by the drama," he said. "Happy birthday, Katherine."

Death of a Condo Commando

Condo commandos and cockroaches are common Florida pests, but if we had our choice, we'd rather deal with palmetto bugs. Condo commandos are as persistent as a summer cold, and just as welcome.

Bang! Bang! Bang!

Death was knocking on our door.

Josh and I didn't know that. We saw something almost as unwelcome as the Grim Reaper – Mrs. Crane, the condo commando. She looked harmless in her square-heeled white shoes and sundress, but she was the most feared woman at the Keelhouse Condo in Fort Lauderdale.

No one ever called Mrs. Crane by her first name. I never saw any sign of a Mr. Crane, not even a wedding photo. The woman was probably baptized Mrs.

"Who's knocking?" Josh asked me. He looked guilt stricken.

I checked the front door peephole and whispered, "It's Mrs. Crane."

"Damn," my husband said. "What if she catches us? She'll know we're doing something illegal."

"You hide in there," I said, pushing him through the bathroom doorway.

"Whatever you do, don't let her in. Take a shower or something."

I waited for him to snap the lock before I opened our front door.

Mrs. Crane was only five feet tall and built like a Humvee. It didn't help that she was wearing bright yellow. The condo commando was a sturdy sixty-two years old. She rolled into our place without waiting for an invitation.

"Do you know water from your kitchen is ruining Millie's ceiling?" Mrs. Crane had flat yellow eyes like a lizard, and her orange hair looked like it was on fire.

"What water? Millie didn't call to say she was having a problem."

"I told her I'd handle it," Mrs. Crane said. "Millie is too nice." She smiled, a sight that sent shivers through the condo residents. "I know the rules. I'm on the board. My committee approves all condo changes and repairs."

"Uh, right." I agreed with her. I had no other choice.

"And your condo is leaking water into Millie's kitchen ceiling," she said.

"It can't be us," I said. "The dishwasher and washing machine are turned off. I'm not washing any pots in the sink."

"I hear water running right now," Mrs. Crane said. It was an accusation, not a statement.

"Josh is taking a shower."

Mrs. Crane eyed the closed bathroom door. I was relieved that Josh had locked it.

The tanklike woman tried the doorknob, then abruptly marched into the kitchen and threw open our utility closet door. Water gushed out and puddled at her feet.

"Ah-hah!" she said, as if she'd found a naked man hiding in there. "Exactly what I thought. It's your water heater."

I was stunned. Another repair. Another debt. "I don't understand," I said. I stared at our hot water heater as if it had turned into an ogre. It was about to devour our last paycheck.

"Your water heater has a hole in it," she said. "You need a new one. It's rusted through. Happens all the time. Especially in this climate."

"Oh, no," I said. "Not now. Josh and I were just leaving for Key Largo. It's our first vacation in more than a year."

"Looks like you're not going," Mrs. Crane said, her face pink with malicious pleasure.

"We'll get a plumber," I said.

"Won't find one on a Saturday," she said. "And if you do, you won't get the permit to put in a new water heater until Monday. Looks like your vacation is cancelled."

"But—"

"And you're responsible for the damage to Millie's ceiling. Her ceiling is bowed with water and the popcorn is falling off in clumps. Looks like a lot of damage to me. You'll need a special contractor to respray the popcorn on that ceiling. You can't do a decent patch job on popcorn, you know."

I silently cursed the inventor of the popcorn ceiling. That spray-on substance made too many Florida ceilings look like they'd been daubed with cottage cheese.

"I'll make sure Millie sends you a bill for repairs," Mrs. Crane said. She would, too.

"How much do you think this will cost us?" I asked, hoping to hide my despair. Josh and I were already in debt, thanks to the move to this new condo.

"You're looking at a couple thousand dollars," she said. "Unless the water shorted out Millie's kitchen lights. Then it will cost even more."

Mrs. Crane sloshed wet footprints across our living room rug and left without a good-bye. The front door slammed shut.

Josh crept out of the locked bathroom wrapped in his terry robe. He was damp and shivering. "There's no hot water," he said, his teeth chattering in the air-conditioning.

"I know," I said. "Mrs. Crane says our water heater died and leaked all over Millie's ceiling. We're responsible for the damage it did to Millie's condo below us."

"We'd better get a plumber to replace the old heater," he said. "The Saturday rates will kill us. We'll be eating peanut butter for months."

"Mrs. Crane says we'll need a permit from the city and we can't get one until Monday."

"To hell with her," Josh said. "I'm not taking cold showers while she pokes her nose into our business. And I'm not missing our trip. Those vacation days don't carry over into next year. I either go now or wait another whole year."

"It took me months of negotiation to get the same days you did," I said. "I had to work six extra Sundays at the bookstore. My vacation will be gone, too."

Josh was the assistant manager at a Fort Lauderdale tourist hotel. That's how he'd gotten a ridiculously low rate at the Key Largo resort. Otherwise, we couldn't have afforded a vacation.

I called a plumber from the approved condo list. At double-time rates, Jackson agreed to install a new water heater. The plumber didn't mention permits and neither did we. By noon, we had a shiny white water heater squatting in the utility closet. Jackson hauled out the dead water heater and loaded it into his truck. I mopped up the water in the kitchen.

Josh and I were ready to leave for our vacation.

That's when we heard three more knocks.

"It's her again," I whispered in Josh's ear.

"Don't answer the door," he whispered back, and dragged me into the bedroom. Unfortunately, it was only to talk about Mrs. Crane.

"We can't keep her out," I said. "She has a duplicate key. We had to give the association our house key at closing."

"She can't barge in any time she wants," Josh said. "This is America."

"Keelhouse Condo is another country," I said. "The condo documents say her committee has the right to inspect any repair work. We signed a statement saying we'd read the documents and agreed to the conditions."

"But she has to make an appointment," Josh said. "It says that, too."

We could hear Mrs. Crane rattling the front doorknob.

"She ignores the rules she doesn't like," I said. "She walks in on everyone at the condo. She caught Mrs. Zimmerman in the shower and Mr. Driver without his false teeth."

"I didn't know Mr. Driver had false teeth," Josh said.

"It used to be the best-kept secret in the condo."

"The deadbolt is on," Josh said. "She doesn't have a key to that. She can't spend the whole day on our doorstep."

Mrs. Crane spent an hour, which was long enough. Every few minutes the woman would pound on the door and demand to come in. Then she'd rattle our doorknob. She was surprisingly strong for a woman in her sixties.

"Please go away," I shouted through the door. In case there really had been a long-ago Mr. Crane I added, "Josh and I are newlyweds. We need some private time."

"Did she used to sell vacuum cleaners?" Josh whispered when Mrs. Crane launched another assault on our front door.

"I think she was a telemarketer in another life," I said. "She is persistent. She spies on everybody in the building. How did she miss the plumber lugging a hot water heater on the elevator?"

"I don't care, but it's about time we had some good luck," Josh said.

The door handle rattled again. The deadbolt held.

By one o'clock, the sweltering Florida sun forced Mrs. Crane back into her condo on the fifth floor.

"Can we go now?" Josh asked.

"Let's give her half an hour," I said.

She was back in twenty minutes. This time, she didn't try to gain entrance. An envelope was slipped under our door.

"I think we got one of her famous warning notices," I said.

Mrs. Crane was notorious for sending threatening letters on what looked like condo association letterhead. Actually, she made her own letterhead on her computer. This one said:

"You have thirty (30) days to repair your defective hot water heater and allow the condo committee to inspect said repairs in your unit, as per section 12(b) of the Keelhouse Condo Association documents. You are also responsible for any repairs to Unit 6265, directly below you, that were caused by your defective water heater.

"If you do not comply, the association has the right to fine you one hundred dollars ($100) per day until you are in compliance. The Keelhouse Condo Association also has the right to repossess your condo unit upon nonpayment of fines."

"She's signed it 'sincerely,'" Josh said.

"Oh, I'm sure she's sincere," I said. "What time is it?"

"One-thirty," Josh said, nuzzling my neck. "We can be at the resort in an hour and a half. We have a king bed."

"That sounds heavenly, but what if Mrs. Crane has staked out the elevator? Or her spy, Clarence the security guard, is working this afternoon?"

"Clarence doesn't work on Saturdays," Josh said, giving me another kiss. "The weekend guard doesn't like her."

"How do we keep her from doing a surprise inspection of our condo while we're out of town?" I asked.

"The deadbolt, remember?" Josh said. "And we didn't give the condo association the key. It's only seven flights down the fire stairs. We can escape without Mrs. Crane finding us. How many suitcases did you pack?"

"Just one. My sandals and bikini don't weigh much."

We sneaked down the hot, dusty fire stairs to the parking garage without encountering Mrs. Crane or Clarence. We threw our bags into our ancient Toyota and were soon on the Florida Turnpike, bound for Key Largo.

"I didn't think we'd ever get away," I said, and stretched. I could feel the tension ebbing away the farther we fled Fort Lauderdale. "Do you think Mrs. Crane has any children?"

"I don't think she has any life," Josh said. "She doesn't work. That committee is her only entertainment. She prowls the condo looking for trouble. She doesn't go anywhere for the holidays and never has any guests. Millie told us Mrs. Crane made the Gonzales family put their parents in a motel at Christmas because she said their condo was over the occupancy limit when they had holiday guests."

"She forced poor Mrs. Daniels to give up her cat because pets are against the rules," I said. "We even signed a petition saying we didn't care if she had Pumpkin in her unit. That cat never bothered anyone."

"Mrs. Crane said there could be no exceptions if the condo documents were going to be valid," Josh said. "I guess that's legally true, but everyone turned a blind eye to Mrs. Daniels's cat. She was a sweet old lady."

"I don't think she died of a heart attack when they took her cat away," I said. "I think she died of a broken heart. She had that cat fifteen years."

"Too bad Mrs. Crane doesn't have a heart to break," Josh said. Then he snickered.

"What's so funny?" I asked.

"Millie told me about the blonde on the boat scandal. Mrs. Crane patrols the docks at night, looking for people who are illegally living aboard their boats. She stopped by the Jamesons' s new thirty-foot sailboat and saw Jack with a blonde. Mrs. Crane screamed that Jack was cheating on his wife. Turned out his wife had dyed her hair a new color."

"That hasn't stopped Mrs. Crane from her nightly rounds along the condo docks," I said.

"Nothing stops her," Josh agreed.

We dissed Mrs. Crane for another twenty miles before Josh turned the subject back to what had been gnawing at us since that fatal knock on the door. "What are we going to do when we get back home?"

"We're going to clean up the illegal mess," I said, "get as much of the evidence out of the condo as we can, then make an appointment to let Mrs. Crane in and inspect the utility closet."

"What about the hot water heater permit?" Josh asked.

"I'll tell her the plumber said he'd handle it. We're using a condo-approved vendor, so Jackson will know how to deal with her. Besides, for what he charged for that new water heater, he should suffer a little, too."

"Can we really afford this condo?"

We'd been asking ourselves that question for six months. Josh and I had been married for five years, since we'd graduated from college. Even with our two salaries, there was barely enough left for our regular Saturday date night. We still had student loans, car payments, and huge credit card bills. But when the housing market took a dive, it was cheaper to buy than to rent. My late Aunt Marie left me twenty thousand dollars, and that cinched it. We started looking for a bargain condo, one that cost less than our apartment.

We found a spectacular deal at Keelhouse Condo. The previous owner was having money problems and needed to sell his condo fast. Keelhouse was in the midst of a two-year renovation project, so Robert's condo didn't show well, as the real estate agent said.

Worse, Robert had painted the inside a flat gray, even the bathrooms. It was like walking into a basement – on the seventh floor. But I saw the possibilities from the moment we entered the door. The living room had eight-feet-tall windows with a stunning view of the ocean to the east and the Intracoastal Waterway below. The master bedroom had a big walk-in closet. The other bedroom would make a fine home office. I thought the place was perfect.

Josh wasn't as sure. He said the rooms were so bright he couldn't watch TV with the sun glaring inside, and it stayed light until after eight o'clock in the summer. Blackout curtains for the huge windows would cost a fortune.

Our real estate agent, Marcia, came up with the solution. "Do you need two walk-in closets?" she asked.

"Not really," I said. "We only have one closet right now. We'd like a little more room, but we don't need that much."

"Then why don't you take the dressing room that's connected to the bedroom you're making into a home office, and turn it into a media room?" Marcia suggested. She whipped out a tape measure. "Take out this double vanity and the wall mirror and the dressing room is a good size – twelve feet by twenty. I don't think this closet wall – she rapped on it and got a nice hollow thud – "is weight-bearing. Remove it and you have a cozy, windowless media room. If you ever sell the condo, it's perfect as a baby's bedroom or nanny's room."

"Works for me," Josh said.

"The only problem," Marcia said, "is that the condo board may not approve the changes."

"If they know about them," Josh said.

"I do know a reasonable contractor," Marcia said. "My other clients love him. Larry would never say a word."

We met with the contractor before we closed the deal. Larry confirmed that he could do the job. "But I do know that old lady, Mrs. Crane," he said. "She will never give you permission."

"Any way we can do it so she won't find out?" I asked. "She'll hear you tearing out the walls. That will be noisy."

"We can make as much noise as we want on weekdays," Larry said. "Until six o'clock at night, we could have a brass band playing in that condo and nobody could do a thing. If you hire me to do the painting and minor repairs, I can do your other project. It's in my best interests to keep my mouth shut. I don't want that old biddy on my back, either."

"How do we remove the debris?" Josh asked.

"You can carry most of it out in your own packing boxes after you move in," Larry said. "There's a Dumpster in the guest parking lot for the condo construction. If you dump broken wallboard, molding, and other junk at night, no one will know. Some of it I can cart out, like the mirror we're taking off that wall, the closet doors, and the marble vanity. We can say you're getting a new vanity. That's considered redecoration and it's legal."

"That's the truth," I said, righteously. "We are getting a new sink." We were relocating it to the second bathroom, instead of having it in the dressing room.

"What do you think?" Josh had asked me.

"Let's go for it."

And so we did. We closed on our dream condo a month later. Robert the owner appeared at the closing, took our money and promptly moved to Majorca.

Once we moved in, we understood why he'd left with no forwarding address. Robert had been a bad home handyman. He had repaired a broken chain inside the toilet tank with duct tape. The night the kitchen ceiling started smoking, we realized that Robert had also done his own wiring. That cost us another two thousand.

While Larry was working on the kitchen wiring, he also took

down Robert's ugly gold ceiling fans in the living room and put in top hats – recessed lighting. It was illegal in most of this building, but it looked terrific. We were now five thousand over our moving budget, and that didn't include the new couch or the sound system for Josh's media room.

The work on the secret media room continued every weekday. Each time one of us left the condo, we carried out a box of debris and emptied it in a Dumpster somewhere along the nearby commercial strip.

It was surprising how much construction trash Larry tore out of the small room. It nearly filled our entire home office. Chunks of wallboard seemed to multiply if we left them alone overnight. Dust settled on everything. All our furniture was draped in plastic.

We were down to four boxes now, plus two eight-foot metal strips that went over the top of the former closet. Those were going to be difficult to sneak out. We couldn't hide them in trash bags or boxes. They were too thick and heavy to bend.

Our time in Key Largo was over too soon. We ate yellowtail snapper and real Key lime pie, which is yellow instead of lime colored. We took walks along the beach and admired the blue-green waters of the Gulf of Mexico. We played in the pool's waterfall. We took a tour on the African Queen, the real boat from the old movie.

I'd brought four mysteries to read – my favorite kind of book – but barely got through one chapter. Josh and I remembered why we got married in the first place. I laughed at Josh's jokes again, and he ran his fingers through my long, blonde hair. We spent a lot of time in bed.

Saturday, there was a knock on our hotel room door. The waiter delivered our breakfast of toast and eggs.

"So tell me," I asked Josh. "Why is soggy toast and lukewarm eggs better than anything we can make at home?"

"Because the hotel has better cooks?" he asked.

I tossed a pillow at him, and soon we were in a full-blown pillow fight, and that turned into something more interesting. Before we knew it, the hotel manager was on the phone, telling us it was two hours past checkout time.

I was glad it was raining when we left. We wouldn't be missing any sun time by the pool. Josh and I had to return to the condo and face Mrs. Crane.

We drove through a gray, dreary rain to Keelhouse Condo. Our old car began bucking and rattling as we approached Fort Lauderdale. It chugged up the parking garage ramp and died in our space, the dashboard lit with warning lights. Smoke poured from under the hood.

"I think our car is shot," Josh said.

More bills.

If the car hadn't died, I wonder if Mrs. Crane would still be alive. Another debt for car repairs was the last straw. Maybe the message we had waiting from Millie downstairs would have made a difference. But we didn't get a chance to hear our phone messages. We were still carrying in our suitcases when Mrs. Crane materialized on our doorstep, arms folded.

"Where did you get those top hats in your living room?" she asked.

"Huh?" Josh said.

Mrs. Crane stepped over our suitcases and walked into our condo, uninvited as usual. She pointed to our ceiling.

"Those are illegal," she said.

"Uh, they were installed by the previous owner," I lied.

Mrs. Crane sniffed. "Where did Robert get a permit? Top hats are forbidden by the city code in this section of the building."

"You'll have to ask him," I said, my voice rising to a terrified squeak.

"I haven't seen Robert recently," she said.

"I think he moved to Majorca," I said, relieved to tell the truth. There was little chance Mrs. Crane would track him down.

"And what about that room?" she said.

"What room?" I said, the dread rising in my gut.

She threw open the door to our home office and pointed to the wreckage of the walk-in closet. "What are you doing in here? You don't have permission from the condo association for a major change."

"You don't have permission to search our condo, either," I said.

"I have the right in the condo documents," she said. "You thought you could lock me out with a deadbolt, but you didn't bother to lock your kitchen window. I opened it and walked right in."

I could see her footprints in the construction dust.

"Now I see why you wanted to keep me out," Mrs. Crane said. "You will restore this dressing room to the way it was when you bought this place. At your own expense. If it's the last thing I do!"

It was. Josh picked up the long strip of metal and whacked her on the head. Her eyes got funny and she dropped on the floor on her back.

"Holy shit," Josh said. "I didn't mean to do that."

We knelt beside her and felt for a pulse.

"I think she's dead," I said.

"No, no," Josh said. "She can't be dead."

"Josh, she's not breathing."

"I guess I'll call the police and turn myself in," he said.

"No! You didn't mean to kill her. There must be a way out of this."

"It was an accident," Josh said.

"Of course it was, but how can we prove that?"

"You read mysteries," he said.

I did. I paced the apartment and looked at the afternoon sun on the water.

"The water!" I said. "She patrols the docks. What if she fell into the water? We'll wait until late tonight. Security leaves at midnight. We'll carry her out."

"How? She's heavy," Josh said.

"We still have that big wardrobe box left over from the move," I said. "And Larry left behind the dolly he uses to carry out heavy things."

"Brilliant! We'll put her in the box now," he said.

"No, we can't have the blood pool in the wrong place. That's an important forensic clue that could work against us. Let her stay on the floor until we're ready to move her."

We threw an old sheet over Mrs. Crane, then spent the rest of the night pacing and unpacking our few things. We did a load of laundry. We checked e-mail and our phone messages. One was from Millie downstairs.

"Listen, kids," Millie said. "Don't worry about my kitchen ceiling. I always hated popcorn and you've given me the excuse to get rid of it. My homeowner's insurance will cover most of it. It was time for a change."

"See," I said to Josh. "Not everyone in Keelhouse is a jerk."

I scrambled some eggs for dinner, but neither of us had any appetite.

It was almost three in the morning when we loaded Mrs. Crane into the wardrobe box and hauled her out with the dolly. She fit easily into the freight elevator. Josh wheeled the box to the edge of the dock. It was silent in the cool, moonless night. Little clouds of mist drifted across the water.

Josh tipped the box into the water and Mrs. Crane slid out with hardly a splash. Just a "blub," and then she was gone.

We hauled the big wardrobe box to the Dumpster, flattened it, and threw it on top. The Dumpster was almost full. Then we loaded up the dolly with the last boxes of debris. I carried out the two long metal strips. We dropped them on top of the wardrobe box, as quietly as possible. No lights came on in the nearby condos. Our neighbors never noticed.

Josh staggered off to bed. I cleaned up all the dust and the little bit of blood from Mrs. Crane.

The next morning, the construction Dumpster with the only evidence against us went off to the landfill.

Mrs. Crane did not show up for the board meeting Thursday night. Her unexcused absence was noted in the minutes. No one asked where she was. Everyone silently hoped she would never return. There were no inquiries and no missing person report. Her spot on the condo committee was filled by Millie. The other condo residents were thrilled. Someone started a story that Mrs. Crane had gone for a round the world cruise, which was true, in a weird way.

Mrs. Crane's body was never found. Josh and I suspected she'd drifted down the Intracoastal and out to sea. Her condo mortgage and fees were paid by monthly automatic withdrawals until her considerable bank account ran out nearly three years later. She was declared legally dead. The association took over her condo for nonpayment of fees and assessments.

We feel she would have wanted it that way.

After the Fall

A friend told me about a coffee taster who could be fired for smoking a single cigarette – it would ruin his taste buds forever. And the man walking down a Manhattan street when a woman fell twenty-one stories and landed at his feet. These two tales became "After the Fall," where justice went out the window.

Mort was walking down the street Monday morning when a woman landed splat! on the sidewalk, right in front of him.

She burst like a water balloon, and Mort was splashed with a tidal wave of blood and little dots of gray-white that he couldn't identify. Then he could and his stomach heaved. He was already dizzy from the coppery smell of the blood. He was starting a sickly sway when a man in a dirty white apron ran out of Sammy D's Deli and said, "Whoa, pal, where are you hurt? You been shot? Don't worry, we've called an ambulance."

"It's not my blood," Mort said. "It's hers." He pointed to the small twisted figure on the sidewalk. That steadied him somehow, and he was able to go on without fainting or throwing up.

"Jesus," the deli man said. "She must have jumped."

They both looked up and saw curtains flapping out of an open window far, far above them.

"You're darn lucky," the deli man said. "A few inches more and she would have landed on you. She would have killed you dead."

The EMS people told Mort he was lucky, too, as they took him to the hospital, where he was scrubbed down with a horrible harsh disinfectant that clogged his sensitive nasal passages. It smelled of cherries, like some perverted candy.

"Sorry," the nurse said when Mort complained of the smell, "but we have to do this for your protection. Bodies are crawling with bacteria."

Mort felt queasy all over again at the unseen horrors invading his sensitive skin, burrowing into his nose and distorting his taste buds. For Mort Heffern was an ordinary man in every way but one. He was average height: five feet seven. He was ordinary looking, with a little round paunch and small brown eyes. His thin, tan hair was receding. Well, to be honest, it had already receded.

Yet ordinary Mort enjoyed many extraordinary delights, including a luscious blonde wife, a five-bedroom house in Nyack, New York, and a bottle-green Range Rover, because of one unusual feature. Mort's sense of taste was superbly sensitive. It was so sensitive that he was a coffee taster for a top New York firm. Mort's taste buds could distinguish Kona (which he considered overrated) from Kenya AA. He could even tell you the slope where the coffee beans grew.

To protect his precious taste buds and their ally, his nose, Mort never smoked. He'd only had one cigarette in his life, back when he was sixteen, before he decided to become a taster and forsake smoking for the rarer and more exquisite pleasure of tasting.

Sometimes, he thought about that one smoke. But mostly he thought about all the good things his taste buds brought him because he didn't smoke.

Naturally, he did not drink. Nor did he wear cologne or use scented soap, and he did not permit his luscious wife, Jasmine, to use them, either. When he first met her, Jasmine was as fragrant as her namesake flower, but he couldn't tolerate living with such a strong scent. She gave it up for him. Mort lavished Jasmine with jewelry to console her for her loss.

Now his taste buds and nose were clogged with the ugly scent of the woman's death and the overpowering odor of that disgusting cherry disinfectant. Mort had no idea what the woman looked like in real life. He caught only a flash of pale arms, flailing legs, and wide, horrified eyes, before she hit the pavement and made a splash.

He didn't mean to be flip about the woman's terrible death. He was shaken, that's all. He called the office of Percardian and Sons from the hospital and explained why he wouldn't be at work that day. Mr. Percardian Senior was sympathetic.

"Take a couple of days off," he said. "Shock can throw off your taste buds."

Mort slept badly that night. He couldn't get that splat! out of his mind. The sound was like something out of a cartoon, except that a woman had exploded like a ripe watermelon on the sidewalk and showered him with her blood.

Finally, after tossing and turning and awakening Jasmine several times, Mort got up and sat in the living room. He wished he had a cigarette. He could see it, glowing in the dark night. He could taste it. But he didn't. He showered three times, trying to remove the smell of disinfectant. But his powerful smelling and tasting apparatus could still detect the faint traces of the cloying candylike scent.

At six a.m., when the newspaper arrived, Mort looked for a story about the dead woman. It was on page six. He learned that she was Patricia Henley Daniels, forty-seven, a special education teacher. She was married to Decameron Daniels, fifty-one, a stockbroker with Wayne-Symmons. The accident occurred at about seven-thirty Monday morning. Her husband told police that he had been dressing in their bedroom when he heard a noise and noticed the living room window was open. He said his wife had been depressed about her father's recent death from cancer. Patricia had jumped or fallen twenty-one stories to her death.

In her photo, Patricia looked small and pretty. She had large dark eyes, curly dark hair and a friendly smile. She looked like the sort of person you would want to teach your child. Mort felt sad that she had ended her useful life on a Manhattan sidewalk.

Mort was also mentioned in the news story: "Police said the deceased had fallen close to a passerby on the sidewalk, Mort Heffern, forty-two, of Nyack. Heffern was not injured."

"Not injured" indeed, thought Mort, as he replayed that awful splat! in his mind and smelled the odor of cherry disinfectant. His hands shook so badly the newspaper rattled.

He stayed home that day as his boss, Mr. Percardian, advised. Mort was pale and tired and everything still tasted of hospital disinfectant. He showered every hour, praying the insinuating cherry scent would leave his nostrils.

He ate sparingly, hoping the blandness of white meat of turkey and whole wheat bread would restore his tortured taste buds. But under the soothing taste of prime turkey breast he caught the corrupting cherry tang. Even sharp English mustard on his sandwich did not remove it.

He tried to nap between his several showers, but every time he closed his eyes, he saw the flailing limbs of Patricia Henley Daniels. Now the dead woman had a face, and he saw those dark eyes, pleading with him to save her in the last dreadful seconds of her life. Then he heard the splat!

"Are you still carrying on about that jumper?" Jasmine was filled with wifely concern. "You should be glad she didn't land on you. You're lucky."

"Lucky!" Mort snapped, his patience at an end. "Everyone keeps saying I was lucky. I was nearly killed. I keep seeing that poor woman hitting the sidewalk. It was awful."

"Poor baby," Jasmine said. "Maybe you need some sleeping pills or something."

But Mort couldn't take sleeping pills. They made his tongue feel as if it was covered with fur, and that interfered with his tasting.

Jasmine made his favorite comfort food that night, homemade tomato-vegetable soup. But the bits of vegetables and rice reminded him of the odd bits and specks the nurse had cleaned off him. And the soup was blood red. He pushed his bowl away, feeling nauseated. Jasmine looked hurt, but bravely tried to understand.

"Not hungry, baby?" She kissed his broad forehead. "You must try to eat something. I got your favorite dessert."

She returned with another soup bowl, this one filled with Cherry Garcia ice cream. He could smell the revolting cherry odor before she walked through the dining room door. His stomach gave a mighty heave and he barely made it to the bathroom in time. Patricia's death resulted in another tragedy. Cherry Garcia had been ruined for Mort for all time, and he mourned the loss.

Mort couldn't sleep that night, either. Or rather, he would doze off until he saw Patricia in front of him, helplessly clawing the air in the last futile seconds of her life. He would hear the splat! her body made and wake up, panting and sweating, sheets twisted around him, with Jasmine blinking unhappily in the light he'd so rudely turned on.

Once more he got up and sat in the living room, staring out the window, wishing for a cigarette, until the morning paper arrived. Today, there were interviews with Patricia's friends and colleagues saying what a fine person she was. There was more news: The police were investigating her death as "suspicious," although the story didn't say why.

Mort spent another day at home, showering, sipping bottled water, and nibbling white meat of turkey. His resilient taste buds were beginning to recover. The dreadful stink of cherries was retreating from his nostrils. Jasmine gave him the comfort of her sweet, unscented self, but did not fix him any food that day. He still heard the splat! in his dreams, and he still sat up most of the night, waiting for dawn and wishing for a cigarette.

It was an exhausted Mort who went out on his porch for the paper that morning. But he woke up when he saw Patricia's name on the front page. The story said the police had arrested Patricia's husband, Decameron, for her murder.

The police said Patricia had not been depressed about her father's death, as her husband claimed. Her friends said she rarely saw the bad-tempered old man and was pleasantly surprised when he'd left her a million dollars. Six days before her death, Patricia discovered that Decameron was having an affair with a woman at his brokerage firm. Patricia had been planning to dump her unfaithful husband without a penny.

The police said Decameron had killed his wife so that he could inherit her million dollars and marry his cookie. They found suspicious-looking scratches on Decameron's hands and arms that indicated Patricia had fought for her life.

The paper showed a photo of the woman Decameron was supposedly having the affair with. She was a blonde of about forty, who looked like a B-movie adulteress. Mort thought she was cheap and obvious compared to pretty little Patricia. As far as Mort was concerned, Decameron had no taste.

But Mort did. His delicate taste buds had recovered, despite his tiredness. He was ready to return to work. But when he got to the block where it happened, he heard that horrible wet splat! rend the air and saw Patricia's windmilling limbs again. He walked two blocks out of his way to avoid the awful vision and ran smack into a coffee cart featuring warm cherry Danish. The smell was so unnerving, he went yet another block out of his way. He arrived at work half an hour late, jumpy as a bishop in a brothel.

His hands shook and he craved a cigarette so badly he could taste it. He knew it would destroy his career, but he thought only a soothing smoke could blot out the horrible splat! and erase the smell of that sickening cherry disinfectant.

After six more sleepless nights, Mort gave in. He drove to an all-night convenience store and found the same brand he'd smoked at sixteen: Lucky Strikes. It was three a.m. He went outside and lit up on his back porch. As he breathed in the first smoke, he felt the nicotine course through him and got a buzz he hadn't felt in years. A pleasant buzz, better than coffee, more soothing. Yet he felt more alive at the same time. It was just the jolt his system needed. He watched the white smoke curl upward to the stars, and smelled only burning tobacco and cool night air. The vile odor of cherries was gone.

Of course, he could never smoke again. He knew that. He finished his cigarette and buried the butt in the garden. Then he washed his pajamas and showered and scrubbed his teeth until the cigarette smell was gone. Finally, exhausted, he fell into a dreamless sleep.

At breakfast, he craved another cigarette with his morning paper. He read a story that said Patricia's husband Decameron had hired Jasper J. Cowell as his attorney. Cowell said his client was innocent and he would prove it.

Mort was afraid. Cowell had a reputation for twisting facts and confusing witnesses so that his guilty clients went free. Poor Patricia would never receive justice and neither would Mort. Patricia's death had shattered his nerves, upset his delicate tasting apparatus, and ruined any enjoyment of cherries forever.

Mort worried that Patricia's husband would escape punishment, as so many wealthy wife killers had before him. The cigarette craving grew worse. At lunch, he went to La Jeunesse, to treat himself to a civilized French meal. But alas, the day's special was duck breast in cherry sauce, and the restaurant was permeated with the fowl odor. Mort left and had a bland turkey sandwich from the coffee shop in his office building. He still wanted a cigarette. He wanted it at one-thirty and at three and at six and ten that night. He didn't give in to his craving until two o'clock in the morning.

As he puffed on the cigarette in his garden, Mort promised himself he'd never smoke at the office.

He kept that promise one week.

It was Mr. Percardian Senior who caught Mort on the third-floor landing of the fire stairs, blowing smoke out the window.

"I am sorry," Mr. Percardian said. "I know that you have been under a strain recently. But you know the rules. Smoking destroys the taste buds. Even one cigarette is enough to ruin them forever, and from the yellow stains on your teeth and fingers, this is not your first cigarette. When I noticed them, I suspected as much, and followed you. I must let you go."

Mort left the office where he'd worked for more than seventeen years, engulfed in shame and rage. He was no longer a coffee taster and he could never be one again. Mr. Percardian would see to that. Mort had loved his job. He was not one more cog in the great mercantile machine of New York, but a big wheel in his world. Now he was a jobless nobody. His beautiful young wife Jasmine, used to the little luxuries he could provide, would leave him when he didn't have any money.

But she did not.

"Don't worry, baby," she said. "I know you're disappointed, but now you can work for my brother's dotcom company. You'll make a ton of money, even more than you did as a coffee taster. And I can wear perfume again."

Mort went to work for his brother-in-law, a grinning dipwad who called him Buddy, just like he called everyone else, because he couldn't remember names. Mort made more money than he had as a coffee taster. But he was unhappy. He hated this meaningless work. He couldn't even drink the office coffee. Diptwit bought it in bulk from an office supply company. It tasted like warm mulch.

Mort missed the prestige of his old job. Decameron the wife murderer had a lot to answer for. He'd killed Mort's career. He'd murdered Mort's sleep. Mort was awakened by that fatal splat! at least once a night. Then he'd sit up the rest of the night smoking.

Mort followed the approaching murder trial in the papers. Decameron's lawyer was using every possible delaying tactic and dirty trick, but the prosecuting attorney promised that the wife killer would get life in prison.

Good. Maybe then Mort would once more sleep easy. Maybe he would get through a day without sneaking around for a cigarette like a teenager. Mort couldn't smoke in his idiot brother-in-law's office, because it was bad for the computers. He sneaked smokes around the Dumpster with half a dozen other nicotine renegades, his sensitive nose assaulted by the stench of garbage, until the healing cigarette smoke blotted out the odor.

Mort returned home each night to find his wife drenched in jasmine scent. The bathroom reeked of jasmine soap, lotion, and bubble bath, and his delicate nostrils itched in protest. But Jasmine refused to give up her perfume, no matter how many blue boxes from Tiffany's Mort brought her.

"It was one thing to give up perfume for your job, Mort. But now, you want me to give it up because you're so sensitive. Well, I'm sensitive, too." Jasmine looked mean when she said that. He didn't remember giving her that tennis bracelet on her shapely arm.

"Where did you get that . . ." he started to say "bracelet," but then realized she might tell him, and changed his sentence to ". . . scratch on your arm?"

"From my kitten, Puss-Puss." She opened the garage door and out strutted a white hairball with malicious blue eyes. "Puss-Puss is a gift from a friend."

The only thing that Mort hated more than perfume was cats. Jasmine had never had one before. The litter box odor permeated the house, even if Jasmine did keep it in the basement. But Mort was afraid to ask who the cat-giving friend was. Jasmine might tell him. In fact, she seemed to be daring him to ask.

Mort began adding scotch to his nightly smokes. The booze blotted out the olfactory assaults caused by his wife's perfume and her cat. After a few drinks, he didn't even mind the tumbleweeds of cat hair drifting around the house.

He started taking a scotch bottle to work to get him through the boredom of his dotcom days. He couldn't seem to negotiate the garage very well lately, and that caused a couple of little dents on his bottle-green Rover, but he thought they only improved it. A tough vehicle was supposed to have a few dents.

When Jasmine complained, he bought her a red ragtop Eclipse. He did not buy her the crystal pendant that she hung on the ragtop's rearview mirror and he didn't ask where she got it. He was certain she was seeing someone else. He wondered when his marriage would be over.

It ended the night he accidentally ran over Puss-Puss in the driveway.

"I'm sorry, Jasmine, I didn't see the cat," he said, as she cried over the crushed body.

"No," she spat back. "You saw two. You've been drinking for months. I can't take it any more."

The next day, when he came home from his dull dotcom job, his wife left him, or rather, she asked him to leave her. His bags were packed and waiting in the garage. The locks were changed on all the doors. He got a good lawyer. She had a better one.

Jasmine got the house, the ragtop, and a staggering amount of alimony. He couldn't possibly pay it, especially after his nitwit ex-brother-in-law fired him. He didn't care. Jasmine would leave him alone if there was no money. He found out she'd moved in with a car dealer – the same one who sold Mort her red Eclipse.

Mort traded in the bottle-green Range Rover for a 1978 Torino whose main color was Bondo gray, got a cheap apartment, and a job delivering pizzas. Not even gourmet pizzas, but junk food made from frozen dough, canned tomato sauce, and cheese that melted like napalm. The smell revolted his twitching taste buds, but he ate the pizzas, anyway. They were about all he could afford. That and scotch and smokes.

At night, Mort would drink and think about how Decameron the wife killer had ruined his life. He had been a happy man until that scumbag pushed his pretty wife out the window. Mort seethed with the injustice of one man ending two lives with a single push.

Mort arranged his life around Decameron's upcoming murder trial. He delivered pizzas after six p.m. By day he sat in on the trial. Mort and Patricia would have justice at last, and he would see it. At first, Mort was afraid he'd be called as a witness, but fortunately, his drinking and employment history made him too unreliable for either side to use. So he was free to be a spectator.

He looked with horror on the prosecution's exhibit photos of the dead woman, splattered on the sidewalk. Her death was even worse than he dreamed. The photos added new color and depth to his nightmares.

He grew queasy as the experts described just how far twenty-one stories was from window to ground, and how long it would take a body to fall that distance. He thrilled with horror at the patholo-gist's description of what had happened to her body as it hit the sidewalk. Every bone was broken. Every bone.

Mort heard her late father's executor testify about Patricia's in-heritance. Her attorney swore that she had made an appointment to change her will and disinherit her husband. She died before she could keep it.

He saw the prosecution's photos of the scratches on Decameron's hands and arms. Poor little Patricia had fought like a wildcat before her husband threw her out the window. It was terrible. The medical examiner found his skin under her broken nails.

But more terrible were the explanations of the defense. The crafty Cowell had a psychiatrist testify that it was "not uncommon to commit suicide within six weeks of losing a family member." Patricia's father had been dead for one month. The shrink also said that two-thirds of all suicides did not leave a note. Patricia had left no note.

Cowell produced a prescription for Prozac from her family doctor. Mort wished the good doctor did not look so much like a water rat, from his beady eyes to his shaggy gray suit. The man was hostile to the defense, insisting Patricia was "not the victim of a major depressive disorder." When Cowell finished with him, the doctor seemed incompetent.

Then Cowell put the woman Decameron was supposed to be having an affair with on the stand. Hannah Higginsworth looked nothing like her photo in the newspaper. Her mousy brown hair was pulled into an unflattering bun. Her suit was inexpensive brown polyester. It turned her complexion an ugly mud color. Her figure was positively maternal. Her nails were short and unpainted. Hannah said she was a victim of vicious office gossip and wept on the stand.

Mort knew the slick lawyer had pulled another of his tricks. He'd dressed Hannah like a frump and ordered her to gain weight. You could imagine her making cookies for the church bake sale, not hunting husbands.

Especially not Patricia's husband. On the stand he looked so smooth, so sincere, so handsome, that Mort knew Decameron had been rehearsed better than a Broadway actor.

The prosecutor could not break him. Yes, Decameron had scratches on his hands and arms. He also had them on his back. His wife had made passionate love to him on the last morning of her life, then said, "Hold me one more time." Decameron thought she meant, "Hold me before I leave for work." He did not realize he was listening to her last wish.

A single manly tear made its way down his face. Decameron bravely ignored it. He loved his wife, he insisted. He would never kill her. He could not imagine having an affair with that woman, Hannah. He said her name with a sneer.

Cowell introduced photos of Decameron's back, slashed with scratches. Cowell claimed these were passion scars made by Patricia. She'd also scratched his hands and arms. Decameron said he did not tell the police about them when he was arrested because he was in shock. How could he remember a few scratches when his beloved wife was dead?

Mort thought that argument was clever, but flawed. The defense couldn't prove the scratches on Decameron's back were made by Patricia. Any woman could have made them any time – even Hannah before she cut her nails. Surely no one was buying that story?

Mort glanced at the jury. The women were smiling at Decameron. The men were nodding their heads in agreement.

At that moment, Mort knew there would be no justice for Patricia or for himself. The prosecutor's inept cross-examination guaranteed it. Mort would never again have a peaceful night's sleep. He had lost his exceptional job, his desirable wife, and his handsome house, all because Decameron had tossed tiny Patricia out a window. One splat! and Mort's own dreams were dashed.

Mort did not wait around the courthouse for the not guilty verdict. He did not want to see the smile of triumph on Decameron's face. As it was, he saw it in the newspaper the next morning.

Mort spent the next month in a cigarette and scotch fog, but even those could not blot out the Technicolor re-enactments of Patricia's last moments. Somehow, he held onto his pizza delivery job. When the debauched fog cleared, he decided if the law could not provide justice, then he would deliver it to Decameron's door.

He spent another month watching Decameron and learning his habits. The killer still lived in the same co-op on the twenty-first floor, but not alone. A lush blonde went in and out as if she lived there, too.

It took a while before Decameron recognized her as the maternal mud-colored brunette who cried on the witness stand. Hannah had lost weight, so that her figure was now curvaceous. Her curves were cuddled in colorful Escada suits. He knew the designer, because his own curvaceous ex-wife used to wear the same suits. Hannah's hair was now a stylish blonde. Her sensible shoes were replaced by spike heels. Hannah was definitely home wrecker material.

She stuck close by her man. Hannah rarely went out without Decameron. She wore him on her arm as if he was another flashy accessory. Mort noticed only one pattern. Every Tuesday night, without fail, Hannah left the apartment at eight p.m. and did not return until midnight. That was Mort's window of opportunity.

He decided Decameron would die next Tuesday night. He was not going to enjoy Patricia's money and Hannah's splendors much longer. Mort would see to that. He would have justice in four days.

Once he decided to kill Decameron, Mort slept better. In fact, for the first time since poor Patricia died, he began sleeping all night through, without that awful splat!

He gave up the booze and cigarettes. He wanted his mind clear the moment he killed Decameron. He wanted his wonderful olfactory apparatus to be working again. He wanted to smell Decameron's fear. He wanted to taste his triumph as the body went out the window.

Mort carefully plotted every detail. On Tuesday night, he drove into Manhattan, dressed in his pizza delivery uniform, which made him virtually invisible. He even found a legal parking space, which he took as a sign that God had smiled on his mission. He saw Hannah leave at eight o'clock. At eight-fifteen, the bored doorman buzzed in Mort. He went up to the twenty-first floor and knocked on Decameron's door.

"Pizza!" he said.

Decameron came to his door and looked out the peephole at the balding, mild-looking man holding the pizza box.

He opened the door and said, "I didn't order –"

Mort had been made ox-strong by months of carrying pizzas in heavy insulated bags up to third-floor walkups. He hit Decameron with the full force of his rage and misery.

A stunned Decameron landed flat on the floor. Mort slammed the door and pulled out the tire iron from the pizza box. He broke Decameron's arms and legs with swift strokes. Decameron screamed in pain and terror.

Mort could taste his fear. It was bitter. Very bitter. And sweet. So very sweet.

"At the trial, the pathologist said your wife fought like a wildcat to live," Mort said. "You won't be able to fight me off. You can't kick me, either. And these broken bones won't be noticed at your autopsy, because all your bones will be broken in another moment, Decameron. You're going to join your wife."

Mort flung open the living room window while Decameron tried to scoot toward the door. He didn't get far. Mort dragged him across the polished wood floor toward the open window. He was careful to hold Decameron by his shoes, so there were no drag marks on the parquet.

Decameron moaned. "Why are you doing this?" he said, sounding like a dead man already.

"Because when your wife went out the window, so did my career," Mort said. "I was the man on the street when Patricia landed. The innocent bystander who was drenched with her blood. The horror that I saw cost me my job, my marriage, and my house. There was no justice for me in court. But I will have justice now."

He flung Decameron out the window. Mort heard him scream all the way down. Then he heard the splat! It was such a satisfying sound.

Mort looked out the window to see his triumph, twenty-one floors below. He saw a man standing on the sidewalk. An ordinary man. Drenched with Decameron's blood.

Mort was horrified. It was as if he was watching Patricia's death all over again, from a different, more terrible view – the same way God must have seen it.

"I didn't check to see if anyone was walking down the street," Mort wept. "I forgot to look."

But he would not forget now.

Blonde Moment

Television is a cutthroat world, where a lucky accident can make a career. Sometimes, Mother Nature gives someone a golden opportunity. This story was inspired by my time as a television feature reporter, where I won two local Emmys.

"Killer," Jason the TV producer said, as he admired the blonde in the blue dress.

"Kill her," is what Evelyn Blent heard.

That's exactly what Evelyn, the six o'clock anchor, wanted to do. Kill Tiffany Tyler Taylor.

It was Jason who gave Evelyn the idea to kill Tiffany. It was Evelyn's grandmother who showed her how to do it.

Tiffany. The little blonde was sitting at her new morning show set for the first time, but she looked like she'd been there forever. Breakfast With Tiffany the show was called, and the new set was created for her. It was all in shades of blue – sky blue and Dresden blue, peacock, azure and sapphire – to set off Tiffany's rich buttery blondeness.

Blonde ambition, that's what Tiffany was. Five-feet-two inches of simpering, slithering ambition. Tiffany was after Evelyn's anchor slot. Evelyn knew it. There was only one reason why she'd get it. She was blonde.

Whenever Tiffany Tyler Taylor walked through station KQZX, every man looked at her like he'd been marooned for a decade on a desert island. From the station manager to the mail clerks, the men stared at Tiffany with dazed looks and sappy smiles. But Evelyn knew the station manager, Mighty Milt, as his toadies called him, was the real problem. In TV, mistakes started at the top. If Milt didn't treat Tiffany like his golden girl, that brown-noser Jason wouldn't fawn over her.

Jason was Evelyn's producer, too, but he had only perfunctory praise for Evelyn. "Nice job," he'd say. Or, "Thanks for covering that light plane crash. Nobody else would be on the scene at five a.m."

Certainly not Tiffany Tyler Taylor. She'd never trudge through a muddy field to get to the crash site. She'd mess up her little blue shoes.

But Jason never looked at Evelyn in that same dreamy way. Even Rick, a cynical, sarcastic cameraman, stared at Tiffany and said with a lovesick sigh, "God, she looks good."

"She's a poodle," Evelyn snarled. "An empty-headed little nothing. What is wrong with you, Rick? You've never fallen in love with the talent before."

Rick shrugged. "Blondes are easier to light," he said.

Evelyn almost believed him. When the harsh TV lights hit Tiffany, her blonde hair glowed like molten gold. She looked like a blue angel with Meg Ryan bangs.

Evelyn looked dark and a little angry on TV. Her brunette hair seemed to absorb light. Her olive skin created strange shadows. TV did odd things to her. If Evelyn gained a pound or two, the camera gave her a double chin and a pouchy stomach. That never happened to Tiffany Tyler Taylor. She always looked petite and perfect.

Tiffany couldn't get a scoop in an ice cream parlor. But Saint Louis viewers were as dazzled as the fools at the station. In six months, Tiffany rose from feature reporter to morning show host.

Now Evelyn was afraid that Tiffany would go after the ultimate prize – Evelyn's own hard-won spot as six o'clock anchor.

Already Tiffany had made two guest appearances on Saint Louis's highest rated news show. Co-anchor Dick Nickerson threw back his head and laughed so hard at Tiffany's mild – (and scripted) – joke about the weather that his comb-over flopped up like a pot lid. Dick got derisive letters from readers, calling him a drape head. He didn't care. Dick adored Tiffany.

Nobody but Evelyn saw the hard little climber under that soft surface. Nobody but Evelyn heard Tiffany's catty remarks.

"Eeuww, are you really eating a bacon sandwich for lunch?" Tiffany said, pointing at Evelyn's BLT. "Bacon has nitrates and nitrites. And it's bad for your skin." Evelyn could feel the zits popping out on her face like dandelions after a rain.

"Bacon makes you fat," Tiffany said, staring at Evelyn's waistline until she felt her gut plop over her belt.

"That's why I stick to salads," she said, smugly. She tapped her green-heaped plate with her fork. Then Tiffany stuck her knife in Evelyn's back. "But I suppose a mature woman like yourself doesn't have to worry about her figure."

"Mature" was not a compliment in television. Tiffany had called her old and fat. No one else heard the insult.

Another time Tiffany suggested that Evelyn get some blond ehighlights in her dark hair. "The lighter color around your face will make you look ten years younger," she said. "Go to Mr. John. He's the best colorist in the city. You'll look so natural."

No one heard that little dig, either.

Only Evelyn heard Tiffany on the phone to her stockbroker every afternoon before the markets closed. Only Evelyn seemed to catch Tiffany calling her agent. That's when Tiffany dropped all pretense of being the city's sweetheart.

"I don't know how I can live on a lousy two-hundred-fifty thousand a year," Saint Louis's sweetie pie hissed. Evelyn would love to have that quote on tape. She'd play it for all the Tiffany fans who said, "She's so down-to-earth."

Evelyn saw red when she heard how much green the gold-digging Goldilocks was trying to pry out of the station. Evelyn didn't make near that, and she'd been at the station ten years.

It was time to have a talk with her mentor, Margaret Smithson. Evelyn would demand to know why she was underpaid and underrated. Margaret would make things right.

Evelyn's anger boiled and seethed as she marched across the newsroom. It burst like a geyser when she opened Margaret's office door, and she spewed out a stream of hot words.

"Stop it!" Margaret said. "Evelyn, you must stop this stupid jealousy."

Evelyn felt like she'd been slapped. Margaret looked small and stern in her smart black suit. She weighed about ninety-five pounds, and most of that was her mop of dark hair. But Margaret was tough. Right now, she turned that toughness on Evelyn.

"Your petty jabs at Tiffany are getting back to the wrong people. I'm warning you. They'll come back and bite you in the ass."

"You're on her side, too," Evelyn said. She knew she sounded whiny.

"I am not," Margaret said. Even when she was angry, Margaret was striking. She had black hair, dark blue eyes, and pale skin. Evelyn often wondered why Margaret wasn't on camera. But Margaret preferred to be a special projects producer. Everything she touched turned to Emmy gold. The lustrous statues lined the shelves above her desk.

"I'm on your side, Evelyn. But you're making yourself look bad. It's contract renewal time, and I have to tell you: Milt is talking about making Tiffany the six o'clock anchor. I think I can head him off, but I don't know for how long if you keep undermining yourself. Milt wants team players."

"It isn't a team. It's a support system for Tiffany," Evelyn said, bitterly.

"See, that's what I mean," Margaret said. "How many times have I told you? Success in television is by the numbers. Right now, Tiffany has them. Viewers will tire of her professional cuteness. They always do. Then Milt will decide she's overpaid and dump her. She'll be gone soon. Sit tight and keep your mouth shut."

But the next morning, while Tiffany was doing a live remote in front of City Hall, a yellow blur of fur raced by her and ran into Market Street. The whole city saw Tiffany run after the dog and rescue it, just before it slipped under the wheels of a truck. In case anyone missed the dramatic rescue, it was shown on the six and ten o'clock news.

The following morning, Tiffany was on the set with the little yellow mutt. Saved and savior looked remarkably alike. Both were small and perky, with yellow hair and floppy bangs. Both oozed cuteness. The mutt licked Tiffany, and Tiffany smooched the dog. Evelyn couldn't decide which one she wanted to kick first.

Evelyn nearly choked on her breakfast eggs when Tiffany announced a contest to name the dog. She lost her appetite totally three days later when Tiffany said she'd received two thousand e-mails. Evidently, viewers also thought Tiffany looked like her dog. The winning name was Tiffany Too.

A week later, Milt sent out a memo that Tiffany and Tiffany Too would be featured at the Fair Saint Louis on the Fourth of July. Tiffany would be the dayside anchor, then do color commentary on the fireworks that night.

Every year, some two million people sweltered on the Saint Louis Riverfront, under the Gateway Arch. The temperature and the humidity were in the nineties – if the city was lucky. Sometimes, it was a hundred degrees or more.

The staff complained about covering the three-day fair in the broiling Saint Louis sun, but they knew it was a career showcase. For four years running, Evelyn had been the dayside anchor and nightside commentator. This year, Milt's memo demoted her to a lowly reporter. She'd be trudging through the almost liquid heat to interview boring people who said things like, "We're having a wonderful time. There's nothing like this in Festus."

Milt gave that sneaky, simpering blonde Evelyn's assignment at the fair. Soon she'd have Evelyn's anchor slot, too.

Evelyn told her mentor Margaret that she felt sick and wanted to go home. She wasn't lying. Her stomach heaved when she read Milt's memo. She barely made it to the restroom before she threw up.

Evelyn had to save her career before that fair-haired fathead took everything from her. She felt hot angry tears. This was dangerous. She couldn't be seen crying in the newsroom.

She ran to her BMW and started driving anywhere, nowhere. She didn't want to think. But Evelyn's driving was not aimless after all. She found herself on Christopher Drive, the road to Granny's house in the country. Granny was common sense itself. She'd help Evelyn.

Granny was the last real grandmother in America. No facelifts and hair dyes for her. Granny had a comfortable figure and crinkly gray hair.

Granny's little white house had yellow plastic lawn ducks and red geraniums. It was surrounded by acres of Missouri woods. Across the street was a horse pasture. Subdivisions were creeping up the road, but you couldn't see them yet.

Granny had grown up on a farm in Tennessee, and she loved to talk about old-time remedies from her girlhood. As a teenager, Evelyn was disgusted when Granny told her that country people used to tie moldy bread to a bad cut to cure an infection.

Later on, Evelyn realized they were using a primitive form of penicillin.

Of course, not all of Granny's old-time remedies were useful. Evelyn didn't believe a pan of water under a bed would break a fever, but it did no harm.

Granny ran outside when she heard Evelyn's car and gave her a comforting hug. Evelyn breathed in her grandmother's old-fashioned violet sachet. Granny's kitchen was perfumed with the warm sweetness of fresh-baked blackberry pie.

"You're too thin," Granny said, which made Evelyn feel better. You could never be too thin on TV.

"And how's my other favorite TV girl?" Granny asked.

"Who's that?" Evelyn said, as she felt her insides go dead. Had that tinselly Tiffany seduced her Granny?

"The little blonde who rescued that dog," Granny said. "She's got a good head on her shoulders."

"Too bad there's nothing in it," Evelyn said.

"Evelyn, is that the green-eyed monster I see in your eyes?" Granny said.

"No," Evelyn lied.

"Then have some homemade pie and tell me why you're dropping in on me in the middle of the day," Granny said.

"Because I haven't seen you in a while," Evelyn said. She couldn't tell Granny the real reason. Not now. Not after she knew Granny was a Tiffany worshiper.

Granny cut a big slice from the blackberry pie cooling on the rack. Warm purple juice oozed out on the plate and dripped on the counter, but Granny ignored it. She was staring out the window.

"Those new people have their white horse in that pasture again on a sunny day," Granny said. "They know that field's full of rue plants. I've told them and told them, but they won't listen to me. Damn yuppies think I don't know anything. If that horse suffers, it's their fault."

"What's wrong with rue?" Evelyn asked.

"It's poisonous to white animals, especially in the sunshine," Granny said. "Grows right there." She pointed to some weedy-looking plants by the pasture fence.

"That doesn't make sense," Evelyn said. "Why would they poison only white animals?"

"Don't know, but they do," Granny said. "Poison white people, too."

"Come on, Granny, plants don't discriminate." Evelyn wondered if age was eroding Granny's sharp mind.

"I mean really white people, like blondes. It won't hurt dark-haired types like you," Granny said. "And that's no old wives' tale. It's a scientific fact. If white animals eat rue, celery, and plants like that, then stand in bright sunlight, they can get real sick.

"But a chestnut horse can eat the same plants and nothing happens. Dark-haired animals and people don't get sick. The plants are only poisonous to very white people and white animals."

"What happens?" Evelyn asked.

Granny loved to describe symptoms. "Their face, throat and eyelids swell up," she said gleefully. "They get dizzy and stagger around like they're drunk." Granny staggered around the kitchen, clutching the purple pie knife to her chest.

"Happened to your Aunt Virginia," she said, solemnly.

Evelyn tried to picture her stout gray-haired aunt staggering. "When?"

"When Virginia was a young girl. At the Cedar Springs church picnic," Granny said. "I know you'll find it hard to believe, but Virginia was a little bit of a thing then, and had platinum-blonde hair down to her hips. Wild as a March hare, too. Some boy dared her to eat a plant in a field. Your Aunt Virginia saw a brown horse eating it and figured it was safe. But it was rue. Her throat swelled up terrible. That girl liked to died. Couldn't get Virginia to touch anything green again, not even a plain old lettuce salad."

Evelyn could see another little blonde eating a salad, then going out into the sweltering Fair Saint Louis sunshine. She could see her white throat swelling and closing up, and the blonde staggering and dying just before the paramedics arrived.

Then Evelyn saw herself taking back the fair assignment that was rightfully hers.

Granny had given her the solution to the Tiffany problem after all. In fact, she'd served it on a plate.

"What's this phenomenon called?" Evelyn asked.

"Photo ... photo ... photo-something," Granny said. Photosensitization.

"A pathological sensitivity caused by eating certain plants that are not ordinarily poisonous," Evelyn's researches at the library revealed.

"A form of light dermatosis," said one old book that was a virtual manual for poisoners. Evelyn couldn't risk checking it out, so she stole it from the library, burying it in her briefcase. At home, she read the section on photosensitization over and over, gloating over each sentence.

"Its symptoms are an inflammatory swelling of the ears, face, and eyelids, with throat and lung disturbances, dizziness and a tendency to stagger," the book said. "When, in rare instances, death follows, it is due to mechanical asphyxia from the swelling of the nose and throat."

Death would be nice, Evelyn thought. But she would settle for seeing the golden girl swell up like a red balloon. Maybe she'd pop, right on camera.

Evelyn giggled, but it was not a cute Tiffany Tyler Taylor giggle.

Her researches only got better: rue and celery, especially the green leafy parts of celery, were rich in furanocoumarins. The name alone was enough to make you turn red and swell.

Some people were supersensitive to them. They'd get a horrible sunburn-like reaction. The lighter-skinned you were, the more intense the reaction. Especially if you went out into the sun.

And if you were taking a drug like Coumadin, it further intensified the reaction, Evelyn read. Lots of people took the blood thinner Coumadin. It was also the main ingredient in rat poison.

All Evelyn had to do was make a nice salad with rue and celery, then spice it with a little rat poison. Not enough to make a brunette sick. Just enough to blow up a little blonde.

It was so easy.

Evelyn knew where to get the rue plants. The pasture near Granny's was filled with them.

Evelyn knew how she would serve them, too. She'd make a field greens salad, then add the rue. It was a field green, too. When people were chomping baby oak leaves and stuff that looked like it had been raked off a lawn, who'd notice some rue? Then she'd sprinkle on green celery leaves for color. Everyone used celery.

A cheese dressing would disguise any bitter taste. I'll make raspberry vinaigrette with Gorgonzola, she thought. I'll add walnuts and dried cranberries to make it nice and healthy.

For everyone but Tiffany.

For good measure, she'd Cuisinart a little rat poison, and add it to the dressing. It would blend in with the herbs and spices. She'd calculate exactly the medicinal dose for a small woman – divided by three salad eaters. Sun, celery, rue – and rat poison. Tiffany would rue the day she went after anything of Evelyn's.

There was one problem. How would she get Tiffany to eat the

salad? Everyone knew Evelyn hated the woman. She barely said hello to Tiffany in the newsroom. She had one month to make friends with her enemy. Evelyn would have to swallow her pride, so Tiffany would swallow her salad.

Next morning, Evelyn walked into Margaret's office and said, "You're right. It's time I buried the hatchet."

"In Tiffany's forehead?" Margaret said, suspiciously.

"For real," Evelyn said. "Yesterday, I had some time to think about what you said. I'm only hurting myself. I want to take Tiffany to lunch. My treat. Would you come as referee?"

"Delighted," Margaret said, her pale face turning pink with pleasure. "I'm so happy you're taking my advice."

Tiffany was wary when Evelyn invited her, even when she explained that Margaret would be there, too. But she could not resist Evelyn's handsome apology. "I've behaved stupidly, Tiffany," she said. "I want this lunch to be a peace offering."

Tiffany looked flattered. She considered Evelyn's olive branch a tribute to her power. During a two-hundred-dollar lunch at a premier power spot, Tiffany prattled on about her favorite subject – herself.

"Tiffany Too and I are the marshals for the Hill Day parade," she said, while the worshipful waiter refilled Tiffany's water glass, and forgot Evelyn's.

The Hill was the Italian section of the city. "Your dog will love the fire hydrants," Evelyn said. "They're painted red, white and green."

"Oh, no, she isn't allowed out of the parade marshal's convertible," Tiffany said, seriously. "Not in those crowds."

Tiffany babbled on. Mentor Margaret smiled benignly. Evelyn cut her swordfish into smaller and smaller pieces until the waiter took her plate away. No one ordered dessert. The reconciliation lunch was over, and declared a success.

Evelyn suffered through two more Tiffany lunches with Margaret's approving company. Because she silently endured Tiffany's monologues, the beastly blonde now considered Evelyn her friend.

"I can talk to you," she said. "You're such a good listener."

Peace was declared. The nasty newsroom rumors ceased, and the gossip mongers went after the noon show anchor, who was having an affair with the consumer reporter. The jokes about what she was consuming were relentless.

At their third lunch, Tiffany finally gave Evelyn the opening she needed.

"I'm not looking forward to covering the fair," Tiffany said, sighing dramatically. Evelyn knew Tiffany was dying for an excuse to talk about her big assignment. At least, Evelyn hoped the twit would be dying.

"It's going to be such a long day," Tiffany cooed. "Almost ten hours. The station is keeping Tiffany Too in the air-conditioned satellite truck. My little puppy will be cool, but I'll be out on the hot fairgrounds all day from eleven o'clock on."

Evelyn ground her teeth as she thought of Tiffany taking over her assignment, but she forced herself to sound sympathetic. "That is a long day. What are you doing about lunch?"

Tiffany shuddered delicately. "I can either eat the station's food – tuna salad and ham sandwiches – all fat – or the fair food, hot dogs and buffalo burgers. Yuck."

Actually, the fair offered delicacies from chicken sate to yes, buffalo burgers. But how would Tiffany know? She'd never covered the fair.

"I come in at noon," Evelyn said. "How about if I bring salads for you, me and Margaret? I have this terrific recipe, with field greens, Gorgonzola, walnuts, and dried cranberries. A good healthy salad will get us through the day."

"Super!" Tiffany said. "You're a lifesaver!"

Yeah, Evelyn thought. I'm saving my life. And my career.

The night before the fair, Evelyn drove to the pasture near Granny's and climbed over the fence. Her pants were full of stickle burrs and her hands were scratched with brambles, but she picked the plants she needed by moonlight. The lights were off at her grandmother's house. Deep shadows along the pasture fence hid Evelyn. Even the night conspired to help her.

In the morning, she concocted the salad, adding the freshly picked rue to the store-bought field greens. She made her salad dressing with a carefully calibrated dose of rat poison. It was the exact dosage for one small healthy woman. Divided by three, of course. Because they'd all be sharing the salad.

She put the salad into a big disposable bowl. She would make sure everyone saw there was only one salad container. At lunch, she served the salad on paper plates, dividing the poisonous portions exactly in three.

"Delicious," Tiffany said, eating her salad greedily.

"Perfection!" her mentor said. Evelyn was too excited to eat. She forced herself to finish her salad.

After lunch, Evelyn gathered up the serving bowl, paper plates and forks, even the napkins. After Margaret and Tiffany left, Evelyn threw the trash into an overflowing can at the far end of the fair. The incriminating remains would be taken away by the trash haulers long before Tiffany's first symptom.

All three women worked in the sweltering afternoon sun. Tiffany, with Margaret's award-winning assistance, was interviewing the big stars performing on the main stage. Evelyn went with Rick the cameraman for what he called "Bubba bites" – sound bites from dreary fairgoers.

After they interviewed a hefty woman from Herculaneum and a downright fat man from Florissant with two chubby children, Rick whispered to Evelyn, "Is there a weight requirement for this fair? Do you have to weigh at least two hundred pounds to get in the gate?"

Evelyn pretended to be shocked, but she secretly loved his misanthropic remarks. The sun was beating on her with almost physical blows. Sweat dripped off her nose. She knew on camera her face would look oily and her hair would look french-fried. She prayed that same sun was working on Tiffany's white skin.

When they heard sirens near the main stage, Rick said, "Maybe one of the fairgoers melted. Let's go see if there's some video."

More sirens screamed. Now police cars, fire trucks and an ambulance were heading toward the main stage. The music stopped abruptly.

"What happened?" Evelyn asked a woman running from the area, clutching her baby protectively.

"Some TV lady started staggering around and grabbing her throat," the woman said. "Her face swelled up something awful. Even her eyes were swollen shut. She looked horrible. I didn't want my Becky to see it."

Yes! Evelyn thought triumphantly, but she made concerned noises.

Rick was running, surprisingly fast for someone with a heavy video camera. He loped past Evelyn. Other fairgoers were running after him, eager to see the tragedy. Evelyn felt a sharp elbow in her ribs. A small boy darted between her legs and she fell on the dry grass.

By the time Evelyn brushed herself off, the excitement was almost over. She saw the paramedics loading a stretcher with a small figure strapped to it. The figure was absolutely still, although the ambulance left with lights flashing and sirens howling.

Evelyn composed her face into a sorrowful mask to hide her glee. She didn't know if Tiffany was sick or dead, but she was definitely out of action. The fair was hers now. Evelyn would return to her rightful place on camera.

She went looking for Margaret. The satellite truck would be the logical choice. At least someone there could tell her where Margaret was. Evelyn was about to enter when the door opened slowly. Out stepped Tiffany. Her hated rival looked disgustingly healthy.

"How? What?" was all a stunned Evelyn could manage.

"Oh, Evelyn," Tiffany said, her blue eyes tearing artistically. "Margaret started gasping and choking and staggering around like she was having some kind of fit. Nobody knew what happened to her, and by the time the ambulance got here, she wasn't breathing at all. It was terrible. They don't think she's going to make it."

"Margaret?" Evelyn said. "Are you sure?"

What had gone wrong? Margaret was a brunette. If rue plants made blondes sick, why was Tiffany well and Margaret dying? Damn Granny and her crazy country remedies.

Blonde Tiffany had eaten more salad than anyone. But brunette Margaret had the severe symptoms. Evelyn had eaten the greens, too, and they'd had no effect on her. They certainly weren't poisonous to one brunette – why another?

"I must see Margaret," Evelyn said.

But Jason, her producer, stopped her. "I'm sorry, Evelyn," he said. "You can't do anything for Margaret. We need you to carry on with the fair coverage."

But she couldn't. Evelyn couldn't concentrate. She missed her first cue for the live remote at the food booths. When she was finally on the air, she looked sweaty and disheveled. Several viewers called the station, asking if Evelyn was drunk. But it was shock, not booze, that slurred her speech.

Evelyn's "Bubba bites," the interviews with the boring fairgoers, were dropped to make room for the special report on the death of Emmy-award-winning producer Margaret Smithson.

Tiffany narrated that report. Everyone agreed that she did a splendid job, showing just the right amount of professional sympathy. Tiffany's story about sharing her salad with the deceased was especially touching.

Evelyn drifted in a fog, waiting for the autopsy results. Maybe the pathologist would find something that would exonerate her. Maybe Margaret had been stung by a bee and gone into shock. Maybe Evelyn didn't kill her mentor and best friend.

But when the report was released, Evelyn knew there would be no reprieve. Margaret had extensive swelling of the face, lips and tongue. She'd suffocated. The details were too horrible to think about.

The pathologist said the severe symptoms were caused by an overdose of Coumadin. Margaret had been taking the blood thinner for her heart. The pathologist believed Margaret had mistakenly taken a double dose of Coumadin and died from it. Her death was an accident.

Only Evelyn knew it was no accident. Only Evelyn knew she'd killed her best friend. And she couldn't figure out how.

At the station, Evelyn stumbled through her standups, missed deadlines, flubbed her lines. She felt numb. She didn't care, not even when the station did not renew her contract. She knew Tiffany would take her anchor spot.

She didn't know why Margaret died, and that made her crazy.

Margaret had only had one-third of a normal dose of Coumadin. It shouldn't have killed her, even if she was already taking the blood thinner. The sun, celery, and rue might intensify the effect, but Margaret was a brunette. It should have been blonde Tiffany who swelled up from the sun exposure. It should have been Tiffany who died.

All Evelyn could do was ask herself, "What went wrong?"

She found out at Margaret's memorial service. Margaret's grieving family displayed photos of their daughter throughout her too-short life.

Evelyn saw the first-grade picture of a grinning gap-toothed Margaret. The little girl was blonde – and not just blonde, but so pale her hair was almost white. In high school, a teenaged Margaret used too much eyebrow pencil and mascara to darken her pale brows and eyelashes.

By college, Margaret was a stunning platinum blonde. It was only after graduation, when she got her first job at a little station in Sedalia, Missouri, that Margaret had dark hair. She was a brunette in every photo after that.

"You were Margaret's best friend," said her mother, a plump gray-haired woman in black. She took both of Evelyn's hands in hers.

"I didn't know she was a blonde," blurted Evelyn.

"Oh, yes," she said. "Margaret had lovely hair. Natural platinum. But Margaret said she couldn't take the dumb blonde jokes at work. She said when she dyed her hair dark, her IQ went up 50 points."

That's where I went wrong, Evelyn thought.

Margaret was blonde. And Tiffany? She remembered why Dolly Parton said she wasn't offended by dumb blonde jokes. "I know I'm not dumb. I also know that I'm not blonde."

Tiffany must have dyed her hair blonde. She recalled her nasty remarks about Mr. John being the city's finest colorist "so natural." Of course. He certainly made Tiffany look natural. That's why the poison salad didn't bother her. She wasn't a real blonde.

It was the ultimate blonde joke on a dumb brunette.

It never occurred to Evelyn that Tiffany was a bottle blonde. She should have known. Everything else about her was fake. And in TV, mistakes start at the top.

Evelyn realized Margaret's mother was still holding her hands and talking. "I told her, 'Margaret, it is a sin and a shame to cover up that beautiful platinum hair.' And you know what she said? 'Mother, I would rather die than be a blonde.'

"Evelyn? Are you OK? Why, you're white as a sheet, dear. Sit down here. It's not healthy to be that white . . ."

Wedding Knife

Most women have worn at least one ugly bridesmaid dress. We suffer the puffed sleeves, dropped waists, flounces, and ruffles for the sake of the bride and her day. This bride may have been guilty of more than a crime against fashion. I hope you'll enjoy one of my favorite short stories. "Wedding Knife" won an Agatha Award for Best Short Story.

The bride stood at the altar, a vision of white lace and billowing silk skirts. Suddenly, she collapsed at Father McLauren's feet, the white silk skirts spreading across the floor like spilled cream.

"Gail!" I said, rushing over to her, but the priest and the groom were already there, trying to revive her.

"Stand back," Father McLauren said, with the authority of a man who'd had twenty years' experience with skittish brides. "Give her some air."

The wedding party, five bridesmaids and five groomsmen, all stepped back. As maid of honor, I hovered a fraction closer than the others. It was my duty to attend to the bride.

Slowly, Gail revived, her face as white as her wedding dress, and not nearly as pretty. She sat up. "Where am I?" she said, in a dazed voice.

"You're at St. Philomena's, getting married," Father McLauren said, smiling gently.

"Shit!" the bride said, loud enough so the first pews heard her. I could hear her mother gasp. It was Gail's mother who had pushed for this wedding to Harold Humphrey IV. It was Gail's mother who was hot for Handsome Harry's social connections, not to mention his money. Gail went along with it because she was twenty-nine, it was "time to get married," and if she had to get married it was better to marry a rich man than a poor one.

And Gail had to get married. She was four months' gone and way too Catholic to even consider abortion. That was probably why she'd fainted. She was pregnant, too sick to eat anything but soda crackers and 7-Up, and Gail's mother had laced her into the dress so tightly she could hardly breathe. But Gail's mother didn't want any ugly rumors. She would try to pass off the baby as "premature," not that anyone but her would care.

The groom went along with the wedding plans because he was thirty-five and it was time he started producing the fifth Harold Humphrey. He was getting family pressure, the kind that resulted in his allowance being cut off. But nobody, except maybe his bride, expected Handsome Harry to be faithful. The man had a roving eye and a wicked little curl that hung down on his forehead. Men who looked like that were meant to stray.

The priest gave the bride a sharp look, and I wondered if he was going to tell her it wasn't too late to call off the wedding. But Gail spoke up quickly. "I'm sorry, Father," she said. "I shouldn't have said that in church. I was embarrassed because I'd made a fool of myself by fainting. I should have eaten breakfast. I apologize for my language. I'm ready to get married now."

It was the priest who helped Gail up, not the groom. I came forward and straightened Gail's dress and ten-foot seed pearl train. Her Alençon lace veil slid to one side, so I righted that, too. Through the white lace over her face, I thought I caught the faint tracks of tears, sliding down her hundred-dollar make-up job.

I would have felt pity for her, but I couldn't forgive her for what she'd done to me. Gail made me a laughing stock in this despicable dress. The other bridesmaids were little blonde Barbie dolls. I was tall and dramatically brunette. Put me in a dress with long, clean lines and I looked sleek and sophisticated. But this getup was pink – pink like a frigging prom dress. It had ruffles all over, and to make it worse, it had a tiny white lace jacket that ended under the armpits. The little blonde bridesmaids looked dainty in pink. I looked like a linebacker in lace.

I begged Gail to let me wear a more becoming style – maids of honor often did wear a different dress from the bridesmaids. But two of Henry's sisters, Junie and Jill, were in the wedding, and they loved the pink ruffled dress. Gail's younger sisters, Heather and Ashley, agreed. The four blonde twits insisted that we all had to wear the same thing to "look right."

Nothing would ever make me look right in that outfit.

"Come on, Vanessa," Gail said, trying to soothe me in the dress shop. "We went to high school together. You know all bridesmaid dresses are hopeless. You can make me wear something horrible when you get married." She thought it was funny.

"That will never happen," I said. "I'm not the marrying kind."

I wasn't either. I preferred married men. No muss, no fuss, no proposals to spoil the fun. I enjoyed sneaking around, and when I got bored with the affair, I broke it off. The men didn't dare complain, or try to get me back. They didn't want their wives finding out.

So although I felt sorry for Gail, I took a small, secret delight in her discomfort. What are friends for?

The rest of the wedding went off without a hitch. Harry pulled back his bride's lace veil and kissed her with a show of passion that left the old women in the front pews fanning themselves. I handed Gail her heavy bouquet of white roses and the oddly appropriate baby's breath, and straightened her seed pearl train again when she turned to face the congregation. Everyone applauded the new Mr. and Mrs. Humphrey.

Then came countless photos and the videotaping, while the wedding guests loitered outside the church. I hated posing for pictures and wondered if I could offer the photographer something to ruin the pictures of me in that dress. I'd caught a glimpse of myself in a mirror in the bride's room at the church and saw the dress was worse than I thought.

At last we ran down the church steps while the guests blew politically correct bubbles (rice hurt the little birdies) and into the waiting white limos.

The reception was lavish. It was held in the main ballroom of the old Mauldin hotel, a fantasy of white and gold trimmed with ten thousand dollars' worth of flowers. My Aunt Marlene had finagled an invitation. Of course, she couldn't resist a jab at me in the receiving line. "That's the ugliest bridesmaid dress I've ever seen," she said, "and I've seen some in my time."

Aunt Marlene was about eighty. Her skin was spotted with warts, moles, and age spots until she looked like a fat speckled hen, with a yellow beak of a nose. The wrinkles under her chin folded up and down like an accordion when she talked. She was wearing her all-purpose navy blue wedding and funeral dress with the rhinestone buttons.

"Thanks, Aunt Marlene. You always know how to make a girl feel good," I said.

"I always tell the truth," she said, righteously. "I know my duty."

"And never shirked it, either," I said.

"That's right," she said, ignoring the dig. "And what was Gail doing cursing at the altar? Disrespectful, I call it."

Exciting, I'd call it. I hadn't seen such malice light up those old dead lizard eyes since Mrs. Dougherty ran off with the Scoutmaster.

"She fainted," I said.

"I'll bet she's pregnant," Aunt Marlene said, and I knew that no matter how tight Gail was laced, Aunt Marlene wouldn't be fooled when the baby came along.

Finally, the receiving line was over. The wedding party scattered to grab a drink, put their bouquets down, or use the bathroom. Gail looked beat. "I need to sit down for a minute," she said.

"Are you okay?" I asked her.

"Yeah, sure." She managed a weak smile. "Just some last minute jitters up there at the altar."

"Can I get you anything? Water? Some food?" The groom should have done this, but he was nowhere to be seen.

"Shoes," she said. "These satin heels are killing me. We still have to throw the bouquet and the garter, cut the cake, and dance. Would you get me my comfortable shoes? I stashed them in the back storage room, by the bandstand."

She pointed in that direction, and I trotted over and opened the door. The light was already on. I saw stacks of beer kegs and soda cases, and a shelf with things the bride would need that night – some lipstick and tissues, a brush and hair spray, comfortable shoes, a short dress she could change into later, and the ornamental cake knife. The storage room angled off to the right.

And there, against a back counter, was the groom getting his own private reception from Ashley, and it was a warm one. In fact, they were consummating their new position as in-laws. They didn't notice me. I grabbed Gail's shoes off the shelf, tiptoed out, shut the door – and ran straight into Aunt Marlene.

"What got into you? You're white as a sheet," she said.

"Nothing," I said, shakily.

"You're lying," Aunt Marlene said, and her chins wobbled like Jell-O in an earthquake. Her old eyes narrowed, and the net of wrinkles around them gathered tighter. "He's in there with his own sister-in-law, isn't he?"

"How did you know?" I said. Aunt Marlene didn't miss much.

"I saw him sneak in there, and five minutes later, I saw her, looking just as sneaky. I knew they were up to no good. I think Gail saw them, too, and that's why she sent you in there for her shoes."

"I'd better get these to her," I said, hoping I could get away, but Aunt Marlene clamped her hand on my arm.

"I hope this marriage lasts until I've paid off their present on my Penney's charge," she said, ominously.

With that, the photographer, who called the shots at all weddings these days, announced it was time to throw the bouquet. Gail had a special "throwing bouquet" made up so she could have the white roses dried and preserved. I handed it to her, then slipped away. I'd made her promise that she wouldn't throw the bouquet to me or make a spectacle out of me. I liked my single status.

When I came back, the girlish squealing had stopped and Harry's sister Jill had caught the bouquet, amid general cheers. "They were fighting over it," Aunt Marlene said. "A regular scrummage."

"Where's the groom?" the photographer asked. "It's time to throw the garter."

"Yeah, where is the groom?" Jill and Heather said. Ashley said nothing. She looked flushed and her hair was coming out of its French twist, and I didn't think it was from the battle over the bouquet.

Gail glared at her guilty sister-in-law. The tension was so thick, you could cut it with a knife.

"I'll get him," Gail said grimly, and it sounded like a threat. She marched straight across to the storage room, flung open the door, and slammed it behind her.

Soon after that, we heard her screams. The bride came out drenched in bright blood, her silk and lace dress splashed with red. There were sprays of red across her face and veil, and her eyes were wide with shock. She was holding a long, heavy silver knife. Blood dripped down her hand and onto her sleeves. She looked like a creature in a horror movie.

"The wedding cake knife," someone screamed, and then I saw the blood-drenched bouquet of ribbons and lily of the valley on the knife handle.

"Gracious, that girl stabbed her own husband," Aunt Marlene said, nearly delirious with delighted malice. She'd never had such a show for the price of a Penney's jelly dish with a silver-plate spoon. "Not that he didn't deserve it, philandering at his own reception."

"No!" I said. "No, it's not true. She didn't do it."

But now I heard the screams of the groom's mother. Her handsome Harry boy was dead, blood all over his starched white pleated shirt and black tuxedo. She couldn't explain why his cummerbund was in his hand. She thought it must have come lose and he'd retired to the storage room to fix it. I couldn't bring myself to go into the storage room again, but Aunt Marlene did, and she gave me all the details. She also spread the word that Harry had been in there alone with his own sister-in-law, doing unspeakable things. Which Aunt Marlene was more than happy to speak about.

The friends of the bride and groom divided themselves into two camps, as if someone had drawn a line down the middle of the ballroom. There were tears and angry voices on each side. Naturally, Harry's family blamed the bride, but I maintained she was innocent. The bride did nothing but cry. Her father, who was a lawyer, told her not to say a word when the police got there.

We stayed at the reception until after midnight, but there was no dancing or dinner. We were all forced to stay there and talk to the police. I didn't tell them what I'd seen in the storage room, but that didn't do Gail any good. Aunt Marlene babbled to the cops, and the police came back to me and threatened me with obstruction of justice unless I talked. The groom was carried out in a black body bag hours ago, and I was still there.

The weeping bride was handcuffed and carted off to jail, but the cops kept her bloody wedding gown as evidence.

Her father had enough clout to get her out on bail and enough money to get her the best defense attorney.

The details of the autopsy were so disgraceful, Aunt Marlene had to whisper them when she told all the neighbors – and me.

"The autopsy showed the groom had had sex just before his death, and not with his bride. At least, those weren't her blonde hairs they found on him," Aunt Marlene said, shivering with glee.

"Anyone could have left blonde hair on him," I said. "He was kissed by a lot of women in the receiving line."

"No, they were female hairs from 'down there,'" Aunt Marlene said, each whisper a stab in Gail's back. "And they found stains and things. He'd been with another woman at his wedding reception. No wonder Gail stabbed him. There won't be a woman in town here blames her."

"I don't care what they found," I said. "She didn't do it."

"You're loyal to a fault," Aunt Marlene said.

By the time of the trial, Gail was eight and a half months pregnant. Her attorney shrewdly insisted the trial go on. Tests had proved the baby was the groom's, and Gail had the sympathy of every woman on the jury – and most of the men, too. The defense had done its homework, and made sure there were several fathers with daughters on the jury. They wanted to kill Harry all over again.

I had to testify to what I saw, thanks to Aunt Marlene's big mouth.

The bride swore she was innocent.

I think if Gail had told the jury she'd stabbed Harry in a fit of rage, they would have understood and set her free. But she said she didn't do it, that she'd walked in there and saw the knife in his chest and heard him trying to breathe. She pulled the knife out and that's how she got blood all over herself.

The jury didn't like that. They didn't mind that she'd killed Harry, but they hated that she'd lied about it. Still, they couldn't be too mad at the poor girl. They only convicted her of manslaughter, and she got the minimum sentence. Her mother will watch the baby after it's born, although her in-laws have sued for custody. I don't think they'll get it, but I do think the kid will get the Humphrey millions in trust.

And Gail was innocent, even if no one believed her.

Because if Harry got lucky at the reception, well, so did I. No one saw me go into the storage room the second time. They were too busy watching who caught the bouquet. I went in there to tell

Harry exactly what I thought of him.

I was already unhappy that I'd caught him with that simp Ashley. I didn't mind sharing him with his wife – as I said, I like married men. But I hated that he had another lover, when he'd promised to love, honor and obey Gail, and he'd broken those vows in an hour.

Anyway, I went back in that storage room and told him what I thought of him. And Harry said, "Can you blame me for cheating on you, Vanessa? You look like a drag queen in that dress."

So I picked up the wedding cake knife and stabbed him in the chest. I didn't mean to do it, but once it happened, I couldn't undo it. Fortunately, there was very little blood. The knife held it in. I thought he was dead, but I was wrong. Harry was just barely alive when his bride came in. She pulled the knife out, trying to save him. Everyone but Gail knew you're supposed to leave the knife in when someone is stabbed like that.

When she pulled it out, Harry's blood sprayed all over his bride. When Gail walked out of the storage room drenched in red, it looked like she'd killed him.

None of it would have happened if she'd let me wear a different bridesmaid dress.

Gail served only two years of a four-year sentence. I consider that just. I think any woman who's ever had to wear an ugly bridesmaid dress would agree.

Good and Dead

The Royalton Hotel in "Good and Dead" was based on a French Quarter convention hotel where I shared a room with a friend. Like private eye Helen Hawthorne's landlady, Doris Ann Norris snuck out for smokes. She saw a young drug dealer operating out of the hotel garage. Between sales, he mingled with the cancer stick crowd. The hotel and the crafty dealer inspired this Dead-End Job adventure in New Orleans. "Good and Dead" was published in Blood on the Bayou, *edited by Greg Herren. The collection won an Anthony Award.*

Landlady Margery Flax was getting gently sozzled on a poolside chaise at the Coronado Tropic Apartments in Fort Lauderdale, Florida. Private eye Helen Hawthorne was one glass of wine behind her.

Margery was a stylish seventy-six, with a springy gray bob, a chunky amethyst necklace, and a purple pantsuit. Her tangerine nails were the same color as her glowing cigarette. She wore her wrinkles as marks of achievement. Helen was forty-two, a leggy brunette married to her private eye partner, Phil Sagemont. The PI pair lived in the two-story building and ran Coronado Investigations out of Apartment 2C.

The two women were munching popcorn by the pool. A light breeze ruffled the turquoise water, sending purple bougainvillea blossoms sailing across the rippled surface. The evening sun painted the old art moderne apartment building pale pink.

Helen yawned.

"Bored?" Margery asked.

Helen nodded. "Phil's working nights and I haven't had a case in a month."

"I have the cure," Margery said. "But you'd have to go to New Orleans today."

Helen sat up, her boredom banished. "Why didn't you say so sooner? New Orleans," she said. "Mm. I'd love to investigate jambalaya, shrimp remoulade, and po' boys."

"Not to mention hurricanes," Margery said.

"Katrina was awful, but the city has made an amazing recovery."

"I meant the drink," Margery said, and took a long drag on her

Marlboro. "Passion fruit, lime juice, 151-proof rum."

"You can have the hangover," Helen said. "I'm thinking beignets at the Café Du Monde. I can almost taste the powdered sugar. So what's the job?"

"A missing person who made off with a hundred grand," Margery said. "I know the missing person – and the woman who wants to hire you. It's quite a tale."

Margery fired up another cigarette and soon fell into her soothing, once-upon-a-time voice.

"Rosalee Alop was a good woman – and she looked it. Her flat shoes and lumpy, colorless clothes announced she was a church lady, a faithful wife, and a hardworking office manager. No lover would dare touch her iron-gray waves."

She absently patted her own gray hair, gently tousled by the breeze, and more than a few men.

"Rosalee lived a life of virtue until last week," Margery said. "Halfway through Holy Week, all hell broke loose. It was Wednesday. Some Christians call the Wednesday before Christ's crucifixion Spy Wednesday."

"Right," Helen said. "Tradition says that's when Judas conspired to betray Jesus for thirty pieces of silver."

"Last Wednesday, Rosalee suffered her own betrayal," Margery said, "and when she went home, her world turned to ashes. There would be no resurrection. At about 8:45 on a steamy Wednesday morning, Rosalee unlocked the turquoise door to Consolidated Worthy Causes."

"Never heard of that charity," Helen said.

"Most people haven't," Margery said. "Tight-assed bunch. Tight-fisted, too. Their motto says it all: 'Helping the deserving poor without making them dependent on handouts.'"

"Oh, right. CWC is near here in downtown Fort Lauderdale. The pink-and-turquoise building on Andrews Avenue."

"That's it," Margery said. "Rosalee thought the building's bright colors were too frivolous for their serious work. Her grim suits more than compensated for the tropical party colors. She was the charity's only full-time employee. Her job description went on for two pages. That morning she was expecting Junie Bea, the shiftless mother of a toddler, KK – Kimmie Kardashian Dillard – to wander in for her child's milk allowance."

"With a mother like that, why did CWC give KK milk money?" Helen asked.

"CWC said it wasn't the child's fault her parents hadn't made it to the altar. Instead of the tube-topped Junie Bea, in stepped Drusilla Cheney, CWC director, sleek as a panther in pink Armani.

"Rosalee blurted, 'Why are you here? The board meeting isn't until next Wednesday.'

"'We've had an emergency, Rosalee,' Dru said. 'I had to call a board meeting by phone late yesterday. Sit down, dear. I'm afraid the news concerns you. We didn't get the Weems-Wells Foundation grant. The one that pays for our office and your salary.'

"'But they always give us that grant,' Rosalee said.

"'Sad, isn't it?' Dru said, but I doubt she sounded sympathetic. 'Fortunately, the board has come up with a super new plan to save CWC. We own this building, and Roger, a director, is a real estate agent. He believes we can get scads for this site.'

"'Where will we be located?' Rosalee asked.

"'Roger says we can use a room at his Plantation office,' Dru said.

"'Plantation! Out in the suburbs! I walk to the office now.'

"'That's okay,' Dru said. 'We're hiring Roger's daughter Audrey as a temp to take your place.'

"'A temp! Do you know how much I do?'

"'A lot, sweetie,' Dru said. 'We've all seen your job description. Audrey is young and enthusiastic and the office is near her parents' home. Plus, donating that space is a nice business deduction for Roger.'

"'But what about me?' Rosalee wailed. 'I'm fifty years old.'

"'You'll do fine,' Dru said. 'We'll write you a glowing recommendation and give you a nice severance package.'"

"Those cheapskates," Helen said. "Real estate in that part of town is sizzling. Roger will make a bundle on that sale. How much severance is Rosalee getting? Thirty thou?"

"Twenty," Margery said. "Rosalee didn't even make minimum wage. She worked for that piddling salary because she had a husband and she believed in CWC. Rosalee started crying and Dru told her to buck up."

"Buck up!" Helen said. "After that poor woman lost her job?"

"Dru told Rosalee she only had one more chore: the next morning, when she came in to pick up her severance check, a manila envelope would be on Rosalee's desk. 'Just hand that envelope to Mr. Rodriguez, the bank officer we always use, and get a receipt. Now you go for a nice lunch, dear, then take the rest of the afternoon off. Tomorrow, pick up your severance check, perform one little chore, and you're free.'"

"Dru is one cold-hearted bitch," Helen said.

"That's no way to talk about your future employer," Margery said.

"I haven't taken the case yet," Helen said.

"You will. Rosalee was shell-shocked. She called me. I invited her over for a screwdriver. I said the orange juice was good for her."

"What orange juice?" Helen said. "Your screwdrivers are six parts vodka to one part OJ."

"Whatever. It was just what she needed," Margery said. "Rosalee let down her hair and told me she wasn't always a drudge. When she was twenty-nine, before she married Dennison and started at CWC, she had an unforgettable Labor Day weekend at the Royalton Hotel in the French Quarter with Bobby, a local she met at a bar. It was a long weekend – accent on long. She said she still thinks about Bobby, even though they're both married to other people."

"That must have been some weekend," Helen said.

"I suspect it got better in retrospect," Margery said. "Rosalee said her husband Dennison was a dependable, faithful man. I translated that to mean he wasn't much fun in the sack. Ol' Bobby must have been some stud. She said he was a trainer, and she was sore for a week from his gymnastics. He was all muscle: broad shoulders, six-pack abs, good legs."

"She remember anything about his face?" Helen said.

"He had thick blond hair, green eyes, a noble nose, and a dimple in his chin.

"Rosalee was a match for him. She showed me a faded photo of herself from that wild September weekend in 1994. She was a stunner – long blond hair, stylish clothes, high heels. Even now, at age fifty, she could still be good-looking. Some make-up and the right clothes and she'd be quite the cougar.

"Too bad when she turned thirty, Rosalee found God and Dennison, and lost her looks. Check out her current photo."

Margery handed Helen Rosalee's CWC employee photo. "She worked to make herself unattractive," Helen said. "That gray hair in an old lady cut adds ten years. Her jaw is clenched and her mouth is a thin line. She could be the cover girl for Prison Matrons Monthly. Any photos of her frisky fling?"

"None. Bobby didn't want to be photographed. He swore he wasn't married, but he wouldn't even take her out for food. He had room service send up their meals for four days. Rosalee thought that was romantic."

"I'd be suspicious," Helen said.

"Rosalee said she didn't need photos: She'll always remember Bobby."

"What's his last name?"

"Charbonnet, a common NOLA name. When he was in the bathroom, Rosalee checked his driver's license. He's definitely Bobby Charbonnet.

"Whatever Bobby and Rosalee did that weekend seems to have started her on the path to godly living, but Rosalee didn't go into details. She'd downed two screwdrivers in a hurry, so I made her eat lunch and drink coffee. She decided she wanted to use her twenty thou severance to move to Costa Rica after Dennison retired this November.

"Suddenly, she looked at her watch and said, 'It's three o'clock. I have to fix a nice dinner for Dennison and tell him the good news.' When she left, Rosalee was sober enough to make it home. Once she got there, she went off the rails.

"Before she could tell Dennison they would be enjoying their golden years in the tropics, he asked Rosalee for a divorce."

"What? Her husband ditched her after twenty years?" Helen said. "She have any idea he was stepping out?"

"None. Dennison said he was going to marry a choir singer he met at organ practice – and don't you dare make the joke I think you're going to." The red eye of Margery's cigarette glared at Helen.

Helen kept silent, thinking of numerous punch lines.

"Dennison said Rosalee spent the night in the guest room. Early the next morning, she packed a suitcase and took his car. She stopped at their bank, but Dennison had already cleaned out their joint account."

"The rat!" Helen said.

"The rest I got from Drusilla. Rosalee drove to CWC the next morning. 'She must have opened the envelope I left for her,' Dru said. 'I didn't seal it. We trusted Rosalee. The manila envelope was closed with brass prongs. Rosalee saw my note to Mr. Rodriguez, the bank officer, instructing him to cash in our hundred thousand dollar CD. Two board members had signed the paperwork and the cash was to be deposited in the CWC account.

"'It was a terrible breach of trust for Rosalee to open that envelope,' Dru said."

"And firing Rosalee without notice wasn't?" Helen said.

Margery snorted. "Rosalee must have seen red – then green – when she read that note. That hundred thousand dollar CD was proof CWC had enough money to run the office and pay her salary for at least a year or two. Instead, the greedy director grabbed that hot property, hired his daughter, and Rosalee was out on the street.

"Rosalee cleverly altered the form so the CD's cash was deposited into her personal checking account."

"And the bank never questioned that?" Helen asked.

"Mr. Rodriguez had dealt with faithful Rosalee for years. Next, Rosalee transferred the hundred thousand, plus her twenty thou severance, to a different bank."

"With branches in New Orleans?" Helen asked.

"You guessed it. Then Rosalee moved the money again, maybe to another account under a different name. Her husband's car was found at the airport on Good Friday. She bought a plane ticket to New Orleans, and no one has seen her since she boarded the flight.

CWC knew Rosalee had skipped town, but didn't realize their money was gone until their regular board meeting today.

"That's when Dru Cheney called. She wants to avoid the police and the embarrassing publicity and hire you to find Rosalee and the missing money. I quoted her double your usual fee, plus our expenses. I hope you don't mind that I'm going along as an operative."

"I like your company," Helen said, "but why do I need an operative?"

Margery grinned. "I'm the only one who can recognize both versions of Rosalee – hot and cold. I'm guessing she's in NOLA for a hot weekend with Bobby. She may even try to get him to run off with her. I think she'll get new ID, if she doesn't have it already, then head for Costa Rica, with or without Bobby."

"Where do you think she is in NOLA?"

"The Royalton," Margery said. "It's still in business. That's where her life changed twenty years ago. I booked us a nonsmoking room with two beds. Dru is standing by to sign the contract and write you a check. A nonstop flight leaves at five-forty."

"You're awfully organized for someone half in the bag," Helen said.

"I can hold my liquor," Margery said. "I've made our travel arrangements online. Text Phil the news. He can take care of your furbag. Throw some clothes in a suitcase. I'm already packed. We can be in NOLA by dinnertime."

And so they were. Helen was used to South Florida humidity, but when she stepped out of the NOLA airport, she was wrapped in a warm, steamy sponge. Margery fired up a quick cigarette while they waited for the hotel shuttle.

"How will you survive in a nonsmoking room?" Helen asked.

"I'll find a cancer stick crowd outside the hotel. I can locate them by their hacking coughs."

By the time they arrived at the hotel, Helen's hair was limp and frizzy and her clothes were wrinkled. "This is the Royalton?" Helen asked the driver as he stopped under the hotel's sagging canopy. Broken neon buzzed over Royalton's Superb Steaks next to the lobby.

"Yes, miss," the driver said, in his soft Big Easy accent. "I do recommend the steakhouse. It lives up to its name – Superb."

Helen and Margery followed a herd of gray-haired tourists into the lobby. The dingy walls were the color of yellowed teeth, the dark wood paneling was scuffed and dinged, and the marble floor was cracked and dirty. Helen and Margery checked in, then waited in a long line for the only working elevator.

Their room looked exhausted: two sagging beds with moss green spreads, dusty velvet curtains, and pictures no one would ever steal bolted to the walls.

"Let's ask the front desk staff if Rosalee is staying here," Helen said.

The twenty-something desk clerk looked like he was born to be an old man. He was skinny, stoop-shouldered, and balding.

He shook his head when he saw Rosalee's photo. "I'd like to help, ma'am. But all the women here look like her." Helen surveyed the flocks of gray-haired tourists, chattering in French, German, and British English and waving brochures, cell phones and maps.

"How about this one?" Margery asked, producing Rosalee's fling photo.

The clerk shook his head. "Believe me, I'd notice someone that hot."

But the lobby was so crowded, Helen wondered if he would. "Let's try dinner at the hotel restaurant. Maybe we'll spot her."

Royalton's Superb Steaks hadn't been renovated since its nineties heyday, but Helen and Margery liked its slightly down-at-heels atmosphere. They slid into a generous booth flanked by the velvet-draped windows.

"Big Brother is watching," Margery said. "I see three security cameras."

Sophie, their red-haired server in a crisp white shirt and black bow tie, asked, "Would you ladies like to join our Superb Steaks Club?" She held up a purple card. "Buy ten steak dinners and get one free."

"Thanks," Helen said. "But we're just visiting." She ordered jambalaya. Margery wanted a strip steak. "Rare. Wave it over the grill and slap it on a plate."

Sophie laughed and brought Margery a sharp, heavy silver steak knife monogrammed RSS.

"Do I have to cut the steak off the cow myself?" Margery asked.

"No, we'll do that for you," Sophie said. "As soon as we wave the steak over the grill, your dinner will be ready. Enjoy your French bread."

"I need a cigarette," Margery said to Helen. "Text me when my dinner arrives."

While Helen slathered her warm bread with soft butter, Sophie settled a couple into the next booth. Helen thought the beefy fifty-something man seemed rigid with anger. Pads of fat hid a once-muscular frame and his expensive blue-checked shirt strained at the seams. His large, fleshy nose shadowed a cratered chin dimple. His brassy hair was badly dyed, but Helen was sure his deep green eyes were real, not contacts.

The woman with him was a babe. A little mileage, but her make-up was expertly applied and shoulder-length blonde hair framed her face. Her stylish black dress showed off her curvy figure.

The couple both ordered steaks. "We're in a bit of a hurry," the man said. "Could you get our dinners quickly?"

"You belong to our Superb Steaks Club," Sophie said. "Do you have your card, sir?"

"Look, I'm in a hurry," he said. "Just get our dinners."

"Yes, thank you, sir," Sophie said, and Helen guessed she'd been tipped. "I'll tell the chef."

As soon as Sophie left, the man snarled at the blonde, "I'm only having dinner with you because I have to eat. Then I want my money and I'm outta here."

This is interesting, Helen thought, leaning back to eavesdrop better.

"You'll get your money, baby," the blonde said.

"I'm not your baby," he said. "And you didn't have a baby. There is no Amy Rose. You've been lying to me for twenty years. Twenty freaking years. I paid you a thousand a month in child support, plus tuition so Amy Rose could become a radiation tech. You got a quarter of a million. I want it back."

"I don't have it, Bobby," she said. "I bought a house. I'm divorcing my husband and he'll get it. But I have a hundred twenty thousand. We can share it. We'll go off together to the Caribbean. Live somewhere cheap."

She was begging. He wasn't buying it.

"Listen, Rosalee," he said.

Rosalee. A woman who wouldn't get her half of the house in the divorce because she was on the run. Rosalee had had a wild weekend with Bobby, a hunk with green eyes, a noble nose and dimpled chin.

Helen texted Margery: ROSALEE & BOBBY IN NEXT BOOTH? CHECK THRU WINDOW.

As Helen reached for more bread, a lone brunette with a flowered silk scarf on her head slid into the cramped table behind Bobby and Rosalee's booth. She was slender, average height, and wore a tailored beige pantsuit with a four-pocket blazer. Scarf Woman could barely wedge herself into the curtained recess. She handed Sophie a purple card and said, "The usual, medium rare."

Helen, who'd spent time in upscale retail, recognized the scarf and suit as Gucci and the brown hair peeking out from the scarf as expertly styled. Who wears a silk scarf on her head in this heat? she wondered.

Bobby and Rosalee's conversation had turned snarly, and Helen tuned back in. "We had some fun twenty years ago," he said, "but that's all. When you said you were knocked up, I did the right thing and supported your so-called baby. I should have asked for a blood test."

"But you didn't, Bobby," she said, her voice soft and syrupy. "Why?"

"Because I'm honorable."

"Or because you didn't want your rich fiancée to find out," Rosalee said. "You married Marie in December and took over her daddy's construction business. What if she knew you were doing the wild thing at the Royalton while she was planning her big society wedding?"

Helen heard a ding! and fumbled for her phone. Margery had texted: IT'S HER. BEST MAKEOVER SINCE CINDERELLA. I'LL STAY HERE. U LISTEN.

The server bustled out with Bobby and Rosalee's steaks, then stopped by Helen's table. "Your meal will be out shortly," she said. "May I get you and your friend a drink on the house?"

"No, thanks," Helen said. "My friend had to leave. Could you pack up her dinner to go?"

Now Bobby and Rosalee's booth sounded like a snake pit. "Who did you get to pose as my so-called daughter?" Bobby hissed. "You must have used at least two blondes. I didn't tumble to your scheme until dear little Amy Rose was in tech school. You sent me a cell phone photo of her at your home. It was so blurry I couldn't see her face, but I definitely saw her tattoo in that tacky tube top: a crescent moon and stars on her left breast. Then six months later, she was going to a dance in a strapless dress. Guess what? She'd lost the tattoo. You'd played me for a fool and I quit sending checks. I want my money back."

"You can have some of your money," Rosalee said. "We'll go away together and share it."

"I don't know you. I spent a weekend with you twenty years ago and forgot about it – except I paid through the nose for a little fun."

"Here's your jambalaya," the server said, setting a steaming plate in front of Helen. She jumped. She'd been listening to the drama in the next booth. Helen inhaled the perfume of spicy chicken, shrimp and andouille sausage.

"I'll bring your friend's to-go dinner in a minute," Sophie said.

"And the check," Helen said. She dug into her jambalaya and listened to Rosalee pleading. "Bobby, I love you. All those lonely years in Florida, you were the only man I thought about. Even when I was with my husband, I was really thinking of you."

"You scammed me, lady," he said. "Give me my money and get out of my life."

"Scammed! What about your wife, Marie? Does she know those payments you made to keep your Great Aunt Emily Bridwell Peyton in a Fort Lauderdale nursing home were really to me? How's she going to feel when she discovers there was no Aunt Emily? Is that worth two hundred fifty thousand to you? It should be!"

"Give me my money," he said, his voice dangerously low.

"No!"

"Then you'll regret it!"

"No, you will."

Rosalee stood up and rushed out of the restaurant. Bobby threw some money on the table and followed.

Helen texted: B&R LEAVING. FOLLOW R. She looked around wildly for the server. Where was Sophie?

"Here's your steak to go," the server said. "And the check." Helen glanced at the seventy-dollar check. Bobby and Rosalee were getting away. She handed Sophie a hundred-dollar bill and said, "There's more when I get back. Wrap up the rest of my dinner, please."

She sprinted for the exit next to the hotel's sagging canopy and was caught in chaos.

A Majestic Minneapolis Tours bus was unloading flowered suitcases the size of steamer trunks. Pale, pleasant people milled about, talking about the humidity. A mud-brown beater blocked the ramp to the hotel parking garage, its radiator leaking green lizard blood. A harried tow truck driver struggled to load the battered car onto his flatbed. A bellman tried – and failed – to clear the crowd.

Where was Margery? Helen saw her fighting her way through the crowd to the parking garage ramp.

"Margery!" Helen shouted, and nearly fell over a yellow striped suitcase. She dodged two more suitcases and a weary, sweating bellman before she popped out of the confusion, next to Margery. "Where's Rosalee?"

"She ran up the garage ramp," Margery said. "He followed about same time that tour bus arrived with half of Minneapolis. Bobby just took off like the devil was chasing him, driving a black Cadillac Escalade. I photographed him." She held up her cell phone.

"And Rosalee?"

"She hasn't come down yet," Margery said. "That dead car has blocked the ramp and they're having a hell of a time loading it on the flatbed. There! Finally."

The tow truck lurched into the narrow French Quarter street and Helen and Margery ran up the crumbling concrete ramp, breathing in the stink of mold and exhaust, as impatient drivers honked their horns.

"No sign of Rosalee," Margery said, sweat running down her wrinkles.

The line of cars stopped at the third level. Helen saw a scattering of parked cars. Two rows from the exit, high-heeled feet stuck out between a white Chevy Malibu and the concrete wall. Helen touched Margery's shoulder, pointed to the feet, and put her finger to her lips. Margery nodded. Helen reached into her purse for her pepper spray, which had made it through the TSA check. The women crept toward the car until they were hidden behind a pillar.

Rosalee was lying next to the Malibu, a thick silver knife in her chest. Death scenes are rarely beautiful, but Rosalee's was an eerie study in black and red. She lay in a dark pool of blood, the white Malibu and the mold-streaked concrete wall spattered with blood. At the edge of the gory pool, a twenty-something man, scrawny as an alley cat, was riffling a small black patent leather purse. He tossed out a lipstick and a room key. His overgrown soul patch gave him a goatish look. He grabbed a fat roll of bills from Rosalee's purse.

Helen shouted, "You! Don't move!"

Margery snapped his photo. He dropped the purse and started to run, but Helen stepped in front of him, pointing the pepper spray at his eyes. "This will hurt," she said. "A lot." He stopped.

"I didn't do it," he said, sweat exploding on his forehead.

"Scum! Robbing this woman after you killed her," Helen said.

"No!" he said. "She was already dead. I took the money. She's not going to need it."

"You let her bleed out and stole her cash," Helen said. "We saw you."

"You saw me taking her money. I found her with the knife in her chest. She wasn't bleeding any more. I watch CSI. I know dead bodies don't bleed. Her heart wasn't pumping any blood."

"What's your name?" Helen asked.

"Squirrel."

"That's what your mother calls you?"

"No, I'm Russell Reed Squires."

"And you didn't call 911?" Margery asked.

"I can't. Because of . . . uh, my business."

"Murder and robbery?" Helen said, grabbing his greasy brown hair with one hand, pepper spray still aimed at his face. He tried to move, but her fingers were too tightly wound in his hair.

"No! I sell a little weed and blow. This is my territory. There are no cameras in this garage. I hang around outside with the smokers until a customer calls me and then I deliver. I got a call from someone up on three, parked in spot sixteen. I made the delivery and he drove off. I saw the dead lady and took her money. But that's all."

He pointed at Margery. "Ask her. She saw me get the call."

Margery nodded. "He took a call and sprinted up the ramp. I bet his cargo pants are loaded with product."

Helen pulled a burrito-sized plastic bag of whitish powder out of the cargo pocket closest to her, and chucked it over the side of the open garage into the alley below. It exploded like a flour bomb.

"Hey!" the dealer said.

"Shut up," Margery said. She liberated a bag of dried plant material from another pocket and tossed it. Helen and Margery quickly emptied his inventory into the alley, then Margery helped herself to a cabbage-size ball of bills.

"Margery, did you see Mr. Squires head upstairs before or after Bobby left?"

"After," Margery said. "This specimen slithers, but he couldn't have killed her. He doesn't have any blood on him. Look at the blood spatter on the Malibu. He doesn't have any blood on that disgusting muscle shirt. He doesn't have any muscle, either."

"Hey!"

"How old are you?" Helen asked.

"Twenty-three."

"Ever been arrested and convicted?"

He tried to stone-face her, but Helen menaced him with the spray. "I did eighteen months for possession," he said.

"Adult or juvie?" she asked.

"I just got out."

"Put that woman's cash back in her purse," Helen said, and he did. "Take his picture again, Margery. The cops will be able to identify him and his sweaty prints will be on Rosalee's shiny patent leather purse. Get out of here."

The dealer disappeared. Margery stepped closer to the blood pool to examine the body. "That's a monogrammed Royalton's Superb Steaks knife. I bet Bobby killed her."

"What's that white thing by the Malibu?" Helen asked.

Margery got closer and photographed it. "A napkin monogrammed RSS with a lipstick smear and a grease spot."

"Bobby hid the knife in the napkin to get it out of the restaurant," Helen said.

"Did you see him running out with the knife?"

"No, I was trying to flag down the server," Helen said. "Let's ask Sophie if she's missing a knife. We need to find out where Bobby lives. She'll know. He belongs to the Superb Steaks Club."

She saw a checkbook sticking out of Rosalee's purse, and used her shirt tail and a pen to ease it out and open it. The account was for Emily Bridwell Peyton at a Fort Lauderdale address. The balance was a hundred fifteen thousand dollars. Stuffed in the checkbook was a driver's license with the same name and address and the glam Rosalee's photo. "I've found the missing money," Helen said, carefully sliding the checkbook back.

Margery was counting Squires's drug money. "Eight hundred twenty bucks here," she said. "Should we call 911 and report the murder?"

"Later," Helen said. "We have a killer to catch."

As the two women ran for Superb Steaks, Helen told Margery about the shadowy woman in the Gucci scarf who sat behind Bobby and Rosalee. Once inside the restaurant, they were grateful it was nearly empty. Sophie greeted them with a smile. "Ladies, you've come back for your dinners."

"We were hoping you could feed us some information," Helen said. "Bobby, who was sitting with the blonde in that middle booth, he's a regular, right?"

"Yes," Sophie said.

"Did he swipe his steak knife?" Helen said.

"How did you know? He's never done that before. Those knives are expensive. The manager counts them every night. I'll be docked a hundred dollars out of my paycheck for that missing knife. The owner can't afford to replace them. And I'll lose twenty-five bucks for the monogrammed napkin the lady with the flowered scarf took. That means I'll make almost nothing this week."

Margery peeled eight twenties out of Squires's stash. "Would that help?" she said. A relieved smile lit Sophie's face. She started to reach for the money, but Margery held onto it.

"We need their names and addresses," she said. "Bobby and the scarf lady. We know they belong to the Superb Steaks Club. Who are they?"

"The scarf lady is Marie. She's married to Bobby," Sophie said. "But they never come here for dinner together. Bobby is a player and brings in so many women, I never acknowledge them and he tips me well. Marie, his wife, has a steady boyfriend named Parker who meets her here. She sees Parker on Tuesdays and Saturdays. Bobby brings his women on Mondays, Wednesdays and Fridays. I think they must have some kind of agreement. I know she can't divorce Bobby. I heard her tell Parker she'd lose her family home if she did. Parker wants to marry her. She told him that Bobby is ruining her family's construction business.

"I expected fireworks when Marie showed up tonight, but she kept her face hidden by the scarf and sat in the alcove. Bobby never knew she was here."

Margery handed her the money and put down two more twenties. "When did Marie leave?"

"As soon as her husband and that blonde he was with ran out. Her dinner was thirty dollars. She left exactly that much – no tip – and then stole the napkin."

"Do Bobby and Marie live together?" Helen asked.

"Yes. Not too far away. Big white two-story on Prytania Street in the Garden District." She looked up the address on the restaurant computer, then added a phone number. "That's Bobby's cell." Margery gave her another twenty and she and Helen ran outside.

The hotel doorman flagged a cab and soon Helen and Margery were at Bobby's house on Prytania, a graceful white brick with black shutters and an airy gallery. Lacy wrought iron protected the palm trees, magnolias and bougainvillea in the manicured yard.

Helen called Bobby's cell and was relieved when he answered.

"Mr. Charbonnet?" Her voice quick and urgent. "I heard you talking to Rosalee about the payments you've been making to her for twenty years. If you don't want your wife to find out, talk to me. I'm right outside your house."

"Who are you?" Bobby demanded. Helen saw a lace curtain twitch and then the front door opened. Bobby met Helen and Margery on the sidewalk.

Helen said she was a private detective, introduced Margery as her associate, and explained they were tracing Rosalee and the hundred thousand dollars she'd stolen.

"She took it from a charity?" he said. "I'm not surprised. That woman is a cheat and a liar."

"She's also dead," Helen said.

"What? How? Where?" Bobby was bug-eyed with shock.

"Where do you think, Mr. Charbonnet?"

He was hyperventilating now. "No! I don't know. I parked on the first floor of the garage and saw her walking up the ramp. She was alive when I left her."

"She was stabbed on the third floor of the garage," Helen said.

"That's not possible."

"I saw her," Helen said.

"My wife must have hired someone to kill her," he said. "Marie's been going over the books for our business. I think she noticed when I quit making payments to Rosalee. She hates me."

"What's your wife look like?" Helen asked.

"Skinny brunette, dresses nice in designer stuff. About that high." He held up his hand at about five feet six.

"Does she own a flowered Gucci scarf?" Helen asked.

"I don't know Gucci from Pucci," he said.

"Really?" Helen said. "You're wearing an expensive Thomas Pink shirt."

"Wife bought it," he said. "Bought this watch, too."

"You're on the outs with your wife and she bought you a nine-thousand-dollar TAG Heuer?

"We were still getting along then. She says I dress like a homeless person and embarrass her. Parker, the man she's been seeing, gave her a designer scarf for Christmas with flowers all over it. I thought it was ugly as homemade sin, but she raved about it."

"I think your wife was at the steakhouse wearing that scarf," Helen said.

Suddenly, Prytania Street was alive with police cars. One jerked to a stop next to Bobby, and a tall, fit cop with buzzed hair got out. His name tag said RUBELLE.

"Mr. Charbonnet?"

Bobby managed a nod.

"Do you know a Rosalee Alop?" Officer Rubelle asked.

Bobby's eyes were wide with fear, his voice low and desperate. "You've got to help me, Ms. Hawthorne," he said. "I've been set up. My wife killed Rosalee."

Officer Rubelle swaggered over to them. "Mr. Charbonnet, I asked if you knew a Rosalee Alop. We got an anonymous 911 tip that you stabbed a woman to death in the parking garage of the Royalton Hotel tonight. Were you at the Royalton tonight, Mr. Charbonnet?"

"Tell the truth, Bobby," Helen said.

"Excuse me, miss," Officer Rubelle said. "I wasn't speaking to you."

"She's representing me," Bobby said.

Helen felt like she'd been punched. She hadn't agreed to take on Bobby as a client. He hadn't signed a contract. She glared at him, and he clasped his hands in prayer and mouthed, I'll pay.

"Are you a lawyer, miss?" the police officer said.

"I'm a private detective from Fort Lauderdale." Helen presented her ID.

"Florida, huh?" the cop said. "I believe Florida is one of the states that has mutually agreed to recognize the right of private investigators to conduct interstate business, but I don't believe that includes representing murder suspects."

"But she found the body," Bobby said, his face white and greasy as steak fat. Helen vowed to take her payment out of his fat hide, strip by bloody strip.

"Did you find the victim, Ms. Hawthorne?" Officer Rubelle said. "Tell the truth now, like you said to Mr. Charbonnet."

"I found her," Helen said. She was relieved her contract with CWC allowed her to disclose that information. Florida law prohibited her from discussing a case without the client's permission.

"The victim's name is Rosalee Alop. She embezzled a hundred thousand dollars from a Fort Lauderdale charity, Consolidated Worthy Causes. I was hired by CWC to find Ms. Alop and the missing money. I tracked her to New Orleans, where she met with Mr. Charbonnet at Royalton's Superb Steaks tonight. They argued and she ran out to the parking garage. Mr. Charbonnet followed her. I ran after them. By the time I left the restaurant, Mr. Charbonnet had driven out of the hotel parking garage. I went up to find Ms.

Alop. I discovered her body on the third floor."

"I discovered the body, too," Margery said.

"And who might you be, ma'am?" Officer Rubelle asked.

Margery was eager to announce she was an operative, but Helen cut her off. Margery would be no help sharing Helen's cell in the NOLA jail.

"She's my landlady, Margery Flax," Helen said. "She wanted to see New Orleans and came along with me."

Margery must have realized she'd be more help out of jail. She quickly softened her expression and did fair impersonation of a sweet, Marlboro-smoking senior.

"So this lady in purple is a tourist," Officer Rubelle said, "and you're a professional investigator, Ms. Hawthorne. And you didn't call 911?"

"I was in a hurry, officer," Helen said. "I believe the killer is at this house."

"You believe? Believe? I believe I just might file a complaint against you, Ms. Hawthorne. You could have called 911 anonymously from a free public phone."

"There wasn't one," Helen said. She figured that was true. Working public phones were as rare as south Florida ski resorts.

"Then you should have used your cell phone," he said. "This is professional negligence on your part. Which department in Florida oversees private investigators?"

"The Department of Agriculture and Consumer Services," Helen said, and waited for the inevitable laugh.

"Agriculture?" the cop said. "Then you've stepped into a big pile of fertilizer, Ms. Hawthorne. If you'd called us, we would have arrested Mr. Charbonnet ourselves."

"He didn't do it," Helen said, her voice shaking.

"The waitress in Superb Steaks said Mr. Charbonnet stole a steak knife from the restaurant," the cop said. "A similar knife was found in Ms. Alop's chest with fingerprints on it. We're running those prints now, but we're sure they're gonna belong to Mr. Charbonnet."

"I'm sure they will, too," Helen said. Bobby looked like he might pass out.

"That same public-spirited waitress said Mr. Charbonnet and Ms. Alop were fighting over money," Officer Rubelle said. "Mr. Charbonnet was furious because the victim had bilked him out of a quarter of a million dollars. He wanted his money back and she said she didn't have it. He said she'd be sorry and the next thing you know, she's dead and he hightails it back home here.

"Fortunately, some responsible citizen did what you should have done, Ms. Hawthorne, and called the police. Now we're going to arrest Mr. Charbonnet and throw you in jail for obstruction of justice."

"Bobby didn't kill Rosalee," Helen repeated. "His wife Marie did. She was at the restaurant. Check the monogrammed napkin that was dropped near the Malibu's tire and you'll find her lipstick and DNA on it."

"Already bagged and tagged," the cop said. "We know how to do our job. Lipstick and DNA are supposed to be on napkins. Anyone could have grabbed her napkin off the table and dropped it near the car."

"Except Bobby Charbonnet," Helen said. "He left while Marie was still eating at the restaurant. She meets her boyfriend Parker for dinner there twice a week. Ask the server, Sophie. Check Marie's and Parker's Superb Steaks Club cards. That same server will tell you that Parker wants to marry Marie, but she doesn't want to lose her fabulous Prytania Street house when she divorces Bobby.

"He's been mismanaging her family business and skimming money to send to the victim. His wife made that anonymous call to 911. A voice print will prove that. Marie set him up. If Bobby was in jail, she could divorce him and keep her showcase house."

"Nice theory, Ms. Hawthorne, but there's no proof."

"I think there is," Margery interrupted. "That steakhouse is loaded with security cameras. Check them, and you'll see a woman in a flowered scarf and fancy suit using her napkin to swipe Bobby's knife off his empty table. That woman is Marie. She followed Rosalee up to the third floor of the parking garage, stabbed her and then drove home. Check the tapes yourself.

"You should also check the data on the Superb Steaks Club cards for Bobby, Marie and her boyfriend Parker and find out how often they ate there. And when you're in this house, look for the clothes Marie wore to dinner tonight. She had on an expensive suit and scarf and they're sure to have blood on them. Is she going to throw away several thousand dollars in clothes?"

"That goes for Mr. Charbonnet's clothes, too," the officer said.

"Absolutely," Helen said. "But he's wearing a checked shirt and khakis, and that's what he wore to dinner. The security camera will back me up. So will the server. There's no blood spatter on Bobby's clothes, though he does have a grease stain on his pants."

"Well, I suppose I can call homicide at the restaurant," the cop said. "They're still working the scene."

"That would be ever so kind of you, Officer Rubelle," Margery said, batting her eyelashes. Helen stared at her irascible landlady doing a southern belle act. It was like seeing an alligator in a ruffled bonnet.

"It's so exciting to watch a police professional at work," Margery purred. "Almost worth missing the Super City Tour, though I did want to see the French Quarter."

The cop preened, then made the call to the homicide detective working the crime scene. "You all stay here while we verify this," he said. "I'll go see if Mrs. Charbonnet is home."

"She is," Bobby said. "She's in the upstairs sitting room, last I knew."

Officer Rubelle and another uniform rang the doorbell and disappeared into the air-conditioned showcase. Margery, Helen, Bobby and two uniforms sweated outside for more than an hour. It was past ten o'clock when Officer Rubelle came out and announced, "We'll take statements from each of you. The search warrant for these premises is on the way."

"You have my permission to search my house," Bobby said.

"We're doing this by the book, sir," the officer said. "Mrs. Charbonnet is now a person of interest."

As Marie Charbonnet was escorted out of her showcase home, eyes glittering with hate, Helen went inside to give her statement in a red velvet parlor furnished with antebellum antiques. Margery was next. Afterward, she and Helen sat outside on the veranda, Margery smoking one cigarette after another.

"I can't believe your Scarlett O'Hara act," Helen said. She mimicked a fake southern belle accent: "That would be ever so kind of you, Officer Rubelle. It's so exciting to watch a police professional at work. Almost worth missing the Super City Tour, though I did want to see the French Quarter."

"Hey, I kept you out of a New Orleans jail," Margery said. "Be grateful."

"I am," Helen said. "But I feel sorry for poor Rosalee. She really loved Bobby."

"The hell she did," Margery said. "You don't blackmail the man you love for twenty years. What are you going to do with the money in her checkbook?"

"Let the police handle it," Helen said. "It's part of a crime scene. I'll write a report letting our client know where it is. But Rosalee is still married to Dennison, so that hundred and fifteen thousand is part of her estate. CWC can fight it out with him."

Margery was tapping on her cell phone. "I'm booking us a flight home for tomorrow," she said. "Two o'clock work for you?"

"That will give me time for a beignet at Café du Monde," Helen said.

At midnight, a badly shaken Bobby tottered out, his checked shirt a wrinkled mess and his hair coated with thirty-weight oil.

He sat down next to them on the front steps. "It's over," he said. "The cops found Marie's bloody clothes and some towels hidden in the dryer. The video of her taking the knife, along with the waitress's testimony are enough to arrest Marie. They're charging her with Rosalee's murder."

"When they prove that's Rosalee's blood on the clothes and towels and Marie's lipstick and DNA on the napkin," Helen said, "they'll have enough for a conviction."

"Don't forget the server's testimony," Margery added.

"Thank you," Bobby said. "You ladies saved me."

"Best way to thank us is to pay us," Margery said. "Nothing says 'I'm grateful' like a stack of cash."

"I'm not sure Bobby can hire me," Helen said. "I don't know if I'm licensed to take a case in New Orleans. I'd have to check the law."

"Well, you can pay me, Bobby," Margery said. "No law against me sharing my good fortune with a friend."

"How much?" Bobby asked.

"Five thousand," Margery said. Helen's eyes bulged.

"For one night's work?" Bobby said.

"We saved your bacon," she said. "Also, I had a thousand dollars' in expenses. Sophie the server was taking a big risk telling us what happened. Thanks to her, we were here when you needed us. I had to pay her for that information."

With two hundred twenty dollars of the drug dealer's money, Helen thought. The crafty Margery had already snagged a profit of six hundred bucks.

"That's a little steep," Bobby said.

"Hey, we were here when the police were going to haul you off to jail," Margery said. "How much would a lawyer have cost if you were arrested? What would an arrest do to your business's reputation? Not to mention a trial?"

Bobby knew when he was beaten. "All good points. May I write you a check, Margery?"

"You may, but you don't have the best financial record. How about you give me that fancy watch as collateral until the check clears? There's a branch of my bank on Canal Street. If your check passes muster, you can stop by the hotel at eleven tomorrow and I'll give you your watch before we leave for the airport."

While Bobby wrote the check and handed his TAG Heuer to Margery, she asked, "Where can I get a good hurricane at this hour? What do you recommend?"

"I don't recommend a hurricane for anyone. They're killers: 151 rum and fruit juice is a lethal combination."

"I can handle it," Margery said.

"Well, Pat O'Brien's is supposed to be the home of the hurricane. But any bartender in New Orleans can make one. The Carousel Bar in the Monteleone Hotel in the French Quarter is fun. The bar looks like a real carousel. It even spins."

"After a drink or two, they all spin," Margery said. "Let's go, Helen."

Red Meat

Jake couldn't believe his sixtieth birthday gift: his wife gave him a twenty-three-year-old blonde. Only later did he realize this dream gift was a deadly pleasure. "Red Meat" won the Anthony Award for Best Short Story.

Ashley had a body to die for, and I should know. I'm on death row because of her.

You want to know the funny thing?

My wife bought me Ashley. For a birthday present.

I was turning sixty that July, and I could feel the cold wind at my neck. I wasn't bad-looking for my age. I still had all my hair. But that semi-permanent twenty pounds of lard around my gut had turned into thirty. I had chicken skin on the insides of my elbows, like an old geezer. And women didn't give me appraising looks anymore.

Not that I need to look at other women. My Francie had kept her figure just fine. She was ten years younger than me, and worked out with a personal trainer. Recently, people had started asking if Francie was my daughter. I'd laughed it off, but it bothered me. I told Francie maybe she should dye her hair gray so she'd look her age. She said, "Maybe you should lose thirty pounds, Jake, so you'd look your age."

I'd thought about going to the gym. We had a good one, right here on Sunnysea Beach, Florida, owned by a former pro linebacker. I'd see Jamal Wellington out running on the sand. You know those fake-heroic chests guys strap on so they look like gladiators? Jamal had a real chest like that, and arms and legs to match.

Francie and I had a beachfront condo about a mile from Jamal's Jym, but beach life makes you lazy. I never got around to walking down there. I'd think about joining the gym, but I'd always lie back down until the fitness fit passed. Instead, I'd pop another brew and watch another movie. I had a state-of-the-art entertainment system with five clickers (Francie put the clickers in a basket so I wouldn't leave them lying around).

Now that I was retired, I had time to catch up on my movies. I'd been comparing the classic Bond films starring Sean Connery to the later ones with Roger Moore. In my opinion, Connery was the one true Bond. Moore looked like a Sears shirt model.

When Francie came home from work that night, I said, "You

can't trust movie critics. This so-called critic says *For Your Eyes Only* is a superior piece of escapism."

"I don't know what you need to escape," Francie snapped, slamming her briefcase down on the kitchen table.

I could tell Francie was peeved, so I put down my beer and took her to the Beachside Bar for dinner. I thought she'd be happy she didn't have to cook. Instead she glared at me when I mopped up my steak gravy with my butter bread. She got testy when I downed my third martini. By the time I ordered Key lime pie with extra whipped cream, Francie was steaming. She didn't say anything, but the air around her got dense and crackly, like she was generating her own personal thunderstorm.

Francie's bad mood was gone by my sixtieth birthday, two days later. She smiled and slipped on her silky leopard-print robe I like so much.

"Happy Birthday, Tiger," she said, handing me a ribbon-wrapped box. "I got you a twenty-three-year-old blonde for your birthday."

"I like my fifty-year-old brunette," I said, patting her rump.

I opened the present. Inside was a gift card. It said I should meet my personal trainer, Ashley, at Jamal's Jym at two p.m. today for my first workout.

"Ashley? What kind of name is that?" I snorted. "She probably looks like a Russian Olympic gymnast. I bet she shaves more than I do." Then I shut up. I realized I was grumping like a sixty-year-old.

"Wait and see," Francie said, smiling.

I walked down to the gym that broiling July afternoon, feeling sorry for myself. I felt like I was walking barefoot across a hot stove. Sweat ran off me like rainforest waterfalls. I couldn't believe my own wife bought me a personal trainer to make me sweat more. I passed the WaterEdge condo building, its units hidden behind hurricane shutters. Those people had the sense to leave south Florida in July. I was stuck here with a bearded woman trainer.

At Jamal's Jym, I presented my gift card to a young guy named Barry. He wore only black gym shorts and running shoes. I wished he would put on more clothes. The guy's bare stomach was so flat you could bounce quarters on it. His muscles rippled when he typed in my name on the computer.

"Your wife got you Ashley," Barry said, with a knowing smile. "Welcome to the club." I didn't know if Barry was talking about the gym, or some other club. I didn't care, either. A blonde walked out of the Staff Only door, and I couldn't stop staring at her.

She looked like a cross between Wonder Woman and the captain of the girls' volleyball team. She was tanned to a golden brown and wearing a black spandex sports bra and short-shorts that revealed eye-popping development, front and back.

She had muscles, but she wasn't gnarly and knotted, like those women in the bodybuilding magazines. Ashley was sculpted like a statue. Her breasts were high and round and real. Her eyes were blue-green, like the ocean on a summer day. Her long golden hair rippled in sunlit waves.

"I'm Ashley," she said.

"Jake," I said, which was all I could manage with my stomach sucked in.

Ashley had me work out with what she called light weights. After that, I had to do two hundred pushups, then run on the sand for two miles.

I went home so exhausted, I fell into bed and slept until the next morning. I missed dinner, but I didn't mind. I dreamed of Ashley, looking like a blonde goddess in black spandex.

I met with Ashley three times a week. Sometimes I slogged through the sand. Other times, I lifted weights. Always, she barked orders: "Slow down! Watch your form! Point those feet straight ahead. No penguining!"

I was lying on a slant board while a beautiful blonde yelled at me. I loved it.

I also loved that all the other guys stared when Ashley and I ran on the sand together. I was the envy of every man on the beach. Even the lifeguards looked at me with new respect.

"How'd you get so lucky to get Ashley?" asked Nick, the bartender at the Beachside Bar.

"My wife bought her for me," I said.

"Yeah, right, and my wife bought me Amy Adams," he said.

Nick didn't believe me. I could scarcely believe it, either.

Ashley had definite ideas about fitness. She wanted me to ditch my Diet Coke for bottled water. "Too many chemicals, dude," she said.

So I laid off the Diet Coke, and started drinking eight bottles of water a day, the way Ashley wanted. I wouldn't tell anyone, but I liked the taste better.

After six weeks, the chicken skin on my arms began to disappear. After eight weeks, my gut began to deflate. Women were giving me the eye again. My Francie started calling me "stud muffin." I hadn't looked this good in twenty years.

"I'm making progress, Ashley," I said. "But I can't seem to lose more weight."

"What are you eating, dude?" she said.

"Not much. That's what is so strange. I skip breakfast and lunch, then eat a big dinner."

She shook her head. "Bad idea. Your body can't run efficiently on no fuel. You're not eating enough."

"That's not what my wife says."

"You need to eat every three to five hours. But you need to eat right," Ashley said, firmly. Everything about her was firm.

She put me on a protein diet. I should have been happy living on mostly meat, but this wasn't what I called meat. Ashley wanted me to eat white meat of chicken and turkey, water-packed tuna, and broiled fish. I could have an egg-white omelet, but no butter or cheese. The only bread was whole wheat, and none of that after three in the afternoon. I could have a baked potato at lunch if I ate the skin, green vegetables like broccoli, and when I was feeling wild, graham crackers. That was it, except for cranberry juice and two cups of coffee a day.

"Where's the steak?" I said. "Where's the hamburger?"

"Red meat's bad for you," Ashley said, looking commanding but adorable, like a dominatrix in a porno movie.

"Ashley," I said, "you are what you eat. I am two hundred pounds of red meat. I am a red-blooded male. I need my red meat."

"Mark my words, dude, red meat will kill you," Ashley said. She was right.

But I loved my porterhouses, filet mignons, even flank steaks. Red meat. Bloody meat, oozing deliciously on my plate.

I ate broiled chicken breast, though it tasted like warm Kleenex. I had whole wheat buns, though they were dry as old attic insulation. And egg-white omelets, though they tasted like nothing at all. I drank bottled water until I felt like one long stretch of plumbing. I sweated at Jamal's Jym, with Ashley barking orders, for two months on this dull diet.

I didn't lose an ounce.

"Hmm," Ashley said. "I know this diet can be slow to kick in, but you must be doing something wrong."

She gave me a little notebook and said, "Write down everything you eat each day."

The notebook was her first gift to me. "My diet diary," I joked.

It's amazing how your sins add up. I saw my life as one unending stretch of virtuous eating. I forgot about the jar of cashews I ate at four o'clock, the candy bar I sneaked at six, the occasional steak to break the monotony. I didn't think a little sour cream and butter on a dry baked potato was a big deal. I sure didn't think a couple of drinks were a problem.

But Ashley did. Lord, the lecture that woman gave me when she saw my diet diary.

"Listen, dude," she said. "I thought you were serious about this bodybuilding."

"I am," I said, mesmerized by her pectoral development. She'd built an amazing body.

"Then you've got to get serious about your food," she said, showing me those fat-free buns as she bent over to pick up a pencil. That improved my heart rate, let me tell you.

Ashley graded my diet diary like a kindergarten teacher. The turkey, fish, and egg-white omelets got smiley faces. The red meat got a frownie face. The martinis got "THIS IS TOO MUCH ALCOHOL!!!"

"Ashley, this is like being in prison," I said, because back then I didn't know anything about prison. "Even the doctors say a glass of wine is good for your heart."

"You can have one – only one – glass of wine with dinner," she said, sternly.

I showed Francie the Ashley-corrected diet diary. I thought she would make sarcastic remarks about the smiley faces, but Francie only patted my newly bulging biceps and said, "Ashley has done wonders, Tiger. Listen to her."

I smiled. Those thirty-two smile muscles were the only ones that didn't hurt.

That was something I didn't talk about. I hurt. All over. All the time. I looked better than I had in years, but those toned muscles let me know how they felt about getting back in shape. My shoulders hurt. My torso ached. My legs hurt.

When I say my legs hurt, I mean my calves, thighs, ankles, even my feet were sore. Each part hurt in a different way. My stretched calves were a dull ache. My sore feet were a sharp pain. My glutes shrieked when I sat down.

I was sixty years old, for god's sake. This was too much.

I told Ashley about the constant pain, but she only said, "No whining, dude."

Francie didn't take me seriously, either. "If that's all you have to complain about, you're doing pretty darn good," she said.

I admit all the compliments made me feel better. Take the night we were having an early dinner with four friends (I had to see Ashley at seven the next morning). They showered me with "you-look-terrifics," and "you've-been working-outs." When I told everyone that Francie had bought me Ashley for my birthday, they could hardly believe it. The guys, Harry and George, winked and nudged each other.

Kaye said, "How do you feel about him working out with a twenty-three-year-old blonde, Francie?"

"Every woman should have an Ashley," she said. "For years, I've been telling him that he eats the wrong food, but would he listen to me? Oh, no, I was just a wife. I was just a nag.

"But when Ashley says he needs to eat more vegetables, it's bring on the broccoli, boys. When Ashley says he's eating too much red meat, he switches to fish and chicken. When Ashley says he drinks too much, he cuts back to one glass of wine a day.

"Could I get him to do that? Not me. I'm only a wife. But Ashley can. That's why every woman should have an Ashley. I wish I'd had her twenty years ago."

Everyone laughed, but I thought I heard a nasty edge. My delight in Ashley diminished just a bit.

I began noticing little things. Like how many times I saw Ashley running on the sand with paunchy guys between forty and sixty. Guys who looked ready to drop from exhaustion. I wanted to talk to them, but Ashley made sure they kept moving. She'd wave at me and never stop. The paunchy guys trotted along beside her.

So I asked her outright: "Those other guys you run with, did their wives buy you as a gift, too?"

Ashley said, "No talking, dude. It breaks your concentration."

Six months into the workout, the pain stopped. That's when I made my final, fatal mistake. I said, "Ashley, it doesn't hurt so much any more."

I wanted to celebrate. But Ashley said, "Then we need to step up the workouts, dude. We can't have you enjoying yourself. No pain, no gain."

When she said those four stupid words, that was the first time I wanted to strangle her.

Then Ashley brought out the blue bands.

They did not look like much: four feet of rubber tubing with triangular handles on the ends. Such simple things, but so many instruments of torture are simple. A simple electric drill in a knee-cap can cause excruciating pain. A simple tire iron can break every bone in your body.

Ashley's exercise bands tripled my misery. She made me wrap them around a palm tree and pull them, while I held my hands and feet at impossible angles. We'd – no, I'd – work out in humiliating poses while fat red tourists, buttered with coconut oil, stood around and laughed.

"Come on, dude, work harder," Ashley would command. "Pull! Pull! Pull!"

I would pull until my arms quivered and my neck ached, but it was never enough for her. "Come on, you're not crippled," she would scream, entertaining the slug-butt tourists.

I smiled through my pain, but that night I went out and had a Diet Coca-Cola. Then I wrote it defiantly in my diet diary. It was my way of getting even. Diet Coke upset Ashley more than beer. She said beer at least had some natural ingredients. "Diet soda is nothing but chemicals, dude."

I felt ashamed when I drank my Diet Coke. I used to down

martinis and single malt scotch. Now I was chugging Diet Cokes – and worse, feeling guilty. All because of Ashley.

I couldn't even get any satisfaction in my rebellion. Ashley only said, "You've come a long way, dude. Who'd have thought an old boozer like you would be sneaking sodas and feeling guilty about it?"

Then she laughed. The cords in her short, powerful neck stood out, ugly as tree roots. I was so mad, I wanted to kill her.

That night, I dreamed I strangled Ashley with one of her own exercise bands. I knew it was time to stop.

Next day at the gym I asked, "Did my wife buy you for one year?"

"A year? No, your wife got the deluxe package, dude. This is a life sentence." She smiled, but her mouth was harder than the Rock's abs.

"Life?" I said. I felt the prison doors closing on me. I would never know another pain-free day. I would never eat another steak without feeling guilty. I wouldn't even drink another sinless soda.

"Look, Ashley," I said. "This has been fun, but it's time to stop. It's been a year. Refund Francie her money and I'll go quietly. I'm sick of all this good health."

"Can't, dude," she said. "No refunds. Francie knew that when she paid upfront."

"Well, I'm sorry she'll lose her money," I said. "But I quit."

It felt good when I said that. I wanted my old life back, and if my old body came back with it, so be it. Maybe I didn't used to look good, but I felt good.

I saw myself ordering one of Nick's straight-up martinis with an oily slick of vermouth and a sliver of lemon peel. Then I'd have a long wet lunch of red wine and rare steak. Red meat for a red-blooded male.

"Quit?" Ashley said, and her lip curled. Even her blonde hair curled in contempt.

"What will you tell everyone? That you're not man enough to keep me? The whole beach knows we work out. Stop now, and I'll tell everyone you weren't tough enough to work out with a girl."

I remembered all those lifeguards and beach bums grinning as I made my proud progress on the sand, Ashley at my side. I remembered Nick the bartender's envy. I saw my friends at dinner, nudging each other. I'd never be able to explain how tired I felt. I'd be a laughing stock.

I'd been given a blonde for my birthday and I was too tired to enjoy her.

"I don't care!" I said.

Jamal came over then. I guess we'd been talking louder than I thought.

"Anything wrong?" he said, looming over me like a mountain.

I shook my head. I was too tired to do anything else. I hurt in places I didn't know I had.

I showed up as usual for my next session. I was tied to Ashley until death parted us. For the first time, I actually looked forward to keeling over on the sand. Eternal rest took on new meaning.

Now that I couldn't escape her, everything Ashley did irritated me. I hated that she called me "dude." I couldn't stand those silly smiley faces in my diet diary. Not that I saw many. I was not only drinking Diet Cokes, I was piling mayonnaise on my grilled chicken – at six fat grams a spoonful. Yet now I didn't gain weight.

"Can't you just lie like everyone else?" Ashley said, as she read my acts of dietary defiance. We were working out on the empty, sun-bleached beach.

"Who's everyone else?" I said, furious at all the frownie faces.

"The other guys whose wives bought me. I'm a paid nag, dude. It's my job to buff up the old boys, tell them to eat their vegetables and drink less. Wives pay me well so they don't have to say those things."

"You mean my wife ... My wife knew that you ..." I could hardly breathe, I was so angry. Ashley ignored my anger, just as she ignored my pain. She kept hitting me with her taunts. Each one was another slam to my tortured body.

"They all do. Every woman in Sunnysea would love to have me, but not the way you would. They know old guys are suckers for sweet young things." She laughed, a cruel, cutting laugh.

"That's what I am – one of your suckers?" I'd never felt more humiliated. Ashley didn't notice that, either. She handed me the hated exercise bands.

"Hey, don't bust a gasket, dude," she said, still laughing. "It's not your fault you can't get it up, old man. Energywise, I mean. Let's work on your upper body strength."

"It's fine," I said, wrapping the blue band around her neck and squeezing as hard as I could. I kept my elbows at a perfect ninety-degree angle. I kept my knees slightly bent to support my lower back. I kept my feet straight out, not splayed to either side, so Ashley couldn't say "no penguining"

Ashley couldn't say anything. She was gagging, gasping, and clawing at her neck. She was strong, but I was stronger. I had another eighty pounds of solid muscle. She'd worked hard to build my arms. I pulled the band tighter. Her struggles grew more frantic. Her legs kicked futilely. I kept pulling, all the pain and rage I'd endured strangling my reason.

Ashley stopped struggling.

She was dead.

Slowly, I became aware of my surroundings again. I'd strangled a woman to death on Sunnysea Beach at two in the afternoon. I was fifty feet from a lifeguard stand. But the guard, whose head was as thick as his neck, was staring at three squealing kids hitting one another with boogie boards. He didn't notice us.

The storm-shuttered windows of the WaterEdge condo were blind, too.

Even the tourists weren't out on the boardwalk in this heat.

If I'd lost my temper in the high season of December, some cop would be reading me my rights. But this was July. In Florida, on a summer weekday, the beaches could be as empty as a gym rat's head.

No one saw me. I was lucky. Better yet, I got out of half my class.

But how long would my luck last? I couldn't leave her there. Everyone at Jamal's Jym knew I worked out with Ashley at this time.

My condo was a mile away. No way could I carry her body there. How was I going to get Ashley off the beach?

Don't panic, I told myself. Think.

I unwound the blue band from around Ashley's throat and shoved it in my pocket. Her face looked awfully red. I put my sweat towel down on the sand, then put Ashley on top of it, lying on her stomach. I turned her head so her long hair covered most of her face. I put my water bottle near her head, to further block the view of her face. If you didn't look too close, she seemed to be napping on the beach.

No one noticed me doing this. More luck. I ran all the way home and got my car. A 1997 Lincoln has lots of room.

I found a meter, another lucky break, and parked a block from where Ashley was on the sand. I only had a quarter, which buys fifteen minutes in Sunnysea.

Now came the hard part, getting Ashley off the beach and into the car. I knelt down on the sand, and shook Ashley gently, pretending that I was waking her from a sound sleep. Then I talked to her, as if she could hear me. I wanted it to look like she was my daughter or my girlfriend, and she was a little sunsick or tipsy.

I rolled her over on her back, then sat her up. She leaned against me. Her right arm flopped back down and nearly dented my quads. Her face looked swollen and awful, but her hair was hanging down, covering it. I got behind her, put my arms under her pits and pulled her into a standing position.

I now knew what a real deadweight lift was. What did Ashley weigh? One hundred-twenty pounds max? She felt like two hundred. I got her up and leaned her against me. She was oddly rubbery, but more cooperative than usual.

I draped her right arm over my shoulder and put my arm around her waist. She leaned against me like a drunk. That was good. I had a little spiel ready. "Out cold," I planned to say, with an indulgent smile. "Too many piña coladas."

I didn't see a soul when I carried Ashley to the car. It was my lucky day. I didn't even mind the ten-dollar parking ticket on my windshield. It was a small price to pay.

I opened the back door, and Ashley fell into the seat. She hit her head with a nasty THWAK! She didn't feel a thing, but I was hurting. She'd strained my already sore muscles. Soon those muscles would never hurt again.

But now I had to get rid of Ashley's body. I wasn't going to risk the ocean – it's too shallow here, unless you get about three miles out into the Gulf Stream. The canals were too risky for the same reason. But if I drove west, I'd be in the Everglades. The "river of grass," they call it. It was full of alligators. Perfect. I wondered if the gators would find Ashley as tough as I did. I smiled at the thought.

In about an hour, I was on Highway 27, which ran through the Everglades. I turned down a gravel road, bumping past a dusty-looking ranch and then a palm tree farm. The road petered out in the sawgrass, mud, and murky water that mark the Everglades. They don't call it sawgrass for nothing. That stuff can literally slice your arm off.

I wrestled Ashley out of the car. I was sweating like a hog. I dragged her into the water, ignoring the mosquito stings and the sawgrass slashes on my arms and legs. The water was shallow and tea-colored. I didn't want to think about what was in there.

I looked for some big rocks to sink the body. But when I got back with my first rock, Ashley was gone. A few seconds later I heard a loud plop! It was an alligator, sliding into the water. My own stomach plopped a bit at the thought, but I knew Ashley was gone for good. I wouldn't have to worry about anyone finding the body.

I was home long before Francie got off work. She found me on the couch watching *You Only Live Twice*, sipping single malt, and eating salted cashews.

"Jake!" she said, surprised. "What would Ashley say?"

"Not a damn thing," I said cheerfully. "She's taking a long rest. So am I."

The scotch made my tongue slip. Francie didn't seem to know what my remark meant, but I'd have to be more careful. I'd have to make sure to go to Jamal's Jym at my regular time Thursday.

I didn't get a chance. Two police detectives, one fat and one skinny, were on my doorstep the next day. They told me Ashley's body was found in the Everglades by a fisherman. Jamal said I was her last appointment, and she never came back. No one had seen her alive since two o'clock yesterday.

I wondered why that alligator had not taken care of my problem, but I didn't say anything. I was cool. I told the cops that Ashley and I worked out as usual. The last I saw, Ashley was running south on the sand to Jamal's. I was headed north, toward my home. I may have sweated a little when I said this, but it was July, wasn't it? The detectives finally left. They seemed satisfied with my answers.

They were back the next day. The fat one asked me to describe my last afternoon with Ashley again. I said we'd worked out on the beach, then I ran home and she ran off the other way.

"You ran home?" the fat cop said.

"All the way," I said, smugly.

"Then why did your car get a parking ticket on the beach about the time that Ashley disappeared?" the skinny one said.

"Uh," I said, and shut up until my lawyer showed up. The cops got a warrant and impounded my car. I wasn't worried. I'd taken it to a carwash.

But the police found three of Ashley's long blonde hairs in the back seat and her sandy footprint on the inside door. I'd tipped the carwash guy ten bucks, too. Good help is hard to find in Florida.

There was no point in claiming we'd had a little afternoon delight back there because the police found traces of some nasty substances on the seat. The body sort of lets go, you know. No, I guess you wouldn't. You've never killed anyone.

The cops also found plenty of motive. Jamal testified that I'd had a "bitter quarrel" – his words – with Ashley at the gym and tried to get out of the contract.

My wife told the court about my strange behavior on the last day Ashley was seen. I couldn't believe my Francie would do that.

The jury, which was mostly men, couldn't understand how I could kill that gorgeous blonde. They didn't understand she was killing me.

So here I am on death row in Florida. Today is my last day on earth. The chaplain asked if I was sorry.

I am.

I am very sorry I didn't come up with a better body disposal plan. You can't depend on alligators. They don't really like humans, and only eat them if they're desperate or disturbed. I learned that in the prison library. I had a lot of time to read while my appeals were being denied.

The warden served up the final irony.

"You can have anything you want for your last meal, Jake," he said. "Even steak."

I couldn't stop laughing when he said that. I remembered what Ashley had said: "Mark my words, dude, red meat will kill you."

That's all we are. Red meat.

And Ashley's one-hundred-twenty pounds of red meat killed me.

Elaine Viets Bibliography

Francesca Vierling series
- *Backstab.* Dell. (1997).
- *Rubout.* Dell. (1998).
- *The Pink Flamingo Murders.* Dell. (1999).
- *Doc in the Box.* Dell. (2000).

Dead-End Job series
- *Shop till You Drop.* Signet. (2003).
- *Murder Between the Covers.* Signet. (2003).
- *Dying to Call You.* Signet. (2004).
- *Just Murdered.* Signet. (2005).
- *Murder Unleashed.* NAL Hardcover. (2007).
- *Murder with Reservations.* NAL Hardcover. (2007).
- *Clubbed to Death.* NAL Hardcover. (2008).
- *Killer Cuts.* NAL/Obsidian Hardcover. (2009).
- *Half-Price Homicide.* NAL/Obsidian Hardcover. (2010).
- *Pumped for Murder.* NAL/Obsidian Hardcover. (2011).
- *Final Sail.* NAL/Obsidian Hardcover. (2012).
- *Board Stiff.* NAL/Obsidian Hardcover. (2013).
- *Catnapped!.* Obsidian Hardcover. (2014).
- *Killer Blonde.* InterMix. (2014).
- *Checked Out.* Obsidian Hardcover. (2015).
- *The Art of Murder.* Obsidian Hardcover. (2016)

Josie Marcus series
- *Dying in Style: Josie Marcus, Mystery Shopper.* Signet. (2005).
- *High Heels Are Murder: Josie Marcus, Mystery Shopper.* Signet. (2006).
- *Accessory to Murder: Josie Marcus, Mystery Shopper.* Obsidian. (2007).
- *Murder with All the Trimmings: Josie Marcus, Mystery Shopper.* Obsidian. (2008).

- *The Fashion Hound Murders: Josie Marcus, Mystery Shopper.* Obsidian. (2009).
- *An Uplifting Murder: Josie Marcus, Mystery Shopper.* Obsidian. (2010).
- *Death on a Platter: Josie Marcus, Mystery Shopper.* Obsidian. (2011).
- *Murder Is a Piece of Cake: Josie Marcus, Mystery Shopper.* Obsidian. (2012).
- *Fixing to Die: Josie Marcus, Mystery Shopper.* Obsidian. (2013).
- *A Dog Gone Murder: Josie Marcus, Mystery Shopper.* Obisidian. (2014).

Death Investigator Angela Richman
- *Brainstorm.* Thomas & Mercer. (2016).
- *Fire and Ashes.* Thomas & Mercer. (2017).

A Deal with the Devil and 13 Other Stories

A Deal With the Devil and 13 Other Stories by Elaine Viets is printed on 60 pound paper, and is designed by Jeffrey Marks, using InDesign. The type is Caslon Pro. The font is a serif typeface designed by William Caslon I in the 18th century. The cover design is by Gail Cross. The printing and binding is by Thomson-Shore for the hard cover and the trade paperback version. The book was published in April 2018 by Crippen & Landru Publishers, Inc., Cincinnati, OH.

Crippen & Landru, Publishers
P. O. Box 532057
Cincinnati, OH 45253
Web: www.Crippenlandru.Com
E-mail: info@crippenlandru.Com

Since 1994, Crippen & Landru has published more than 100 first editions of short-story collections by important detective and mystery writers.

- *This is the best edited, most attractively packaged line of mystery books introduced in this decade. The books are equally valuable to collectors and readers.* [Mystery Scene Magazine]

- *The specialty publisher with the most star-studded list is Crippen & Landru, which has produced short story collections by some of the biggest names in contemporary crime fiction.* [Ellery Queen's Mystery Magazine]

- *God bless Crippen & Landru.* [The Strand Magazine]

- *A monument in the making is appearing year by year from Crippen & Landru, a small press devoted exclusively to publishing the criminous short story.* [Alfred Hitchcock's Mystery Magazine]

Recent Publications

The Columbo Collection by William Link.
New stories written by the creator of television's greatest
sleuth. Trade softcover, $18.00.

Ten Thousand Blunt Instruments by Phillip Wylie, edited
by Bill Pronzini. Lost Classics Series.
Wylie's stories were, in the words of editor Bill Pronzini,
"controversial, provocative, iconoclastic." His detective
fiction was among the most ingenious and innovative of
his generation. Full cloth with dust jacket, $29.00. Trade
softcover, $19.00

The Exploits Of The Patent Leather Kid by Erle Stanley
Gardner, edited by Bill Pronzini. Lost Classics Series.
The Patent Leather Kid is an elegant crook, hiding his
identity with mask, gloves, and shoes made out of black
patent leather. In truth, he is a wealthy, seemingly indo-
lent socialite, who becomes a terror to the underworld.
Full cloth in dust jacket, $29.00. Trade softcover, $19.00

Valentino: Film Detective by Loren D. Estleman.
Valentino has a perfect job for a film buff — he is a film
detective who locates lost movies so that they can be preserved for future generations. And often he has to become
an amateur sleuth as well. Full cloth in dust jacket, signed
and numbered by the author,
$43.00. Trade softcover, $17.00.

*The Duel Of Shadows: The Extraordinary Cases Of Barn-
abas Hildreth* by Vincent Cornier, edited By Mike Ashley.
Lost Classics Series.
"One of the great series of modern detective stories." So

wrote Ellery Queen when he introduced American readers to the writings of Vincent Cornier. Full cloth in dust jacket, $28.00.

Shooting Hollywood: The Diana Poole Stories by Melodie Johnson Howe.
Melodie Johnson Howe was "one of the last of the starlets," making movies with Clint Eastwood, Alan Alda, James Caan, James Farentino and others. Hollywood is brutal, and it is a place, as Marilyn Monroe said, "where they'll pay you a thousand dollars for a kiss, and fifty cents for your soul ..." Diana Poole finds crime in that world of glitz, glamour, and greed. Full cloth in dust jacket, signed and numbered by the author, $43.00. Trade softcover, $17.00.

The Casebook Of Jonas P. Jonas And Others by E. X. Ferrars, edited By John Cooper. Lost Classics Series.
Stories by a mistress of the traditional mystery. "She remains," wrote one reviewer, "one of the most adept and intelligent adherents of the whodunit form." Full cloth in dust jacket, $29.00. Trade softcover, $19.00.

Nothing Is Impossible: Further Problems Of Dr. Sam Hawthorne by Edward D. Hoch.
Dr. Sam Hawthorne, a New England country doctor in the first half of the twentieth century, was constantly faced by murders in locked rooms and impossible disappearances. *Nothing Is Impossible* contains fifteen of Dr. Sam's most extraordinary cases. Full cloth in dust jacket, signed and numbered by the publisher, $45.00. Trade softcover, $19.00.

Night Call And Other Stories Of Suspense by Charlotte Armstrong, edited by Rick Cypert and Kirby Mccauley. Lost Classics Series.

Charlotte Armstrong introduced suspense into the commonplace, the everyday, by writing short stories and novels in which one simple action sets a series of events spiraling into motion, pulling readers along, breathless with anxiety. Full cloth in dust jacket, $30.00. Trade softcover, $20.00.

Chain Of Witnesses; The Cases Of Miss Phipps by Phyllis Bentley, edited By Marvin Lachman. Lost Classics Series.

A critic writes, "stylistically, [Bentley's] stories ... share a quiet humor and misleading simplicity of statement with the works of Christie .... Her work [is] informed and consistent with the classic traditions of the mystery." Full cloth in dust jacket, $29.00. Trade softcover, $19.00.

Swords, Sandals And Sirens by Marilyn Todd.

Murder, conmen, elephants. Who knew ancient times could be such fun? Many of the stories feature Claudia Seferius, the super-bitch heroine of Marilyn Todd's critically acclaimed mystery series set in ancient Rome. Others feature Cleopatra, the Olympian gods, and high priestess Ilion blackmailed to work with Sparta's feared secret police. Full cloth in dust jacket, signed and numbered by the author, $45.00. Trade softcover, $19.00.

The Puzzles Of Peter Duluth by Patrick Quentin. Lost Classics Series.

Anthony Boucher wrote: "Quentin is particularly noted for the enviable polish and grace which make him one of the leading American fabricants of the murderous comedy of manners; but this surface smoothness conceals intricate and meticulous plot construction as faultless as that of Agatha Christie." Full cloth in dust jacket, $29.00. Trade softcover, $19.00.

The Purple Flame And Other Detective Stories by Frederick Irving Anderson, edited by Benjamin F. Fisher. Previously uncollected stories by one of the premier mystery writers of the 1920's and the 1930's. Full cloth in dust jacket, $29.00. Trade softcover, $19.00.

My Mother, The Detective: The Complete "Mom" Stories by James Yaffe. Second edition enlarged. Trade softcover, $19.00.

All But Impossible: The Impossible Files of Dr. Sam Hawthorne by Edward D. Hoch. Full cloth in dust jacket, signed and numbered by the publisher, $45.00. Trade softcover, $19.00.

Sequel to Murder by Anthony Gilbert, edited by John Cooper. Full cloth in dust jacket, $29.00. Trade softcover, $19.00.

The Zanzibar Shirt Mystery and Other Stories by James Holding, edited by Jeffrey Marks. Full cloth in dust jacket, $29.00. Trade softcover, $19.00.

Subscriptions

Subscribers agree to purchase each forthcoming publication, either the Regular Series or the Lost Classics or (preferably) both. Collectors can thereby guarantee receiving limited editions, and readers won't miss any favorite stories.

Subscribers receive a discount of 20% off the list price (and the same discount on our backlist) and a specially commissioned short story by a major writer in a deluxe edition as a gift at the end of the year.

The point for us is that, since customers don't pick and choose which books they want, we have a guaranteed sale even before the book is published, and that allows us to be more imaginative in choosing short story collections to issue.

That's worth the 20% discount for us. Sign up now and start saving. Email us at crippenlandru@earthlink.net or visit our website at www.crippenlandru.com on our subscription page.